"*What You See* is the third AMAZINGLY THRILLING book in Cherise Sinclair's Sons Of The Survivalist series and is Bull's story. And what a fantastic, compelling, and soul melting romance it was too!" ~ Marie's Tempting Reads

She will risk everything to rescue her friend.

Frankie's BFF and four-year-old son are trapped inside a fanatical militia's compound. In Alaska, no less. Wilderness rescues are so not in the New Yorker's skill set. But she'll figure it out. She must.

Bull's new roadhouse server is a mass of contradictions.

The city girl's reasons for being in Alaska don't add up. Bull's been burned by liars before. So, why is he falling for this crap again? Maybe it's her big brown eyes, exuberant personality—or her generous, compassionate heart. Whatever the reason is, he cares. If she's in trouble, he'll do his damnedest to get her out.

The huge Alaskan is terrifyingly compelling--and heart-warmingly concerned for her.

But Frankie refuses to involve Bull in the deadly mess. Her plan to rescue her bestie will work without anyone getting hurt. As she tries her best not to fall in love, she doggedly acquires each skill she'll need.

Getting shot, though...that hadn't been on her to-do list.

WHAT YOU SEE

Sons of the Survivalist: 3

CHERISE SINCLAIR

VanScoy Publishing Group

What You See
Copyright © 2020 by Cherise Sinclair
ISBN: 978-1-947219-30-4
Published by VanScoy Publishing Group
Cover Art: I'm No Angel Designs
Edited by Red Quill Editing, LLC
Content Editor: Bianca Sommerland

ACKNOWLEDGMENTS

Thanks to Fiona Archer and Monette Michaels for critting Bull's story. When you both yell at me for the same problem, I know I'd better fix it.

To my beloved Alaska authorities, JJ Foster and Kathleen Cole: You are so good at keeping me from making any horrible cheechako goofs. (Any errors that slipped in are my very own).

Daniela Gardini, thank you so much for helping with the Italian. You rock, girl! (Any errors are because the author is stubborn).

Many hugs to my wonderful beta readers, Marian Shulman, Lisa White, and Barb Jack.

So much appreciation goes to my Red Quill editors—Ekatarina Sayanova, Rebecca Cartee, and Tracy Damron-Roelle. Because of your hard work and superb skills, Bull's story will be released before winter...and will be readable. Thank you!

It's been a rough fall for my team—loss of furbabies, bronchitis, infections, even cancer—and I can't believe how you each insisted I send the manuscript anyway. Because you wanted to help.

I love you all.

PROLOGUE

The sweet smell of pineapple, coconut, and hot oil jerked nine-year-old Kana Peleki to a stop in front of the small, brick-fronted restaurant. "*Dad?*"

A woman bumped into him from behind, then stepped around him with an annoyed sigh.

He didn't apologize. All he could see was the restaurant. All he could hear was an echo of a deep voice, "*My little sous chef. Look, hold the knife this way...*"

Kana shook his head hard. No, his father wouldn't be in that restaurant making Samoan half-moon pies. Wouldn't be giving that booming laugh and pulling over a stepstool so Kana could help.

Dad was dead. Gone.

Kana leaned against the building and scowled at his feet. Big feet.

"*I can't believe how fast you're growing.*"

Dad had said that too.

Would he even know me now? He'd grown a lot since his father died.

Because of that woman.

1

Anger roused inside him. Dad had died because the owner of the LA restaurant wanted him, always calling him her "handsome chef" and touching him. But after they'd done the sex stuff, she'd changed and got all mean and called Dad names and hit him, even though he never yelled back or anything.

In the car that night, she'd shouted at Dad and slapped him real hard. The car had gone sideways and—

Kana's belly lurched, and he put his hand over his mouth. Heat ran over his skin, then cold, like he'd fallen in the icy stream outside Mako's cabin.

Don't puke.

He pulled in long breaths and fought off the sickness. He wasn't a little kid anymore, not like when Dad died. He'd been in foster care, been on the LA streets. He was tough now, not a wimp.

He walked on.

"Hey, Bull. *Bull.*"

He jumped—because Gabe was yelling at *him*. *Bull's my name now.*

Bull. Frigging good name, right? He puffed up his chest to look bigger. Yeah, by the time he was grown up, he'd be as big as the bull moose that Mako had shot last week. The one that had given Kana—no, *Bull*—his new name.

He raised his hand to show he'd heard Gabe but didn't move. Did he want to hang out with his kinda-sorta foster brother—or the other two?

Mako called them a team. *A-huh.* Bull wasn't so sure.

Okay, maybe the four of them had fought back against the foster home perv, even though they hardly knew each other. And when Mako said he'd bring them to Alaska and raise them, they'd all agreed. Better than being homeless on the streets, right?

It still didn't make them no team or a family either.

"C'mon, Bull!" Dark-haired Gabe, a year older than Bull, motioned toward Caz and Hawk who were surrounded by big-ass

2

teens. The pushy jerks weren't a gang, though. Not here in bumfuck Seward.

Bull didn't move. Did he want to get in a fight for the other boys in the sarge's log cabin?

Gabe was okay. Bossier than anything, but he made up good games—and played fair. Made sure they all played fair.

Caz? Yeah, he was okay, too, even if he didn't speak English so good. When a bird's nest fell down off a tree, Caz kept the babies alive, getting up early to feed them and everything.

Hawk? Well, Hawk was weird. If anybody looked at him funny, he'd hit them. Bull had some good bruises since the kid hit hard. But he'd sneak bugs and worms to Caz's baby birds...and then pretend he hadn't. Why'd he want them to think he was an asshole?

Wondering what they thought of *him*, Bull waited to see what'd happen down the street.

Trash-talking, the local kids surrounded Caz and Hawk. "City brats. Go back to the Lower 48 where you belong." The pimple-faced town boy must've been around fifteen, same as the other three circling Hawk and Caz.

Bull growled. Hawk was a jerk sometimes, and Caz just a shrimp, but they were all living together. *Kinda makes them, like, mine, right?*

"Ugly-face, don'cha got nothing to say?" Another teen poked his finger at the scar on Hawk's face.

Caz slapped the kid's arm away. "*Chinga su madre, hijo de puta!*"

The Alaska dumbasses got even madder. They could probably tell that he'd called them nasty names.

Caz had some guts.

Turning a pissed-off red, Hawk lifted his fists. *Uh-oh.* When he lost it, no one was safe.

As Bull headed toward the group, the fight busted out.

The pimple-faced kid punched Caz right in the face.

Hawk kicked the jerk's leg, and then *all* the town kids jumped in.

Like that was fair?

With a yell, Gabe grabbed a bike from the sidewalk and clobbered one teen right off his feet.

"Go, Gabe!" Bull launched himself into the fight and hit a ginger in the side, knocking him onto his ass.

Next to Bull, Hawk pushed the asshole who'd called him *ugly-face*. Shoving his head into the kid's chest, Hawk punched him in the gut, right-left-right-left. Getting hit back didn't slow the crazy hawk down any. Screaming bloody murder, the teen fell over, got up, and ran like a chickenshit.

Cheering, Bull realized he was bouncing on the ginger's back and had rammed the kid's face into the pavement. *Oh, crap.*

The weenie was crying.

"Yeah, scram." Bull rolled off, and the ginger ran.

Caz was fighting pimple-face and, *shit*, using one of his knives!

Coming from behind, Gabe bashed the bike into the teen. Bleeding already—*go, Caz!*—the teen staggered back and ran after his wannabe gang.

Gabe scowled. "Put those knives away before someone sees them."

Slicker than snot, Caz made the knives disappear.

Bull snorted. If he'd been littler, he'd want knives, too. And Caz could sure work those blades.

"Fighting, huh?" The deep gravelly voice made Bull jump and spin.

Mako stood right behind him. The big-shouldered man used to be in the military and was hard as steel. His blue eyes saw everything.

Fuck.

He'd promised he would keep them till they were grown up. Maybe they shouldn't've got in a fight the first time he brought them to town.

Tensing, Bull backed up until his shoulder was against Gabe's. Caz was on Gabe's other side, and after a second, Hawk wiped the blood from his mouth and stood next to Bull.

They'd done okay, Bull decided, against all those bigger kids. Felt kinda good.

Gabe looked Mako straight in the face. "They were picking on Hawk and Caz. That's not right."

"No, it's not." Mako eyed the street. The teens had disappeared. "Doubt they'll try it again."

Bull folded his arms over his chest. "Cuz we won."

"You did." The sarge actually grinned. "You'll do even better when you learn to work together."

They all looked at each other. Together?

Maybe.

"You got a fat lip, boy." Mako slapped Hawk's shoulder. "An ice pack'd help—but winning a fight deserves ice cream."

They all grinned—even Hawk, although it made his lip bleed more.

A bit later, with a strawberry ice cream cone, Bull sat with the others at a patio table outside. It was a cool town. The sea gulls strutted around at their feet, begging for food and acting like clowns. Big planters had dark blue and yellow flowers matching the colors of the flag hanging overhead from a light pole.

While Bull slowly licked his ice cream, Mako told them to guess stuff about the people who walked past. What they did for a living. If they were good people. If they could fight.

Bull pointed his chin at a guy in mud-covered clothes who was leaning on a lamppost. "Homeless, no job, asshole, probably he'd fall over if he tried to fight."

Mako snorted. "You're seeing the dirt and the clothes. Look past that shit, boy."

Bull scowled.

"He's wearing fancy cowboy boots. Good ones." Gabe tilted his head. "An' his jeans 'n' shirt aren't new, but not cheap, either."

Mako nodded. "Better. Keep going."

"Got knife in boot," Caz said.

Bull blinked, and yeah, there was a hilt at the top. So much for being worthless in a fight.

A big pickup pulled up to the curb. The big shell on the back had ten tiny doors in it, and dogs were whining behind them.

The guy climbed into the passenger side and leaned over to kiss a really hot woman.

Mako said, "He owns the sports store. He and his wife aren't millionaires, but well enough off. That's a dog truck, and he's muddy from training his new sled-dog team, fixin' to race them. Probably took himself a spill."

"Crap," Bull muttered. He couldn't have been more wrong.

"Exactly. Learn to see past the surface—with men *and* women. It'll save you a world of hurt."

Hurt. Bull turned away, mouth tight. If Dad had really *seen* the restaurant owner who wanted him, maybe he'd have stayed away from her. Maybe he'd still be alive.

And Bull wouldn't be in Alaska with a bunch of strangers.

CHAPTER ONE

*I*t is not your outward appearance that you should beautify, but your *soul, adorning it with good works.* ~ Clement of Alexandria

"I'll speak to the stylist about her schedule and see if she can fit in more time for you," Frankie Bocelli told the woman in the doorway, who was afraid the newer and younger models were getting more attention from the stylist than she was.

Che cavolo. What the heck? How petty. Typing a reminder to follow through, Frankie put a stranglehold on her mouth. She must be polished and gracious. Always. No matter what.

Besides, fighting amongst the models was to be expected. To them, hair and makeup stylists were as important as her organizational software was to her. *So, don't be judgy.*

"Thanks, Francesca."

Francesca. Ugh. "You're very welcome." Watching the model strut out of the office, Frankie rubbed her face. Why in the world was she so grumpy these days? It seemed as if everything irritated her recently—although her annoyance with her given name was long-standing.

Fran-chess-kah. Could anything sound fussier? And it had so many letters. In preschool, she'd still been printing her endless name as the short-named classmates like Eve and Ann headed out to play.

In elementary school, hadn't she just adored being called Frankenstein or Frankfurter? *Not.* But it was worse when her breasts appeared, and the boys took to calling her *Chesty.* Really, her breasts were awesome—*thank you, Italian genes*—but at the time, well...

Things changed when she started college. Her new friends decided her stuffy name didn't suit her, and her roommate, Kirsten—Kit—dubbed her Frankie. When everyone started calling her Frankie, her world expanded.

Names were important, a kind of acknowledgment. *"I see you."* Being called the wrong name constantly felt like a slow erosion of her identity.

But after graduation, she'd fulfilled her parents' expectations and returned to work in the family business. Mama insisted her daughter mustn't be called something as masculine-sounding as Frankie. No matter what Frankie wanted, she'd be known by the name on her birth certificate.

Lucky me. Needing a moment, Frankie walked over to water the plants that lined her window. The African violets were blooming in bright lavenders and pinks as if to urge her to cheer up. Beside them were two plants her bestie had given her—a so-called "money" plant and one to clean the air. Kit was all about useful plants.

From outside came the low hum of traffic, punctuated by honks and beeps. New York cabbies loved their horns.

She braced her hands on the sill. Through the drizzling rain on the glass, her tenth-floor office window gave a dreary view of skyscrapers. Spring was late arriving in New York.

The gray, smoggy sky suited her mood.

However, moods could be improved by food—and she had

something to eat. She'd bribed one of the gofers to get her a Shake Shack burger.

Back at her desk, Frankie opened the sack and grabbed a crinkle-cut fry. *Yum.*

"Francesca, I need your help." Birgit, her oldest sister, entered with the signature catwalk strut that'd made her famous. A second later, she reclined in a chair in such a perfect picture of anguish that there should have been a violin accompaniment.

"What's up?" With a sigh, Frankie set her burger to one side. Alas, it'd be cold by the time she got to eat it.

Her sister gave the food an appalled look. "You can't seriously be planning to eat that disgusting monstrosity. Think of your hips. You're already way too—"

"You don't have to eat it." *My burger. Mine, mine, mine.*

"Come to my exercise class tonight. It's weightlifting and aerobic dance. That'll sweat the pounds away." Birgit patted her concave stomach.

Honestly, my family. All of them obsessed with schedules and nutrition and exercise.

"I prefer my aikido classes, thanks." Way back in grade school, she'd won a rare battle with Mama and was allowed to take aikido instead of following her oh-so-graceful older sisters into dance classes. "And I jog, too."

At Birgit's skeptical expression, Frankie smirked. "Just yesterday, in fact."

A friend's crazy kids loved to fly drones. Unfortunately, the so-called drone obstacle avoidance stuff didn't always work, and there were plenty of drone-meets-light pole crashes. She'd gotten plenty of exercise while chasing after the silly machines.

"Stunning bodies take dedication, Francesca," Birgit said.

Don't roll your eyes; don't roll your eyes. Both of Frankie's siblings approached exercise like a nun would the rosary. Why couldn't Mama have been a lawyer or doctor? Or a farmer. Farming would be cool.

But *nooo*. Norwegian and gorgeous, Mama had been a top model, married her favorite fashion photographer, *the* Bocelli, and opened a modeling agency.

Birgit and Anja resembled Mama and were models.

Frankie, the baby of the family, got Papà'sItalian DNA. Brown eyes, brown hair, and big breasts. At least she'd managed to be five-six, or she would've felt like a Hobbit. Papà's mama was only five-one.

"Really," her sister continued, "you need to get into HIIT and alternate that with Pilates and—"

"Birgit." Years of experience let Frankie interrupt the rant. "What was it you needed?"

"Oh, darling." Birgit sat up. "You *have* to help me. Tomorrow, I have a fitting for an exercise clothing shoot, but there's an afternoon reception for that new *Vogue* photographer, and I want to go. Can't you talk with the wardrobe stylist and get her to move the time? She's a self-centered putz, but everybody listens to you."

Frankie smothered a sigh. Despite the fancy "human resources coordinator" title, her job was basically running around and making sure everything went smoothly, even though problems should really be handled by the models' agents. Even worse, her siblings always came to her, rather than their handlers.

"Let me give Alsace a call and see if we can slide the fitting forward an hour. I'll arrange a driver, so you won't have to wait for a taxi."

"Perfect. Thanks, sis."

"Sure."

Birgit sauntered out of the room, her predatory runway strut so much a part of her that she probably couldn't walk normally at this point. The high heels on her feet brought her height to well over six feet.

Just looking at those shoes hurt. Frankie wiggled her toes. No matter what Mama thought about dressing up and wearing makeup to enhance an image, Frankie stuck to professional, but comfortable. There was a benefit to being in administration rather than on the catwalk.

Before she could start on her lunch, two more models stopped in for advice on dealing with an overly handsy agent.

Then a male model got sent to her office to discuss his temper, which was causing problems with...oh, just about everyone. After a chat, she gave him a card for a therapist who understood the odd stresses of the modeling profession.

He scowled. "This'll ruin my rep."

"Hey, this is New York." Frankie motioned to the skyscrapers outside the window—probably still a great sight to someone from Nebraska. "Everyone's in therapy."

His lips curved, and he grinned reluctantly. "Yeah, okay. Thanks, Francesca."

"Sure."

Before she could snatch a bite, a new model stopped in, an eighteen-year-old who was having problems coping. So young.

Frankie dealt out her usual advice—having friends elsewhere and cultivating hobbies. If a person's only form of validation came from her career, then any upset in the job world could be devastating. Someone with a variety of interests could shrug off an ugly comment about her appearance by thinking, *maybe I messed this up, but I'm a good cook and great with people and can beat anyone at Monopoly.*

Once the girl was settled and thinking more clearly, Frankie rearranged schedules and recruited an older model who agreed to serve as mentor.

The office empty again, she glanced at her burger. *Cold. Yuck.*

Oh, well. Ruined lunch or not, she did enjoy keeping people happy and making things run smoothly. This was what she was good at.

What her family needed from her.

"Baby, you're the sweetest thing I've seen today." The silky-smooth voice from down the hall was all too recognizable—as was the line. Her ex-husband was trying to con another woman in his quest to get to the top.

Giggles, murmurs.

Wanting to gag, she considered shutting her door. Trying to warn Jaxson's newest target wouldn't work—Frankie would simply be considered a vindictive ex. Then again, if he hadn't had an ironclad contract with Bocelli's, she really *would* have asked Mama to show him the door. So, yes, maybe she was a little bit vindictive.

Stopping in the doorway, Jaxson gave her a patronizing smile. He knew he was drop-dead gorgeous and could have any woman in the world.

Except her, at this point.

These days, *oh-so-perfect* males froze her emotions like a midwinter blizzard.

"Did you need something, Jaxson?"

"Love, Francesca, I need love." His voice was raised enough for his latest conquest to hear.

She snorted. "I think you're getting adoration mixed up with love. Buy a dictionary."

He scowled, then spotted her lunch. "Pitiful. You know, if you'd go on a diet, fix yourself up, *you* might get a little love—or even adoration. Try it some time."

"Really?" she cooed in a breathy voice. "You really think so?"

Before he could respond, she gave him a thin smile and turned her attention to her in-basket. "I'll take it under advisement."

With a grumble that sounded insulting, he disappeared.

She shook her head. *Not your best moment, Frankie.* She didn't usually let his slurs or her family's obsession with appearance make her feel like the ugly runt of the litter.

No, she wasn't up to model standards, but she didn't *want* to be a model. *I'm healthy, pretty, have a lovely, lush body, gorgeous hair and eyes, and even better, a marvelous personality.*

Exactly so. Now move on.

Exasperated with herself, she tossed the cold burger and fries into the wastebasket and returned to perusing her mail.

Announcements. Office supplies. Schedule changes. Usually applications and resumes went to Mama, but, currently, Frankie received the business-related ones. If she ever wanted a vacation, she would need an assistant who could take her place, not a shared admin. Right now, anytime she mentioned time off, everyone in her family insisted she couldn't be spared. That she was needed there, making things work right and smoothing over the entitled-diva messes.

Frowning, she picked up the last piece of mail. Addressed to Francesca Bocelli, care of The Bocelli Agency.

Frankie,

I need help so bad.

I'm trapped. Obadiah joined a militia—the Patriot Zealots—and brought us into their compound. He won't let me leave. In fact, we moved someplace even more isolated—Rescue, Alaska.

You were right, Frankie; he was such a mistake. He's getting meaner, and he lets the leaders—

The rest of the sentence was blotted out.

If I don't make it out, can you try to get Aric away from them? Here are papers I managed to fix up in case you need them.

I know you'll want to call the police for me, but you mustn't. One of the Rescue police is a member of the Patriot Zealots. Don't call the FBI or others. Just don't.

But...please, Frankie. Get Aric out.

Kit

Frankie realized her palms were pressed together in front of her chest. As if prayer would fix this. *Kit, what have you fallen into?* She opened the other papers. There was a form, witnessed by a couple of people, giving guardianship of Aric, Frankie's godson, to her.

It made sense. Aric wasn't Obadiah's birth son; the boy was three when Kit fell prey to the creep.

There was also a handwritten list of the reasons why Frankie had been nominated as guardian and why no one else, especially Obadiah, should get oversight of the child.

Pictures of Kit and Aric were enclosed. Frankie picked one up.

Blond, blue-eyed Aric resembled his birth father—a man who'd been in Kit's life for less than a week. She'd never even learned his last name.

Since the picture of Aric showed him as around two years old, Kit's first husband had probably taken the photos. Even though Aric wasn't his, he'd been good to the boy, even when addicted to narcotics. He'd died of an overdose before the marriage was a year old.

Poor Kit had crummy luck with men. While she was still reeling from her husband's death, Obadiah scooped her up and married her.

Frankie riffled through the photos and found none from this year. The religious fanatic of a spouse probably didn't believe in cameras.

Aric would be turning four this summer. *"Get Aric out."* The little boy was in danger.

Oh, Kit.

As the words on the papers blurred, Frankie realized her hands were trembling. *Cazzo.* Fuck! She didn't know what to do—but she had to do *something*.

Roommates for much of college and a couple of years afterward, she and Kit were sisters-by-choice.

Frankie'd been Kit's birthing partner and helped raise little Aric until Kit married the first time. When the newlyweds moved to Texas, Frankie had bawled her eyes out.

Sure, she had lots of friends, but none like Kit. No matter how much time or distance—and Texas was certainly distant—they always picked up where they'd left off.

"*Amica mia*, you should have come back to New York when your husband died." Instead, Obadiah had deluded Kit until she'd disappeared into "the little woman". The perfect wife.

Frankie had met the *bastardo* only once for a few seconds at the wedding. The conservative crackpot had already decided she was a bad influence on Kit. He'd pressured Kit until she'd stopped calling, writing, or visiting.

Unwilling to cause problems, Frankie had honored Kit's withdrawal. Obviously, that had been a mistake.

Before Obadiah, they'd always been there for each other. Through missed job opportunities and celebrations and relationship disasters. After Kit moved, they'd spent hours on the phone. When Kit's husband died, Frankie had flown to Texas, cared for Aric, and kept things going while Kit mourned.

When Frankie's marriage fell apart, Kit had come to New York. After lots of handholding and enduring the wailing and weeping—because Frankie wasn't a silent sufferer—Kit had pushed her out of the house and back into living.

Although not back into dating. Kit had always been more of an optimist there, which seemed strange since she had lousy taste in men. The dominant guys she fell for inevitably turned out to be creepers or controlling or basic assholes. Kit's miserable childhood had left a glitch in her nice-guy radar.

But Obadiah? "You really picked a bad one, this time."

Frankie read over the letter again.

Alaska—seriously?

But there was no way she'd leave her bestie or her godson with some abusive asshole. With luck, all Kit needed was someone pulling strings to get her and Aric out.

I'm good at making things happen.

If Kit needed more than that, well... Frankie pressed her lips together, determination rising inside her. She'd do what she had to do.

She punched the office intercom button and waited until the shared administrative assistant answered. "Hey, Nyla. How would you like to hold down the hot seat for a while?"

Her family would just have to cope.

CHAPTER TWO

B *y failing to prepare, you are preparing to fail.* - Benjamin Franklin

No taxis, no skyscrapers, no people. And now that she was off the Sterling Highway, there weren't even paved roads.

Welcome to Rescue, Alaska, huh?

Admittedly, the scenery on the drive from Anchorage had been spectacular with stark, snow-covered mountains and foothills, deep river valleys, and miles of lush forests. Every time the road curved, another view had taken her breath away.

As Frankie turned off Dall Road and onto a muddy dirt road, branches from the dense forest on each side clawed at her rented sedan. She winced at the harsh scraping noises. *Sorry, car.*

Was the Patriot Zealot property around here? The teenaged gas station attendant in Rescue had given her directions, but there were an awful lot of small roads that branched off of Dall.

She drove around another corner, and there it was. The home of the Patriot Zealots.

Six-foot fencing topped with razor wire—seriously? Talk about unfriendly. A gate barred the way, and inside the fence, a small shack stood next to the road. Somehow, she doubted it was a bus stop, more like a guard hut.

Up the slope, the cleared forest still lay under snow. High tunnel greenhouses dotted the fields. Farther away, log houses mixed with prefabs in an unsightly mess. The buildings were too distant to see the people. *Are you there, Kit? Is Aric?*

At the gate, Frankie turned off her car and stepped out, avoiding a patch of ice. *Brrr.* The cold, damp air smelled like evergreens and snow with a hint of wood smoke—and was so clean her city lungs might go into shock.

As she approached the gate, she heard barking. Two dogs jumped out of the hut, followed by a man who held a *rifle*. Frankie knew Obadiah was a Christian fundamentalist fanatic, but this place felt like a third-world prison camp.

Her plan to loudly demand to see Kit was a bust. The isolation here and the guard's rifle wiped out that strategy. In fact, telling these people she knew Kit would be a mistake. She needed more information first.

Wearing a black winter jacket, jeans, and black boots, the scruffy-bearded guard scowled at the big black dogs. "Shut *up.* Sit." After the dogs obeyed, he turned his attention to Frankie in a long, leering study. When his gaze lingered on her mouth, she was glad her coat covered her curves.

To her relief, he angled the rifle so it didn't point directly at her. "Are you lost?"

"I don't think so." Frankie gave him a wide smile—something she rarely had to force, but everything about this place was creepy. "Is this where the Patriot Zealots live?"

His face went cold. "Yeah, who wants to know?"

"Uh, I do." *Duh. Am I not standing right here in front of you?* "I heard my aunt joined and was here, and I thought I'd pop in for a visit. She's getting old and—"

"No visitors allowed." He moved the rifle to cover her again. *Cavolo*, that was a big gun. Didn't they have any laws in this state?

She widened her eyes, all girly shock. "No visitors? Like, at all? How am I going to say hi?"

He shook his head. "If yer aunt wanted to be around the modern world, she'd be out there. She wants to be here with no contact with the outside. No contamination, just peace."

"Huh. But what if she gets sick? She's not young anymore."

"We care for our own."

"Can I leave a messa—"

"You can fuckin' leave." He gestured with the rifle—such an unsafe move.

"Okay, right." She huffed out a breath and lifted her lips into another brainless smile. "Sorry I bothered you. You have a good day."

Followed by the dogs, he swaggered back to the guard shack.

Turning the car, she drove back down the road, suppressing the urge to peel out and splatter mud and rocks over the hut and stupid guard.

So much for her idea that she could just make noise and get Kit and Aric out.

Once around the bend of the road and out of sight, she pounded her fist on the steering wheel hard enough to hurt her hand. "*Cazzo, cazzo, cazzo!*"

Her Italian grandmother would've had a fit at such swearing. Women didn't use the *f-word*—no matter what language. Then again, there had been that summer when the nasty rooster spurred Nonna, and Frankie'd learned a whole bunch of new Italian swear words.

The rooster had made an excellent escarole soup, and the experience taught Frankie a valuable lesson—a sweet personality could exist side-by-side with a steely core.

With a grunt, Frankie sat back. The swearing might relieve stress but didn't offer any solutions.

She pulled out onto Dall Road and headed back to Rescue. Contacting Kit would be difficult with that no visitors rule and no way to get a message into the place. For all Frankie knew, Kit might not even be in that—that *compound*. The *cult* compound.

However, those Zealot members must visit town, sooner or later. For groceries, mail, gas. Or...maybe to go to a bar?

She tapped her fingers on the wheel. Being discreet would be essential while making inquiries about the cult.

Obtaining information and coming up with a safer plan might take a while. So...how to keep from sticking out like a sore thumb in the tiny town? The gas station owner had said this was the dead month for tourism. Ski season was over, and the fishing was just starting to pick up.

Not that I resemble a fisherman, anyway. Cooking fish? She was a pro. Catching? No. Absolutely not. Pretending to be a tourist would be her last resort.

She might need to find a job to blend in. If the summer season was starting soon, they'd be hiring, right?

Even weird cult types had to buy food. They'd talk to clerks and salespeople. Being all self-sufficient and stuff, they probably didn't go to restaurants. Did religious conservative types go to bars? Kit had told her that Obadiah didn't drink.

She'd better try for salesclerk jobs.

Hmm. What if she ran into Obadiah? Would he recognize her?

She pulled on her lip. *Nah, probably not.* The only time she'd met him was a moment in the reception line after his and Kit's wedding ceremony. He'd already been swamped with introductions to all of Kit's co-workers at the garden nursery. Honestly, why hadn't Kit seen that as a big red flag—that the guy hadn't made the effort to meet any of her friends?

No way would Obadiah remember her face.

So, first step, find a place to stay. Tomorrow, get a job. She rolled her eyes. *Mannaggia. Damn me, for sure.* This so wouldn't go over well with Mama, who'd thrown a fit about Frankie taking vacation time. *"You're needed to be the liaison with the runway show next week. Some of our girls need your handholding. And who will deal with the fighting backstage? And that new photographer has everyone in tears. How can you just walk off and leave me saddled with all these problems?"*

Frankie's jaw firmed. All those problems could be handled by a perfectly capable staff. No one was indispensable.

And I haven't had a vacation...well, ever.

It hurt that her mother thought she was being selfish.

Of course, she didn't know that Frankie was here to help Kit. That Kit was in trouble. She wouldn't understand. Over the years, Mama had cut Kit to the quick with valid, but tactless comments about her poor taste in men. Kit was sensitive to criticism—and when this was over, she wouldn't need Mama's "helpful" remarks reminding her of another mistake.

At least Papà had been supportive of Frankie taking time off and had chided Mama about treating Frankie more like an employee than a daughter. But that was Papà; he had a soft heart. When she was little, she'd wished he'd been home more. But famous photographers traveled.

And took pictures of gorgeous Norwegian models and fell in love. The thought still made Frankie laugh. Two more unsuited people could never be found, yet, somehow, they were still married.

Frankie sighed. It'd be nice to have someone she could talk to about this mess. Someone to cuddle with at night. Someone who might even reassure her that everything would be all right.

Because right now, she was feeling really alone—and drowning in doubt.

What might those people do to Kit if Frankie made too many waves?

CHAPTER THREE

*B*e the person your dog thinks you are. ~ JW Stephens

Blood singing in his veins, Bull was on the cooling-off portion of his run. This was his favorite place to jog—from his roadhouse, down to the lakeshore, through the town park to Dante's cabins and back. It was off-season with the number of tourists beginning to pick up.

Dante's pickup and a sedan had been parked by the four cabins, so the old Okie might have a new renter.

Gorgeous Friday. Under a vivid blue sky, the sun glinted off the bold line of the Kenai Mountains. Bear Mountain and Russian Mountain to the south were spectacular and so white he had to squint his eyes.

The temp was mid-thirties with air crisp enough to crackle—exactly what he needed to clear away the remnants of battle nightmares from the night before.

Pulling his attention from the view, he checked his surroundings again since bears leaving hibernation tended to be irritable as were winter-skinny moose. He'd started wearing his bear spray belt.

Voices near the trail caught his attention.

"Yeah, just bought the damn dog. Bernese mountain and German shepherd mix. Its owner died, and the son didn't want the mutt, so it was cheap. He said the brute fights like a demon, but, Jesus, look at it cringe. I was robbed."

Another man spoke. "Good thing you brought him here to test him first, or you would've been fucking embarrassed at the fights."

Two other voices joined in, agreeing.

"Let's try this again," one said. "Maybe it'll do better this time."

Bull slowed, an ugly feeling crawling up his spine. Fights?

"And go!" Growls and snarls mixed with shouts. "Get him, you fucking mutt. Attack!"

Oh hell, no. Not in my park. Not in my town.

In a slushy clearing, two dogs circled each other while several men watched.

One dog attacked, the other yelped, then the two were fighting for real.

Only four guys. He could probably take them, although it'd be nice to have one of his brothers at his back.

Moving closer, Bull eyed a pile of old buckets someone had forgotten last fall. The melting snow had revealed them—and left them filled them with water. *That'll work.*

He picked up a bucket and tossed the icy water at the dogs.

Shocked, the mutts broke apart.

Still pissed off, Bull tossed the second bucket of water at the men.

"What the fuck!" The yells were satisfying. And then all four charged Bull.

Fine. He was warmed up and ready to fight.

He sidestepped the leading man. A hard punch to the guy's gut folded him over, and he started puking. *Jesus.*

Retreating to keep from getting splattered, Bull tripped the second one, so he could concentrate on the third. Twisting to take the third's punch on his shoulder, Bull hit his chin hard.

Laid him out cold.

The second man scrambled to his feet just in time to get Bull's boot in his gut, leaving him curled up like an armadillo.

Good enough.

The last one was the asshole who'd bought a dog for the sole purpose of fighting it. The one who hadn't even jumped into the brawl. The man's eyes widened like he suddenly realized he was the only one standing, and he backpedaled rapidly.

"You wanted a fight," Bull growled as he advanced. "Try doing it yourself, you cowardly bastard."

Even as Bull slapped aside the man's wimpy punch, his buddies abandoned ship, staggering away. One dog followed them. The other stood, paw in the air.

Seeing his friends fleeing, the cowardly owner yelled a protest.

Bull raised his fist and smiled. "Happens we like dogs here. Assholes, not so much."

"Fuck you." The guy retreated a step, then sprinted after his friends. Leaving his dog behind.

Rather than following, the dog whimpered, lay down, and watched Bull warily. Obviously, there was no bond between the dog and the owner.

Dammit, I don't have time for a dog, let alone a fighting dog.

The mud-covered fur appeared to be long—a mix of reddish brown and black. Bleeding from a couple of bites, the dog whined at Bull, appearing more bewildered than vicious. *Hell.*

Bull went down on one knee and held his hand out, speaking slow and low. "I don't know much about the Bernese part, but shepherds are good working dogs. You want to come interview for a job at the Hermitage? We've got chickens and a kid you can guard. You'd have to set up a truce with the cat."

At Bull's quiet words, the dog's ears perked up, and its bedraggled tail moved back and forth tentatively.

"Then again, the shape you're in, the cat might win a fight," Bull murmured as the dog rose and took a few steps forward. The black fur over his back and sides didn't hide sunken flanks. Bull spotted a dick. No balls.

The dumbass owner had thought to fight a neutered dog?

"You'll be better off with us," he said. "Guess a name for you might help."

The dog inched closer.

"My niece, she's into those Harry Potter stories. Named her cat Sirius." Bull reached out slowly. The dog's thick fur was patterned like a shepherd. Black over his back and tail, dark muzzle and ears, russet around the eyes, cheeks, ruff, and legs. A white blotch of fur marked the center of his chest.

After a second, the dog wagged his tail, bowing his head so Bull could ruffle the soft flopped-over ears. "How about we name you something Potterish to get Regan on our side. Maybe Gryffindor—and call you Gryff for short. If Regan pushes for you to stay, Caz and JJ won't argue—not that Caz would anyway. Audrey has a soft heart, so Gabe will be in."

It was amazing how the Hermitage had gone from being just Mako's sons to adding in women and even a kid.

"Now Hawk, he might be a trickier sell on the surface, but if you whine and show him your injuries, he'll go belly-up. He knows what it's like to get beat up."

A black nose lifted to sniff Bull's neck. A quick lick told him he had himself a dog. Not what he needed in the least.

Ah, well. At least he got to punch some assholes.

Standing in the slush-filled parking lot on Friday, Frankie unhappily studied the restaurant-bar in front of her. It was a massive building made of logs with a sign on the front: Bull's Moose Roadhouse. Thankfully, there was a HELP WANTED sign in a front window.

This was her last chance to get a job.

Over the last day, she'd worked on the items on her to-do list: Gather information, secure a place to stay, and find work.

The information gathering would be an ongoing and long process. With her first attempt, the postmistress and other store owners had been easy to lead into gossiping about the Patriot Zealots, commonly called PZs. It seemed that the *men* from the compound showed up in Rescue often enough. The women didn't get out much except for shopping at the grocery store—with male escorts. The women weren't allowed to drive, and the children didn't attend public school.

Anger burned in Frankie's stomach at the thought of little Aric being subjected to the fanatics. Damned if she'd let that continue.

List item two was easily achieved. Dante, the grocery store owner, had several lakeside cabins he rented to fishermen, but the season hadn't started yet. She questioned her sanity about living in a rustic log cabin, but Dante'd assured her that the Chicago woman he'd rented to last year had loved the place.

Frankie shook her head. Whenever one of the locals looked at her, she knew they were thinking *city girl*.

At least she'd managed to avoid a thick New York accent. Growing up with a Norwegian mother and Italian father, being around models from everywhere had helped. If anything, she sounded Italian, thanks to spending summers in Italy with her grandmother—and imitating Nonna. Having discarded her own Norwegian language like last year's apparel, Mama didn't approve.

Papà had laughed and taught her new swear words.

Her mother would be even more appalled about Frankie

applying for a job in a bar. However, waitressing was something Frankie knew how to do. *Thank you, Kit.* When Kit first arrived at college and started work in a restaurant, the quiet, shy eighteen-year-old had been overwhelmed. So, Frankie'd gotten a job at the same place, thinking she'd work there long enough for Kit to relax. Even after Kit grew comfortable with the restaurant, Frankie remained—because she'd loved it. Loved everything from washing dishes, bussing tables, waitressing and hostessing, to working in the kitchen on the line. She'd even graduated to being one of the chefs, now and then. A restaurant was a totally different atmosphere than her mama's image-happy modeling company.

Frankie shook her head, wistfully longing for a return to those years and the wonder of learning and exploring new ideas. The drunken nights where they'd sit in the dorm hallways and debate politics. The camaraderie of working in a restaurant. The joy of having friends who liked the same things she did, who saw who she really was—and liked her that way.

Those years were long past.

She eyed the roadhouse and was quite sure that working in a restaurant now wouldn't be nearly as fun as when she was a college student.

But she wasn't here for fun now, was she? This place would serve her purpose, since the postmistress said the PZs were often at the bar.

Time to hit the runway and walk the walk. Pulling in a fortifying breath, she crossed the lot, pulled open the door, and stepped inside.

The place was nicer than it appeared from outside, and she was glad she'd worn nice black slacks and her favorite royal blue sweater.

The restaurant and bar were spotless, and the air held the tempting aroma of grilled meat. With golden-stained log walls and wagon wheel chandeliers, the rooms held an Alaskan hunting-lodge ambiance. The nightclub took up about half of the right side of the building with a glossy, wooden bar along the back and distressed-wood tables and chairs in the center. Mounted on the log walls were huge antlers interspersed with wild animal photos.

Although only mid-afternoon, there were a couple of guys at the bar, and a few people seated in the restaurant.

Frankie stopped at the hostess station and waited for someone to notice her arrival.

"Oh, hey." A slim, young man in a pink button-up shirt walked over. His nametag said Felix. "Bar or restaurant?"

"Actually, I saw the *help wanted* sign in the window."

His face lit up. "Awesomeness. We're already short-handed. The ski season might be ending, but the summer tourist season will be kicking in soon. Help we need."

She smiled. "Perfect. Do you have an application or—"

"Wylie can talk with you now." Felix motioned her into the room. "He's a good guy. Maybe a bit grumpy today. Night owls hate working lunch shifts. Given the choice, I don't think he'd get up until mid-afternoon."

Great. An interview with a grumpy guy. Ah, well, this Wylie couldn't be worse than diva models, screaming photographers, and irritable event organizers.

A few minutes later, she sat across from the middle-aged chef being interviewed. Thankfully, she'd already worked out her evasions about why she was in Rescue and could answer the question he'd asked.

"It's one of those things. I've only lived in cities"—true enough except for her summers in rural Italy—"and I want to try something different for a while." If she was here for reasons other than rescuing Kit, she would've been delighted to visit Alaska. And meeting new people was always wonderful.

However, even if she had to hide her complete reason for being in this state, an employer deserved as much honesty as she could give him. "I doubt I'll stay permanently. Do you hire seasonal workers?"

"Yes, we do. Absolutely." Wylie was clean-shaven, had a bit of a gut, typical of chefs, but otherwise was in fair shape. "Right now, we've barely begun hiring for the longer summer hours and will have more positions open in the restaurant in a couple of weeks. If you don't want to wait until then, I currently have an opening for wait staff at the bar, Wednesday through Saturday nights."

Exactly where she wanted to be. Frankie grinned. "Sold. When do I start?"

"How about tomorrow night?"

CHAPTER FOUR

*S*ometimes it's not the people who change, it's the mask that falls off. - Haruki Murakami

On Saturday morning, Bull's family was hard at work. Winter on the Kenai Peninsula in Alaska was winding down with spring on its way. Seemed like breakup came earlier every year, and the lakes and rivers were almost ice free. Time to assess snow damage and put things to rights.

It was also time to inventory the freezer and pantry so he could finish off last year's meat and fish before the new harvest season. They'd all dealt with their own freezers, but Bull had volunteered to go through the one at Mako's cabin.

Stopping on the deck, Bull took off his muddy, Xtratuf rubber boots. "Yo, Gryff. Come on in, buddy. You might as well get familiar with this place, too."

Still favoring his sore paw, Gryff bounded up the steps into the big two-story cabin. Bright, open, and all one room, the house was vastly different from the tiny, off-the-grid log cabin where the sarge had hidden after his discharge from the military. A decorated Green Beret, Vietnam vet, and drill sergeant, Mako had put in his twenty years, then disappeared into the wilderness to deal with his PTSD and paranoia on his own.

Bull shook his head. No one in their right mind would've approved a crazy survivalist for adoption—not that Mako had wanted kids. However, nearly twenty-five years ago, when the sarge was in LA for a teammate's funeral, he'd heard screams from the next-door foster care home and entered to find an unconscious man with his pants around his ankles and four terrified boys. Caz was still holding the baseball bat. Figuring no one would take their word against their foster father's, the four had planned to run and live on the streets—where most of them had been before. Mako offered to take the boys to Alaska and raise them himself.

Bull shook his head at the memory. That pretty much summed up Mako's core belief—a man protected the weak.

The sarge kept his word and raised them to stand on their own. To be strong and honorable. To fight together as a team and then as brothers.

After his "sons" left to enlist, Mako's PTSD and paranoia worsened, and eventually, they'd convinced him to move to Rescue where he had an old military buddy. His paranoia wouldn't let him live in town, so they'd pooled their resources and bought up a good portion of the lakefront. Their five homes formed a half-circle around a communal space that faced the lake.

Mako built his place, planning to live upstairs and use the downstairs for family. He'd wanted room for them all to gather for meals and evenings. The equipment in the weight room and dojo rivaled some gyms.

He ruffled Gryff's fur. "I miss that tough old guy."

Gryff whined in sympathy and licked Bull's hand.

A year and a half ago, Mako had chosen a quick death rather than a slow one to cancer, but damn, Bull would've liked to have said goodbye. To have told the sarge how much he meant to him. To all of them.

But hell, Mako had known. He might have been a crazy survivalist, but he could also read people. *Miss you, Sarge.*

Time to work—Mako's answer for all ills.

A couple of hours later, Bull had a list of what needed to be eaten soon and what should be restocked. Odd how all the packages of salmon steak and chicken were gone, leaving less popular items like soup bones—which, come to think of it...

He pulled out a package and grinned at Gryff. "Guess what you get after it thaws a bit."

"Hey, Bull. You in here?" That was Gabe's voice.

"In the pantry," Bull called.

Gabe's footsteps approached the kitchen. "The chickens are laying like crazy. Maybe you could make deviled eggs? Audrey and I have older eggs in the fridge."

Because hardboiled eggs from fresh eggs were fucking impossible to shell.

"Sure, I can do that." Bull left the walk-in pantry, followed by Gryff.

Gryff stopped dead at seeing Gabe.

Even without wearing a uniform, Gabe had the appearance of the law—short brown hair, clean-shaven, hard-set stern jaw. And a cop's wary cynicism in the sharp blue eyes staring at the dog. "I think you have something to share, bro."

Bull grinned at the order for information.

The oldest of Mako's sons by a year, Gabe had always been their leader. Even as youngsters, Gabe would give the orders, then Bull would muster the troops—the other boys—and resources. Sneaky, tender-hearted Caz would handle recon and deal with injuries. Always more of a loner, Hawk was their pilot—and sniper. The years in various military forces had only strengthened those roles.

And speaking of the devils, there came his two other brothers, across the deck and into the house.

As Hawk and Caz stepped in, Gryff caught their attention—and backed up until his hind end was against Bull's legs.

A year younger than Bull, shorter and slenderer than the others, Caz smiled at Gryff, his brown eyes kind. "There's a pretty boy."

Bull glanced at his last brother. Beneath the scars and tats and blond beard, Hawk wore a scowl, of course, since he reacted to *change* the way he would a bunch of insurgents breaking into his home.

Not a problem. There were ways to scale Hawk's guarded castle.

Catching the dog's eyes, Bull made a high, almost inaudible *ooo-ooo-ooo* whine.

Raising his muzzle, Gryff imitated the sound with a most pitiful, mournful howl.

"Ay, *pobrecito*." Caz went down on one knee and held out a hand. Trained as a medic by the Special Forces, now a nurse practitioner, Caz had an especially soft heart for pets.

Still pressed against Bull, Gryff started to wag his tail.

"Go say hi, buddy." Bull motioned toward Caz, and Gryff advanced...carefully. A sniff, a caress, and Caz had himself a new furry friend.

"Where'd he come from?" Gabe also knelt and held out a hand to be assessed.

"In the park. Some assholes were trying to get him to fight another dog—and Gryff wasn't into it. The one who bought him was told he was a great fighting dog."

"He's neutered," Caz pointed out.

"Yep. When I broke up the fight and busted the humans up a little"—his brothers grinned—"the owner left Gryff behind. I couldn't leave the pup there—and we could use a dog."

Hawk snorted his disagreement.

Rubbing his jaw, Gabe scowled. "I'll check around. Make sure we're not having any dog fights around here."

Bull had counted on that. Rescue's Chief of Police took his job seriously.

"He's torn up a bit." Caz was already checking the dog's injuries as Gryff nosed Gabe's hand for more petting.

"Yeah. The other dog ripped up Gryff's paw, got him a few times on the neck and shoulder. He's hurting, Doc."

"*Sí*. I'll give you some ointment for him," Caz said.

"Hell. Let me know if you see the bastards again." Hawk's blue eyes softened, and he went down on one knee for his own introduction.

Leaning against the kitchen island, Bull grinned at his deadly brothers. Gabe—a retired Navy SEAL like Bull and master of all weapons. Cynical, damaged Hawk—army sniper and pilot for anything that would fly. Cazador—Special Forces medic, silent and deadly with blades.

And all three hardasses turned to putty in a dog's fuzzy paws.

"That whine-on-command is pretty effective," Gabe said, having noticed that Bull instigated the *I'm-a-poor-puppy* sound.

"He's damn smart," Bull said. "Whoever had him before the asshole did some training. It won't take much to teach him to bark on command."

Caz groaned. "Don't tell Regan how to—"

As if summoned, Caz's daughter trotted across the deck in a flurry of light footsteps. All of ten years old now, she had long, dark brown hair, brown eyes, and light brown skin—like a mini-me Cazador. Her mother died last fall. Discovering he was a father, Caz had brought her to the Hermitage—and now she owned all their hearts.

"That's a dog." She stopped in the door.

"*Sí, mija*." Caz rose and held his hand out to her. "Bull rescued him. He has some sore spots, so be careful when you're petting him."

"Oh, he's all fluffy and pretty." Regan walked forward

cautiously—and damn, Bull hadn't realized just how big Gryff was. The dog probably outweighed the girl by ten to twenty pounds.

"Look to one side, not directly at him, and hold your hand out," Caz murmured.

When she did, Gryff walked over, tail already waving because...yeah, he could tell she was just a pup.

Regan grinned as the dog sniffed her hand, and she squeaked with the lick of the tongue, then set to petting the happy mutt. "What's his name?"

"Gryff—short for Gryffindor."

When the Harry Potter fan squealed in delight, Bull didn't miss the narrow-eyed stare from her father who recognized the manipulation.

Ha. Grinning, Bull watched as Regan and Gryff bonded. Her smile was huge.

There were days he really envied his brother. Caz not only had Regan but had found himself an incredibly strong woman with a big heart. Speaking of ...

"Where's JJ?" Bull asked Caz, then glanced at Gabe. "And Audrey?"

"JJ's starting the packing process." Caz was amused. "Two weeks away apparently requires a lot of forethought in what to take."

"Ah, I forgot she was leaving on Monday." The officer was headed to Sitka to learn all the nuances of Alaska law enforcement.

"Lillian offered Audrey a bribe of her special fertilizer mix to get help transplanting seedlings into bigger pots," Gabe said. "She won't be back for a couple of hours."

"Not if she has little seedlings to play with." Bull grinned. Gabe's woman, Audrey, had fallen head-over-heels in love with gardening. Lillian—whose arthritic knees weren't happy with kneeling on cold ground—loved the young woman's help and had taken the city girl under her wing.

"Since you're all here, and since I found a surplus of moose steak in the freezer, and we have too many eggs, how about chicken-fried steak and eggs?" Bull asked.

"I'm in," Hawk muttered. He loved everything country, from the food to the music.

"Can I help?" Regan asked hopefully.

Bull's heart turned the consistency of pudding. As if anyone could say no to those big brown eyes. "I wouldn't dream of cooking for a group without my junior sous chef." He motioned toward the kitchen. "Let me introduce you to the wonders of cream gravy."

Before Regan could rise, Gabe bent over and whispered in her ear, "See if you can talk him into making biscuits."

Bull smiled because...no persuasion needed. There was nothing as satisfying as feeding people—especially his family.

That night, Bull pulled into the back parking lot at his roadhouse, got out, and did his usual quick scrutiny of the surroundings. An itch tickled his monkey brain—someone was watching him—but whoever it was didn't feel dangerous. Then again, maybe he was paranoid simply from lack of sleep. Fucking PTSD. He'd left the military a good seven years ago. Shouldn't an escape from nightmares accompany the DD-214 discharge papers?

At least Gryff woke him up before he'd descended too far into the abyss. *Good dog.*

With narrowed eyes, Bull checked the area for movement. Seemed quiet enough. By the roadhouse, the patio area overlooking the lake wasn't open for dining yet. Movement caught his attention. Near the forested path to the town park, two people stood hand-in-hand, watching the water.

Music from the bar trickled out into the night along with the clamor of voices inside. Sounded as if it was getting busy. Time to rev up to tend bar.

Owning the roadhouse suited him, since he could alternate bartending with being a chef, or not do either on the days he needed to be in the office. Damn paperwork. Owning two other restaurants and a brewery, plus managing Mako's trust, was getting to be too much.

Maybe he could re-enlist?

Off to the right, a car door opened with a creak. "Bull!"

His muscles tightened. *Oh, hell.* Guess he knew who'd been watching him.

His ex-wife Paisley hurried across the slushy, gravel lot. Her blue eyes were alight, her smile big. She clasped her hands together. "Honey, it's so good to see you."

Sure, it was. His mouth flattened. Once upon a time, he hadn't been a cynical bastard, but his first wife and various girlfriends had introduced him to disillusionment. His second wife, Paisley, had put the icing on the cake.

Unable to avoid her hug without pushing her away, he turned his head to escape her attempted kiss. Even the wind off the snow-pack-fed lake couldn't cool down his annoyance. "What do you want, Paisley?"

"Oh, darling, don't be angry with me." Ignoring his step back, she patted his arm, then his chest.

Irritation bit into his self-control. "For fuck's sake, woman, when a person moves away from you, it's a polite way of saying *don't touch*. What part of that don't you understand?"

She stared at him with hurt on her face. "You love my touch and always want my kisses and to make love."

"*Not. Any. More.*" He took another step back and crossed his arms over his chest. Fucking-A, they'd been divorced for over two years.

"But..."

"Why are you here?" The struggle for patience felt as though he was slogging through the endless sands in Afghanistan with a full pack.

She curled a strand of hair around her finger and looked up through her lashes. "I miss you, Bull. I want to get back together." Her voice dropped to a mere whisper. "I think we made a mistake."

We made a mistake? He stared in disbelief. Had she forgotten so easily? He sure hadn't.

He'd been so in love with her. So damned blind. He'd let slide the times she said she had to show a house and been out late. He'd explained away the occasional whiff of unfamiliar aftershave when he'd kissed her neck, telling himself she'd touched her neck after shaking hands with someone. Despite knowing she was obsessive about checking her phone, he'd excused the times she didn't answer his texts.

Until one day.

Until he had trouble pissing, got checked, and was told he had an STD.

Trailing her for a few days, he'd learned that loyalty and fidelity were merely words to her, donned for appearance sake, and discarded as easily as her last month's purse.

Now she was here, saying they made a mistake?

There had been no mistake, except marrying her in the first place.

He gritted his teeth to keep from flaying her with sarcasm. What would be the point?

After a calming breath, he said evenly, "Paisley, we'll never be together. We had this talk." The one where he told her that he'd never be with someone he couldn't trust—and she'd broken that trust. Irreparably.

"But...but I miss you. I need you." She latched onto his arm and clung. "You love me. You said you did."

"It's over. I don't love you." He pried her fingers off. "Go home —and don't come back."

When she burst into tears, he hardened his heart and walked away.

As he reached the back door of the roadhouse, someone cleared their throat. Aw, fuck, someone had witnessed that clusterfuck of a scene? *Hell*.

"My boy, are you all right?" Lillian's crisp British-accented voice was as clear as if she were still performing Shakespeare in London's West End.

"Hey, you two." Discarding the morass of his past, Bull straightened his shoulders and brought out his smile for her and the wiry, white-haired man next to her. "I'm good, yes."

Lillian gave him a skeptical frown.

Diversion time. "You look great, Lillian." She'd gone back to London to have knee surgery and recuperate there. Alaska winters and walkers didn't mix well. "Tell you what—if Dante isn't treating you right, let me know, and I'll take his place."

Lillian's smile cleared the worry from her face.

"In yer dreams, boy." Dante, Mako's old friend, was on the downhill slide toward seventy but as tough as old shoe leather. Absently tugging on his beard, he watched as Paisley drove her car out of the lot, spewing gravel everywhere. "Would that be your ex-wife?"

So much for a diversion. "Yes, that's her." Bull ran his hand over his shaved skull. "Gotta admit, I was a fool. Her beauty shut my brain down completely; it took me a while to wise up."

"Happens to the best of us." Dante slapped his shoulder. "Eventually, you learn that what you want in a spouse is just like what you want in a teammate—someone to fight at your side. A partner who'll have your back and can be relied on."

The old soldier smiled down at Lillian. "A sense of humor doesn't hurt either."

"You knotty-pated old fool," the Brit murmured, but the way she leaned her head against his arm contradicted the insult.

Envy ran through Bull. That easy affection was what he'd

hoped to find with Paisley.

And hadn't.

"Enjoy your evening, you two." Bull managed a smile and pointed a finger at Dante. "Don't you kids leave any used condoms in my parking lot."

He walked through the door to the sound of Dante's sputtering and Lillian's laughter.

As he donned the denim vest that served as his roadhouse's uniform, he glanced around the bar. Very nice. The wagon wheel chandeliers, the antlers, and the distressed wood all made for a friendly atmosphere. The sawdust on the floor to impart a nostalgic ambiance hadn't lasted past the first few months. Too much of a pain to sweep up.

Since he only hired a band on weekends, the tiny dance floor was often wasted space. However, the raised stage and sound equipment came in handy for the activities he'd tried during the long snowy winter when people needed diversions. Karaoke, poetry and fiction-reading, open mic for music had all proven popular.

Once behind the bar, Bull called to the other bartender, "I'll take this half, Raymond."

Canadian Raymond Yang was working to save for grad school next year. He gave Bull a frazzled glare. His shoulder-length black hair, which his Taiwanese mother kept telling him to cut, had come loose from the leather tie. His long-sleeved shirt had wet stains on the cuff. "It's crazy tonight."

Good. Just what I need. Bull rubbed his hands together. "Fun times."

One of the servers, Felix, stepped between the curved rails of the waitstaff station. The blond young man—today in a flamboyant metallic print shirt that was dimmed only slightly by the vest—grinned and slid his pad of orders to Bull. "You're late, Boss."

"Sorry 'bout that." Bull used to worry about Felix, who openly played on gay stereotypes, saying he preferred that people knew exactly where he stood. He'd caused more than a few fights, but damned if there weren't more men than Bull realized who swung that direction. Felix never lacked for partners.

Bull kept an eye on him though. The sarge had taught him that a man watches out for the people on his team.

With the energy in the room fizzing like champagne, tonight would be a good night. As Bull filled drink orders, he exchanged banter with some customers, handed out compliments to others, and paused to simply...check in...with the quieter ones.

Best job in the world. Aside from cooking. And running businesses and—

"Bull, my favorite bartender!" A masseuse from McNally's Resort gave him a wide smile and a toss of her hair.

His mood soured slightly.

The woman's friend, also an employee of McNally's, leaned forward, pressing her ample breasts against the bar. "Now that the ski season's over, you'll see us in here more often."

"Good to hear," he answered. "It's nice to have a break between tourist seasons."

The masseuse reached across the bar to attempt to stroke his arm.

Pretending not to notice, he moved out of range, grateful for the bar between them.

I like people. Really, I do. Admittedly, sometimes he wished that *people* didn't include those of the female gender who touched without permission. Actually, a person's space should be respected, no matter the genders involved. "Can I get you anything else?"

"No, we're just waiting for some nachos from the—oh, here they are now," the woman said.

"Ma'am, here is your order." The brunette server set a platter of nachos on the bar top, all her attention on the customers. She didn't even glance at Bull.

Tilting his head, he studied her as she dealt with the payment. Wylie had mentioned he'd hired new waitstaff.

Intriguing-looking woman. Medium height and full-bodied rather than slender. She wore the roadhouse's denim vest over a rich blue shirt. A tooled leather belt wrapped around her black jeans. Gold earrings twinkled against dark brown hair that fell to mid-back in a long braid. She wore no makeup from what he could tell, but her gorgeous brown eyes, with stunningly long black lashes, were the color of melted dark chocolate.

She had a strong face with an assertive chin...and her perfectly curved mouth was made for smiling.

He wanted to see her smile.

Unfortunately, when she glanced at him, he got nothing. In fact, her big eyes were cold. It appeared here was one beauty who wouldn't be flirting with him. After giving him an unreadable look, she walked away.

He rubbed a thumb and finger down the sides of his goatee as he watched her.

Interesting. Did she dislike men with shaved heads? Or was the color of his skin a shade too dark?

Or maybe bartenders were on her shit list? If so, she'd certainly picked the wrong profession.

She stopped at a table to take orders and talk with the customers.

He was right—her smile was beautiful.

That *man* was here. The one who'd been so cruel to the woman in the parking lot. And he was a *bartender*.

Earlier, on her break, Frankie'd been outside and strolled around the building in time to witness the huge and hotter-than-hell *bastardo* coldly crushing his lover's heart and tossing her aside. Like she was nothing.

Like Jaxson did with me. Frankie's mouth tightened at how similar the parking lot drama had been to Jaxson's leaving.

How many nights had she cried herself to sleep at the memory of her husband's—ex-husband's—vicious words when he told her he was leaving.

"Hey, we had some good times, and hell, I know you liked the sex. You didn't seriously think it'd last, did you? I mean, I like you—I married you, right?—but this living together isn't working for me. It's time to move on."

Move on? He'd leave her? "B-but you love me, Jax. You said you did." She moved forward...somehow. Her legs didn't feel as if they belonged to her anymore. Taking his arm, she stared up at him.

With an irritated sound, he pried her hands off. "You're nice. Pretty and all that. Really. I just, kinda realized I don't love you. Yeah, you deserve someone better, right?"

He didn't love her.

But they made love just last night. She wrapped her arms around herself, against the chill in the air. In her heart. Had he forced himself to have sex with her?

Her hands fisted. "Did you ever love me?"

He flushed, and the dark red across his chiseled cheekbones only made him more striking. When they first met, she'd wondered what he'd seen in her. After all, he was so very handsome, a man who could be...

Could be a star among male models.

Oh. She stared at him as the future she'd imagined with him shattered.

Mama had signed him on with the agency last month, saying he was family now and deserved to have a chance. Now he would walk the runway in the upcoming fashion show. He was already receiving tons of exposure.

Her lips felt numb. "You got what you wanted from me—a contract with Bocelli Agency—and now you're dumping me."

"Jesus, don't get all butt-hurt. We had our fun. Now, it's time to call it quits." And he walked away. Out the door. Out of their marriage.

As a woman's piercing laugh came from a table near the bar, Frankie shook her head, trying to escape the memories. *Cavolo,* that ugly scene in the parking lot brought everything back, as if it'd been yesterday when Jax sliced her to pieces with his words and indifference.

Just like the bartender had done with his lover.

Frankie had hoped he was a tourist. Someone she'd never have to see again. Instead, he worked here in the bar. Did that suck or what?

Taking orders for drinks, she whispered insults between tables. "*Brutto pezzo di merda, bastardo*".

The bastard was definitely a piece of shit.

"*Vai a farti fottere.*"

Yes, he should go f-bomb himself.

She could see why his poor lover had fallen for him, because the guy was very much sex-on-a-stick. Start with that resonant, cavernous voice. Add in appearance: massive and hugely muscled. His skin was just slightly darker than her Italian heritage had given her. His mesmerizing black eyes, shaved scalp, and black goatee with a sprinkling of silver reinforced he was all man.

No one viewing him would realize he was such a jerk. Yet, five minutes after emotionally gutting a woman who loved him, he was flirting with every woman at the bar. It was typical behavior for shallow, heartless chick magnets like her ex.

Over at the other section of the bar, Felix caught her gaze. "Doing good, Frankie."

She smiled back. The effervescent waiter was such a darling. He'd helped orient her to her job earlier.

After working for a bit, she noticed drink orders were getting filled faster. The new bartender was very efficient. And, even if she hated to admit it, his arrival had changed the mood in the place. Everyone seemed friendlier. Happier.

As she walked up to the waitstaff station, two people slid onto empty stools—a curvy blonde woman and a black-haired man who reminded her of a stunning, young Antonio Banderas.

"Good evening," she greeted them.

"I see the roadhouse has a new server. Welcome to Rescue. How long have you been in town?" The man had a smooth, Hispanic-accented voice.

Was he flirting? No, he just seemed friendly. "This is my third day here."

"Oh, I bet you're the woman who rented a cabin from Dante." When Frankie nodded, the blonde held out her hand. "I'm Audrey. I run the library—and sometimes help with waiting tables here, too."

"Frankie." Frankie shook her hand. "It's good to meet you."

Audrey motioned to the man beside her. "Caz, commonly known as Doc, runs the health clinic."

"*Chica*, I'm not a doctor." He frowned at Audrey. "How did you manage to convince Gabe you're so sweet?"

She smiled. "Love. It's blind."

Laughing, Frankie turned to check on the bartenders. Still busy. She smiled at Caz and Audrey. "You have a very friendly town."

It'd surprised her how much she enjoyed being here—and even working in a bar. Handing out drinks was much better than dealing with oh-so-entitled models, photographers, and agents.

"It is friendly, especially now. After a long Alaska winter, everyone's happy to see new faces," Caz said.

"I bet." Before she could say more, the big asshole bartender slipped the drink orders from her hand and grinned at the new customers. "Where's Gabe?"

"He's on his way in," Audrey said. "He was playing with paperwork and budgets."

"Now, that's just sad." The bartender flipped through Frankie's orders.

"Hey, Caz is here," someone farther down the bar shouted, then slapped the bar top. "Song, song, song."

"*No mames, güey.*" Caz lifted his hands in exasperation.

The chant spread from around the bar to everyone in the room. "Song, song, song."

Despite the words Frankie had translated to mean something like *seriously, dude*, Caz shook his head in resignation and asked Audrey, "You in?"

Snickering, she shook her head no. "My throat is sore. Lillian made me help act out a book for the preschoolers."

Frankie leaned on the bar. What in the world was going on?

With one hand, the bartender was drawing a beer, with the other, he slid a wireless microphone down the bar top. "You're up, Doc. "Let's have 'Hakuna Matata'."

Caz sighed and picked the mic up. "You owe me, *'mano*. That beer better be cold."

"Always."

At the bartender's dazzling smile, Frankie's heart completely skipped a beat. *Cribbio—sheesh.* All that intense confident masculinity was intimidating.

She forced her gaze away and saw Caz flick the mic on...and start the bouncy tune from *The Lion King*.

When the bartender picked up a mic and joined in, Frankie's mouth dropped open. The man had a gorgeous bass voice.

The two were spectacular. They sang harmony, added their own sound effects, and when they reached the chorus, the bartender waved at the room and yelled, "You bastards have had plenty to drink. Join your asses in—or I'm cutting you all off."

Laughter ran through the room, and everyone in the place started to sing.

Mouth open, Frankie stared. It was *amazing*.

As she returned to serving drinks, Caz and the bartender sang another tune, and this time the customers didn't wait to join in.

When she returned to the bar the next time, the music was still bubbling in her veins. She'd sung along, too. Everyone in the place was smiling.

"That was incredible," she said to Audrey as she set her drink orders down.

Audrey grinned. "It's fun, isn't it?"

"Does that happen a lot? He"—Frankie motioned to the giant bartender—"he kept working as he sang and didn't seem to think anything about it."

"He didn't." Audrey took a sip of her drink. "He and his brothers grew up singing together. Even more than the rest, Bull thinks music is meant to be shared."

"Bull? He's called Bull?" Frankie took stock of the bartender. At least six-four with muscles piled on muscles. There was a wrestler-actor named the Rock, and Bull was like Dwayne Johnson's bigger, deadlier brother. A lot deadlier. Despite the man's easy smile, those dark eyes were watchful, always aware of everything and everyone in the room. His stance and his body language were always in a ready state. Yes, she'd guess he'd lived through some ugly stuff. "Bull seems like a good name for him."

"Apparently, he had an encounter with a bull moose when he was a child—and wanted to grow into the name."

"An encounter? Is that what we're calling it?" A man put his arm around Audrey, kissed her cheek, and grinned at Frankie. "The moose chased Bull through the trees and would've stomped him good if Mako—our father—hadn't dropped it."

"Wait, what? He was chased by a moose as a kid?" Frankie's eyes were probably popping out of her head.

"*Viejo*, you're scaring the cheechako," Caz chided.

"Sorry." Audrey's guy chuckled. "It didn't catch him. He laughed his ass off afterward."

"Of course he did." Audrey rolled her eyes. "You idiots have no common sense about danger. None whatsoever."

"So harsh, champ," Bull said to Audrey before setting the last drink on Frankie's tray. "It's Frankie, right?"

She nodded, keeping her expression cool. He might be an

awesome singing bartender with an interesting background, but he was also a heart-destroying *bastardo*.

"Are you doing all right? Any problems out there?" His dark eyes held concern. As if he'd flatten any trouble-making customers for her.

Which was lovely, but she didn't want his concern or his attention and was tempted to tell him exactly why.

No, Frankie. She needed this job and letting loose her hot temper would be a quick way to the door. She could be polite and work with this man.

But...why did he have to be so sexy?

"No problems. Everyone has been great." She added a reluctant, "Thank you."

Catching the chill, he stiffened slightly, nodded, and returned to his work.

"Whoa, I didn't know there was anyone on earth who didn't like Bull," Audrey clapped her hands over her mouth. "Sorry."

"It's—" There was no way to explain. Frankie shrugged.

Amusement in his dark blue eyes, Audrey's guy held his hand out. "I'm Gabe MacNair, Chief of Police here—and I won't arrest you for not liking the bartender."

Frankie stiffened. Kit's letter had said a Rescue cop was in the PZs. "Well, I'm glad I won't get locked up. It's good to meet you, Chief." She managed to smile and shake his hand. "Now, I'd better get these drinks delivered."

She picked up her tray and headed for her section, hearing Monty Python's Knights chorusing, *"Run away. Run away!"* in her head.

After delivering the drinks, she checked her section, cleaned tables, and picked up empties. There weren't many dirty glasses since the restaurant section had closed, and their busser had moved to the bar.

Spotting three men taking over a corner table, Frankie headed that direction.

One man was a tall, skinny ginger, complete with a long beard. One was short and slim with short brown hair and a trim beard. The third had a black buzz cut and was clean-shaven. All three wore boots, jeans, and work shirts.

As she smiled at the men, she noticed Felix had moved into her section. "Welcome to the roadhouse, gentlemen. What can I get you to drink?"

The red-bearded guy leered at her. "Are you on the menu?"

Mannaggia, did servers have to put up with such tired lines every night?

"No." She didn't bother to soften her reply. Lifting her brows, she waited, pen hovering over the pad.

Although the ginger scowled at her, they gave their orders without further wayward comments.

As she left, she heard them talking about women getting above themselves. How women were created to serve men.

She stopped short. *Merda.* Yes, *shit,* exactly. That was the same drivel Obadiah had used on Kit. Could those men be Patriot Zealots? Instead of treating them like creepy sexist assholes, she should've been polite and exchanged banter. She could have slid in a few questions and gotten a feel for them.

"Frankie, my sweet." Resembling a California surfer boy, Felix joined her and started to lift the drink orders off her tray.

"Hey." She slapped her hand on the pad. "What are you doing?"

"The boss doesn't want our female waitstaff to have to deal with Patriot Zealots—*PZs.* They're...hmm. Let's just say they're total Neanderthals."

"Felix, that's an insult to Neanderthals everywhere."

Laughing, he patted her shoulder. "Exactly right. So—"

She didn't release her grip on the drink orders. "I can handle cavemen."

"But—"

Felix didn't have a shy bone in his body, and his preference for the same sex was obvious. "Honey, if they're like that with women, they're probably just as rude to you."

Why should he have to put up with their behavior?

He flushed. "Yeah, but I'm closer to their weight class than you are."

Those *bastardi*. "I knew Alaska was a frontier, but I'm surprised the owner puts up with—"

"Eh, he doesn't." Felix leaned against an empty table. "I should have gone over this with you. If anyone touches you inappropriately, you can boot his ass out or tell the bartenders and they'll handle it. We tolerate mildly rude comments. After all, the customers are drinking and hey, *Alaskan*, right?"

She laughed. "As far as I've seen, the customers in here are nicer than New Yorkers."

"I'm *so* not going to vacation in New York."

"Oh, no, no. You'd be fine. New York is all about equal opportunity rudeness. With equal amounts of nice, really."

"Good to know." Felix glanced back at the PZ table. "After the boss banned, oh, a half-dozen PZs, they learned to keep their hands and crude insults to themselves. But their misogynistic, bigoted behavior makes the female servers uncomfortable, and I'm okay with—"

"No, Felix. Let's see how it goes with me waiting on them. If I'm bothered, I'll ask you to take over." She needed to talk with them, see if Kit was inside their compound still—and how to get her and Aric out.

"*Girlfriend*." Felix shook his head reprovingly.

Frankie gave him a slow smile. "I grew up in New York, my friend, and learned my insults from cabbies and street vendors. I can hold my own."

"Huh. In that case, they're all yours."

She timed her arrival at the bar so the nice bartender named Raymond would fill her orders.

Then she took the PZs their drinks. "Here you are."

More leering looks.

She smiled cheerfully. "I hear you guys are Patriot Zealots, but I don't know what that means."

The red-bearded guy started, "It means we take women like you and—"

He grunted when someone kicked his leg.

The older, clean-shaven one took over. "The Prophet has directed us to return to the traditions of our forefathers. To follow the Bible and the Constitution. Our people find peace in letting go of modern ways."

He seemed oh-so-sincere. She'd bet he did a fine job of recruiting people.

"Hmm. That sounds different. Interesting." *Don't appear too enthusiastic, Frankie.* The crazy cultists would be suspicious otherwise. She needed to let them chase *her.*

Even if everything in her urged her to get Kit and Aric out now.

She took their money for the drinks—no credit cards for these boys—and handed back change. Modeling herself after a younger cousin, she assumed a pitiful, wavery smile. "After the month I've had, peace would be awfully nice."

She left without waiting for their response. They'd be back. It sounded as if the PZs were frequent customers.

Stopping near the center of the room, she pulled in a breath to release her anger and frustration. Boy, did she need a drink to erase the foul taste of the fanatics.

Hang on, Kit. I'm going to find you and see that you're safe.

One more breath, and she was able to get moving again.

As she headed for the next table of customers, she noticed the bartender—Bull—watching her with a concerned expression, as if making sure she was all right.

The realization sent a tiny blossom of warmth through her. Because, despite her brave words to Felix, right now, it felt like home was awfully far away.

CHAPTER FIVE

The truth of the matter is that you always know the right thing to do. The hard part is doing it. - LTG Norman Schwarzkopf, U.S. Army, Retired

The town cleaned up nice, didn't it? With Gryff at his side, Bull strolled down Rescue's main street. Checking on the businesses was another of the responsibilities on his plate.

When Mako had first moved to the failing town of Rescue, he'd bought up a bunch of properties to help the business owners escape. Then McNally's Resort opened, bringing tourists back to the area. When Mako died, he left everything to Bull, Gabe, Caz, and Hawk along with orders: *Revive the town.*

It was why all four of them moved to Rescue. Bull opened the roadhouse; Gabe, the police station; Caz, the health clinic. Hawk had only come back last fall and was picking up jobs as a bush pilot. Since Bull had an MBA, his brothers dumped the administration of Mako's trust and managing the properties to him.

Bull considered the street. On each side were piles of dirty snow that would take a while yet to melt.

The business owners had started their spring spruce-up. The two-story hardware store was now forest green. Obviously inspired, the sporting goods owner used the same color to paint the trim on his white building. The art gallery was pale yellow, the coffee shop green and white. Brightly colored, boxy clapboard buildings mingled with reproduction Victorian architecture creating a picturesque downtown, especially against the backdrop of snow-topped peaks to the south.

It'd taken a year of hard work, but the town was more tourist-friendly, as well. The sidewalks and streetlights had been repaired. Gabe had talked the town council into hiring the local handymen, Chevy and Knox, to build wooden benches.

Bull had purchased a batch of whiskey barrels, cut them in half, and handed them over to Mayor Lillian for the town's gardeners to use as planters along Main Street. Now, they were filled with soon-to-bloom snapdragons.

With the snow beginning to melt, the locals who'd holed up for the winter were emerging to mingle with early fishermen and a spattering of tourists. The summer season would soon be in full swing.

It was good the roadhouse was hiring new waitstaff.

And one server, in particular, was fucking intriguing.

Bull had checked out Frankie's paperwork before sending it off to his administrative assistant in Anchorage. Ms. Bocelli was a born-and-bred New Yorker. After high school, she'd worked in a restaurant, then in an office at a modeling agency. Gabe, being a paranoid cop, had run a background check, and Frankie had no record.

Bull nodded at a man coming out of the post office and held up an acknowledging hand to the postmistress's hail. He should visit Irene; she knew almost as much gossip as Lillian.

Business by business, he made his way down Main Street, asking about sales, vandalism, shoplifting, and any other problems. He noted down suggestions and complaints.

Since he needed supplies, he visited Dante's Grocery. In Anchorage, he bought in bulk for his three restaurants, but shopped locally for his own stuff. No one in Rescue wanted Dante's to close.

"Sorry, Gryff." Bull tied the dog's leash to a street pole. "You have to wait out here. Food and fur make a bad combination."

Gryff gave an anxious whine. It was the first time Bull'd left him when in town.

Bull went down on his haunches to talk on the dog's level. "Listen, buddy. You're on our team now, and we never leave anyone behind. I'll grab the groceries and be back out. There's a dog biscuit in your future if you're patient, yeah?"

He got a long lick on his hand and chuckled. "Good enough."

Entering the store, he did a quick survey. Thanks to Mako's training and years in special ops, he doubted he'd ever lose the edgy awareness of his surroundings.

Behind the counter, Gabe's woman, Audrey, was ringing up groceries for Lillian. Audrey stopped by the grocery each day to give Dante a break. She was a sweetheart—as all of Rescue had come to realize.

Down one aisle, a couple of Patriot Zealot men were shopping. Mirrors showed their women in another aisle.

Bull strolled over to the counter. "Audrey. Lillian."

"Hi, Bull." Petite and curvy, Audrey wore a gray T-shirt that matched her smoke-gray eyes. The writing on it made him grin —"*I see you research without the librarian's help. I, too, like to live dangerously.*"

"Good morning, my boy." Lillian tilted her head to accept a kiss on the cheek. Her smile faded to a small frown. "Your skin is brown enough that dark circles under your eyes aren't as obvious as mine"—she patted her cream-white skin—"but I can see you haven't gotten enough sleep."

She was an observant woman. His dreams had been plagued with explosions from IEDs, rattled with gunfire, and streaked with blood. He'd woken, covered in sweat, and still feeling the grit of sand in his clothing and between his teeth. The nightmares had been his fault this time. He hadn't banked the fire in the wood-stove before going to bed, and the house had been too warm. Heat brought back...everything.

"Although I *am* a god among men"—he stroked his goatee—"even *I* occasionally have trouble sleeping at night."

"What?" Audrey shook her head. "Uh-uh. I hate to tell you this, but Gabe is our local god."

"No way." He gave her an outraged stare. "To think you used to be my favorite."

Her snicker stopped abruptly. "Just a minute...does losing favorite status mean you won't make me smoked salmon chowder anymore?"

Crossing his arms over his chest, he waited.

She huffed. "Fine, fine, you're a god among men. Even Gabe would agree—as long as he gets that chowder."

"Well played, my boy." Chortling, Lillian patted his arm. "I'll see you at poker night. Get some sleep before that."

"Yes, ma'am." Grabbing a basket, Bull headed for the produce aisle. The greenhouse at the Hermitage provided most salad makings, but he craved fresh fruit—even if it cost an arm and leg.

Near the potatoes were three Patriot Zealot women, two older and one in her twenties, all three in typical drab PZ attire.

He'd always wondered why the long hair when it was always in a bun. And the ankle-length skirts were so impractical, probably mandated simply to handicap their women.

The roadhouse's new employee, Frankie, was chatting with the women.

Now what could a New Yorker and members of a religious militia have in common? Interested, he started picking through the apples, pretending not to listen.

"I love your clothes." Frankie gestured to their long-sleeved blouses and skirts. "Sometimes I feel as if I'm...oh, flaunting myself...in what I wear. Do you feel safer when you wear more coverage?"

Bull blinked. Last night, she'd seemed completely comfortable in her skin. More than most women. Then again, he was male. What did he know?

He glanced at her from the corner of his eye. She had a fantastic body, all lush curves, and compelling brown eyes framed with long dark eyelashes.

She was so very female, yet not at all delicate or frail. Watching her work, he'd gotten the impression of resilience. Sturdiness, even. She wasn't someone who'd fold under pressure. That was a character trait the Navy SEALs valued.

But...she did appear tired, and her eyes were red, as if she'd been crying. The thought was worrisome.

"The Prophet has told us what a good woman should wear, and our safety comes from following his guidance in all things," the woman with gray streaks in her hair told Frankie.

While the younger PZ woman remained silent, the other two spoke in low voices of their contentment that God, the Prophet, and their husbands would handle everything. Their joy was in obedience.

Bull didn't react. To each his or her own, and they sounded content. He and his brothers—especially Gabe—worried about the women behind the high PZ fences, but this group didn't act as if they were imprisoned or unhappy.

"Your lives sound just wonderful." Frankie beamed at them. "Do you suppose I could visit sometime? Maybe even talk to some people about...I don't know...joining or something?" Her voice sounded higher than normal, her face guileless, and she came off as years younger. More innocent.

She wanted to visit the fanatics? For fuck's sake. Still stalling, Bull dropped some oranges into his basket. The New Yorker hadn't seemed like someone susceptible to a fucking cult. His muscles twitched with his urge to yank her away from the PZs.

She might not take that well.

Yet the staff in the restaurants was his responsibility, almost like an extended family. Damned if he wanted to think Frankie would imprison herself inside high fences where some asshole would dictate all her choices, from clothing to what to think. What would drive her to even consider that shit?

Well, he'd keep an eye on her. However, since she didn't like him, maybe he could get Felix to talk with her.

Whatever was wrong, Bull would help if he could.

Kit. The shock of seeing her best friend still reverberated through Frankie. She'd walked into the grocery, and there was Kit. Unfortunately, her friend was accompanied by not only the women, but male PZs.

Emotions pelted Frankie like a hailstorm. The same height as Frankie, Kit had always been more slender. Now she was emaciated, with hollowed cheeks. Her fair skin was sallow, her gold-brown hair yanked back tightly in a bun. She wore an ankle-length, heavy, black skirt and a white shirt buttoned to the neck. Her amber eyes were haunted and exhausted. A yellowing bruise covered her left jaw, and she moved...carefully. Like she hurt.

Cazzo, Kit.

Frankie kept smiling and talking, trying to appear as if she was eating up what the middle-aged Patriot Zealot women said. Kit had yet to speak. Maybe the younger PZs weren't allowed to talk when out in public? Or the older women wouldn't let her.

Frankie's palm tingled because... *No, you mustn't slap anyone. Concentrate.*

She nodded at appropriate moments. "That makes sense." No, no, it didn't. How could anyone take orders from some male nutcase on how to dress and who she could talk to? *Count me out.*

When one of the women stiffened, Frankie followed her gaze. The giant bartender moved away and turned the corner to a different aisle. How long had he been in the produce section? Had he heard their conversation? What must he think of her?

Then again, why should she care?

She turned her attention back to the women. To Kit. They needed to talk.

But how? Obviously, nothing would be said in front of Kit's babysitters. Okay, then. How inventive could Kit be?

"Oh, oh, shoot." Frankie interrupted one of the older women. "I might have left my car unlocked." The near falsehood bothered her, but it wasn't...exactly...a lie. She hadn't left the car unlocked, but she *might* have. "There are a lot of tourists in town."

"City people are all thieves," one woman said. "You'd best go check."

A thief, am I? Frankie smiled. "Nice to meet you all."

At the front, she walked past the bartender who was talking with Audrey. "Audrey, I need to check something in my car. I'll be back for my groceries." She set her basket down near the counter and headed out.

She could feel Bull's gaze on her back.

Outside and away from a big brown dog that was tied to a streetlight, she stood by the wall. Would Kit be able to come up with an excuse and lose her watchers so they could talk?

Her breathing sped up at the thought of Kit trapped in that place. Being hurt. Unable to call for help.

The door opened, and Kit stepped out and looked around. In the grocery, someone called, "Stay right outside, woman."

Staying out of sight of anyone inside, Frankie called softly, "Here."

"Frankie, Oh, sweet Jesus, Frankie!" Kit started to rush over, then halted when Frankie held up her hand. *Stop.*

"Lean against the building by the door, so your asshole PZs can see your back but not your face." Frankie remained close to the wall. The minute someone came out, she'd walk away and not appear as if she'd been talking to Kit.

As Kit turned and stood in sight of the window, Frankie frowned at the bruise. "Did Obadiah hit you?"

Kit nodded, her shoulders rounding as if the facial damage was the least of what she'd suffered.

"*Amica mia,* you mustn't go back there. Come with me now, and I'll have you in—"

"They have Aric. I can't leave without him." Kit's voice, normally bright and clear, was a pain-filled, hoarse whisper. "They only let me out today because they want my advice about buying berry bushes from Soldotna."

All plants grew better with Kit's help. Under her hands, even the worst soil grew wonders.

"Then we should go to the police to get Aric out." Frankie held up a hand. "Right, I remember. Someone in the police is a PZ, so we'll call the FBI or—"

Kit shook her head frantically. "The guards would kill Aric before the cops could get through the gate. Eventually, maybe, someone would find his body in the forest, and they'd say he ran away and got killed by a bear or something."

Gut-wrenching horror propelled Frankie forward. Her godson wasn't even five years old yet. "No one would do that."

"They would." Kit swallowed. "They *have.* At least twice in the Texas compound before I joined them."

How long could someone live in such fear? "Just take Aric and run."

"It's...impossible. First, all the young ones stay in the children's barracks, day and night, with a matron. The women sleep in a building next door unless a husband wants..." Kit wrapped her arms around herself.

Unless a husband wanted his conjugal rights? A flare of anger shot through Frankie. No, concentrate. "So, you don't get to see him?"

"Well..." Kit hesitated. "Aric sneaks away to be with me. A lot."

"But you can't just...escape?" Frankie frowned. "I saw the fence and gate in front. How far does it—"

"All the way around the compound. With guards and watch-towers and guns." Kit shook her head, shoulders sagging. "Maybe we could hide from the guards...at night...but I sure couldn't climb that fence, especially with Aric."

All that razor wire on top. No one could. Frankie scowled. "Why don't the other women do anything? If all of you revolted..."

"Some women would leave if they could get their children. But some are there because they want to be. Like them." Kit motioned toward the grocery store. "They believe with all their heart in the Prophet, Reverend Parrish. They tell Captain Nabera if anyone talks about leaving or criticizes anything."

Before Frankie could ask, Kit added, "Nabera likes hurting people—especially women."

Madonna, how was she going to get Kit and Aric out? "I'll tell the FBI, and they'll surround the place so no one—"

"No. It'd end up being another Waco or Ruby Ridge shootout where kids got killed along with the adults. No."

"Then"—Frankie's hands fisted—"how can I help?"

Kit's gaze was despairing. "You can't. I'm so sorry; I shouldn't have dragged you into this."

I won't accept that answer. "What if I cut a hole in the fence? At night?"

Kit blinked. "A hole. To let us out through the fence. Maybe... maybe. Our two buildings are next to the fence. If we could crawl out through the fence behind the buildings, we'd only have to dodge one patrolling sentry."

"Okay, then. One hole coming up. When?" Frankie hesitated. "I need time to figure out how to get to the right place." Her courage vacillated. That area was all forest.

"Frankie, this isn't safe for you. You could—"

"When, Kit?"

"Ahhh, it needs to be a Saturday—that's when Obadiah drives the captain and other lieutenants into town for drinks. There'll be fewer guards, and with the Captain gone, they get lax on their rounds. Today's Thursday. So not this Saturday."

"Okay."

Kit's wry expression held some of her old spirit. "I'm afraid the forest doesn't have street signs. You'll need to figure out how to get to the compound...at night. Maybe a week from this Saturday? As soon as it's full dark?"

"Yes." Frankie whipped out her phone. "Saturday, May eleventh. Full dark." Full dark didn't occur until late at night. She'd have to take that into her calculations. "If something happens, either on my part or yours, is there a way to make contact?"

"No. Only the Prophet and Nabera have phones."

"*Stronzi*," Frankie hissed. "Fine, if something happens, we'll rain check until the next Saturday...until the time it all comes together."

Relief filled Kit's face even as her brows drew together. "It's not safe for you. Frankie, I don't even know how long I'll be here. Obadiah plans to take us back to Texas sometime this summer."

Just then the grocery door opened.

Even as Kit turned, Frankie shot her a look—*We have a plan*—then strolled away down the street as if that's what she'd been doing all along. All she wanted was to confront those PZs. Hit them and show them what it felt like to be beaten-up.

Swearing under her breath, she circled the block and returned to Dante's Grocery.

The PZs were gone.

Still tied up, the pretty brown dog stood and wagged its tail.

"Aren't you a sweetie." Frankie held her hand out. She'd never had a pet, but quite a few of her friends had pets—usually apartment-sized ones. "I'm Frankie, and I'm friendly, too."

After a good sniff, the dog thrust its head under her hand.

She laughed. "All right then."

Seeing a few healing gashes on his ears, paws, and muzzle, she stroked him carefully, avoiding anything that might be sore. "Whatever you've been doing, you need to be more careful, okay? Now, I need to get my groceries before everything melts. It was nice to meet you."

She got a dog-smile in return.

Inside the grocery store, the bartender—no, she needed to stop thinking of him like that. He was Bull. She was so slow-witted, it'd taken her a whole day to put Bull the bartender together with Bull's Moose Roadhouse and ask Felix if Bull, the bartender, owned the place.

The man was her employer, and everybody liked him, except her. Then again, people showed a different side of themselves to work associates. She'd just been lucky—unlucky—enough to see him with his lover.

After all, everybody at the modeling agency liked Jaxson—except for the women he'd screwed over who thought he was the biggest wart on the face of the planet.

"Was your car all right?" Audrey asked, turning toward Frankie.

What exactly had she told Audrey and Bull about her car? That seemed ages ago. "Um, fine. All fine."

After a searching stare, Bull picked up her basket of groceries and set it on the counter for her. "So, how are you settling in?"

Oh, no, not conversation. It was the last thing she wanted right now when all her thoughts were focused on Kit.

Get it together. You're a tourist who took a job for fun. Focus, Frankie.

She unpacked the basket onto the counter. "Well enough, thank you. I have to admit it's disconcerting to wake up to birds singing instead of traffic and horns and sirens." Where was the rumble of the subway under her feet, the wailing of sirens, chiming church bells, and blasting car radios? Where were the street and subway musicians?

Homesickness hollowed out a place beneath her sternum. She'd cried last night like a little five-year-old away on her first sleep-over. *Cavolo.* Definitely holy crap. Her eyes were still red. Hopefully, they hadn't noticed.

The bartender didn't seem to miss much.

She set a loaf of French bread onto the counter. "I never thought I'd miss the sound of traffic. Or pigeons cooing or even a screeching gull."

"I understand all too well." Audrey started ringing up the groceries. "I've only been here about a year—from Chicago. Would you believe I rented your cabin on the lake before I moved in with Gabe?"

"Really?" Another city person. "Then you get it—about the lack of noise. And strange sounds around the cabin?"

A frown creased Bull's forehead. "What sounds?"

"Like someone or something is moving around outside. And there are weird hoots and sometimes a scream."

A faint smile deepened the sun lines beside his eyes. "You're on a lake. Lots of animals will wander down to get a drink or to hunt. Moose and bear don't care how much noise they make. The hoots are—"

"Excuse me. *Bears?* Bears...outside *my* cabin?"

"'Fraid so, yeah." The amusement in his eyes increased.

"I saw a few when I was there. One evening, I walked out of the cabin and a moose stood right beside my car." Audrey shook her head. "I learned you shouldn't try to get one to move. You'll only make it so mad that it'll attack."

"Half-a-ton of weight stomping on you can do serious damage," Bull agreed.

"You really did get chased by a moose when you were little?" Frankie asked him.

"Yep. We enjoyed moose stew all year." Bull's lips twitched, drawing her attention. Wasn't it funny how a goatee could make a man's mouth look...kissable?

Uh-oh, don't even go there, Frankie Bocelli.

"I better get to work," he told Audrey, then his gaze settled on Frankie. How could black eyes get even darker? "You're working at the roadhouse tomorrow night. Come in a few minutes early. I'd like to talk to you."

Her mouth dropped open.

Maybe he was the boss, but it was worrisome that he'd know her schedule offhand without checking it. Why would he want her to come in early? Maybe to put the moves on her now that his lover was gone?

Her jaw tightened. Whatever he wanted, he could tell her during her work hours—when there were lots of people around. She'd show up exactly on time and not a second early.

Giving them both a nod, Bull headed out, carrying his groceries and a giant bag of dog food.

As all the muscles of his arms and shoulders flexed into boulders, Frankie stared, then yanked her gaze away. *"Santo cielo."*

Audrey's laughing eyes met hers.

Caught. Frankie gave her a rueful shrug. "All those muscles. Who wouldn't drool?"

Grinning her agreement, Audrey started bagging the groceries.

A high voice came from outside, "Uncle Bull, we want to cook!"

Frankie checked the front window.

A young girl, maybe ten years old, charged at Bull.

He set his bags down on the sidewalk, caught the child, and swung her around. As she patted his shaved head, her little girl giggles mixed with his deep masculine laughter.

"Madonna," Frankie muttered. "I think my ovaries just exploded."

Audrey busted out laughing.

Frankie shook her head. "Not an expression common to libraries?"

Audrey wiped her eyes. "Not even close."

Frankie turned to the window again. A boy and another girl had appeared and were obviously asking Bull for something.

"He's teaching Regan how to cook." Audrey continued checking out the groceries.

"He can cook? Like something besides weightlifter protein shakes?"

Audrey gave her a startled look. "He's a superb cook."

That did make sense, considering he owned the roadhouse. Outside, he unleashed the dog from the light pole, then helped the children scramble into the red pickup. Then the dog jumped in, getting a quick ruffle of his fur before Bull shut the door. He acted like he liked the dog, yet it was so skinny and battered. Why didn't he take better care of it?

Frankie shook her head and noticed that Audrey had finished ringing up the groceries.

"By the way, do you read?" Audrey asked. "We have a book club—several, actually—and—"

"I'm in." Frankie winced. "Well, as long as you're reading something besides literary stuff. I read to escape reality, not wallow in it."

Audrey's eyes were dancing. "I feel the same way. We have a romance group, one for mysteries, and one for thrillers. Oh, and Tina and Lillian want to start one that's only for subversive women."

"I gave up on romance." After Jaxson, she'd lost hope there were any nice guys in the universe. "But I love thrillers, and the subversive women's group sounds like a blast."

Books—and a way to meet people, gossip, and get information. Perfect.

"Awesome." Audrey gave her details of the meetings and upcoming books, and Frankie entered everything into her phone. Where would she be without her smartphone to-do lists?

Audrey handed over the grocery receipt. "Your total comes to $105.83."

"Aaah, right." She waved her phone over the card reader. "I forgot that the price of stuff here was higher."

"Sure is. Having to fly or ship everything in makes for high costs." Audrey eyed Frankie with worry. "Working in the bar doesn't pay all that well."

"I'm doing all right." Her savings account was quite healthy, especially compared to her sisters who'd blow their earnings on clothes, furniture, cars, vacations, and expensive alcohol. Crazy. She preferred quality over trends—and stocks and bonds over spending. Even if she hadn't gotten the roadhouse job, she'd be fine.

But that wasn't what a real server would say. To ease Audrey's worries, Frankie said, "The tips have been good and will get better if the tourist season is as busy as people think."

"It sure seemed that way last year."

"Now that you've been here a year, do you like living in Alaska? It's got to be different from Chicago." Frankie snorted. "The whole town of Rescue has fewer people than are in my apartment building back home."

Audrey's eyes lit. "I love living here, especially because it's so small. I feel like I belong, and I get to help decide what happens with the town. In Chicago, I was...oh, just another ant in a colony. One of the masses. Here, people know me. They notice if I'm ill. They worry about me."

"Hmm." *Who would notice if I were sick?* Hmm. The people at work—after all, her family was there. Then again, her sisters didn't usually notice if she wasn't feeling up to par. Aside from them—and they did love her, even if it seemed sometimes like that love came second to their careers—she had some good friends. Just not anyone she saw every day. "I think I envy you."

"No need." Audrey smiled. "You're here now. Give Rescue a shot and see if you don't end up staying forever."

"You have book clubs and bars and friendly people. How could I not love it here?" With a grin, Frankie picked up her groceries and headed to the car.

Even as disquiet crept over her. *Not return to New York? Leave her job?*

Never. Uh-uh, never.

CHAPTER SIX

T *eamwork is essential; it gives the enemy other people to shoot at. -* Murphy's Laws of Combat

The next evening at the roadhouse, Bull noticed that Frankie hadn't come in early. In fact, she not only showed up exactly on time but persisted in avoiding him. All her drink orders were handed to the other bartender.

Amused, Raymond shot Bull a grin as she headed off with a full tray. "She hates you and loves me. I like this."

He couldn't punch an employee as he would've if it were Gabe poking at him. "Maybe she only likes short, ugly men."

Raymond made a hissing sound in pseudo-annoyance. Far from ugly, he was beloved of the customers.

Bull started building a black and tan, his gaze half on Frankie. Aside from steering clear of him, she was an excellent server. Efficient, didn't mix up orders, kept the tables bussed. She was cheerful and friendly without flirting...and dodged the occasional roving hand without making anything of it.

Not that she should have to put up with that kind of crap,

dammit. Case in point, the four college-aged boys down from McNally's Resort who sat at a center table. They had more money than sense, and even their few wits had disappeared with alcohol.

"You're so pretty," one said loudly. "Want to go do something after you get off work?"

Frankie shook her head, enough that the gold hoop earrings danced against her neck. "Sorry, but I don't date customers. Would you like a refill on that beer?"

In a typical one-upmanship move, the guy's friend said loudly, "Hey, no need to date. How about we get together, and you sit on my face."

Even as Bull's temper rose, Frankie gave a merry laugh. "Seriously? Is your nose that much bigger than your dick?"

When everyone within hearing roared with laughter, the young man turned red and sank down in his seat.

Bull nodded approval at how she'd taken the kid down with humor, not aggression. That was one guy who'd be more careful with his off-color remarks.

When she returned to the bar and handed her drink orders to Raymond, Bull walked over. "That could've been awkward. Nice job of handling the situation."

Her face lit, then her expression turned cool. "Thank you," she said politely.

Orders filled, she moved away.

Raymond glanced at Bull. "What'd you do, Boss, piss in her beer or something?"

"Damned if I know." Admittedly, his size bothered some people, but she didn't appear intimidated. Bull watched her, irritated that the smile she gave so freely to everyone else was never turned in his direction. She had a beautiful smile, warmer than a wood fire on a snowy day.

Raymond studied her. "She must be the only female in the world who doesn't think you're a sex god."

Bull snorted and returned to bartending.

Still irritated.

It was such a human reaction that he had to laugh. He'd complained about women pushing themselves on him. And when one didn't? He sulked like that college student.

The music in the bar was the soundtrack from the original *Footloose* movie. Smiling, Frankie did a little spin as she delivered drinks and headed for a newly filled table.

Would Bull sing tonight? Even when he wasn't performing for the crowd, she'd noticed how he hummed or sang along with whatever was on the playlist. He had such a deep voice—a bass— the sound rumbled right to her bones.

What must he sound like in bed? *"More, sugar."* The words were imaginary; the heat streaming through her veins sure wasn't.

Bad Frankie.

She shook the sound of his voice away and put her attention where it belonged—on the people waiting to order. "What would—"

A shriek of pain came from the back of the roadhouse where the kitchen was. Someone shouted.

What in the world?

Abandoning the bar, Bull headed there, walking...but moving incredibly fast.

I hope whoever that was is all right. Needing to help, she took a step that direction and shook her head. They didn't need her, but how odd it seemed not to be the one fixing everything.

"Let's try this again." She smiled at the older couple. "What can I get you to drink?"

After collecting a set of orders, she headed back to the bar.

"Frankie." The chef Wylie hurried up to her, white hat still on his head, ruddy skin flushed from the kitchen. "You mentioned you did line cooking in the past. Any chance you could fill in for that position? It's mostly grill and fry backup. Our regular got burned and needs to see the doc."

Little scorches were common on the line, but the noise had implied more. "That bad?"

"That stupid." Wylie's mouth twisted. "He was swirling a pan of oil—and his phone rang."

She knew the outcome, oh yeah. "Swirled the oil right over his hand?"

"Bingo. He'd already been warned twice that phones aren't allowed in the kitchen. Guess he figured the rules didn't apply to him." The chef looked toward the kitchen. "I need to get back. Can you help?"

"But...my job here?" She gestured toward the bar.

"We'll move one of the restaurant staff over to take your place. Aside from Bull, you're the only one here who's worked the line before. Can't spare him—the bar's crazy tonight."

True enough. Raymond wouldn't be able to keep up with mixing drinks by himself. "Sure, I'll come play in the kitchen."

"Thanks, Frankie. We really appreciate this." He motioned to a slender young man waiting by the hostess stand. "Give Easton your drink orders and come on back."

Two hours later, Frankie heard Wylie announce the restaurant was closing and the cooks should finish the last orders, do their shut down and clean-up.

Madonna, thank you.

Wylie grinned at Frankie. "You did great. Want to switch jobs and join us here?"

She was overheated; her head itched under the cap, and oil had impregnated her skin. There was a painful red line on her arm —*oven door*—and stinging blisters on the back of her hand—*duck meets hot oil.*

71

Cooking wasn't for wussies. Yet she'd had a good time. Feeding people made her happy.

So did serving, and she needed to be out where she could meet any Patriot Zealots. "I'll stick to being a server. But for emergencies like this? I'm your girl."

"Got it. We won't abuse your good nature, but it's good to know who to call in case of trouble. Thank you."

"Sure." She started shutting down the grill. "You know, I bet Italian food would be popular here, or even an Italian theme night."

"Italian? God, I love lasagna." He scratched his cheek. "I'm all for changing things up. You should talk to the boss about it."

Wait, what? "Ah...no. It was just a thought." She wrinkled her nose at him. "You know, it took me a day or two to realize you weren't the boss."

"God forbid." He guffawed. "I just help out with hiring until Bull gets off his ass and finds us a manager."

"Ah, but you rule the kitchen. I think chefs are probably far above bosses."

"I so agree." Wylie's grin was wicked.

Smiling, Frankie turned to get cleaning supplies and ran right into Bull. Her breasts, then her head bounced off his very solid body. "*Oomph!*"

She tottered back.

"Steady now." His giant hands curled around her upper arms to hold her up. "Are you all right?" His deep voice rumbled in his chest.

He smelled of sandalwood and cedar, like dark carnal nights and heated kisses.

Oh, honestly.

How could she think of having sex with a man she didn't even like?

"Um, I'm fine, thank you." She pulled at his grip, and he released her instantly.

Even as she tried to rub away the tingles from his touch, he spoke to Wylie over her head. "We should hire a manager. I agree. But we need to talk about the hierarchy of chef above boss." His low chuckle indicated he wasn't threatened in the least by her comment.

The man had far too much self-confidence.

Look how he took up all the free space in the kitchen. The way his shirt stretched over the chiseled muscles of his chest was simply mesmerizing. She took another step back.

He gazed down at her. "I appreciate your helping out here in the kitchen. You have a choice now—you can call it a night or return to serving."

"I'd be happy to finish my shift in the bar." Maybe the PZs would be in.

"Good enough. Easton hoped he wouldn't have to break his date." Bull gave her a faint smile, not his usual big grin.

Come to think of it, after the first night, those were the only kind of smiles she received from him. Aside from the one compliment, he'd kept his distance. Had he picked up on her animosity and honored her wish to avoid him?

The realization was disturbing.

As Bull headed back to the bar, the chef frowned. "Problem between you two?"

She wouldn't speak of Bull's callous behavior toward his lover in the parking lot. Wylie obviously liked his boss.

"No. I've hardly spoken to him." She shrugged. "I just prefer to steer clear of"—*womanizers, asshole players*—"hot guys."

The chef barked a laugh. "He sure is that." The frown returned. "But the big bull is more respectful toward women than...than hell, any of us."

"Of course," she said politely. To be fair, what she'd taken for flirting with female customers turned out to be Bull's manner with everybody, no matter the gender, age, or appearance. He was simply extremely outgoing.

Frankie pulled off her apron and the chef beret they'd provided for her hair. Her scalp seemed to cheer at being released from the sweltering, heavy confinement. She picked up her server vest. "I'm going to clean up in the ladies' room and get over to the bar.

And boss or not, she'd continue to avoid "the bull". Because what she'd told Wylie was the absolute truth—she totally avoided man candy.

Chocolate was far better for a girl.

CHAPTER SEVEN

*I*f *the enemy is within range, so are you.* - Murphy's Laws of Combat

This should be fun. Not.

On her knees in the dense undergrowth, Frankie studied her brand-new drone, the one she'd named Iron Boy. The drone wasn't the cheapest model but wasn't too expensive either—because she knew she'd probably fly it into a tree.

It was all hooked up to the controller and her phone, calibrated, and ready to go. The streamlined white body, the rotors, the high-tech gizmo on the front made her feel as if she was in a science fiction movie.

Wouldn't that be cool? Well, as long as she could be a heroine like the ever-so-competent Ripley from *Aliens*.

I don't feel like Ripley.

That wasn't who she was. She was no courageous kick-ass woman.

She was a city girl. She *liked* being a city girl. Still, no matter what it took, she'd get Kit and Aric out of that PZ compound. Because helping her friend was also who she was.

Why, oh why, couldn't it have worked out that she could call in the police, FBI, or DEA. But Kit had been very vehement about not doing that.

After reading about Waco and Ruby Ridge's disastrous shoot-outs, Frankie understood why. At Ruby Ridge, the white supremacist leader had survived the battle, but his poor wife and a fourteen-year-old boy were shot and killed. At Waco, the siege caused seventy-some deaths, including twenty-five children.

The PZs had that big fence and gate. If they refused entry to law enforcement, there could be a nightmare of guns and fighting. Bullets would go right through those flimsy houses—and kill children and women.

So, fence cutting was the plan of the day, which meant finding out where the women's and children's barracks were.

One drone flyover, coming up.

Thankfully, she'd found a good launch site.

Dall Road ran from Rescue to McNally's ski resort high on the mountain and had a myriad of small dirt roads branching off to various houses and cabins. The PZ compound sat a third of the way up in a valley between two foothills.

On Thursday and Friday, she'd driven down all the tiny roads on each side of the compound, putting on an embarrassing *I'm-a-stupid-female-tourist* act whenever she ended up in someone's front yard. Finally, she'd found a poorly maintained road that wound past several properties and dead-ended at an abandoned cabin. A strenuous hike through vicious underbrush brought her to this spot where she could...barely...see a corner of the compound far below.

Let's not think about all the rules I'm going to break. Her drone wasn't registered. Wouldn't always be in her line of sight. Would fly directly over people. Would be snooping over an area where the residents had an expectation of privacy.

She grimaced. Since Kit said a PZ was one of the Rescue cops, if Frankie got caught, she'd probably be locked up forever.

If the PZs caught her, it would be worse than that.

Heart pounding hard, she powered on the drone, hovered it, and sent it off the cliff down to the target zone. A quick check ensured everything was being recorded to her phone.

I can't believe I'm doing this.

She watched the screen and kept the drone high up. Wasn't it nice the PZs had all that cleared land and those big plastic greenhouses? It was easy to find the compound in the forest.

Iron Boy flew past the southern fence toward the rooftops.

Now, which building will have the children?

"Down, boy." She worked the controls to decrease the elevation.

Iron Boy dropped low enough she could see people. Men with rifles. Women. A couple of big dogs. *Right, mustn't forget the guard dogs when planning.*

There—there were the children. Kids were playing games between two houses near the east fence. One building had two ugly shrubs in front, the other one a flagpole.

Score! The children's barracks must be one of those two houses.

The kids started pointing at the sky. At the drone. *Uh-oh.* The adults noticed. Suddenly, fireworks sounded. The snapping and crackling echoed off the mountains.

Her screen went blank.

She stared at her phone and shook it. The drone display was gone. That hadn't been fireworks. *Merda*, it'd been *gunfire*.

They'd shot Iron Boy. Killed her little drone. Her hands went cold. Numb.

They'd come searching for the drone operator—for her.

Run.

She shoved her gear into the bag and sprinted through the

thick underbrush. A branch scraped across her face in a flare of pain. Eyes tearing, she bounced off a tree.

Faster.

She leaped over a dead log and tripped on the uneven ground. A rock tore her palm open, and her ankle twisted with a blast of pain. She scrambled up and forward, shoving her way through the dense growth, collecting more stinging scratches and scrapes. Her arm bumped into the spine-covered stem of a tall, ugly plant. *Ow, ow, ow.*

Panting, heart trying to burst from her chest, she staggered into the open area around the cabin.

No one was there. Not yet. *Move.*

She jumped into her car and sped down the narrow dirt road. Branches lashed the sides of the vehicle. The bottom of the car scraped as the wheels dipped into the ruts.

Don't get stuck, don't get stuck.

At Dall Road, she started to turn north toward town. To go home. To hide.

No, no, she couldn't. She'd have to drive past the turnoff to the PZ compound to get back to Rescue and her cabin. What if someone was watching the road?

She turned to the right and headed up the mountain. There was a bar at the ski resort...with alcohol. Maybe she'd even buy a bottle to bring home with her.

In the rearview mirror, she saw a car pull out onto Dall Road from the PZ turnout. Another car pulled out, and another and another. Heading both ways.

She stepped on the gas. In the resort parking lot, her little car would be just one of many. She'd be one of many. They wouldn't find her.

Anger was a sullen burn in her chest. The *bastardi* had trapped Kit and Aric.

And they'd killed Iron Boy.

In the Patriot Zealot compound, Captain Grigor Nabera walked outside. His lieutenants stood waiting for him in a rigidly straight line. "Report."

"Sir." Hair freshly buzz cut, Luka stood straight—and Nabera almost smiled, knowing the fool's shoulders ached from the lashing he'd received yesterday for questioning the Prophet's scriptures. "The drone pieces were recovered. The device isn't military or law enforcement. It's one that can be bought from any store."

Nabera gave a nod and saw him relax. "Obadiah, what about the perimeter?"

The obedient soldier of the Prophet had a straggly yellow-brown beard, short brown hair, built heavy, like a Texas bison, and he was just as slow moving. "The perimeter has been searched with no tracks found."

"Good. And farther out?"

Tall, skinny Conrad had a reddish beard that reached his belt buckle. "Sir, my team went up Dall Road. Three dirt roads had fresh tracks, so we checked 'em. The last...it had a shithole of an empty cabin. Somebody pushed through the undergrowth to a spot that overlooks us. They couldn't've seen more 'n a corner of the compound though."

"Except the person was using a drone," Reverend Parrish said as he joined them. The Prophet seemed tired with lines around his mouth and deep-set eyes.

Nabera gave him a worried look. If their leader faltered, so would they all. Their plans to shake up the country, bring back the traditional ways were just beginning to come together.

With a reassuring smile, Parrish set a hand on Nabera's shoulder, warming him to his soul. "In this godless world, technology like drones will be an increasing problem to the faithful."

"We'll catch the bastard." Nabera's lip curled up. "He'll end up in as many pieces as his hellish spyware."

His lieutenants all nodded quickly.

Conrad stirred.

"Speak," Nabera ordered.

"When we got onto Dall Road, we saw a truck almost at Rescue. A SUV comin' down the mountain, and a little car going up to the resort. Some of our faithful went after them and reported back." He held up the reports.

Nabera took the papers and glanced at them. Both vehicles were owned by Rescue residents, ones with families. Not the type to spy on them with a drone.

Conrad waited for Nabera's nod and continued, "At the deserted cabin, the tire prints were small—and the vehicle must've been low. It scraped bottom a time or two."

Nabera eyed him. "You think it might've been the little car?"

"Yeah, mebbe." Conrad scowled. "We found footprints. Small." He held his hands up to illustrate the size. "Could be the spy's a teenager or a woman."

Obadiah shook his head. "Women don't do such things."

"Yours might've before you broke her." Conrad sneered at him.

Obadiah glanced at Nabera uneasily.

Nabera felt a stirring in his manhood...because Obadiah's woman, Kirsten, wasn't broken. Not yet. A spark of defiance still glowed inside her.

He wanted to be the one to snuff it out.

But this wasn't the time to think of such matters.

The Prophet frowned. "A woman. Spying on us."

"She might be a reporter like the ones who plagued us in Texas," Nabera said. Along with the rage that someone had invaded their privacy came a sense of anticipation.

When one of their women had escaped and claimed she'd

been abused, reporters had swarmed to the Texas compound. Not that they could get in.

Naturally, after the escapee disappeared, the news dried up. The police had decided the woman had gotten frightened and left the area.

Nabera scratched his chest and smiled. She *had* been frightened...after he'd caught her. He'd had a most pleasant night.

And she had certainly left the area. Her body was now rotting in one of the east Texas deep-water swamps.

Gators were God's cleanup crew.

May in Alaska...such a fine time of the year.

Standing at the grill, Bull breathed in the scents of hickory smoke and sizzling meat. Along with the conversation of his family came the contented clucking of chickens and the quiet lap of water against their small dock.

It was a starkly beautiful day. Under a clear blue sky, the white-clad mountains were mirrored in the calm turquoise lake. On the banks, the grasses and reeds were turning a vivid green.

Summers were short here and meant to be savored—which was why his family was gathered on the Hermitage patio for supper. Although the temp was in the fifties, the heat of the grill and the sun's warmth kept them all comfortable. Sure beat the winter when a warm day made it barely above freezing.

"Serve them up, Regan." He set the last burger on the stack.

"Yes, sir." His ten-year-old niece carefully lifted the platter. As usual, she'd been his assistant chef. Today, because she'd been missing JJ who was out of town for a while at some cop seminar, he'd graduated Regan to actually helping him at the grill.

She might follow Caz into the medical field, but the ability to cook never hurt anyone.

She was as proud of the food she'd grilled as he was of her.

With JJ gone, Caz had helped his daughter braid her long brown hair up and out of danger. The girl had scrapes on her hands where she'd fallen into the brush on a fishing expedition this morning. Her nose was sunburned. Her red sweatshirt had a picture of Leia with a blaster, saying, *Don't mess with a princess*.

Bull grinned. Feistiest niece ever.

The rest of his family made appreciative noises as she set the platter of burgers and sausages on the long picnic table.

Not that they were starving, since Hawk had brought raw veggies and crab dip to munch on while Bull and Regan grilled.

Being a firm believer in the importance of vegetables, Caz had raided the greenhouse to make a salad of baby greens.

Gabe and Audrey had contributed cheesy scalloped potatoes and a chocolate cake. From the smears of frosting on Regan's cheek, she'd helped bake.

"Dig in, people." Bull said—and grinned as they did.

Yeah, there was nothing as great as feeding people. He watched Audrey try a testing nibble of the caribou—aka *reindeer*—sausage. Surprise filled her face, then she handed a small chunk to Regan. "It's really good. Try it."

Regan sampled. "Huh. Like a really spicy hot dog." Making a hungry sound, she grabbed a sausage for herself and wrapped it in a bun.

Laughing, Bull passed her the catsup before taking some burgers for himself. Feeling something rub his shin, he pulled off a piece of meat and dropped it to the ground.

Sirius's tufted ears pricked forward, and the cat batted at the tidbit experimentally with a big paw, before deciding the offering was adequate.

The long-haired stray had filled out nicely after a few months of regular meals. The beast was descended from monster-cats—Caz thought it had Siberian Forest cat genes—and was big enough the hawks wouldn't bother him.

Having Gryff around would help, too. The canine had taken

up watchdog duties with all the enthusiasm of a new SEAL team member. Turning and seeing the big brown eyes, Bull tossed a piece of burger, and the dog snapped it out of the air.

The introduction of cat and dog had gone well, and a tentative peace had already been established. On first spotting Sirius, the dog had stalked forward...and Regan burst into tears. Gryff had flattened to the ground in obvious worry he'd screwed up. Sensitive guy, Gryff was. Bull turned and fondled the soft ears. "You're a good dog."

Over the next hour, the conversation ran around the table, adhering to the sarge's protocol for meals where each person shared the high and lows of their day.

Hawk had flown a busted-up guy to the Soldotna hospital. The man had swerved his car around a moose in the road, skidded on ice, and hit a tree instead.

The doc had treated a woman for a concussion. She'd been dipnetting for the first of the hooligan runs, slipped, and smacked her head into a rock.

"Dipnetting? That's like fishing?" Regan asked.

"More like scooping little fish up with a big net." Bull mentally made room for some fishing time. "The hooligan are thicker in May. We'll spring your papa from his clinic and go then."

The kid had the best smile.

"Hey, Uncle Bull, is that your new waitress?" Regan pointed at the other side of the lake.

In jeans and a red jacket, Frankie was perched on the small picnic table behind her cabin. Something sat beside her—a bottle and glass? Her shoulders were slumped unhappily. She was drinking alone. She was too far away for him to see her expression, but her posture was a picture of loneliness.

A shame she didn't like him, or he'd bring her here. Feed her.

"Yes, that's Frankie," he told Regan. "Dante rented her a cabin."

"Is she nice?" Regan's brows drew together. Although she'd

come a long way from her defensive attitude last fall when Caz had brought her to Alaska, she was still slow to warm up to strangers. Reminded him of Hawk, sometimes.

"Nice, well..." Bull hesitated. His new employee was friendly to everyone but him.

"Frankie seems really nice," Audrey said. "It can be scary to be all alone in a place like this—so different from the city. She's from New York."

"Oh. Yeah, I get it." The Los Angeles child cast a sympathetic look toward Frankie.

Caz grinned at Bull. "Does your server still not like you?"

"Nope. Damned if I know why."

Regan's small face scrunched up. "If she doesn't like you, then I won't like her."

For fuck's sake. Bull scowled at Caz who'd started this mess, and his brother gave a very Hispanic shrug, denying all responsibility for fixing it.

"Maybe you should ask her why she doesn't like you." Gabe tossed a piece of sausage to Gryff.

"What?" Bull eyed Gabe. Of them all, Gabe was the best strategist—but wasn't exactly known for having long heart-to-hearts about emotional matters. "*You're* saying that?"

"It's a self-serving suggestion." Gabe chuckled. "Dante strained his back delivering firewood to the cabins. He asked if we could drop off some wood for Frankie, since he didn't make it to her place."

After an idiot renter used an ornamental tree for firewood, the old Okie had taken to stocking the cabins with wood.

"You want me to make the delivery for you, eh?" Bull scowled at his brother.

"Well, yeah."

Fuck. However, it wasn't a bad suggestion. "Okay, sure." He'd wanted to discuss her idea for theme nights at the roadhouse, anyway. "First thing tomorrow morning."

"We'll hold off on not liking her until Bull reports back, yeah?" Gabe grinned at Regan.

Regan's mouth set into a firm line. Someone had already made up her mind. His niece was extremely loyal.

Hawk snorted, not speaking, but amusement showed in his steel blue eyes. If not the target, Hawk enjoyed Gabe's maneuvering.

Bull studied him, then Gabe.

Hawk, who'd suffered more as a kid than most humans ever endured, had emerged with a caring heart even if he kept it armored and hidden. He and Gabe had been close when growing up. But when they'd been on the same team in a mercenary outfit, something had happened. Gabe didn't know why Hawk had quit the team and pulled away, and Hawk sure wasn't talking about it, the taciturn bastard.

Bull eyed Gabe. It might be that Gabe's unhappiness with Hawk's silence was why he'd set Bull up to talk to Frankie.

Audrey had obviously come to the same conclusion. She winked at Bull, before leaning into Gabe who automatically put his arm around her.

Too fucking sweet. So were JJ and Caz.

Bull turned away, trying to ignore the empty feeling in his chest. Why the hell was he regretting not having a relationship too? He'd tried it, hadn't he?

Married twice, burned twice.

Done with that shit.

CHAPTER EIGHT

*Y*ou make mistakes. Mistakes don't make you. ~ Maxwell Maltz

The deep-throated sound of a big vehicle woke Frankie from sleep—which hadn't started until dawn. Anxiety could keep a person awake even better than caffeine.

She couldn't forget the snapping sound of weapons and Iron Boy's death.

Of course, she knew the little drone hadn't been a person, but he'd seemed alive. He whirred and flew and responded to her orders. At least until those *stronzi* had killed him.

What would have happened if they'd caught her?

She shivered. *This isn't my thing—I'm no warrior.* Maybe she practiced aikido, but she'd chosen the martial art because it didn't revel in violence.

I'm not Ms. Nature Girl, either. She was a pro at figuring out subway times, at picking up adorable sculptures on Bleecker Street, at laughing at the *"you broke my eyeglasses"* street scams, and at finding hidden green areas to refresh her spirit.

A wilderness jungle ninja? So not her.

I made a little progress, though. She'd narrowed down the location of the children's barracks. Next step would be to figure out how to get in there. How to get little Aric out.

Fear slid through her chest because she had no clue how she'd go about that. And they had guns.

Oh, please, Kit. Manage to sneak out. Please.

Outside, the truck engine stopped. A car door slammed.

Right. Outside. Her. Cabin.

She sat up in a rush, and her head spun. *Bad Frankie, too much wine.*

Strained muscles and bruises and scratches from her escape set up a painful clamor all over her body. She whimpered, wanting only to burrow back under the covers.

Someone was here. Who?

Up, up, up. The room was still dark—only due to the blackout curtains covering the windows. Because the sun rose crazy early around 5:30 in the morning and didn't set until after 10.

The wood floor was cold against her feet. She stopped. *Naked.* Right. Maybe sleeping in the buff in this wilderness wasn't smart, but nightgowns and pajamas hated her. Tried to strangle her or wrapped around her waist or breasts.

She yanked on a pair of jeans, then donned a flannel shirt as she slid on fluffy slippers.

There, she was dressed. Sort of. Her shirt was buttoned crooked; she was commando and braless. Whoever it was should've called first if they wanted a put-together appearance from her.

She opened the front door a crack.

No one was in sight.

A big red pickup had been backed into her gravel drive far enough the truck bed was out of sight around the side of her cabin.

Thunk. Thunk. Thunk.

Oh, it was Dante. Her landlord had said he'd be over to fill the lean-to with firewood. He was so sweet.

She started to head around the side, then paused. Her flannel shirt didn't hide her braless state. Perhaps she should change.

But Dante had mentioned his back was acting up—and he was moving a bunch of wood? Really bad idea. She could handle unloading the stuff.

She hurried around the side of the cabin. "Dante, you shouldn't be lifting—"

It wasn't Dante.

Clad in a tight black T-shirt, Bull was stacking firewood neatly in the shed—and her breath seized in her throat.

Whoa. Shoulders shouldn't be that wide, and his biceps and triceps were so pumped up the man could be a model for an anatomy class.

She sure would've enjoyed the subject a lot more.

Aaand, he noticed she was staring. *Cazzo*, she was probably drooling.

Framed by his black goatee, his lips quirked up. "Haven't had your coffee, yet?"

Lovely. Her hair probably resembled a rat's nest. Hopefully, she didn't have drool marks down her cheek. "Not even close. Your truck woke me up."

Even to her own ears, she sounded grumpy.

His gaze swept over her, and there was no way he'd miss that she was braless—and that the cold had her nipples jutting against the flannel shirt.

When she crossed her arms over her chest, a dimple appeared in his cheek. "It's good when you can sleep late," he said mildly.

His gaze lingered on her face, reminding her of the vivid red scratches across her cheek and chin. The bruise on the left where she'd bounced off a tree trunk probably showed, too.

"My job requires late hours." She added a scowl to keep him from asking about her face.

He huffed a laugh. "You could complain to your boss—except he knows you were off last night." Despite her grumbles, he spoke with his usual good nature.

"I guess that excuse won't work then." Pushing away her mood —whatever odd mood she was in—she chuckled. "Sorry for grumping. And thank you for bringing wood. What do I owe you?"

"No charge. We have plenty and owed Dante a favor." As he walked past her to the truck for another armload, his big dog bounded over.

We. Did that mean Bull had a girlfriend? And why was she wondering about that? She bent down to pet the shaggy dog and he leaned against her legs so hard she almost toppled over. "Good morning, dog."

"Gryff—that's his name."

"Gryff." Such a sweetie.

"Say hi, buddy." Bull said to the dog. "Bark."

Gryff let out a loud woof, then trotted to Bull, obviously expecting a compliment.

"Good job, boy." Bull bent and petted the dog until Gryff spun in happy circles.

Dammit, she didn't want to like the man. "Well, thank you for the wood. I do appreciate it." She could enjoy her first cup of coffee by the woodstove. "I never realized how comforting a fire is. The heat is...I don't know...warmer?"

"Seems that way to me, too." His smile tugged at her.

But a gusting wind blew her hair in her face, again making her aware of her bedhead, unwashed face, sloppy clothes, and lack of underwear.

Cazzo. She took a step back. "Thank you again. Have a nice—"

"Frankie." He leaned a shoulder against the shed's post and pinned her with a black gaze. "You don't like me. That's your prerogative, but if I'm doing something that's annoying you, it'd be a relief to know what it is."

Her mouth dropped open. "What?" She threw her hands into the air, her voice rising. "Were you raised in a *barn*? If someone dislikes you, you're not supposed to comment on it. Or question it."

That dimple appeared again, so incongruous in such a hard face. "Not a barn—a log cabin. By a Green Beret veteran. Lessons on manners were few and far between.

A log cabin. That explained *sooo* much.

He folded his arms over his wide chest. "I have heard it mentioned that answering a question is considered polite."

Her chin lifted. If he wanted the truth, then fine. That's just what he'd get. She'd tried to be polite—okay, no, she hadn't, but she hadn't called him a *stronzo* to his face. She hesitated and mentally ran through the past few days. No, no, she hadn't. *Whew.* "All right then."

But how was she supposed to even start explaining?

After a few seconds, he made a noise low in his throat. "Spit it out, Frankie."

"*Stronzo*," she muttered. *Asshole it is, right to your face.*

He didn't react.

Fine. "My first night at your roadhouse, I went outside on my break, and there you were in the parking lot. You and your lover. And, Mr. Alaska man, I watched you gut her feelings like you would a deer. Then you strolled inside like you hadn't left a woman bawling her eyes out behind you."

He stared at her, then ran a hand over his shaved pate. "Fuck."

There was an impressive explanation.

The sharp line of his jaw turned harder than the mountains behind him. "If I have to explain this shit, I could use a cup of coffee."

He was inviting himself in for coffee? *Che palle.* How annoying. She pulled in a breath to refuse, but...she wanted that explanation.

"All right." Her aikido workout could wait until later. She inclined her head. "Build me a fire, and I'll make coffee."

He nodded, smile totally gone.

Apparently, he did have a temper after all.

Crouching by the small woodstove, Bull heard the hiss of the coffee maker in the kitchen corner. Gryff had joined Frankie, having discovered that food frequently fell from the sky in kitchens.

As the fire caught, Bull took a seat on the armchair and scowled. Talk about his marriage. Right. He'd rather roll down a jagged slope and rip up his skin.

Even now, he couldn't believe how thoroughly Paisley had snowed him.

Years ago, the sarge had said that most people concealed their true selves as thoroughly as a mama fox would hide her den. *"But, with you, boy, what you see is what you fucking get."* Maybe that was why he could read people well enough but wasn't inclined to be suspicious— especially of a lover.

Live and learn.

With a sigh, he glanced around the one-room cabin. Dante had remodeled last winter, smoothing the log walls and wood floor to a satiny patina. The back half of the room held the kitchen corner with new appliances. A movable divider sectioned off the bedroom corner.

In the cabin's front half, a colorful green and brown rug, two brown overstuffed chairs, and a matching couch made up the sitting area. With a fire crackling in the woodstove, the room was nice and cozy.

The New Yorker had made herself at home. A bright sweater hung over a kitchen chair. There were books and an eReader on the coffee table. The kitchen table had bright wildflowers in a glass jar...and an empty wine bottle.

"How do you take your coffee?" Frankie asked.

"Black, please."

She walked over and handed him a heavy mug.

A sip told him she knew how to brew coffee. "Thanks."

She tilted her head in acknowledgment, then studied the fire. "You did it differently than what Dante showed me."

City girl. "We all have our own techniques to start fires, and each woodstove has its own quirks."

"Huh. Who knew?" As she curled up in a corner of the couch in the boneless way shared only by women and cats, her gorgeous breasts wobbled enticingly.

Fuck, he really *was* trying not to notice them. Or that her hair looked like she'd just had headboard-slamming sex. But, hell, he was only human.

Human or not, he wouldn't act on his urges. That wasn't why he was here—and even if things were different, he was her boss. He didn't mess with his employees.

She took a sip of her coffee, then lifted an eyebrow at him. Her husky voice held a slight taunt as she repeated his order, "Spit it out, Bull."

He really did like her sense of humor.

It still wasn't easy to talk about Paisley. What *had* he said in the parking lot that night? He mostly remembered being irritated to hell and back. "You called her my lover."

"Well, yes. She talked about you loving her touch, kissing, making love..." Frankie's face darkened with a flush.

A modest New Yorker? Oh, he liked that.

But now he remembered what he'd said. "I can see how you might think we were lovers." Bull watched the fire gain height as the flames moved from kindling to thicker sticks. "What you're missing is this: she's not a current lover. She was my wife. We divorced two years ago."

Frankie's expression changed from surprised to appalled. She lowered her cup. "Two years? But surely... She acted like..." She flushed.

He knew what she hadn't asked. "We haven't been together since the divorce. I saw her in passing a year ago at the symphony. We were both there with other people."

"Oh, *che stupida che sono.*" Frankie tapped her forehead with the palm of her hand. A man did have to enjoy how her emotions played out in her expressions, showed in her big brown eyes, came out in her very Italian gestures. "She played you, and I was the one who fell for it."

"So, it seems." As his tense muscles relaxed, Bull extended his legs. "She wanted to get back together, and I lost my temper."

"Um, it's not my place to say anything, but maybe she misses you? People do reconcile sometimes."

"I wouldn't have her back on a bet," Bull grated out.

Frankie blinked, obviously startled at the growl in his voice.

"Before we married and while we were married, she told me she was all about loyalty and faithfulness. That people who cheated were scum. I believed her until she gave me an STD."

Frankie's mouth dropped open.

"She was fucking her clients when showing houses." He felt like a fool. Why the hell had he shared that with—

"Showing houses?"

"She's a realtor."

"I hate liars." Frankie scowled, then her nose wrinkled. "I guess that's one way to ensure a sale."

A snort broke from him, and then he was laughing, roaring, because...*yeah*. It felt as if sharing—and the humor—had shaken loose a knot that'd been inside for a long time.

"Sorry, that was rude," Frankie said to her cup.

"The truth can be." Still smiling, Bull lifted his mug to her. "Now you know why I reacted badly when she showed up."

"I would say you showed a lot of restraint." Frankie got up and fetched the coffee pot to refill their cups. "Here, I thought my breakups were bad."

Bull spotted the flicker of pain in her liquid dark eyes. She'd been hurt...and he had a wayward notion to find the bastards and teach them the error of their ways. "Breakups. More than one?"

As she resumed her seat, Frankie studied Bull. He was all man—his shoulders wider than the back of the big chair. It was easy to see he was the sort of person who preferred to keep emotional baggage to himself, but he'd shared about his wife and their divorce.

It was a gift, in a way.

One that perhaps should be reciprocated.

She rose. "I'm half-Italian—and my grandmother always cooked when she got upset or unhappy. Can I make you breakfast?"

"If you let me help." He stood, dwarfing her.

When some guys loomed over her, she wanted to punch them. Bull, instead, made her feel like moving...closer. She took a step back. "Sure. In Nonna's house, everybody pitched in." Even the men. Sharing the cooking and clean-up had been the only feminist directive her Italian grandmother had embraced.

In the kitchen area, she set out mushrooms, onions, and bell peppers. "You get to chop."

She started on frying the bacon.

He washed his hands, then diced the onions in a way that said he knew his way around a kitchen. No wonder Audrey had been startled when Frankie'd doubted he could cook anything other than protein shakes.

A woman could learn a lot about a man by observing him cook. Bull was skillful. Precise. Everything went into tidy piles. When she'd told him what to do, he'd simply agreed. He was a team player.

Catching her watching, he prompted, "How many breakups have you been through?"

He was also too good at multi-tasking.

"A few, I guess. Two were serious. One marriage."

He shot her a keen look. "Still hurts?"

After a moment of checking her emotions, she could tell him, "Not nearly as much as during the divorce period."

His smile agreed. "Your ex cheated?"

"Actually, no." She could feel her chest tighten around the pain and humiliation. Was this how Bull had felt when he'd told her about his wife? "It's complicated."

"Tell me," he said softly and pushed the onions over to her to sauté as he started on the peppers.

"My mother owns a modeling business. My father is a fashion photographer."

His expression didn't change. He'd obviously never heard of *the* Bocelli.

That was incredibly freeing. "Modeling is extremely competitive. They fight to get the right photographer, to be picked for the big fashion shoots. Getting into a high-end agency is...important."

Bull had paused to watch her face. As he returned to chopping, he frowned, then shook his head. "I forgot—there are *male* models, aren't there? Did your ex play you to get into the business?"

"You got it."

"What a fucking *bastard*." Scowling, Bull set a hand on her shoulder. "I'm sorry. That had to have hurt."

"Thanks." Her eyes started to burn with tears. *Onions.* Really, it was just the onions, and not the understanding gesture or sympathy in the deep voice. More than she'd had from her family. When she'd raged about what he'd done, her mother had told her she shouldn't swear or speak in Italian—but hadn't said a word about Jaxson's deceit. Hadn't tried to break the contract and get rid of him.

Needing to move, she dumped the peppers into the bacon grease and laughed at the sizzling sound. "My sisters would be scolding me about how unhealthy this is."

Rather than complain about bad fats, Bull chuckled. "Not me. I love bacon."

She smiled back and then blinked. *No, Frankie. Bad, bad, bad.*

No matter how likable he was. Or lickable—*stop it.* First, she was here for Kit, not for anything else. Especially not a gorgeous man who could be a real complication.

She turned her attention to sautéing. Much safer. Cooking always was.

Bull glanced at her. "I wanted to talk to you about your idea of an Italian theme night. How'd you come up with that?"

Wait, she'd just tossed that out there to Wylie. "It was just a thought, not anything to really..."

"Frankie. That wasn't my question." He rested a hip against the counter and waited.

That much self-assurance should be outlawed.

So, how to explain. She sure wasn't going to mention that part of her agency job was to come up with inventive ideas in ways for models to present themselves, transform their portfolios, create unique brands. Apparently, that part of her brain didn't stop, even in Alaska.

"Fine, it's like this... In a city, restaurant theme nights aren't that common since there are tons of specialty restaurants. But here, there's only your place and McNally's restaurant. Oh, and the pizza place."

"Thank fuck for pizza." Bull pushed over the mound of mushrooms and started grating pepper jack cheese.

"True. I'd be desolate without pizza." She grinned at him, added the mushrooms, and started breaking eggs into a bowl.

"Themed specialties." Bull considered. "Perhaps a night a

week?"

"That would be good. So, someone craving Italian knows he should visit on, say, Thursdays."

"Hmm." He considered for a moment. "I like it."

His approving nod lit a glow inside her, much like when she'd been ten, served her first lasagna, and been cheered by everyone at the table. She smiled back, regretful she couldn't simply enjoy feeling...valued. Making her place at the roadhouse. But she wasn't here to stay or to do anything but get Kit and Aric out.

When she closed the egg container, he chuckled and put his hand over hers. "Three more eggs, please, sweetheart. I'm a big eater."

His warm, callused palm was so wide it covered her hand completely.

A disconcerting need flared inside her as her hormones bubbled to life.

No, no, no.

"Three more it is." She tried to lift her hand, but he had it pinned down, then slid the sleeve of her flannel shirt upward. Exposing all the red scratches and scrapes from yesterday.

With his other hand, he tucked her hair behind her ear and studied her face. "You look like you got tossed into a blender on the chop setting." He ran a finger down her cheek beside one long scrape. So gentle a touch, yet his grip on her hand was as unyielding as his gaze.

She swallowed and considered lying, but simply couldn't. Evasion, then. "I was exploring your Alaska wilderness and ended up off the trail." Her smile made the scratch on her chin pull painfully. "Some of those bushes are pushier than rush hour, subway riders. One of them had spines all over it—the stem, the leaves, everything." Thank God she had tweezers with her since a whole lot of those spines had ended up in her arm.

"I bet you met up with some devil's club." A line formed between his black brows. "Unless you're an experienced hiker, leaving the trail is unwise. It would be my pleasure to show you around."

She couldn't think of what to say. He was strong, competent, and knew his way around the wilderness. How she wanted to simply beg him to help her get Kit and Aric, but...that would be foolish.

They barely knew each other. She thought of the way Iron Boy had died and cringed inside. Helping her would mean risking his life.

And there was always the risk he'd do the logical thing—like call the police.

So... Pulling him into her problems wouldn't be smart. Neither would spending time with him. No matter how appealing he was —a man who had a sense of humor, had been hurt by his ex, was a good listener, and could cook.

Yet, despite all her arguments and logic, she wanted him. She could feel the heat growing between them and how her excitement fizzed with the slightest brush of his skin, with the deep sound of his voice.

She shook her head. "I've decided that wandering around a forest where the foliage is more aggressive than I am isn't my thing." True enough, even if she'd be doing exactly that in a day or so. A chill ran through her. Alaska wilderness areas were fantastically beautiful...and very scary. And then there were the PZs...

His gaze narrowed slowly as if he could see the quiver deep in her bones. As if he knew how scared she was. Why did he have to be so good at reading people?

She shook her head. "I appreciate the offer, but no."

They both knew she was turning down more than his offer to go hiking. Unfortunately, she had a feeling he would be keeping an eye on her. Which would be so very comforting—except she couldn't afford that.

"All right." His expression didn't change, so why did it feel as if he was disappointed?

CHAPTER NINE

Try to look unimportant; the enemy may be low on ammo and not want to waste a bullet on you. - Murphy's Laws of Combat

Bull led the way down an animal path, followed by a happy Gryff. Hawk brought up the rear. The still-damp trail was a bit rambling, but it'd get them to the PZ compound eventually, and he was in no hurry.

An Alaska forest in May was the best of times. The snow receded until only remnants remained in the shade. The weather was drier. The spring-green new birch leaves were bright against the black spruce. The underbrush of bearberry and currants was still sparse, making it easier to see the wildlife—like a skinny black bear emerging from hibernation with its odiferous, scruffy winter coat.

The trees were noisy with migratory birds, and over the leafy canopy, a trio of squawking ravens were dive-bombing a bald eagle out of their territory.

Laughing at the sight, Bull paused and glanced back at his brother. "Teamwork wins the war again, yeah?"

"Yeah." Hawk watched the battle with a slight smile.

Bull decided to try for conversation. "You think Gabe is right? The PZs numbers are increasing?"

Hawk stepped over a fallen log, slick with rotting bark. "Why? Got more shootings out here?"

"Not recently. The locals have learned that anyone close to the compound is liable to get perforated. Drives Gabe nuts." Bull started walking again. "The victims never see the shooter. They're always fairly sure the gunfire comes from the compound—but the PZs insist the shots couldn't have come from their area."

"Without a witness, he can't arrest anyone." Hawk sounded disgusted.

"Yep." Bull grinned and cautioned the former sniper who was almost as silent as Caz, the former assassin, "Do me a favor and don't get noisy."

An annoyed grunt answered him. "Their numbers might be increasing. There're more new faces in town."

The trail branched, and Bull stopped to calculate distance and direction. "Not what I wanted to hear." There was only one new face that interested him these days. A woman with big brown eyes, a stubborn chin, and a smart mouth. Someone who worked hard, enjoyed the customers, laughed like she meant it, and didn't take crap from anyone.

He chuckled, and beside him, Hawk lifted an eyebrow.

"Ah, I was thinking of another new face—a recent hire at the roadhouse—"

"The New Yorker who doesn't like you?"

Right. Audrey mentioned her during one of their patio meals. "That's the one. She's a delight to watch in action. The other night, when she leaned over to put a drink down, an asshole tourist shoved his face against her breasts."

"You kill him?"

"I didn't have to." Bull had been a second from vaulting the bar to do so. "She dumped the entire tray of drinks in his lap, then sweetly told him and his buddies that the only service they'd get from that moment on would be from the giant bartender at the bar itself. And she pointed to me."

"Nice." Hawk gave a nod of approval.

"Yeah, she did good." Frankie'd leashed her temper just enough to get her point across without it escalating into a brawl. And, hell, now he had a craving to see her when she let her emotions loose. No matter what emotion. Actually, he had one emotion in mind.

Because he was an asshole. *Employee, remember? Hands off.*

After giving Gryff a quick pat, Bull turned down the trail to the right.

Hawk followed.

Bull had been surprised when Hawk volunteered to come today. He seemed set on annoying Gabe whenever possible—and Gabe was the one who'd asked for periodic recons of the Patriot Zealot compound. "A shame we don't do more hiking with everyone. Caz. And Gabe."

A glance back showed Hawk's expression had gone cold.

"Want to tell me what happened between you and Gabe?"

"No."

"What the hell? You mean there aren't going to be any brotherly confidences on our little walk?"

"Asshole." Hawk's mouth twitched. He might be a withdrawn hardass with a shitload of triggers to set him off, but one of his redeeming traits was his ability to laugh at himself.

"Fine." Bull ducked under a low-hanging branch. "Now winter's over, you got any plans on what you're going to do? I can use you in the restaurant or bar. Or with managing Mako's foundation."

"For fuck's sake, get real."

Not an unexpected response. Hawk didn't hate people, but wasn't exactly sociable, mostly because he hated to talk.

"I'm picking up work as a bush pilot." Hawk stepped around a patch of snow. "Deliveries, mostly. Some taxi stuff as long as it's not that sightseeing crap where I'd have to give an idiotic tourist spiel."

"Sounds good." Relief made Bull's voice come out gruff. If Hawk had flying jobs, he wouldn't return to being a mercenary. They'd all been worried.

A while later, Bull slowed and held up a hand in the 'stay quiet' signal. They were within hearing distance of the compound. Time to go silent.

The fence marked the edge of the PZ's property line, so Bull and Hawk weren't trespassing. But that had never stopped the fanatics from acting like pissed-off yellowjackets. Only these wasps had bullets instead of stingers.

In the late afternoon, Frankie left her car safely hidden behind some bushes, sat down on a log, and used a compass to mark her starting location on the map.

There, it hadn't even taken her too long. She was improving.

Taking another reading, she set off toward where the Patriot Zealot compound should be.

It'd sure be easier if there were some actual hiking trails in this area—or cell service so she could use a GPS. But noooo, it was all wilderness.

Between quick heart-lifting glances at the gorgeous mountain to the south and east, she concentrated on her navigation. The vegetation was annoyingly thick until she blundered onto a thin animal-created path. With a sigh of relief, she checked her compass and marked her map, then followed it. It was much better walking, only what was that? *Ew.*

In the center of the path was a huge steaming pile of poop. Nose wrinkled, she stepped over it. *Please, let whatever beast made that be a long, long way away.*

Something thudded off to her right, and she jumped. But... okay...it was moving away. A rustling sound came from her left. She jerked—and a bird burst from a bush. Frankie put her hand over her racing heart. Only a bird.

Oh, I want to go home. At least in New York, she knew what she was doing.

She'd tried to figure out all this wilderness hiking by researching her ass off since talking to Kit almost a week ago. In the little Rescue coffee shop, she'd watched videos on her phone on how to navigate in a forest, then bought a compass and topographical map in the sports store.

Her goal today was to reach the compound—without getting lost.

And then see what would be needed to sneak up to the fence behind the children's building.

The muddy patches of the trail showed prints. Cloven hooves. Maybe a deer or something? But that...that was a boot print. Her stomach tensed. Did those fanatics hike around outside their property?

She still hadn't worked out how she'd navigate the correct paths when rescuing Kit and Aric. In the dark. There were way too many little animal trails. It'd be awfully easy to get lost. But, obviously, if the PZs were out here at any time, she couldn't tie bright ribbons or something to the trees to mark her path. That'd be like waving a flag saying someone was sneaking around their compound.

Never mind. The nighttime navigation plans would have to wait. She'd figure something out.

Her dark green cargo pants pockets were stuffed with basic hiking survival essentials—*thank you, Google*—like matches, a space blanket, and bear spray. The spray would probably work against PZs, too, right?

Voices sounded in the distance, and when the trail branched, she left herself a small unobtrusive marker of sticks and kept moving. She veered around a big patch of spine-covered devil's club. *Ha, I know you now, demon plant.*

Finally, something glinted off to her left. She pushed some branches aside to see. Yes, that was chain-link fencing sparkling in the sunlight.

Triumph bubbled up inside her, but breaking into a victory song might be...unwise.

There was a wide, cleared space between the fencing and the tree line. Probably so no one could approach the fence during the daylight hours without being spotted.

Merda, that was a very tall, heavy fence. A discouraging one. There was no way she—or Kit—could climb over that thing, especially with the rolls of razor wire strung along the top. Maybe wire cutters would work?

This was the west fence, the one closest to Dall Road, but the buildings where the children had been playing were on the east side. She'd have to hike all the way around to decide on the best place to sneak in—or out. She headed south.

Frustration built inside her. The animal trails didn't always follow the fence line. And if she didn't watch carefully, she was liable to end up lost. Just the thought dried up all the spit in her mouth.

Inside the compound, she saw fields and the long greenhouses. A raised wooden tower elevated on stilts sat at the corner of the west and south fence. She examined it warily, trying to stay out of sight.

After a minute, she retreated back into the forest and followed the south fence toward the east. This place was way too big.

Thankfully, she was off tonight and tomorrow. Aikido kept her in fair shape, but hiking in this rugged terrain called for different muscles. And those muscles were starting to complain.

Bull could probably run this trail without breaking a sweat.

Bad Frankie. We're not going to think about that man.

But thinking about him was far too easy to do. Sex with him would be like the scream-worthy moment a roller-coaster dropped over the highest peak.

But a relationship? More like the slow, clattering climb up the roller-coaster tracks to the top, giving a person too much time to wonder about how bad things could get. And inevitably, the carnival ride would end with the cars coming to a jerky halt.

She avoided handsome men for good reasons, starting with them being shallow and self-centered—like her ex. Bull...didn't seem to be like that. He was certainly smart. Charming. Friendly. Fun. Caring.

However, no matter how compelling he was, she wasn't here for a man; she was here for Kit and Aric.

There—there was another wooden tower—the southeast corner. *Yes!* Staying hidden, she turned to follow it up the east side.

Are those the women's and children's buildings?

Too much underbrush was in the way. Skirting a patch of snow, she worked her way forward to where the undergrowth was thinner, and she could see across the bare area between the forest and the fence to the buildings inside. She could hear men talking and occasionally see a child between the buildings. The children made almost no noise at all.

Wait, was that *Aric*?

Without thinking, she parted the bushes so she could peek out.

There was a horrible loud *bang*. Then another. Something went *thunk* ahead of her, and bark splintered on a tree trunk. *Cazzo,* someone was *shooting* at her.

Another *crack*. Something tugged at her sleeve, scraped across her deltoid.

She dove back into the woods, running directly away from—

The ground disappeared out from under her. She fell, down

and down, trying to grab branches, dirt, and nothing slowed her tumbling.

She landed hard, almost in a tiny stream bed and gritted her teeth to keep screams from escaping.

Hearing men shouting, she scrambled farther into the underbrush. Would they come after her?

Panting, she frantically checked her surroundings. Even if the bushes were springing back into place, she could see the track of her fall.

Everything hurt, especially her arm that burned like fire. They'd *shot* her. No time to check it. *Get out of here, Frankie.*

She shoved to her feet and ran upstream on the bank. Her boots slipped and slid in the mud and snowy patches.

Glancing back, she saw her footprints that would point the way right to her. *No, no, no.*

She'd read thrillers about fugitives walking in the water to hide their tracks. Here was a stream. Would it work?

It might. She had to lose whoever was after her. That came before anything. She jumped into the calf-high stream. As the frigid water washed over her boots and trickled inside, she sucked in a breath and broke into a stumbling run downstream—the opposite direction of where she'd been going.

The minutes passed, an eternity of minutes, and the sounds of people behind her grew louder, faded, then disappeared. Relief swept through her. She'd lost her pursuers.

She'd also lost any sense of where the road might be. *Cazzo, cazzo, cazzo.* A new fear crept up her spine.

The forest darkened around her. It couldn't be sunset already. No, not sunset. Black clouds filled the sky. It was going to rain; she just knew it.

She stumbled up onto the bank, and the icy water drained from her boots. Her feet were numb. Her sleeve was wet—and red—because her upper arm still bled. A deep furrow cut across her deltoid and burned like fire.

Stop the bleeding was a basic first aid rule. And she sure didn't want to attract bears or anything.

But with what? Her socks were wet and muddy. She wasn't wearing anything that would—okay, maybe she was. No one was around to see her breasts, right? She pulled off her shirt and bra and wrapped her bra around her arm, then awkwardly used her teeth and free hand to knot it. An icy wind whipped over her bare skin.

As she eased her shirt back on, she shivered. That bullet could easily have struck her chest. Or her head.

Keep moving.

Farther down the stream bank, a small trail disappeared into the forest. A hobbit trail—because hobbits were a lot less scary than bears. It finally wound its way to a bigger trail. Um, did that mean it had bigger animals?

Maybe it would eventually reach a road. She kept trudging, her boots squishing with every step, her feet cold and blistering within wet socks.

An odd feeling ran down her spine and raised the hair on her nape. She halted. What a creepy feeling, like...like someone was watching her.

A low growl came from the side, and she spun. *Wolves!* In terror, she stared at the undergrowth.

"Frankie?" The deep rumbling voice was the most wonderful sound she'd ever heard.

"Bull!"

When he stepped out of the forest onto the trail, she ran straight at him—and he pulled her into his arms.

Into safety.

The little New Yorker was twined around him tighter than a morning glory vine...and shaking so hard her bones should've rattled. At his feet, Gryff whined, tail whipping furiously.

Jesus, what'd happened to Frankie? Bull's jaw clenched. They'd heard gunshots a while back...

"Easy, Frankie. You're all right." But was she? "Hawk, is she hurt?"

"Yeah, bro. Bloody sleeve. Clever girl wrapped a bra around the wound. Clothes are ripped."

Bull stiffened.

Hawk said hastily, "Torn up from the brush, not a person."

Frankie pulled back, gripped Bull's arms, and gave him a shake. "*Quiet*. They'll hear. They have guns."

His suspicions confirmed, fury rose inside him. Someone had *shot* her.

"Sweetheart." He tilted her chin so he could meet her eyes. He kept his voice low and easy, despite the boiling in his blood. "No one is close to us right now. Trust me on this."

"You're sure?" She checked his expression, then Hawk's.

When they both nodded, she started to sag in his arms.

"Hold still a minute." He moved her bra-dressing enough to check the wound on her arm. A bloody groove across her deltoid. The bullet had missed shattering her shoulder joint by mere inches.

Hawk's mouth tightened, and he drew his pistol.

Reacting to their anger, Gryff growled, and the fur down his spine rose.

Gently, Bull put the dressing back in place. It would serve until Caz could do a better job.

Wrapping an arm around Frankie's waist to keep her upright and moving, he headed down the trail toward his truck.

"Who shot you?" Bull asked.

Hawk fell in behind, guarding their six.

She hesitated and said slowly, "I didn't see whoever it was. I just heard shooting, and I ran."

Bull turned and considered the direction she'd come and saw Hawk doing the same. Their gazes met. The only people back there would be PZs. It wasn't the first time someone had been fired on for getting too close to their area.

Bull's jaw clenched. He'd kill the bastards and raze their buildings to the ground.

She wasn't a local; she wouldn't know to avoid the assholes. But...it wasn't hunting season, and there was nothing around to attract a tourist. She'd said she didn't plan to do more hiking, so why was she out here?

He bit back the question. This wasn't the time. "Running was smart. You didn't see the shooter at all?"

"No." She shook her head. "I fell off a ledge. That's how I got scraped up. But since I wasn't sure who was wandering around the woods shooting, I didn't go back to that trail."

"Another wise decision." Bull studied her pale, scratched face. A vivid bruise marked one cheek. He could feel the tremors shake her at intervals.

"I was, maybe, a *little* bit lost, so I'm glad we ran into each other."

"Just a little, hmm?"

Her mouth curved, and she held up her hand, thumb and forefinger an inch apart. "Hardly worth mentioning, really."

A resilient personality. A sense of humor. Even when terrified, she'd coped with her wound and being chased. He'd known soldiers who would've run until they bled out.

Unable to resist, he bent and kissed her beautifully full lips and felt her lean into him. Felt her respond. "I'm glad we found you, then. Let's go get your arm taken care of."

With Gryff's furry body resting on her bare feet, Frankie sat, warm and dry, on a kitchen chair in Bull's home while Doc Caz worked on her arm. Gritting her teeth against the pain, she stared out the huge front windows. Rain was dancing over the waters of the lake, turning the turquoise to gray.

It'd started drizzling a while back, soon after Bull and Hawk found her in the forest. Although she'd gotten soaked, the hike out to the south—on a different trail—had been easier.

Despite being exhausted, she'd made mental notes of the distinguishing landmarks—a massive fallen spruce, a streamlet. Next time—and there would be a next time—she'd use that trail to get to the PZ compound.

The path had ended at two cabins owned by Knox and Chevy, the town's handymen. Bull's red pickup was there—and he'd tossed her car keys to his rather menacing buddy, Hawk, who said he'd retrieve her car.

Bull would've taken her to the health clinic, but the doc had already left for here. It seemed that Bull, Cazador, and Hawk were brothers, and each had a house at this place—the Hermitage— where five two-story cabins curved around a shared lakeside courtyard.

Now, freshly showered, hair wet and straggling down her back, she sat in the kitchen in her boy briefs and Bull's T-shirt that was longer than a dress. She was braless, too, since her bra was soaked with blood—*her* blood, which really should be kept safely inside her body, not ruining her clothing.

Let's not repeat this experience.

"All done." Caz finished dressing the gunshot wound and sat back. "Are you sure you don't want something stronger for pain?"

"No. Ibuprofen is fine." She wrinkled her nose. "Pain meds mess with my mind—and I get more anxious than I would without them. The pain's not that bad, and I'd rather stay clear-headed." *Especially now.*

To change the subject, she studied the tidy white wrap around her arm. "I've never had a doctor make a house call before. Do you do this often?"

"Not often, no, but I would not want the mean bull to pound

on me. He punches too hard." His warm brown eyes danced with laughter.

Standing beside Frankie, supervising, Bull patted her shoulder. "The doc already informed me his bill for the house call will be three jars of high bush cranberry jam."

Frankie frowned. "But I have money. You shouldn't have to pay him."

"Not a problem." A dimple appeared with Bull's smile. "I canned extra last fall to use as bribes."

Caz scowled. "There is no generosity in his soul."

"Not for you assholes." Bull shook his head and told her, "My brothers are worse than locusts. Given a chance, they'll eat me out of house and home."

"It is true." Caz nodded solemnly. "When the bull was small, we stole his food. Starved him. It's why he's so undersized, now."

Frankie burst out laughing as she looked up...and up...and up at Bull.

He was grinning.

She loved the way the two teased each other. Nonetheless, she'd never seen brothers who resembled each other less.

"You should have some of his jam, *chica*," Caz told her. "And if you're still here in September, we'll draft you to pick cranberries for next year's batch."

Caz's phone made a muted sound, and he checked the text. "Ah, I must return to the clinic. A hiker's feet got up close and personal with a pot of boiling water."

"Oh, ouch."

"I'm glad you're here where Bull can keep an eye on you." He gave her a quick, blinding smile.

"Thank you again, Doc."

"De nada." Caz picked up his bag and headed out the sliding glass door, passing a tall, muscular man with a badge on his chest. A police officer.

When the man walked into the kitchen area, Bull set a hand

on her shoulder. "Frankie, this is another of my brothers. Chief MacNair. Francesca Bocelli."

Another brother? Smiling, she shook the chief's hand. "We met at the bar on my first night there."

"That we did." He pulled up a chair and sat facing her. Notepad in hand, he inclined his head. "If you wouldn't mind, Ms. Bocelli, I'd like to hear what happened."

She gave him the same information she'd given Bull and Hawk. Out hiking. Didn't see who shot her.

The last thing she wanted was to focus attention on the PZ compound. Not until Kit and Aric were out—and then she'd come down on them like a runaway subway train. Because the *bastardi* had shot her, and she wasn't even on their land.

"Just wandering around, hmm?" The chief's blue eyes sharpened. "No idea where you were?"

"That's ri—"

Bull set his hand on her shoulder, his expression unreadable. "Hawk backtracked you. He said you half-circled the PZ fence. Why?"

She averted her gaze, hearing again the snapping sound of gunfire, felt the fiery line a bullet carved into her arm.

No, don't think about that now.

"Frankie?" Bull prompted.

She was all about honesty, but...as when cooking, a bit of spice could make anything easier to swallow.

"This is a little embarrassing." She wrinkled her nose. "I like knowing what makes people tick. I even like listening to gossip"—*totally the truth*—"and there's a lot of talk about your crazy fanatics."

After all, Bull had seen her talking to the PZ women in the grocery store. "Since I've wanted to learn to hike—"

Bull frowned, undoubtedly recalling she'd said she wouldn't go out in the woods.

Oops.

She hastily added, "I got tired of being viewed as the city girl and watched some YouTube videos about hiking. Anyway, I took my stroll in the direction of the Patriot Zealot's so-secret compound. Just to see what was in there."

The police chief's jaw went hard—and so did Bull's—and now she had two men frowning at her.

No matter how uncomfortable, she preferred that they believed her to be an idiot rather than think she was surveying the PZ land for a real reason.

"Could you tell if the gunfire came from inside the fence?" the chief asked.

"I couldn't say. It wasn't from behind me, but..." She shrugged and winced as the movement pulled on her wounded arm.

The cop glanced at Bull.

"Hawk wasn't sure," Bull said. "Her tracks at that point were buried underneath a batch of other footprints."

The ones who'd chased her.

The chief's expression turned sour. "I'll speak to Reverend Parrish...and will get the usual run-around. That they don't know anything. That they heard gunfire and went out to see if someone needed help."

Oh, sure they had...out of the goodness of their little hearts.

She just checked the cop to see if he had more questions.

"I wish I could say I'd arrest the shooter, but it's unlikely. Other hikers and hunters have been fired upon when in that vicinity. The Zealots are practiced at making sure no one sees exactly who did the shooting. I'm damned sure it's them, but I can't prove it." Chief MacNair appeared as if he'd like to tear the compound apart with his bare hands.

Huh. This law enforcement officer certainly didn't like the Patriot Zealots. He couldn't be the one who Kit had written about in her letter.

Eyes simmering with fury, Bull wore the same frustrated expression as the cop.

The chief rose. "Thank you, Ms. Bocelli. I'll let you get some rest." His voice took on an edge of command. "Now that you've seen the compound, please stay away from it."

Not going to happen.

She put on a friend's thick southern accent. "But, Chief, it's such a pretty fence, and the people are so hospitable, bless their hearts." She put a hand on her chest and sagged back into the chair. "Although, I do say, being shot at has quite reduced my sense of adventure."

Bull's deep laugh sent a shiver of pleasure up her spine.

Chief MacNair grinned at her, then left the way he'd come in —across the deck to the courtyard.

Frankie turned to Bull. "Don't tell me, he has a house here, too?"

"'Fraid so."

"How many brothers do you have?" Remembering how they'd just strolled in, she eyed the deck door. Her city paranoia was outraged. "Don't you lock anything up?"

"Just us four." He grinned and tugged a lock of her hair as he answered her second question. "Anything that faces the outside is battened-down. Doors into the courtyard, not so much. Usually only at night."

She'd noticed how their tall wire fencing connected the houses together and then continued down to the lake on either side, totally enclosing the semi-circle, leaving it open only to the water. "Why does the fencing around the PZ compound feel like a prison but yours feels like safety?"

Bull tucked a hand under her undamaged arm and pulled her to her feet. "Because our fence is to keep out moose and bears and intruders, but not to keep anyone inside. If someone wants to leave, they can."

The Patriot Zealot fencing really *was* a prison, holding Kit inside.

Frankie frowned. Today had sure been one major setback.

How *dare* the *bastardi* shoot at her.

But she'd located the compound and knew more of what she was up against now. Like guards in those watchtowers. Her foray hadn't been a complete failure.

To Frankie's surprise, Bull didn't lead her toward the garage and his pickup but took her between the two kitchen islands into the living room area.

He had an interesting home. The back half of the big two-story house had a hallway to the garage. A staircase led to the second floor. The entire front of the house, open to the ceiling rafters, had windows facing the lake. She could even see her cabin across the water.

Inside, the room's warm brown and cream colors were echoed in the river-stone-lined corner nook that held a black wood stove. Rather than a traditional couch and chairs, a U-shaped leather and suede sectional curved around a big-ass television. Far too inviting. "Um. I should go home."

"No, you should have a seat and relax for a while." He smiled, but his arm around her waist was unyielding as he seated her where she could see out the huge display windows. On the deck, planters held cheerful pansies that brightened the gray day.

"Bull, I really do appreciate all your help, but—"

"Caz wanted you to stay here for a while to make sure you're recovered. And I want you here." Bull sat beside her and took her hand. "Caz and I have been in combat. Even if you deal well at the time, the shock of getting shot will catch up with you."

His black eyes trapped hers. "If you have trouble, I want you here with me."

"Listen, I'm perfectly—"

"Is the yorkie yapping at you?" The sandpaper-rough voice made her jump.

Hawk walked in from the deck.

"She's a mouthy one, yeah." Bull smiled.

Hawk had remote blue-gray eyes in a scarred face. Thick

blond hair was yanked back in a tie. His beard was short. Full sleeves of tats and more scars decorated his arms. This fair-skinned brother certainly didn't resemble Bull or Caz. Neither did Gabe.

"It's good to officially meet you, Hawk."

He gave her a quick assessing look, nodded approval at the dressing on her arm, then handed over her car keys. "It's in Bull's driveway."

"Thank you. I really, really appreciate it." She caught a half-smile on his face before he glanced at Bull and jerked his head toward the deck.

Bull rose and followed him for a talk outside.

When he returned, Frankie asked, "What was that Hawk called me when he came in?"

Bull flashed a smile. "Ah, he's a bit sparse on words. He shortened New Yorker to yorkie." Plucking the keys from her hand, Bull tossed them into a coffee table basket that held his wallet and keys.

"Yorkie? Like the fluffy dogs that bark all the time?" *Yappy* dogs. Her eyes narrowed as she glanced toward the door.

"Mmmhmm, soft, fluffy dogs with big dark eyes. Known for being bold and brave despite their size." His fingers danced over her hair, fluffing it.

She looked up to object, and he took her mouth, kissing her so gently, so carefully, so...thoroughly, that she melted back into the couch.

Ooooh, such a kiss, even better than the one she'd gotten on the trail.

Even as she lifted her hand, intending to pull him closer, he straightened with a reluctant sigh. "Sorry, sweetheart. I didn't mean to take advantage."

"You didn't." She gave him a wry smile. "I think you know that." Because she wanted him as much or more than he wanted her—and he was too astute to misread the signs. Even now, the feeling of his arm against hers was making goosebumps rise on her skin. He'd taken a shower and each breath brought her the crisp, clean scent of his soap.

She'd always been attracted to him, but this almost dying stuff? Somehow, all she wanted right now was to have him take her. Hard. Pound away and let her know that she'd survived. The need was almost primal.

Biology was a bitch, wasn't it?

"Nonetheless." He shook his head. "Hang out for a while. Read a book; take a nap. You're safe here—and you can relax."

"But I can't just intrude on your evening and—"

"Sure, you can." He smiled easily. "All I'd be doing tonight is paperwork anyway. I'll be at the dining room table."

"Oh." Despite the smile, his expression was uncompromising. She might as well give in. "Well. Thank you."

"Very good answer." He pulled a golden Sherpa-lined fleece blanket off the back of the sectional. The feeling of his hands tucking it around her, being so very gentle, sent another frisson of desire over her skin.

No, don't grab him, Frankie.

From a bookshelf against the wall, he brought over a mix of books. "I don't have a large selection of genres."

Setting aside her naughty thoughts, she glanced at the titles. Children's books, thrillers, and... "Horror?"

"The kid's books are for when I have my niece over. The rest are mine. I also have gardening or recipe books if you'd prefer."

"Much as I like gardening books, my only plants are on my apartment balcony." Grief stabbed her heart. How she missed her summers gardening with Nonna where they'd pick produce and then cook together. Her sisters had never wanted to spend time on the farm; it'd been just Frankie and Nonna—and the rest of the Italian clan.

Bull's eyes softened. "Frankie..."

"But I love thrillers and horror, and you have one of my old favorites." She picked up *The Watchers* by Koontz, wiggled into a comfy position on the corner, and smiled up at him. "Thank you. For your rescue—and your care."

"My pleasure." He brushed his hand down her hair in a caress that was as soft as the blanket around her. When she leaned into his touch, his eyes heated, but then he stepped back with an almost inaudible sigh. "Gryff, want to keep her company?"

At the invitation, the dog jumped up and curled into a ball with his head on her feet.

"You're just a big softie, aren't you?" she murmured, patting his soft fur. *And so is your owner.*

Bull disappeared for a minute and returned to leave a travel cup of tea in the sectional console, then moved away again. He sat down at the dining room table and opened a laptop.

Leaning her head back on the cushions, she took in a slow breath, feeling the low hum of desire in her veins. She shouldn't let him kiss her, touch her, and somehow, after being almost killed, she no longer wanted to be prudent. She wanted to celebrate being alive...with the one man who tangled her emotions and wakened her lust in a way no one had in, perhaps, ever.

No. Behave yourself, Frankie. She shouldn't start something. Not here. Not now.

Grumbling under her breath, she petted Gryff, let the simmering desire fade, and listened to the sounds around her. So quiet, she could hear the light clicking of his laptop keyboard. Through the open deck door came the soft lap of waves against the lake shore, and birds calling to each other. No traffic, no sirens, no neighbors talking or shouting or playing loud music.

Slowly, her muscles loosened as she sipped the tea. After a minute, she opened the book and started to read about a dog.

CHAPTER TEN

W ords are slicker'n grease, boy. Don't listen; watch. What does the
guy do? It's actions that'll show who he really is. ~ First
Sergeant Michael "Mako" Tyne

Finished with work, Bull motioned Gryff off the sectional and
settled in his place beside Frankie. Such a pretty sight.

She'd fallen asleep not long after she'd started reading. Gradu-
ally, the strain had disappeared from her face.

Damn the PZs. All the same, it could be the assholes hadn't
realized they were shooting at a woman—or even a person. Bored
guards were known for taking potshots at anything that moved in
the surrounding forest. Frustration simmered inside him because
simply destroying the place wasn't possible—not with innocent
women and children there. There might even be new recruits who
hadn't realized what they'd signed on for. Maybe. He doubted a
person would remain ignorant of their purpose for long.

As if she'd heard his violent thoughts, she stiffened in her
sleep, her hands twitching, her breathing speeding up. A crease

between her brows and her whimpers indicated she wasn't having a good dream.

Fuck knew, he had the bad kind all too often.

"Frankie," he murmured. He set his hand on her leg over the blanket, letting the warmth penetrate. Slowly, he glided his palm over her thigh, up and down. "I'm here. You're safe."

Her breathing halted for a second, before she wakened. Her gaze focused on him—"Bull"—and desire rose in her eyes.

Tempting, tantalizing desire.

Fuck. "Yeah. You're in my home—and safe. You had a nightmare."

"I did, only it wasn't all a dream." Her voice rose with amusing indignation. "I got *shot.*"

"So, you did." He kept stroking slowly. Wishing—as he shouldn't—that the blanket didn't cover her bare leg. "Hell of a day, hmm?"

"There's an understatement." She turned toward the front windows that faced the lake, and her eyes widened. "It's dark."

"It's after 11:00." Night had fallen while she'd slept. Enjoying the sunset on the lake, then the moon-shimmer on the snowy mountains, he hadn't turned on the inside lights. Only the various kitchen electronics provided any light in the house.

When Frankie struggled to sit up, Bull pulled her to a sitting position. And enjoyed the sway of her full breasts under his T-shirt.

Her mouth curved up...because she'd noticed the direction of his gaze.

He shrugged. "I'd say I'm sorry, but it wouldn't be true. You have beautiful breasts."

Her laugh was low and husky. "Okay, yes. I do."

Yeah, he really did like her.

"Thank you for insisting that I stay." She pulled in a long breath that had him checking out those breasts again. "Knowing I could have died... Being here, somewhere safe, let me get past it."

"That was the plan." It'd helped him too, knowing nothing would hurt her here. Not with him around. He'd needed that assurance as much as she had.

She leaned forward, running her hand up his shoulder, behind his head, and gave him a straight-forward, heated look. "Thank you. For the rescue. For handling everything and giving me a quiet space to recuperate."

Her lips pressed against his, warm and soft, opening to him. When he put his arm around her and pulled her close, her body went boneless, letting him have all the control.

She tasted of cinnamon-apple tea as he took the kiss deeper, exploring and teasing, before drawing back.

In the dim light, he could see her eyes were filled with desire, and damn, but he wanted more. Shaking his head, he drew away.

"What?" Her frown was delightful, dark brows together, mouth twisted in an adorable pout.

"Gratitude sex...let's not go there." If and when they hooked up, he wanted honest emotions.

Her eyes widened, then she grinned at him. "That *kiss* was your thank you. Nothing more."

"A kiss is good. Beats getting a card in the mail." Cards had been forwarded to him a time or two after hostage rescues.

Her tongue ran over her upper lip. "Um, more kisses would be good."

"I only rescued you once."

"Moving on from that..." Her skin darkened with a blush. "Maybe, as two consenting adults, we could possibly indulge in some simple sex with...um, no expectations for anything afterward. With the caveat that nothing intrudes into work."

"Simple sex." Nothing about this woman was simple. He studied the sultry look in her dark eyes and admitted that the attraction between them had been there since they met.

He rubbed his lips lightly over hers and murmured, "I could do with some indulging."

Her lips tipped up with her smile. Framing her face with his hands, he kissed her. Invading. Demanding.

She had a luscious mouth.

More.

Rising, he snapped his fingers for Gryff and let the dog out into the grassy shared courtyard. "Go enjoy the evening, buddy." Closing the door, he flipped the lock and glanced toward the sectional. With the lights off, nothing would be visible from outside.

As Bull rejoined her, Frankie laughed. "Don't want to corrupt your baby?"

"He's an innocent li'l pup, all hundred pounds of him."

"I did notice he was lacking some...equipment," Frankie said. "Perhaps I should make sure that you haven't suffered the same fate."

"We *did* have people shooting in the forest," he said in a judicial tone. "It would be best if we performed an inspection for missing or damaged parts." He pulled her shirt off, sat beside her with one hand behind her back and the other on her breast.

He kissed her.

Sensory overload. Her lips were full and soft. Her breast was full and soft. Both equally appealing. *Jesus.*

"Mmm. This part seems functional. Let me check the other one." He cupped her other breast, enjoying the heavy weight on his palm as he kissed down her neck, taking care to miss the scratched spots. "Yes, this one seems to be fine."

When he ran his thumb around her velvety nipple, she pulled in a shaky breath. Nicely sensitive. Yeah, his mouth needed to be there.

Slipping off the sectional onto his knees, he flattened her on the cushions, hand in her hair. Lowering his head, he licked around one soft nipple, blew a puff of air, and tongued the heady peak.

. . .

Ohhhh. When Bull stretched her out on the couch, she felt like a virgin sacrifice on an altar. And as if in response, her naked breasts were throbbing and tingling. He closed his mouth over one aching nipple, and the bloom of lust made her back arch.

He switched to the other breast, rubbing his slightly scratchy goatee against the tender underside before drawing the nipple into his mouth. His mouth was far too skilled.

Her body was melting into a carnal pool. If this was what happened during pagan rituals, she'd volunteer to be tribute. Even though she wasn't a virgin.

She ran her hands over his head, enjoying the feel of the shaved scalp. Not stubbly, but ever-so-soft skin, like sun-warmed, buttery leather.

Moving up, he kissed her again, even as he teased her nipples with his fingers. "I can report that the above-ground equipment seems to be in good order," he murmured. When he rolled one nipple between his thumb and forefinger, her mind hazed at the pleasure.

"Well." She blinked, then gripped the back of his T-shirt. "Hold still. I mustn't slack off on the job."

He ducked his head, letting her pull the shirt over his head and off.

Oh, *santo cielo.* Good God, she might not survive this. His body was male perfection, from the strong, corded neck, the smooth bronze expanse of his wide chest, to the hard slab of his ribbed abdomen. One shoulder had a tattoo with an eagle perched on an anchor, clutching a rifle and a trident. The other shoulder had a frog skeleton. A friend's husband who'd been in the Navy SEALs also had one of those eerie tats. A long scar ran over his upper chest, a circular white one on his lower abdomen.

He was a warrior.

Unable to keep from touching, she flattened her palm against steely pectoral muscles, started to sit up—and winced as her back pulled.

His dark brows drew together. "You're hurt."

"No, not really."

"Frankie." His voice was a low rumble of warning.

"Fine, my back is a little sore. New York streets aren't a good preparation for hiking and falling off Alaskan cliffs."

Even his low chuckle was sexy? "I daresay not. Roll over, sweetheart, onto your belly."

Ignoring her whine of complaint, he moved her. The cushions were plush against her bare breasts and abdomen, making her very aware that all she wore were her small briefs.

"Stay right there." He rose. When he returned, the cushion dipped as he sat beside her hip. A second later, his callused palms stroked up on each side of her spine. A sweet scent like tropical fruit wafted through the air, and a second later, heat spread over her skin.

"That feels wonderful."

"Mmm, the stuff has a warming agent in it." He pressed gently, at first, easing her muscles, then his powerful hands squeezed the knots, tightening to the point of pain, then releasing.

She moaned as each painful spot relaxed. Slowly, he worked his way down her back, avoiding the bruises.

"You're great at this," she murmured.

His laugh was a dark rumbling sound. "When I was a sex-driven young man, Caz said giving a massage was a wonderful way to get a woman's clothes off and please her as well, and he gave me lessons so I wouldn't break anyone."

She snorted because he easily could. Yet his strength and gentleness combined was incredibly arousing. So was his generosity. Despite already being on the way to having sex, he'd put his own desires on hold to make her feel better.

It would be easier if he were ugly.

"Excuse me?"

"Oh, *che palle*, did I say that out loud?"

"'Fraid so." He was laughing as his hands glided over her skin. "Do you normally have sex with ugly men?""

There was no way to answer that.

When she stayed silent, he rolled her to her back and massaged the front of her shoulders. His dark gaze met hers as he waited for her answer.

"Bull, I don't..." She sighed. "I don't really trust good-looking men."

He blinked, then his eyes sharpened. "Because of your ex who's a model and undoubtedly handsome?"

"He's one. There were more." Just the thought of them made her tense. "One cheated on me. Another stole money. Another man—besides my ex—wanted my influence to get ahead in the business. I know you're not them, but it's difficult to fight the feeling that pretty men are all about themselves and no one else."

She turned her head. As the memories of the betrayals surfaced again, they hurt even more. Her emotions were already scraped raw from the day.

I shouldn't be here.

Ugly emotions didn't excuse her behavior. Bull had rescued her, and now, she'd essentially said he was untrustworthy and shallow. How rude and ungrateful could she be? "I'm sorry, I didn't mean—" She tried to sit up.

His hands tightened on her shoulders, holding her in place... and he resumed gently rubbing her shoulders. "Frankie," he said softly.

"I'm sorry," she repeated, staring at the back of the sectional. How could she excuse herself gracefully with one foot in her mouth?

He chuckled and cupped her face, turning her head toward him so easily. All those muscles. So damned gorgeous. "Sweetheart, look at me," he said firmly.

She had no choice.

A line had deepened between his brows, but he showed no

anger. His dark eyes studied her. "If you grew up in the business, that's where your dating pool is from, I bet. Were those gorgeous, shallow men all models or wannabe models?"

Her ex, yes. The rest, mostly yes. "I dated students in college. That's how I found out that the less...hot...men were nicer."

"Ah, got it." He smiled at her. "Might I point out a small flaw in your hypothesis about the character of good-looking men."

It wasn't fair that the man was as smart as he was attractive. "All right."

"Your sampling came from a subset of handsome men. You dated male models, people whose careers are dependent on their appearance. Because of that, a high percentage of models—probably both male and female—likely possess a certain kind of self-centered personality."

Wait a minute, now. "You mean... What you're saying is that male *models* are possibly shallow and untrustworthy, but that might not apply to gorgeous men who aren't models?"

"It might; it might not. People are...people." He ran light fingertips over her cheek. "I learned early on not to judge a person by outward appearance. And really, Frankie, women get pissed off when guys judge them on how they look."

His quiet words felt like a blow because of the accuracy. She'd done exactly what she found so appalling from men. Or even women. If someone said, *I don't date ugly men*, Frankie would've called her small minded. Stupid, even.

She was the stupid one. "I hate it when someone—besides me—is right. You know that, don't you?"

He had such a great laugh.

She grumbled under her breath and took a moment to consider her past dating history, seeing the relationships, the men, through a new lens.

"One other thing," he murmured. He skated his thumb over her lips, making her realize she'd been rubbing her cheek against his wide, hard palm. "Your past is telling your head not to trust me. But you already do, don't you?"

Damn him. She did. How did that happen? Maybe because he'd saved her from the forest, taken care of her, and been wonderful with his dog, his niece, and the people at work. She'd come to know him better than she realized. He didn't go for the easy slick choices, didn't depend on his charm, but...did the work. He was sincere...and careful with people.

"Maybe," she said, grudgingly. "Yes, all right. I do trust you."

He rewarded her for her honesty with a kiss. Such a great kiss. Firm, seductive lips turning so hungry and demanding that her senses spun.

She curled her uninjured arm around his shoulder and felt his back muscles flex as he braced himself on one hand and covered her breast with the other. His palm was still slick with the massage oil...and as he teased her nipple, her skin began to tingle and warm.

"What?" She wiggled. "What's in that stuff?"

"Just something for fun." He rubbed his nose against hers and kissed her again. "It's good for sore muscles—and for other areas, as well. Like lady-bits."

He ran his fingers around her other nipple, tugging it to a point. When he bent and blew air across the jutting peaks, the sensation of heat and the cool air made her toes curl. He cupped a breast in each hand, then squeezed, tightening the skin, so when he circled a nipple with his tongue and suckled, pleasure shocked through her.

"Bull..."

Never slowing, he moved back and forth between her breasts, sucking, teasing, tugging.

Madonna, she might die of pleasure. Moaning, she ran her fingers down his back, over rippling muscles beneath velvet-smooth skin, down the deep furrow of his spine, to his tight buttocks. *Mmm.* Twisting slightly, she slid a hand between them and under the waistband of his jeans. He was so hard, so thick that there wasn't any room in there at all. "That must be very uncomfortable."

He broke out laughing. "Woman, you have no idea." He sat up and tucked his fingers under the waistband of her briefs and paused to give her a chance to object.

Object? Not hardly. Her whole body wanted those skilled hands on her pussy. She lifted her hips. His smile flashed, and then her briefs were off and tossed onto the coffee table.

He sat back, studying her body with an open appreciation that sent a flush over her skin. "You look delicious in that position." He ran a finger from her breast, down her stomach, and...down her right thigh.

She glared. *Stronzo*. Whatever happened to a man going straight for the target? For a change, it was what she really wanted and...he was going to play?

She grabbed his big-boned wrist—her fingers couldn't even close around it—and moved his hand to her pussy. "There."

Oh, bad Frankie. Some men felt threatened by—

"There, hmm?" His mouth quirked.

His unshakable self-confidence was even sexier than his body.

He gripped her ankle, lifted her right leg over his head, and set it down in his lap, so he was seated sideways between her thighs. Reaching over to the bottle on the coffee table, he pumped more lotion into his palm. "I forgot. We're in the middle of a massage."

Her mouth dropped open. She wanted sex, not a massage.

Smiling slightly, he ran those big hands up and down her thighs, across her stomach, down again—missing her pussy entirely.

She groaned, and her hips tilted up in demand.

"Really?" A corner of his mouth curved.

His fingers were still slick as he moved from her belly down over her mound—and wasn't she glad she'd shaved that morning? He slid his fingers up and down the plump outer folds, and the skin began to tingle, reminding her of the strange lotion he'd been using. Slowly, he opened her, exposed her, and slid those lotion-coated heavy fingers right over her throbbing clit.

"Aaaah!" Her hips bucked up, and with one hand over her pelvis, he held her down.

Her legs were kept open with his huge body between them, and he circled a finger around her clit. As the lotion heated the swollen tissues, and her sensitive nub began to tingle, she started to squirm. The feeling was...intense.

"Look at me, sweetheart."

Her gaze was caught by his black eyes, held in the same way he held her hips down.

His fingers never stopped moving. Although his hand was so powerful, his touch was light. Teasingly firmer, then only a brush as he drew all the blood, all her focus to that one spot.

Wait, no, making love should be equal. She ran her hands up and down his arms, over his chest and down.

He slid farther away. "Next time. I want you badly enough that I'll wait." He grinned. "It's a guy thing."

Without waiting for her answer, he bent down, and his lips closed around her. Between the tingling lotion and his mouth, her whole clit seemed to burst into glorious flames.

She cried out, knew she was making noise, and couldn't stop.

Chuckling, he ran his jaw over the crease between her thigh and pussy, the goatee a rough scrape on the tender skin, then returned to tormenting her. Flicking licks of his tongue alternated with rough suckling.

"More. More, *now*." She shot from aroused to urgently needing to come and grabbed for his hair to pull him closer. To make him do what... Her fingers found only warm skin. No reins.

At her frustrated growl, his head came up. His gaze swept over her and filled with amusement.

If he didn't touch her, she'd die. And he was amused? "You, you *bastardo*."

"Not according to my mother, sweetheart." Watching her face, he slowly slid one finger inside her, sending her right to the brink of orgasm.

She gasped at the overwhelming sensation.

"Oh, yeah," he murmured, then bent his head and took her into his mouth, sucking and licking even as his finger slid in and out.

"*Ooooob*." The explosion of pleasure was so intense it drove all the air from her lungs. She gasped for air and screamed as she convulsed in a blinding climax.

His finger thrust deeper, sending her over, again and again and again, until she was reduced to quivering jelly.

As she pulled in lungfuls of air, he smiled down at her. "Jesus, I love the way you sound when you come. How you look." He kissed her mound lightly and moved her leg from around him so he could rise and shed his jeans.

Mmmm. His cock was fully proportional with his size—thick and long and very erect. His balls hung between his legs, potently full.

His wallet was in the coffee table basket, and he slipped out a condom and sheathed himself.

Easing himself down, he settled on his knees between her thighs, lifted her hand, and curled her fingers around his cock. *Cazzo*, he was big. He made a low rumbling sound of enjoyment when she tightened her grip and gave an experimental pump.

His gaze assessed her expression. "You all right with continuing, Ms. Bocelli? We can stop now if you want."

She snorted and answered by pulling his cock toward her.

His laugh rang through the room. "All right then." Setting a hand beside her shoulder to brace his weight, he used the other hand to set his cock at her entrance and slicken the head. "I love how wet you are for me."

His deep voice, his care for her comfort added layers of excitement. Her arousal rose under his touch, his voice.

Slowly, he worked his way in, inexorably stretching her, filling her until her whole lower half throbbed with excitement.

"You feel amazing, city girl." Bull kept a firm grip on his control, enjoying the little sounds she was making—the tiny inhalation as he pushed deeper, the almost inaudible moan as he withdrew. Yeah, it'd be far too easy to shoot before he was ready—and he intended to take his time and savor this moment.

Damn, he enjoyed her—her courage, sure, but also her sense of humor, her ability to laugh at herself, her kindness to Gryff. How she talked to Hawk without acting afraid. The way she lost herself in her orgasm with a scream. Fuck, he'd almost come right then like a horny teen.

He pressed in, slow and sure, going balls-deep until she was a hot, tight fist around him. And he felt her tighten her pelvic muscles to make it even better for him, because that was the type of woman she was—as generous with giving as she was enthusiastic in receiving.

Braced on one arm, he cupped one lush breast with his free hand, plumping it, kneading it, smiling as her muscles clenched around his dick. Sensitive breasts were his favorite. "The way you feel around me is fucking wonderful."

The corners of her mouth tipped up, and he could see the pleasure in her big brown eyes.

Slowly, he started to move in and out, enjoying the slick feel of her cunt around him. Her nipple jutted into a peak in his hand.

He moved faster, harder, keeping a careful eye on her. He was big—yeah, no denying it—and it was worth taking a little extra time to ensure a woman was ready. But her hips were rising, meeting him with every thrust.

The sound of sex, wet and slapping, filled the room. Her face was flushed, eyelids at half-mast, as she ran her hands over his chest.

Close, but not quite there, and he'd give his next breath to see her come again. Fuck, he'd never seen anything sexier, and he damn well wanted to be inside her this time.

Let's take a bit of control from her.

Releasing her breast, he lifted her left leg, setting it on his shoulder and holding it there—eliminating her ability to move or lift her hips. Forcing her to take what he had to give. As he drove harder, he watched her swallow, saw her color deepen, her nipples bunch tighter.

Her eyes closed as the muscles of her torso tensed. A thrust, another, and then her neck arched as she went over. Her cunt squeezed his cock, released, squeezed as she came in waves and "ohh, ohh, ohh, fuck, ohhhhh," filled the room with her gorgeous voice.

The fantastic buffeting around his dick shoved him right over the edge. With a low roar, he slammed into her, deep, deeper, as heat engulfed his balls, then his cock, and he came with hard pleasurable jets.

Jesus fuck.

He pulled in some air, then gently lowered her leg to wrap around his waist. She did the same with her other leg and drew him even closer, holding him inside her with the same generosity that she made love.

Easing himself down on one elbow, he brushed her hair from her damp face and traced a finger around her swollen mouth. "Sweetheart. That was amazing."

Under his touch, her lips curved up. "Hmm. It was...pretty good. Maybe we should go again, so I can be sure."

He burst out laughing and hugged her to him. "We will definitely have to go again and see."

It was well past dawn.

Frankie was curled up against Bull's side in his bed, drowsing off and on from the last bout of sex. When they'd come upstairs to his bedroom, he hadn't closed the wide doors that overlooked the living room below and had a view out the two stories of windows facing the lake. As the rising sun turned the snow on the distant mountains to golds and pinks, he'd woken her, reminding her she'd asked for a repeat. His hands had already been busy, and she'd been far too aroused to protest.

The slow, sweet, sensual second time had been even better than the first, leaving her feeling as if her body had melted into syrup.

Sleepily, she skated her palm over the warm satin of his chest, feeling the hardness of the muscles beneath. His arm tightened around her in an affectionate squeeze.

In the corner, Gryff lay in a big cushy dog bed, his fluffy tail over his nose.

"Good morning, sweetheart," Bull murmured.

"It is, isn't it? And you have such a beautiful—quiet—view. I can't believe the lakeshore isn't crowded with houses."

"That's because we own most of it. We wanted enough land that the sarge wouldn't feel crowded."

"The sarge?"

"Ah, he was basically our adopted father—and a recluse and paranoid as all get out." Bull smiled slightly. "He raised us in an off-the-grid cabin, but when we all left, we talked him into moving here where he'd be closer to his friend Dante. It turned out that Dante had bought a lot of lakefront property when land was cheap, and he was eager to sell us this side. My brothers and I pitched in to buy it and build here, so we could be near the sarge when time allowed."

"You miss him."

After a long moment, Bull sighed. "Yeah. We're combat vets and know how short life can be, but we never expected *him* to die. He always seemed indestructible."

Grief. Why did the sound of it in his deep voice pull on her heartstrings? "I'm sorry, honey."

He smiled, then his eyes seemed to darken. "Speaking of dying, do you want to tell me more about your trip to the PZs yesterday?"

"No, I think my curiosity about them was satisfied." And that was all she was going to say about it. She couldn't lie to him and didn't want to.

Besides, she was just someone he'd had a nice bout of sex with. No entanglements, remember? She could hardly tell him the truth and ask for help. There was no way to predict how he'd react. He might well ignore Kit's objections and call in the FBI and cops.

She could handle this. Her desire to have someone hold her hand while cutting a fence could get Kit and Aric killed.

Bull didn't make the obvious comment—that curiosity had almost killed this cat. When she checked his face, his gaze was far more thoughtful than she liked. Not surprising, really. Under that good-natured, sociable front was a frighteningly intelligent man.

With a fingertip, he traced a scratch so lightly that it barely hurt as if to remind her of the danger she'd been in. "I think there's more to it than curiosity...but you don't know me that well, do you?"

A much better subject to pursue.

"Not exactly. For all I know, you could be a serial killer who's leaving corpses all over the mountainsides." She gave him a half-smirk. "Maybe I was out there searching for all those dead bodies."

His dimple appeared for a second, but then he ran his fingers through her hair, moving the heavy strands to fall down her back. "When you're ready to share the rest, I'll be here. Ready to listen."

She wanted to share. To tell him everything. And couldn't.

At the burn of tears in her eyes, she hastily slid out of bed. "It's morning. I should get moving. My shift starts early today."

"Frankie." He lifted those black eyebrows, his gaze steady. "You're going to be too sore to carry trays. You'll have the next two nights off from work. *Stay*."

But if she didn't leave right now, they'd probably do...sexy stuff...in that bed. And that was the problem.

Cazzo, she knew this would happen—that she'd start feeling all emotionally vulnerable and get attached. Just because of a few orgasms. And the way he felt inside her. That deep voice calling her sweetheart. His hand on her face. Those black eyes and...

No, no, no. Casual sex. Nothing more. She needed to concentrate on getting Kit out of that place. He was a distraction she couldn't afford.

"I have lots of other stuff that must be done." She pulled on her clothes, still astounded he'd not only washed everything for her yesterday, but had managed to get all the blood out, as well.

He rose from the bed, intimidating in size, yet so very tempting. Because she knew the feeling of his fingers on her skin, the taste of his mouth, his skin, his—

"Let me make you breakfast." He adjusted her shirt sleeve, easing it over the bandage on her arm.

"No, no, thank you. I need to get home." She wanted to settle her feelings, get past the sadness that this was all there could be.

She forced a smile. "This was a one-time thing, remember? No complications or entanglements. No expectations for anything afterward." She bent to pet Gryff, taking comfort in the soft fur and wagging tail. Dogs were so straightforward.

When she straightened, Bull had pulled on a pair of jeans and stood watching her.

She hadn't noticed before, but when he didn't smile, he appeared dangerous—like the soldier he'd been. She drew in a breath. "Thank you for the rescue and one wonderful night away from reality."

When he nodded, she knew he'd caught her meaning—that they were back in the real world. She had Kit and Aric to rescue. After that, well, her home was in New York as was her job and her responsibilities.

This night...had been just a dream.

CHAPTER ELEVEN

S uccess is not final, failure is not fatal: it is the courage to continue that counts. - Winston Churchill

The next morning, Frankie walked down Main Street, needing coffee more than she needed her next breath. She'd run out of coffee for the tiny coffeemaker in the cabin. Not that it made particularly good brew anyway.

She scowled at the blue sky, the cheerful snapdragons in the barrel-planters, and the bright clapboard storefronts. How dare everything be so happy.

Despite a dose of ibuprofen, her muscles still ached slightly from the unfamiliar hiking, and her arm throbbed. Nevertheless, she was past ready to return to her roadhouse job, but *noooo*. The boss said not until tomorrow.

I need coffee. And people. And to do something besides fail.

Maybe she'd just lay herself down on the sidewalk and have a temper tantrum.

"Morning, Frankie," the postmistress called, herding her grandchildren into the grocery store.

"Good morning." *Well, merda.* Guess it wouldn't be appropriate to give Irene's toddlers the example of a screaming tantrum. Besides...big tits, sore arm. It'd hurt too much.

Hands stuffed into her fleece jacket's pockets, Frankie continued down the sidewalk. Nothing was going right.

Like the failure of her visit to the PZ compound. The chief was probably grateful the PZs weren't located on a public road. Just imagine if visitors to Alaska decided the place was a tourist attraction.

A thrill a minute. Visit the notorious Patriot Zealot compound. See if you're fast enough to dodge speeding bullets. Terror will strike on our featured cliff-ride when you fall right off the trail. Caution: Adults only. Possibility of death. Not recommended for the faint of heart.

Despite reaching the compound, she hadn't figured out which building the children were in.

Then again, she'd gained essential information. Like if she wanted to cut through the fence, it'd better be done out of sight of the guard towers and at night because there was a big wide space between the fence and the tree line. She knew—all too well —that the guards had guns and would use them.

She'd found the right trail to use—the one that started at two cabins close together. What were their names? Chevy and Knox. Bull had called them the town's handymen. If she could find them, would they give her permission to park there?

Then...she'd have to manage to walk that trail at night. The thought sent a shiver up her spine. She'd either end up lost forever or killing herself in the darkness. But using a flashlight would be like painting a target on herself. Where were her see-in-the-dark superpowers?

Wait... One of her friends had gone on a bat walk in Central Park, and the organizers had given her night vision goggles to use. She'd said it was amazing how much she could see.

Yes, yes, yes.

In the coffee shop—her favorite place to use the internet—

Frankie did her research. So much research. Finally, she decided a night vision monocular would work best along with head mount equipment so she could wear it hands-free. Tomorrow, she'd visit sports and hunting stores in Soldotna to get the equipment. She just wished she had more time to learn to use the stuff.

With a sigh, she leaned back in the booth and made the call she'd been dreading. "Anja, I got your voicemail."

"Francesca, finally. I'm so fed up with my manager, and I'm thinking of letting him go. Instead of fixing things, he seems to think I need to apologize to one photographer, and he actually ordered me an alarm clock and said to start using it. Can you imagine? You need to get back here and deal with him."

Closing her eyes, Frankie searched for a tactful answer. Because it sounded as if—without Frankie present—the manager was finally doing the job he was supposed to do.

Worse, Frankie had been enabling Anja's unprofessional behavior. That wasn't a surprise. It was one of the reasons her family insisted she stay. Although she preferred to think of her job as partly crisis consulting, her family used her more like a Mafia fixer.

When her sister's ranting slowed down, Frankie managed to interject, "I'm sorry you're having a rough time, Anja, but you'll have to deal with it. Learn to use the alarm clock and show up on time."

That got a fresh spate of screaming, and Frankie lowered the volume. Why, oh why, did she feel guilty that she wasn't there to help Anja out of the mess her crummy behavior had caused?

Well, if Frankie got Kit and Aric out of the compound this Saturday, it was possible she'd be back in New York by next week. She could get everything back to normal.

She opened her mouth to say so, then shook her head. Making promises that might fall through wouldn't be wise.

Instead, she made soothing noises and eventually managed to conclude the phone call.

However, Anja's griping reminded her to check in with her friend who was dropping into her condo once a week to water the plants. Friends were truly the best gifts in the world.

That done, she tried to drink more coffee, but it was all gone. *Che cavolo!* She'd barely gotten a chance to appreciate it.

Outside, she headed toward her car and noticed a couple of men in the next block painting the outside of the pharmacy. Painting...like handymen might do.

She strolled that way.

The men were probably in their thirties. The brown-haired one was short and incredibly muscular. The other was tall and lanky with a bushy red beard and drooping mustache.

She caught an interested glance from the red-haired guy and smiled. "Hi. I love that color of teal blue."

"Yeah, it's pretty, isn't it?" He tilted his head. "You're the new server at Bull's place, right?"

Such a small town. "That's right. Um, would you guys happen to be Knox and Chevy?"

He brightened. "Good guess. I'm Knox."

"Chevy, here." The shorter man set his brush down. "Were you needing work done?"

"Oh. No. Actually, I have a favor to ask." This felt so strange. "I know Bull parks his truck at your place so he can use the trail there. Could I do the same now and then? I saw a couple of birds —and bats—I wanted to photograph."

It was the best excuse she could come up with on short notice.

"Huh." Knox looked disappointed that she hadn't come over to flirt or something. Then he shrugged. "Bats, huh. That's different, but sure, not a problem. Did you see where the bull parks?"

"Mmmhmm. I did."

"Use that spot," Chevy said, his voice a deep bullfrog sound. "It's out of the way. Watch out for kids and dogs."

"I will. Thank you." Turning, she headed back to her car.

"Hey, New York!"

Recognizing the tenor, Frankie turned in a circle. No Felix.

"Up here."

Frankie spotted her fellow bar server standing in an upstairs window over the hardware store. "Good morning." She frowned. Felix looked positively disheveled, hair standing up, a beard shadow. "Rough night?"

His laugh was more grumpy than amused. "Rough two days. On Monday, a friend and I flew up to Godwin Glacier to help set up the dog sledding camp. I twisted my ankle on the ice."

"Oh, that sucks."

"Yeah, pretty much." He grimaced as he moved away from the window.

He was hurting.

And...hadn't he mentioned he loved working at the roadhouse because he hated to cook. It didn't even bother him that his rental had only a tiny microwave and mini fridge.

A mini fridge. This was Wednesday. Did he even have food left at home?

A minute later, in the coffee shop, the man behind the counter smiled. "Back again? Did your caffeine wear off already?"

She laughed. "I can always use more. Do you know Felix?" When the man nodded, she added, "What does he usually order —for his drink and pastry?"

"A latte and whatever the scone of the day is."

"Perfect." Frankie eyed the counter's display window. "Then a large latte, a half-dozen of the scones, and one pecan sticky bun. And, since I totally deserve it, how about a large cappuccino with a shot of hazelnut, please. Can you make all that to go, please?"

"My pleasure. Coming right up."

By the time she arrived back at the hardware store carrying all those goodies, she was glad Bull had given her the night off. The gunshot wound made her arm ache—and didn't that sound badass?

On the side of the building, she climbed the stairs to the second-floor landing and tapped on the door to the left. "Felix? It's Frankie."

"It's open."

Balancing the takeout box, she entered the older one-bedroom apartment with a high ceiling, off-white walls, and brown shag carpet. It was probably pre-furnished since she doubted Felix would have chosen the bland blues of the uphol-stered furniture and landscape paintings.

She glanced at him and grinned at his purple running pants and pale green T-shirt.

On the couch, he pushed to a sitting position. "Girl, what's up?"

"I brought you some breakfast. And coffee. Obstacles cannot be vanquished properly without coffee."

His face flushed, a gleam of tears appeared in his eyes, then he smiled. "You're an angel from heaven."

"No, my child, from New York, which is a completely different location." Relieved he'd chosen to laugh, she opened the box and handed over his latte. In the kitchen corner—which needed cleaning—she dug out plates and napkins and arranged the pastries.

"The scones are for you." After tossing her jacket onto a chair, she fixed him with a stern gaze. "No touching my sticky bun, boy."

He snickered. "That calls for a filthy response, but I'm not at my best."

No, he really wasn't.

Frowning, she sipped her drink, nibbled on her pastry, and studied her surroundings. The rest of the apartment wasn't truly dirty, just messy.

First things first. She got a pillow off one of the chairs. "Lean back against the armrest and put your foot up on the couch."

When he did, she tucked the pillow under the one that was all strapped-up. "Did you see the doctor?"

"Doc Caz? Sure." Felix grinned. "He's such a hottie."

"I'd have to agree with you there"—although Bull was much sexier—"but I'm surprised he didn't arrange for someone to help you."

Felix flushed. "I said I had it covered, and...he started to ask how, but somebody brought in a guy who'd missed the tree with a chainsaw. Blood everywhere."

"Ew."

Felix pointed to her. "See? Exactly how I felt. I hauled ass out of that place."

"Without getting the help you needed. Bad Felix." Frankie fixed up an ice bag out of the puny supply of ice in the mini fridge. After laying it on his ankle, she headed for the kitchen. "I'm going to tidy up in here a little." Most of the mess was containers of food he'd microwaved and dirty glasses and cups.

"Girlfriend, you don't have to do that."

"I know. And you didn't have to help me learn the ropes at the roadhouse." She grinned at him over her shoulder. "Gratitude paybacks are hell, aren't they?"

He laughed and relaxed, seeming less lost.

Here in Alaska, she'd learned how it felt, being alone with no one to call. None of her work buddies should ever feel like that. Not if she had anything to say about it.

As she finished up in the kitchen, there was a knock on the door.

Felix shook his head. "That staircase hasn't seen so much action since the 1900s." He raised his voice. "It's open."

Frankie frowned. "It's not safe to leave your door unlocked."

Audrey, the curvy blonde librarian, walked in with filled grocery sacks. "Felix, you should lock your door."

He burst out laughing. "I'm surrounded by city girls."

Audrey smiled across the room. "Hi, Frankie."

A petite older woman with chin-length white hair walked in. "My boy, what have you done to yourself?" The elegant British accent made Frankie blink.

"Lillian, my sweet, would you believe I tangled with an icy glacier and lost?" Felix gestured to his ankle. "Someone told you?"

Audrey nodded. "Caz asked Bull if he needed to write a doctor's excuse for you, but Bull said you were already scheduled off for most of the weekdays this week. He was pretty unhappy you hadn't called to tell him you were laid up."

Just the mention of Bull's name made Frankie's heart race.

Audrey continued, "He got called to Anchorage for some financial thing, or he'd be here scolding you."

"Uh, oops?" Felix shook his head. "He would, too. He's such a great boss."

He was. Frankie sighed. It'd almost been easier when she believed the handsome face and friendliness were only camouflage for a nasty person underneath. Instead, he was just what he showed the world—outgoing, smart, and concerned about others. Including his employees.

Felix should have called Bull. Scowling, she picked up the glittery phone on the coffee table, pushed Felix's finger against the reader to unlock the device, and added her phone number to his contact list. "Next time, call me."

"I—" He blinked as Audrey took the phone from Frankie, added her own number, and handed it to Lillian who entered hers.

Felix bit his lip. "Thank you."

"We brought some easy-to-heat food and staples." Audrey picked up the sacks and headed for the kitchen.

As Lillian sat on the couch to check and rewrap Felix's ankle, Frankie finished tidying up the apartment.

"Still swollen," Lillian shook her head.

Frankie walked over. It was bruised, as well. "Ouch."

He shrugged. "It's a lot better today. I'll be able to take my regular shift tomorrow night."

"Keep your ankle wrapped for a few more days," Frankie advised. Her years in aikido had led to a lot of sprains and strains. "It'll twist again otherwise."

"I will. Stupid ankle." Pouting slightly, he took a sip of his coffee.

As Lillian pulled out a new ACE wrap, she frowned at his drink. "The coffee shop is farther than you should walk today."

"I didn't go there." Felix smiled. "Frankie took pity on me and brought me breakfast."

"Did she now?" The woman turned to Frankie. "I'm quite sorry. We simply barged in here without introductions. I'm Lillian Gainsborough. It's lovely to meet you."

"She's also known as Mayor Lillian to the Rescue citizens," Audrey said.

Felix grinned. "She's also your landlord's ah...friend, if that's what we're calling it these days."

Lillian looked down her nose at him. "Such a lackluster word, but I suppose it will suffice."

Felix simply laughed.

Frankie stared. The old Okie who owned the grocery had this sophisticated Englishwoman for a girlfriend? "I'm Frankie Bocelli, also known as one of the waitstaff in the roadhouse."

"Ah, that's where I've seen you," Lillian said.

Audrey laughed and told Frankie, "A guy reached for your ass when you were wiping down a table, and you towel-whipped his hand hard enough we heard him yelp all the way across the bar."

"Quite nicely done." Lillian nodded her approval. "You were perfectly dignified when you asked him if anything was wrong."

Audrey was snickering. "Really, what could he say?"

"Was it the Patriot Zealots giving you grief?" Felix asked with a frown.

"No, just a tourist who overstepped the boundaries." She'd worried that Bull would be upset, but he'd just congratulated her on handling it herself—and reminded her to call for him anytime

145

she wanted him to take care of a problem. His trust in her and his protectiveness were a devastating combination.

"Actually, the PZ crowd won't be bothering your fair establishment for a couple of weeks," Lillian said.

"Really?" Audrey paused in putting groceries away. "Did they leave?"

"Unfortunately not." Lillian folded her hands in her lap. "I spoke to Reverend Parrish to schedule a town council meeting, and he said the entire compound is going into a lockdown for training exercises. *Maneuvers.*"

"They certainly take themselves seriously—like an army." Audrey banged the cupboard door as if to express her opinion.

A lockdown for two weeks? Frankie scowled at the floor. Surely, they weren't on heightened alert because of *her*? Because of the drone, and then spotting her near the fence. Could they think federal agents were suspicious and scouting them?

Had she caused this? "Is this normal for them?" she asked Lillian.

"Oh, now and then. It's some sort of readiness evaluation. Chevy said once that there is a lot of shooting going on during their scenarios. The members are restricted to the compound while they test their ability to respond to attacks." Lillian's brow wrinkled. "There is a gray area between the practical preparation for trouble or going overboard."

"I can guess which side the PZs fall on," Frankie said, her stomach sinking. Kit had chosen Saturdays because the PZ officers would be out drinking. But they wouldn't leave if they were restricted to the place. And the guards would be extra alert during a readiness evaluation. It would sure be the wrong time to be trying to escape—or cut a fence.

There was no choice. Kit and Aric's rescue would have to wait until after the lockdown. It was good they'd mentioned rolling the date forward in case of problems.

Rapid footsteps on the staircase caught her attention. Someone thumped on the door.

Felix rolled his eyes. "Come on in."

The young girl Frankie had seen with Bull danced in. She was short, slender, and maybe nine or ten years old with long brown hair and big brown eyes. She hugged Felix. "I'm sorry you're hurt, F-man."

"Yeah, me, too, baby." Felix kissed the top of her head. "Have a scone—I know you like them."

Lillian sniffed. "The rapscallion is playing favorites. He didn't offer any to us."

"Cuz he likes me better." Chortling, the girl grabbed a scone, settled on the floor beside Felix, then turned a curious gaze on Frankie.

"You two haven't met yet, have you?" Groceries put away, Audrey sat down in an armchair. "Frankie, this is Regan, Caz's daughter."

"*You're* Frankie?" Regan scowled before her face closed down.

What did I do? At a loss, Frankie glanced at the others.

Audrey got an *oh-shit* expression, whereas Felix and Lillian appeared confused.

"So, Regan, what'd Frankie do to make you mad?" Felix asked, reminding Frankie of how Bull had asked nearly the same question. What was with these guys?

Regan gave Frankie the evil eye. "She doesn't like Bull. He said so."

Oh, *merda*. "Um, actually, I didn't like him at first. Later, I found out I was wrong, and now we're friends." She could feel the heat rising into her cheeks.

"Friends? Again with the insipid descriptor?" Ignoring Felix's snickering, Lillian pursed her lips. "I am certain our Bull would prefer to be known as a swain, beau, paramour, suitor, or an innamorato, instead."

There were no words.

Frankie took a sip of her coffee.

Felix grinned. "See, Audrey, you should have Frankie's skin color. She doesn't turn nearly as pink as you do."

After a moment, Regan focused on Frankie. "Are you going out with Uncle Bull?"

Frankie choked on her drink. "No. No, I'm not. No."

"Why not? He's really nice—and a hunk. Women are always all over him." Regan said.

"Oh, *really*." Frankie had to unclench her jaw. "Well. I'm sure he's exceedingly popular with women, but I'm too busy to date anyone—and I'll be returning to New York once the summer is over."

"Now, doesn't that have a familiar ring?" Lillian wagged her finger at Audrey. "However, I'm afraid Bull hasn't found anyone to capture his interest, which is a shame. He would be much happier with a good woman, don't you agree, Regan?"

Oh, wait a minute here. Dragging in children to make a point was *cheating*. Frankie gave Lillian a frown to show her she'd broken the unspoken rules.

Regan studied the woman who had just given Lillian a dirty look. Only, her mouth had tipped up, kinda like she was almost laughing, too.

Frankie'd been all embarrassed when she talked about Uncle Bull. Almost like how Niko had turned all red when he sat beside Delaney at lunch, and stupidhead Shelby made smoochie noises. But Shelby'd been right, cuz Niko totally liked Delaney.

Was this Frankie crushing on Uncle Bull? *Maaaybe.* Uncle Bull wasn't usually interested in women, but he sure kept watching her across the lake last weekend. Maybe he was like...lonely. Papá had JJ now, and Uncle Gabe had Audrey. Uncle Hawk didn't act like he'd want a girlfriend, but Uncle Bull might. Grammy Lillian said he'd be happier with a good woman, and she knew, like, everything about love stuff.

But would this Frankie be okay for Uncle Bull?

Papá said Uncle Bull was married two times, but sometimes people didn't stay together cuz it turned out they didn't like the same stuff. And that made sense, Regan decided.

Maybe she should check...? Okay, so, Uncle Bull liked cooking and fighting. "Do you like to cook?" Regan asked Frankie.

She blinked and then smiled. "I love to cook. My grandmother taught me a lot, and then, I worked in a restaurant when I was in college and learned a lot of their specialties. How about you? Do you like being in the kitchen?"

"Yeah." Regan grinned. "I made donuts last week. It was way chill."

Audrey snickered. "The guys found out, and the donuts were gone before lunch."

"Four men—I bet." The way Frankie rolled her eyes made Regan laugh.

"I shared," Regan said. "I could've guarded my donuts if I wanted to, cuz Papá's teaching me to fight—and Uncle Bull's helping him."

When Frankie wrinkled her nose, Regan's heart sank. Guess she didn't like to—

"Your father's probably a good teacher for you, but Bull is huge, and the way he fights wouldn't be right for you. He's used to being a lot bigger and stronger than just about anyone."

Grammy Lillian tapped a finger on her cheek. "You sound as if you've had some experience with fighting?"

"Some. I've taken aikido classes since I was Regan's age." Frankie grinned at Regan. "I like aikido because it lets me throw people around without having to punch them in the face. But that's just me."

Fun! Maybe Papá would let her learn aikido. Regan grinned back, then frowned. "No one teaches that aikido stuff here."

"No, but I still practice. There are a couple of grassy areas in the town park, where I practice in the mornings. You'll have to join me, and I'll teach you a few moves." Frankie smiled. "If I tried to practice kicks in my cabin, I'd break a window, and Dante would throw me out."

Regan laughed. Dante was all proud of his rentals.

When Audrey asked Frankie how she liked the cabin, Regan sat back and considered. Frankie was really pretty when she smiled, and she wasn't wearing a bunch of stuff on her face or rings and necklaces, and she just wore jeans and a blue sweater. Not all fancy. Uncle Bull wasn't into fancy stuff.

And she liked to fight and cook.

Regan nodded.

If Uncle Bull was lonely, this Frankie might do.

CHAPTER TWELVE

W atch their hands. Hands kill. (In God we trust. Everyone else, keep your hands where I can see them.) ~ Rules for a Gunfight

A graveled path from Frankie's cabin ran alongside the lake, in and out of trees, straight to the city park. Carrying her *aiki-jo*, the four-foot aikido staff, she jogged slowly, grumbling with every step. Her legs felt more like brittle branches than flesh, and her body sure wasn't what a person would call willing. She was still sore from her...adventure, the one where the *bastardi* shot her. But the wound was doing fine. She mustn't let her body get out of shape, not when Kit and Aric's lives might depend on her.

She wanted to work out anyway. Back in college, she'd stopped doing her aikido exercises, stopped jogging—and not only gained a bunch of weight, but also became winded from just walking up a flight of stairs. That had made her do a long hard study of what she wanted from life—to do stuff and eat stuff.

She wanted to be able to play the occasional soccer or baseball game with friends. Or fly drones with kids. Then, as Nonna said, eating was one of life's pleasures. Bacon. Lasagna. Wine. Sticky buns. She wanted to savor her food, which meant burning some of those calories off. So, she'd returned to aikido and jogging.

The jogging wasn't helping with her mopey feelings today. She'd been here in Alaska for just over two weeks. Kit still wasn't free, and everything was stalled now, what with the PZ lockdown.

Then again, the delay would give her time to figure out how to use those night vision optics. Her trip to Soldotna yesterday had been successful, and last night, she'd worked on getting the head mount to fit and attaching the monocular.

She grinned, reminded of when she and Kit had tried to assemble a stroller for Aric. *This strap goes...no, not there, it must go... no, not there either.*

With a lot of lubrication from swearing, the night vision equipment was put together. Next step, get outside and learn to walk around without killing herself. She was going to need a lot of practice. Even with enhanced night vision, she wasn't sure she could follow that windy, narrow path at night.

So...at night, she'd practice with the NVM. During the day, she needed to hike the trail to the PZ's compound enough times so she could manage even after dark.

Surely there was an inconspicuous way to mark the trail, one the PZs wouldn't spot. She grimaced. Well, she'd figure it out. It was just one more little frustration in a pack of them.

Like the very personal frustration that today was Friday, and she hadn't seen Bull since early Wednesday morning.

How could she miss him so much?

Okay, sure, ever since the first day in the roadhouse, she'd listened for his deep voice and stole glances at him. Come on, who wouldn't? The man was a walking advertisement for masculinity. And sometimes, he'd hold her gaze—a long look across the bar that was as palpable as a caress.

But, after spending the night with him, bare skin to bare skin, having him inside her, his hand moving over her skin, his skillful lips driving her crazy... The need to see him, to be with him, had grown into an addiction.

With a grunt of exasperation, she increased her pace. The swathes of shade were almost frigid, making her grateful for jogging pants. In the sun, the temperature rose a good ten degrees. By the lake was a huge brown bear, too much like in a grizzly horror film. But its attention was on the water and the glints of fish. Easing carefully away, she put a good distance between them before managing to breathe.

Back to jogging, she passed a Frisbee golf area, then a horse-shoe pit. To her right, a loon flapped slowly off the water, a trail of sunlit droplets in its wake. As the bird lifted into the sky, so did Frankie's mood.

About halfway through the park, she veered off the trail, down a short path that opened into a wide grassy field with picnic tables dotting the perimeter. Old chalk markings indicated the space was used for soccer or football games.

Level ground. Nicely private. Perfect for her aikido practice, especially when she used her jo. Carefully, she did her stretches. Her wound pulled a bit, but it'd be all right.

Starting the kata, she gripped the jo lightly, feeling it become part of her body. As she went through the twenty *suburi* of thrusting, striking, countering, and figure-eights, energy rose and flowed from her center outward and into the staff.

Balance and grace—the heart of aikido—were what would turn an opponent's attack into defeat.

The sense of being watched intruded on her peace, and she spun smoothly to scan her surroundings.

Gryff beside him, Bull was leaning against a tree, studying her, scarred arms over his chest. His tank top clung to his thick pectoral muscles, damp with sweat. He'd obviously been jogging with Gryff.

Like a giant wave, her blood surged in her veins, roared in her ears, and tumbled her senses. Bull. *Santo cielo*, the very air seemed to sparkle.

The dog trotted over, and she smiled in relief. She knew how to talk with *him*. "Hey there, Gryff."

He accepted her enthusiastic petting with a wagging tail and a quick lick to her wrist.

"You're a good dog. A fine dog." As her brain rebooted and came back online, she straightened and smiled at Bull. "Good morning. Did you enjoy the show?"

How long had he been watching her?

"Why, yes, I did, thank you." That too-sexy-for-words dimple appeared as he smiled. "You're exceptionally good, but I assume you know that. How long have you been practicing?"

"I started in elementary school." She grinned. "My mother wanted me to take dance like my sisters, but there were bullies in my class, so my father said I could learn self-defense. Mama chose aikido because it's so 'pretty'."

Later, Frankie had stayed with it because the philosophy agreed with her own.

"Aikido really is beautiful." Bull's brows drew together. "But it's not the most effective fighting style."

How many times had she heard that criticism? Unhappily, it was true, in many ways. Not that she'd admit it. A girl had her pride. "Is that a way of saying you want to spar?"

His eyes lit. "Well. Sure. I never turn down a chance to fight."

No leer, no cracks about getting his hands on a woman. From the pleased smile on his face, he meant it sincerely. Maybe he didn't get to spar very often. Who in their right mind would take on someone his size?

If he could really fight—and from the way he moved, she figured he could—she was seriously outclassed. He was incredibly muscular, taller by seven or eight inches and outweighed her by close to a hundred pounds.

This was going to be fun. "All right. Rules are you pull your punches and kicks, no blows to the face or crotch."

"Good rules." Bull walked over to the dog, unfastening his jogging belt. She saw it held an aerosol can against his back. Seeing her interest, he said, "My wallet—and bear spray."

Duh, she should carry spray. "I guess if the spray doesn't work, they'll be able to ID the remains."

He grinned. "There's that, yeah."

She laid her jo beside the dog. "Tell Gryff I'm not attacking you, okay?".

"He's shown he can tell the difference between fun and anger."

Uh-oh. That comment implied Bull's skills weren't rusty. He probably sparred with the other guys at the Hermitage.

She was doomed.

They started off easy, punching, kicking, easy one-two forms, and then, he sped up. His moves grew faster, more aggressive. She blocked, danced around him, her speed mostly making up for his overwhelming strength. She caught some blows that would've been disabling if they'd been real.

Weaponless aikido was superb at turning an attack, but not so good at really hammering an opponent. However, she did have a weapon. She dodged a kick, swiped her jo off the ground, and kept sparring.

She lunged with the end of the staff. If not pulled, the blow would've taken his liver out—and he gave an approving laugh.

Now, the fight was equal, and if anything, the slight smile he had at the beginning grew bigger. He caught her a few times—and grinned when she spat curses at him—and she dished a few out herself.

She'd never had so much fun in a fight.

Spinning him off-balance, she swung and stopped the staff a few inches from his throat.

"Very nice." His smile held only respect and approval. "The

moves with the staff are far more aggressive." After a quick glance for permission, he examined her jo.

"I have a couple others, but this is my 'street' staff." It was painted in swirly Celtic designs with rubber on one end. "When I use it as a walking stick, no one gives it a second glance."

"Clever. And if you don't have it, you could use anything else about the right length."

Canes, umbrellas, branches. The world was full of potential weapons. "That's the idea." Wiping her face with the bottom of her shirt, she belatedly realized she'd flashed him with her bare stomach.

For which he rewarded her with a very masculine look of appreciation.

Oops. She straightened her shirt and felt her cheeks heat.

Smiling, he handed her back her jo. "So much for trying to show you that aikido isn't enough to keep you safe."

Huh. No wonder he'd agreed to fight her. The big guy was so very protective.

Laughing, she sat cross-legged beside Gryff who laid his head on her knee so she could properly pet him. "I learned the inadequacies of aikido the first time I had to fight someone in real life."

Bull's face went still, and he went down on his haunches in front of her. "Tell me about it."

"It's okay, *orsacchiotto*," she murmured. He really was a teddy bear, all concerned and warm—and deadly. "We survived."

"We?"

The teddy bear was persistent. "In college, my roomie broke off with a guy—a vindictive kind of guy." *Kit, dammit, you never did learn.* "He came to pick up his stuff from our apartment and started hitting Ki—*her*. Jumping in, I learned aikido's good at keeping me from getting hit, but less useful at really disabling an attacker."

"It lacks the predatory moves," Bull agreed.

"And I lack a predatory instinct." She shrugged and stroked Gryff's soft fur. "I considered Krav Maga."

Bull nodded. "Good choice."

Naturally, the guy would think so. Krav Maga was all about wiping out the opponent. She shook her head. "That's not who I am. I'm a pacifist at heart. So, my instructor talked me into the jo as a compromise."

"Ah." He studied her for a second. "Actually, I do understand. I enjoy fighting for fun, but I'd rather no one gets hurt."

She'd seen that. Even when she'd landed a blow, he never stopped grinning. "I hoped you'd be a typical big guy and rely only on your size to win, but your skills are even better than mine."

Bull rocked his hand back and forth. "I'd win in pure offense, but I'm not as good as you are at defense."

"Where did you learn? If you were raised around here, does that mean there's a gym and classes?"

"Not hardly." He sat down beside her. With a small whine, Gryff scooted over to be between them and heaved a sigh of bliss when Bull ruffled his fur.

Frankie had to suppress her own whine. Because she knew all too well that Bull had awesome, gentle, strong hands, so very skilled at touching.

"We had our own personal instructor when growing up. The sarge—our adopted father—started us on morning PT the day after we arrived in Alaska." Bull huffed a laugh. "I was nine and thought I was in great shape. After Mako got through with us, I wasn't sure I'd be able to walk again."

"Morning PT?" Frankie frowned. "You were just *children*."

"He was career military and spent years as a drill sergeant." Bull grinned. "Honestly, even the SEAL's BUD/s course wasn't all that bad after the sarge. Once he had us in shape, he taught us to fight."

A jay landed in a nearby tree, obviously hoping for picnickers. When no food appeared, it scolded them and flew away.

"You didn't compete in tournaments or anything?" Frankie asked, smiling when Gryff set his paw on Bull's leg. *More petting, less talking.*

"No, we rarely went into town. But with four of us, we had our own type of tournaments—also known as brawling."

Good memories, Bull thought as he petted Gryff's silky fur. The four of them had been hardened by rough foster care homes, by trying to survive in the worst sections of LA, by attending schools with inadequate supervision. They'd all been damaged in different ways.

"Caz could barely speak English and would pull a knife at the drop of a hat." Actually, he'd still perforate anyone who pissed him off enough. "Gabe had a smart mouth and bossed us around, which we mostly liked, since he's a natural leader, but...not always."

"And when you didn't like it, you'd fight?" Frankie was staring at him with wide eyes.

"Oh yeah. Then there was Hawk who had a low tolerance for anyone infringing on his space." That hadn't changed either. "Being young assholes, we'd push just to set him off."

Frankie rolled her eyes. "Of course you would."

Badgering Hawk to get a reaction had ended with Hawk losing it and battering the shit out of Caz. Two days later, Mako's friend Zachary Grayson came to visit for a while. The doc took them on long hikes—especially Hawk. Did chores with them—especially Hawk. Hawk would sneak out of the loft to watch the fire late at night, and Grayson occasionally joined him.

Being snoopy brats, Bull, Gabe, and Caz eavesdropped—and learned why a casual touch or too much proximity bothered Hawk so much. Fuck, some parents didn't deserve anything other than the deepest of hells. Jesus, they'd felt so fucking guilty.

After that, they'd done their damnedest to make him part of

the team—whether he wanted to be or not. Hawk had learned what it was like to have someone on his side against all comers.

Now there wasn't anyone Bull trusted more to guard his back.

"How did Mako come to have the four of you? He...uh... doesn't sound like a typical adoptive father."

"As it happens, he rescued us from an abusive foster care home in California and brought us to Alaska. Not exactly legally."

The way her eyes widened was adorable.

"It took a while, but we turned into a team, then into a family." Bull sighed. "It was about a year and a half ago when we lost the sarge. That was..."

There were no words.

Frankie's expression turned soft. Rising onto her knees, she kissed him gently.

Her sympathy drew away the rough edges of his sorrow. He was left with a gentle sense of loss and gratitude he'd had the rugged old survivalist in his life for so long.

Bull wrapped his arms around Frankie's waist and pulled her closer. "Thank you, sweetheart."

When she started to draw back, he smiled slightly. Mako always said a warrior should take advantage of ground and position and weakness. Maybe he hadn't meant the lessons to apply to sex, but...

Bull smiled, thinking of his little niece, who insisted Frankie was "into him" and he should make some moves.

Let's see if Regan is right.

Cradling Frankie's head with his palm, Bull fell sideways, rolling to put her beneath him, and kissed her again. Soft lips, soft body.

Soft heart.

Yeah, she appealed to him on all levels. He brushed his mouth against hers and nibbled down her cheek to her neck. All woman, with the taste of salt. "Mmm."

"Crazy man." Her voice had gone husky, even as she pushed at his shoulders. "We're in a park."

"Woman, you picked this site because it's private." If Regan hadn't told him she worked out in the park, if he hadn't been watching for her, and if Gryff hadn't caught her scent, Bull would have jogged right past. Would have missed seeing her practice. She'd been a hell of a sight with the short staff flashing around her so effectively he could almost see her imaginary attackers and hear their bones breaking.

She was gorgeous, graceful, and sexy as hell.

As he settled his weight on top of her, her legs opened. She could undoubtedly feel his bulging shaft against her pelvis.

She swallowed, her gaze on his.

"Guard, Gryff," Bull ordered.

The dog moved to the only trail into the small clearing and lay there, ears forward. Whoever trained the dog before the asshole got him had done a fine job.

When Bull turned his attention back to Frankie, her face was flushed a dark rose color. "Um. I thought we'd agreed we weren't going to..."

"To fuck?" he asked gently. "No, we agreed to no entanglements and that nothing would intrude in work. On your way out, you might have mentioned something about a one-time thing, but I didn't agree to that."

"Oh." Her small hands stroked his shoulders in a way he remembered...and enjoyed.

He nibbled on her jaw. "I think we can maintain a boss-employee dynamic at the roadhouse and still have a friendlier connection outside of work."

"A connection?" Her lips quirked.

"Precisely." Damned if he could resist her. Even though she'd only stayed one night, he missed her in his bed.

"You're crazy. You know I'm not going to stay in Rescue."

"I did hear that, yes." They'd see where they were when the summer season ended. Plans did change, after all.

"Well. All right." Her big brown eyes searched his for a moment, then her mouth curved into a sultry smile. "Yes, let's *connect.*"

He kissed her again, slow and sure, taking possession even as he slid a hand beneath her black tank top and black sports bra to savor her perfect breasts.

More. He sat back on his heels so he could pull her shirt and bra up and off.

"Fuck. You are incredibly beautiful, woman." The sunlight glowed on her damp olive skin. Her lush breasts, a shade lighter, were tipped with large pink-brown nipples that practically begged for his touch.

Words were inadequate. He bent to pay homage with his mouth, licking between the soft mounds, kissing up and over the nipples, sucking on each until they peaked...and she squirmed in need of more.

Perfect. But stripping her completely naked in a park, even with the dog on guard, wasn't wise. He eyed the area, grinned, and rose. Partly naked would work.

"Bull?" Frankie stared up at him, and damn, but he seemed even bigger than normal, standing over her.

He closed his hands around her waist, lifted easily, and set her on her feet.

Had he changed his mind?

He noticed her expression, and a dimple appeared in his cheek. "We're not done, Ms. Bocelli."

"Oh. Good." Wrapping her hands behind his neck, she pulled him down. The long, exploratory kiss led her mind to other things she wanted to do, to touch, to lick.

Step by step, his mouth on hers, he moved her backward until her butt bumped into a picnic table. "Stand right there for a minute." He pulled off his shirt and covered the surface.

His arms brushed against her naked breasts as he reached down to untie her joggers. Oh, this was so unwise. And somehow, she didn't care. She ran her hands over his bare chest, leaning forward to lick over taut, salty, damp skin, to swirl her tongue around one of the flat male nipples.

His growl sent hunger rolling up and over her.

Hands cupping her face, he kissed her long and hard, then spun her around. With his hand between her shoulder blades, he bent her down until her breasts flattened against the picnic table.

On his shirt. Because, being Bull, he'd made sure she was protected from dirt and splinters.

He yanked her pants down and rumbled in satisfaction. "I love your ass."

She could only grin because...such a guy.

There was the sound of his sweatpants being untied. The crinkling of a condom wrapper. Then he pressed against her entrance and made an appreciative purr.

She was really, really wet.

"Now," she ordered.

"Oh, it'll be now, city girl." His thrust inside her was long and hard.

The full, slick sensation sent pleasure rippling along every nerve pathway in her body. *"Cazzo!"* She extended her arms and gripped the sides of the tabletop.

"I know that much Italian." He chuckled and squeezed her hips. "In fact, I intend to *cazzo* you very, very thoroughly."

"Try this one. *Di più*." She pushed her butt up to get him to move.

"Oh, not just yet, sweetheart."

With a powerful hand, he gripped her right hip, holding her still. Reaching around with his left, he slickened a finger between her folds, then with unerring precision, he stroked her clit.

A glorious wave of heat swept over her, and she shuddered at the exquisite sensation of being held in place and forced to take the pleasure he was dealing out. "*Di più*, Bull, please," she gasped.

"Not yet. I want you higher." His lips brushed her ear as he whispered, "When you come this time, my pretty screamer, you do it without making a sound. Understand?"

The edge of command in his voice shook her, but she nodded. No screaming in the park. *But, but, but...*

His finger continued the slow circling of her increasingly engorged nub, even as his shaft filled her to overflowing. As everything inside her tightened, as the sensations became overwhelming, she started to tremble.

A scream threatened, and he covered her mouth, even as his finger pressed harder on her clit. The controlling hand on her mouth and the way he had her pinned to the table with his weight somehow increased every sensation, tipping her over the precipice. A fireball of pleasure erupted and roared through her so hard that the world went white around her.

"Very nice," he rumbled in her ear, moving his hand from her mouth.

Panting, she rode the last waves of sensation—and then he gripped her hips with both hands and began to thrust, hard and fast and deep. Plunging in, pulling out, his hold on her unbreakable, unyielding.

She could only grip the edges of the tabletop and hold on as another orgasm rolled over her, flattening her with mind-shattering pleasure. It lasted and lasted as he worked her with a glorious hammering.

By the time he lifted her hips for an even deeper penetration as he came inside her, she was a limp, sated body.

"Mmm." Rather than pulling out and moving away, he lay with his chest over her back. His chin rubbed against the top of her head as he...cuddled...her. "You've ruined me for any sparring sessions. I'll think of the way this one ended, get a hard-on, and not be able to fight at all."

When his words registered, she busted out in giggles. "Try taekwondo with a wide stance. That'll leave room for your massive equipment."

She could feel his chest shake with his laugh. "Massive equipment, hmm? Pump my ego like that, and we'll end up with another round or two on this picnic table."

That would be amazing.

It also reminded her where they were. "We should move, actually, before someone finds us."

"Gryff would give us warning. But you're right." Bull lifted up —and pulled out, the sensation making her spasm inside. How could she have come so hard and yet want more?

He moved away to the garbage container to deal with the condom. With a sigh, she started to push up off the table.

"Let me, sweetheart." He bent, squeezed her buttocks with an appreciative hum, and pulled up her pants for her.

"Thanks." As she stood all the way up, her head spun.

He steadied her with an arm around her waist. "Okay?" His frown created a deep line between his dark eyebrows.

"I'm good. Those were just really good orgasms." At his chuckle, she grinned up at him, then patted his bare chest. It really was mesmerizing how his tanned skin stretched so tightly over the rock-hard pectorals. She could even run a finger between each horizontal line of abdominal muscle.

With a guttural growl, he took her hand in his. "We can continue this back at your cabin if you want."

"We shouldn't—" Disappointment stole her breath as he donned his shirt. *He should never wear clothes. Ever.*

Unfortunately, she had her own clothing to deal with. She picked up her bra. Before she could pull it on, he turned her so he could check her wounded arm. "Appears to be healing all right. I noticed you didn't let it slow you down."

"It's fine. Just a bit sore." His concern made her feel...funny, and she hurriedly pulled her damp sports bra over her head. Naturally, the tight elastic band rolled, and the fabric squished her full breasts into odd positions. Somewhere a demon laughed and rubbed its hands in sadistic delight. She hissed in exasperation.

"Need help?" Laughing, Bull unrolled the mess in the back. Putting her back against his chest, he slid his hand down the front of the bra and lifted her left breast, then the right to settle them comfortably.

As he teasingly ran a finger around one nipple, her skin flushed. "Bull, behave."

"You think I should?" His arm tightened around her waist... and his finger kept circling. "I didn't get a tour of your cabin the last time I was there."

"Ah." She swallowed at the throaty promise in his deep voice. "You know...I have a very nice bed." Her words came out sounding like she'd just woken up in that damn bed.

"I'd enjoy seeing this fine bed." Releasing her, he grinned and pulled her tank over her head.

As she picked up her jo, he called Gryff. "Good job, buddy. You did a fine job of guarding us" Bending, he gave the happy dog scratches and pets.

In the deepest part of her chest, Frankie's heart did a long slow slide.

Oh, no, no, no. She was falling for this big Alaska man.

CHAPTER THIRTEEN

If at first you don't succeed, reload and try again. - Unknown

On Monday night before the book club meeting, Frankie turned off the car. *Cribbio,* she was tired.

Earlier today, she'd parked her car at Chevy's house and tried the trail that Bull had used after she'd been shot. It turned out she might have been just...a bit...overly optimistic about how easy that trail would be.

It was a good thing she had her compass, or she would've been totally lost. And this was in daylight. Trying it at night, even with the NVM? No way.

She needed to figure out how to mark that trail.

With a sigh, she laid her head on the steering wheel and pulled in a breath. Rain pattered down on her car, turning the interior to a gloomy gray...just like her mood.

It was only a few days into the PZ's lockdown, and already she was so frustrated her head might explode. Who knew what Kit and Aric might be enduring in that ghastly place?

Then there was Bull. She laid her hand on her chest because just the thought of him made her heart happy. Then sad. Since last Friday's sparring sessions, Bull had joined her in the park for morning workouts—he called it P.T.—and then sweaty, amazing sex in her cabin afterward. Damn her for a fool, but their times in bed were becoming more than just friendly fuck-sessions. At least on her part.

But what if he started to really care for her?

Maybe, if the stupid PZs hadn't done their war scenarios, she would've been too busy to let Bull sneak under her defenses and into her bed. Into her heart.

But nooo, she'd been so anxious, so lonely, so unhappy that the comfort of his mere presence had been overwhelming, even without adding in the sex. Now, here she was, totally falling for him. A man she wouldn't hurt for the world...and that was what appeared to be in the cards. A whole bucketful of hurt for them both.

Straightening, she wiped her eyes. At least, she'd held firm on not spending evenings or nights with him, and she'd been clear about why—that she'd be leaving, and they didn't have a relationship. She refused to have a relationship. He kept telling her he understood, then kissing her, touching her, until all her worries disappeared.

Shaking her head, she slid out of her car. Fat raindrops splattered her face and hair, and she yanked her hood up. One tiny beam of sunlight escaped through a thin gap in the dark clouds. The sun wasn't anywhere close to setting.

Hurrying into the municipal building, Frankie saw that the reception desk in the center of the lobby was empty. The police station doors to the left and the health clinic to the right had CLOSED signs. Police station and health clinic. Bull's brothers had both sides covered, didn't they?

She shook her head. Honestly, it was a good thing that their "Sarge" had managed to instill so much...honor...into them, or this town would be in trouble.

Gabe was an amazing police chief. She should still find out if his officers were PZ members like Kit thought, just in case. She wouldn't call them in, even if they were all good guys since the last thing she wanted was a siege situation, but if something bad happened during the rescue, it might be good to have some sort of...secondary plans.

Upstairs, the library was tiny and cozy with gray-blue walls and off-white trim. There were bookshelves, areas for children, computers, and magazines. In one corner, a group of people in comfortable armchairs were in a circle. Some had travel cups with them as well as their books. She should have brought coffee, too.

Next time, she'd be more prepared.

"Frankie, I'm glad you could make it." Audrey rose and waved her forward. "Everyone, this is Frankie from the roadhouse."

"Welcome, Frankie. It's good to see you again." Silver-haired Lillian rose and held out both hands. "Do sit beside me."

As Frankie took a seat, people introduced themselves.

"I'm Guzman." The gray-bearded man laughed, showing silver fillings. "Welcome to the best of the book clubs."

"Glenda Johannsen. I own the arts and crafts store." The stout middle-aged brunette smiled. "It's nice to get another reader."

EmmaJean was in her thirties, slender and bouncy. "Hi, Frankie!" Frankie knew EmmaJean and her husband ran one of the B&Bs.

"I'm Cecil. It's good to see another city girl settling in." White hair, white beard, weathered ancient face. He tapped his black cane on the floor for emphasis.

Frankie liked him immediately.

With long, gray hair and an adorably garish, tied-dyed T-shirt, Zappa hadn't left his hippie days. She'd met him at his gas station a few days ago. He gave her a bright gap-toothed smile. "You're here just in time for fishing season. Then there's hunting season after that. All sorts of things to show you."

"Hear, hear," Guzman said.

Hunters. She eyed them. *I bet they'd know a lot about trails.*

"Welcome, Frankie. It's good to see you again." Tina, Chevy's wife, was an energetic redhead. They'd met earlier today when Frankie parked near her house to hike the trail.

And it would be best to head off any commentary about that. "Is this your escape from the little ones?"

"It's *such* an escape." The petite woman snickered. "Every minute with them, there's some cataclysmic meltdown. Reading about world-ending disasters helps me put everything back into perspective."

Frankie couldn't help but laugh.

As people settled in, the discussion started. So *fun.* There were occasional forays into gossip until Audrey would bring them back. Frankie had rushed to finish the current book and was able to contribute.

Before they broke up, Audrey asked them to pick the next book—which set off a whole new set of discussion.

"I like the one with the engineered plague," Tina said. "It's very different, and—"

Frankie frowned, seeing Audrey cringe a little.

After a glance at Audrey, Lillian spoke up. "I quite adore psychological thrillers, and we haven't had one of those in a while."

Cecil pulled on his beard. "Mebbe, mebbe. There was one that Guzman favored with hostages."

"Yeah. A bomb and hostages in the New York subway system." Guzman winked at her. "Our city girl here could tell us how real-istic it is."

"You're giving me nightmares at just the thought, you evil man," Frankie told him to his delight.

"It doesn't sound too bad. It's centered around a mercenary group, so it'll be all shooting and stuff." EmmaJean wiggled. "A team of guys. I love bromance, don't you?"

"What's not to love?" Frankie's comment got a laugh, and the discussion continued.

Her thoughts had been derailed.

Mercenaries. Soldiers for hire. Could she hire some—an outfit or whatever they were called—to rescue Kit and Aric?

If Kit couldn't manage to get to the fence, that might be one way to help her get out. However, the risks would go up. As she knew, the PZs would shoot at trespassers, and the mercenaries would probably shoot back. That's how innocent women and children could be hurt or killed. Better them...probably...than calling in the Feds and instigating a siege-type situation, but neither scenario sounded safe.

Okay, she'd keep that as a backup plan.

As everyone rose, she moved to where she could walk out between Guzman and Zappa. "Hey, guys." Now, how to phrase this? "It sounded like you're both hunters, and since I have you here, I had a question. I heard the best hunting is at night, but don't you get lost? I mean, there's night vision goggles, but still, don't you get turned around if you're following a trail?"

Zappa beamed at her as they walked down the stairs. "That's a righteous question. I lost my way a couple of times getting to my stand."

"You can get lost on your way to the outhouse," Guzman stated and held the door for her.

Zappa drew himself up in insult. "Dude."

At the sight of the rain, they all stepped under the shelter of the overhang.

"There are ways to mark a trail—or...the path to a kill so it's easy to find the way back," Guzman said.

A kill. Ew. Personally, she'd rather think of her meat as dropping into the grocery store all prepackaged. "I thought there must be a way, but it seemed like going around and spraying trees with fluorescent paint wasn't a good thing, especially if you're hunting on someone else's land."

Zappa had the cutest laugh, a *heheheheh* sound. "You'd be right. But there are ways."

"There's chalk—even reflective chalk which will wash away within a day or so." Guzman pulled at his beard. "I like reflective tacks. Or...if it's somewhere I prefer to keep hidden, I use a clear reflective trail marking spray. Can't be seen in the daytime."

Clear? Now that had possibilities. She smiled at them. "I knew there must be a way. Thank you." She smiled at them. "I might have to use one to find my picnic table in the dark, huh?"

As they laughed, she waved and dashed to her car.

One trip to the sporting goods store coming up in the morning.

CHAPTER FOURTEEN

Your enemy is never a villain in his own eyes. Keep this in mind; it may offer a way to make him your friend. If not, you can kill him without hate—and quickly. - Robert A. Heinlein

Bull could hear the hum of the refrigeration units as he gave the counter surfaces the old "white glove" treatment. Not a trace of grease or dirt. *Good work, cleaning crew.* Might be time to hand out some bonuses.

The sound of gravel crunching and a car engine came from the rear parking lot. The little New Yorker was here.

The anticipation of seeing her made his temperature rise and muscles tense, rather like hearing a call to arms.

Fuck, he had it bad. When first dating Paisley, had he felt this way? He'd thought he loved her, but he'd loved a person who didn't exist. People put their best foot forward when dating—that was human nature. But, in Paisley's case, the façade concealed someone totally different.

He had to wonder if his brothers would've seen her more clearly. Only Hawk had met her, just for a few minutes. He'd been headed back to the mercenaries. Gabe, in the same merc unit, had been overseas, and Caz'd been doing volunteer health care in South America.

Paisley'd presented herself as being honest and loyal, a person who believed in service to others. Hardly. She'd implied that she volunteered her time at a hospital. Turned out her only time in a hospital was to have her appendix removed.

Now, much wiser, he could see the red flags he'd missed. Including the one where she'd pushed for marrying so hastily.

Now, here was Frankie. Her past—and reason for being in Rescue—was a mystery. Yet...unlike with Paisley, he'd seen Frankie when she was stressed and in pain. After being shot. Harassed at the roadhouse. She'd handled herself in a way he could respect.

She had a temper, oh, yeah. She'd also given him quite a few cold looks in the beginning—because she thought he'd crushed someone's feelings. That spoke of a compassionate heart.

Her sense of humor and ability to laugh at herself matched his. She had the determination to work out hard enough and long enough to be damn good at aikido.

Whenever Gryff was around, she was petting him—and the dog adored her.

Maybe he didn't have the whole story, but he was certain of her character. Over the past few days, they'd been together a lot. They'd meet in the park, work out, return to her cabin for a different kind of workout, and then cook breakfast—or some-times lunch—together.

Unfortunately, he couldn't talk her into spending nights together. She was holding firm on the casual, not-a-relationship stance. Stubborn woman.

She was going to find he was an equally stubborn man.

As he strolled out the back door, she was opening the trunk of her small Toyota rental. He shook his head. "Your car is too low for our gravel roads."

"I don't drive around much. Here, can you carry these?" She

handed him two grocery sacks, took two for herself, and slammed the trunk.

Didn't drive much? She hadn't talked about visiting any tourist traps, had she?

He followed her inside, enjoying the mesmerizing sway of her ass. Hell of a body.

Hell of a mind.

And he still had questions about why she was in Alaska by herself. She wasn't typical of those intrigued by the frontier life. Hadn't arrived with a boyfriend. Wasn't one of the youngsters who were traveling for the hell of it. That type usually grabbed a job at the resort or in Anchorage.

No, she'd picked a tiny town named Rescue.

In the kitchen, she started water to boil and pulled out a sauté pan.

He planned to help as needed and also assess the dishes she'd make for the first "Italian" night as well as seeing what to order as far as food, spices, and equipment.

Speaking of which, "Do you have the store receipt so I can reimburse you? Would you prefer a check or a direct deposit to where your paycheck goes?"

"Yes, thank you." As she handed the receipt over, she bit her lower lip. "The price of everything was pretty high."

"Welcome to Alaska." He tugged a lock of her hair. "Not to worry. When I buy in bulk, the price goes down, and if this works, my Homer restaurant will have theme nights, too."

"Your Homer restaurant." Holding a big pot, she gazed over her shoulder at him. "You know, I heard you say restaurants—as in plural—before, but thought it was just a slip of the tongue. You own more than one?"

"One in Homer, this roadhouse, and a restaurant-brewery in Anchorage."

Bending over, she pulled out a long casserole pan, saying in a grumpy tone, "At one time, I thought you were just a plain old bartender."

He laughed.

They worked well together as he'd already discovered when they made breakfasts. She took over as chef, directing and putting everything together while he stepped in to do some of the prep work in between making notes.

She was cooking a complete menu to be added to a pared-down roadhouse menu. An antipasto platter, crostini appetizers, and soup. A caprese salad, garlic bread, and bread sticks. Then the three main courses—lasagna, an herbed fish dish, and a chicken parmesan variation. There would also be some side dishes like garlic-prosciutto Brussels sprouts that he couldn't wait to sample. The dessert menu would have tiramisu and pistachio ice cream added on.

"What are you going to do about the Mexican night?" She was layering the lasagna noodles, ricotta, and meat sauce. "Do you have a chef for that?"

"I'll handle that night. Cazador brings back recipes whenever he visits Mexico. We might add in a Russian theme night—or even an Asian one, since Hawk picked up some good recipes when he was stationed there."

A noise caught his attention. Someone had tapped on the back door.

Frankie opened the door, then stepped outside to talk to whoever it was.

After a second, Bull recognized the voice—nineteen-year-old Amka, one of the restaurant waitstaff.

"I saw the cars and thought Wylie was here," Amka was saying to Frankie. "I wanted to give him my resignation...you know, quietly. Can you take it and give it to the boss?"

"Sure," Frankie said. "But why are you quitting? You said you really liked being a server and that the roadhouse was more fun to work at than fast food places."

"I did. It is."

At the unhappiness in her voice, Bull moved toward the door. Whatever was wrong, he'd fix it.

"Hmm." Frankie said slowly, "You live with a longtime friend, your family is up in Barrow, no boyfriend. That makes me think the problem is here at work?"

Oh, hell. Bull stopped before reaching the open door.

Amka burst into tears. "He—he's always making jokes that creep me out, and he won't stop touching me, even though I asked him not to."

For fuck's sake. "He" was obviously someone here at the road-house. Who the hell was harassing the girl? Anger rose in Bull fast enough it felt as if his blood had turned to lava. But if he stepped outside, he'd only scare the youngster worse.

"Ah, I can see how that'd make you want to quit." Frankie's words were calm, full of empathy. "You know, if the *stronzo* is treating you that way, he's probably harassing the other women, too. Tell me his name so I can protect them."

Bull almost smiled. Sneaky New Yorker. For herself, Amka might not have given up the name, but to help the others? How could she not?

"It's Harvey." Amka said in a rush, "He's not grabbing my boobs or anything, but he kind of slides his hand on my arm, or pats my butt, or puts his arm around my waist. I can't get near him without him doing something like that."

"*Men.*" Frankie's mutter was loud enough that Bull heard.

He winced. Too many of his gender were assholes.

He wouldn't have thought Harvey'd be one. Fuck, he hated firing people.

"Listen, I know giving up this job will put you back financially," Frankie said. "Why don't you let me talk with the boss—and maybe with Harvey? Sometimes guys don't understand how offensive their behavior is, and I have a method I've used before to get through to them. Give me—and him—another week, and if he doesn't improve, I think Bull will show him the door. Can you give me—us—a chance to see if that'll work?"

"I...I don't want to leave, not really." Amka's sniffles broke Bull's heart.

Damn him that this had happened in his place. He wanted to pound Harvey to paste, but he knew the guy. He wasn't a bad guy. Did the idiot not realize what the hell he was doing? For fuck's sake, was he really that dense?

With an effort, he left the women to talk. To distract himself, he pulled out the Italian sausage and ripped it to pieces.

A couple of minutes later, Frankie returned and stopped when she saw his face. "Uh-oh. I take it you heard some of that?"

"Enough, yes." Bull evened out his voice. "You did well with her, Frankie. Thank you."

Frankie shrugged. "Sexual harassment happens all too often. I've had to deal with it at my New York job."

"You were—"

"No, no. My mother taught me and my sisters how to deal with office predators." She shook her head. "Unlike Amka, I've never needed money so badly I was forced to be polite to *bastardi*."

Bull had seen how she handled customers with wandering hands. Overly familiar co-workers were probably humiliated with equal ease.

He leaned on the counter. "You said you had a method to deal with harassment. Want to take a break and pay Harvey a visit?" There was nothing in the kitchen that couldn't be put on hold for a while. And he was too angry to want to cook.

"Sure, let's do it." Frankie started putting food into the refrigerator. "Will you let me help?"

The need to deal with everything himself was there, but... "Our culture—especially in Alaska—teaches this behavior, hell, even encourages it. Even knowing that, I still want to punch him.

So, if you can manage to resolve this without a firing or broken faces, that'd be good."

"Violence and sexism—you men are all screwed up." Her bubbling laugh lightened his anger.

She picked up her purse. "If Harvey has an imagination, we *might* be able to teach him something and change his behavior. I'll give you your role-play lines on the drive over."

Role-play? What the fuck?

Frankie settled into the seat in Bull's pickup. The vehicle was the size of a tank, yet sitting beside him felt almost intimate. The cab smelled of clean leather and the wonderful sandalwood-and-cedar of Bull's aftershave.

As he closed her door and headed for the driver's side, she sighed. Somehow, he managed to treat her as if she was equal and still someone to be protected. One more thing to like about him.

Starting the pickup, he headed down Dall Road. He drove fast, but carefully, in control at all times. His sleeves were rolled up, and the light brown skin of his muscular forearms boasted ample scars. His jaw was tight, and deep lines had formed between his black brows. He didn't just look concerned; he looked deadly.

Cavolo, Harvey had better be ready to see reason.

He turned down a rutted dirt road and stopped in front of an aged, manufactured home. An old pickup was parked off to one side. "Harvey's home. He lives alone—divorced a while ago—and she has their two teens."

Hopefully, the boys hadn't become infected with their father's attitude toward women.

As Bull and Frankie reached the house, Harvey opened the door. In his forties, the burly man had a beer belly, an outdoors-man's leathery skin, and receding, collar-length brown hair. He bent to grab the collar of a thickly furred, black dog.

"Yo, what brings you two here?" Harvey asked, and she remembered why she liked him. He'd always been friendly, stayed on top of the work, and helped with whatever needed to be done.

"Got a problem, Harvey, and we wanted to talk to you about it," Bull said.

"Sure, anything I can do." Harvey frowned, obviously picking up Bull's unhappiness...in a way he hadn't with Amka. Because Amka was female.

No, don't give in to anger.

"Have a seat, folks," Harvey said. The tidy living room was pleasant with well-worn furniture in browns and greens.

As they took chairs, the dog sniffed Bull's boots. "There's a good dog," Bull murmured and stroked its head, getting a wag of the tail.

"He is a good mutt," Harvey agreed. "Found him with a busted leg on the road a few years ago."

And kept him. Frankie sighed. Why couldn't people be all evil or all good? A mixture of traits made things so much harder.

"So...what's the problem?" Harvey prompted.

Bull inclined his head at Frankie in an unspoken invitation for her to handle it.

Okay, she could manage. "Harvey, I enjoy working with you. You're always on top of the job, give a hundred percent, and are friendly with everyone—customers and staff. However, your friendliness is making some of the staff uncomfortable."

He stiffened. "How's that?"

"Some of your jokes and comments are sexual in nature. In addition, I'm afraid that touching another person, male or female, in the workplace isn't appropriate."

"For God's sake. Is someone sayin' I'm...what's it called...sexually harassing them? I would never—" He turned to Bull. "I never grabbed anyone's ass or anything."

Bull didn't respond. He really was leaving it to her. *Best boss ever.*

Frankie leaned forward, resting her elbows on her knees, recapturing Harvey's attention. "You touch the young women, Harvey. Shoulders, arms. You'll put your arm around a woman's waist and tell them how pretty they are."

"I'm just being friendly!"

"To you, it's friendly." And she...mostly...believed that was how he meant it. "To *them*, you're a big, strong, older man who is touching them without permission."

He shook his head, not seeing what she was getting at...which was why she'd come up with this role-play.

"Do you agree that you're bigger and stronger than the young women we have working in the roadhouse?" When he shrugged agreement, she nodded toward Bull. "Kind of like how Bull is bigger and stronger than you?"

Harvey snorted. "Bull's bigger than just about anybody."

"That's the truth," she muttered.

A corner of Bull's mouth tugged up.

"So, Harvey. I want you to imagine...oh, let's say you're in prison." Frankie smiled at his surprised expression. "Hey, the staff think the kitchen feels like a prison sometimes, right? Just bear with me, here."

That made him laugh. "Okay, I'm in prison."

"You just got dumped in there, and naturally, you're worried about the really hardened criminals. Like Skull." She pointed to Bull. "A mass murderer from one of the worst LA gangs."

Bull rose without her asking, and she blinked because he appeared...different. Cold, dead eyes. His expression was cruel, his body language predatory, as if he really did torture his victims.

He stalked over to Harvey and clapped a hand on his shoulder. "Oh, look, fresh meat." His deep voice held a brutal anticipation.

Harvey froze.

"Fuck, aren't you a pretty one." Bull's hard mouth curved up, and somehow grew even meaner. "Even better than that new guy last week. Had me a *good* time with him."

Harvey gave him an appalled stare, cleared his throat, and edged sideways on the couch. "Listen, I—"

Bull ran his massive hand up and down Harvey's arm. "Nice shirt. Soft. I like it."

Harvey shoved his hand away. "Jesus, stop. This isn't—"

"Bet all the girls think you're hot shit, huh," Bull said. "You got a great mouth, you know that?"

The implication, totally unspoken, was that the mouth could be used for sex—the same kind of suggestive comment women got all too often from men.

Harvey had apparently never been on the receiving end of that kind of innuendo.

"Always like the ones with soft hair." Bull tugged on Harvey's wavy hair, something Frankie realized she'd seen Harvey doing to servers in the kitchen.

Harvey turned pale.

Bull glanced in inquiry at Frankie. *Done?*

She nodded and motioned to his chair.

As he sat, she waited a moment for Harvey to process his feelings. "If I was to ask Bull what he was doing, he'd say he was just being friendly."

"Yeah, friendly." Harvey scrubbed his hands over his face. "Felt like I was being set up for a gang-rape in the shower

"Because you're not sexually attracted to him, and he's a lot bigger and stronger. When there's a discrepancy like that between two people, then what feels friendly to the powerful person comes across as intimidating—even frightening—to someone smaller."

Harvey stared at Bull, then Frankie, before turning his gaze to the window. Hopefully, he was recalling the way he'd behaved with the women employees and realizing they hadn't seen his actions as friendly at all.

"Holy hell." He met her gaze. "I get your point."

"You're not the first or last man to have discovered he…"

"Tripped over his own dick," Bull contributed.

Yes, that. Frankie shook her head. "I don't think you deliberately scared them...although you probably thought their discomfort was a bit funny."

Because most guys thought that way.

"I never thought of myself as an abusive asshole." Harvey scowled. "My old man was one. Hit my mom. I never wanted to act like him. Ever. And I have been."

Progress. "If Bull agrees, let's see how it goes." Frankie paused. "What you must remember when you interact with other employees, especially women, is simple. Don't do or say anything you wouldn't want to receive from a giant convict named Skull."

"That's a different way to look at things, but, yeah, okay." Harvey eyed Bull. "I'm sorry. I'll apologize to the servers. You okay with that?"

Bull nodded. "I learned something, too. Make it right with the staff, treat them with respect, and we're good."

"Thanks, boss."

Frankie smiled. Bull really was a good boss.

"Yeah, just don't start calling me Skull." Bull rose, then bent to give the dog a rib scratching that made it wiggle happily.

What was there about a man who'd take the time to make a dog happy?

"Time to get cooking, Frankie. Try to impress me with your Italian menu."

Frankie rose, winked at Harvey, and said, "Sure, *Skull*. Let's go."

When Harvey laughed, she had a feeling things were going to be all right.

As Bull pulled into a garage, Frankie parked her little Toyota in the driveway. And sighed. In the PZ compound, Kit was probably going through hell, and here Frankie was, planning to feed people.

Cazzo, I hate waiting.

The book club had given her the last piece of the puzzle—how to mark a trail at night—as well as the idea about mercenaries. She'd check into the mercenary stuff with her friends back in New York. Just in case she ended up having to call in help.

If everything went to hell, she'd ask Bull for assistance. She'd sparred with him, and he was scarily competent. A military veteran. He'd help; she knew that right down to the bottom of her soul.

Nonetheless, she still had ten more days to practice everything, and hiking in and cutting the fence—just her alone—was the best plan with the least risk to others. Gambling with her own life was her choice. She'd pull in others only if she couldn't manage on her own.

Sliding out of her car, she walked over to his pickup. "I'll have you know that my Toyota had a few nasty things to say about your road."

"Sorry. To discourage people from using our private road to get to the lake, we keep the section near the highway in rough condition."

"That almost makes sense." The "Hermitage" was well named.

She frowned. Hadn't Bull's cabin been near the other end of the semi-circle of five houses? "This isn't your place, is it?"

"Nope. This house belonged to the sarge." Grief filled his dark eyes for a second. "The upstairs was his private quarters, and the downstairs is the communal area for all of us."

Frankie put her hand on his arm for comfort. "How many is *all of us*, then?"

Before he could answer, the interior door to the house opened.

"Yay, you're here. I'm hungry." Regan, Caz's daughter, bounded down the three steps, her brown eyes shining. "Hi, Frankie and Uncle Bull. I can carry stuff."

"Sounds good to me." Bull tousled the girl's hair, then picked up the heaviest box and headed for the door. He called over his shoulder, "You can give the kid all the heavy stuff to cart—she's strong."

"Hey!" But the girl's expression said she loved the compliment.

Laughing, Frankie eyed the boxes of food and pulled one forward. "Why don't you take in the antipasto."

"The what?"

"It's an Italian appetizer. If you put the platter out on the table, we can all nibble on it as we unload the rest. And you'll be first to have a sample."

The girl's face lit. "Awesomeness. I got it."

Regan disappeared into the house.

As Frankie pulled the next box forward, someone reached around her to take it. "Got this one." It was the tall, hard-faced chief of police. "Welcome, Frankie."

Gabe gave her a smile and headed away, clearing the space for Audrey.

"Audrey." Frankie smiled. "I was hoping you'd be here."

"It's good to see you again." Audrey held out her hands for the insulated lasagna container. "In case no one told you, everyone's thrilled to have something new to eat, both at the restaurant and here today."

"That's great to hear." Frankie hesitated. "Bull said to figure on around eight people for the taste test, only he didn't mention exactly who they would be."

"Men." Audrey rolled her eyes. "There are the four brothers, JJ and me, Regan, and you. How's that?"

"Perfect. I know almost everyone." Pleased, Frankie dragged out the freezer box as Audrey moved away with her load.

"Got it." Hawk, the dangerous-looking blond guy from when she'd been shot hefted the container and walked away.

Huh. Still just as talkative as before.

With a snort, she leaned into the truck bed to pull out another box.

Regan ran back into the garage.

Caz followed. "Frankie, it's good to see you."

She smiled, remembering how his smooth Spanish-accented voice had been so calming when he was dressing her gunshot wound. "Hi, Doc."

He put his hand on his daughter's shoulder. "*Mija*, Bull said there was another kind of appetizer. Why don't you talk the chef out of that one?"

Regan gave Frankie a pleading gaze out of eyes the same dark brown as her father's. "The ant-ant-pasta is super, but Uncle Bull said I'll like the other one, too."

"I bet he's right." Frankie picked up the box with the crostini. "Your papa needs to carry this dish since it's heavy." And the bread toppings wouldn't survive being tilted.

Caz took the box and grinned when Frankie handed Regan the basket filled with garlic bread.

As they disappeared, an athletic-appearing woman with short, curly auburn hair and turquoise eyes came down the steps. "Hi, Frankie. I'm JJ, and I live with Caz and Regan. I love Italian, so you're my new best friend."

"It's nice to meet you." Frankie grinned and offered a box. JJ would be an easy person to like.

With a smile, JJ took it and disappeared back into the house.

Bull strode across the garage and joined Frankie. "I put the garlic bread in—there's a timer set for that."

"Perfect." Every cook in the world knew the secret to good food was using timers.

Bull leaned into the pickup to drag out the last box.

As his arm rubbed against her shoulder, the awareness of his body sizzled across her nerves like wildfire. She sighed.

Too loudly.

Abandoning the box, he straightened. As he looked down at her, heat stirred in his midnight-dark eyes. "I missed working out with you this morning, woman," he murmured. "And missed everything that usually follows."

Oh, so had she.

His fingers tangled in her hair, his thumb brushing her cheek.

Her breathing stopped, and she leaned in, every skin cell tingling and anticipating his touch.

He bent an infinitesimal amount, then paused. "No, this is not the time. I won't want to stop." He made a sound of masculine frustration. "Do you have any idea how many times I had to step back while you were cooking today? You're hard on a man's control, woman."

She laughed. "Me, too. I was annoyed you were so very professional in the kitchen."

"I'll make it up to you...later." He tapped her chin and stepped back. "Come, my chef. Let's feed the hungry masses before they begin to howl."

He handed her the smaller container, took the last big box, and led the way into the house. They went down a hallway and out into a huge open room beneath a high vaulted ceiling. The design was similar to Bull's home. The kitchen area was to the right. Past it, a long dining table stood in front of the two-story wall of windows facing the lake. To the left was the wide sitting area with a long U-shaped sectional, one even bigger than Bull's— as was the television that took up much of the wall.

Hawk was setting the table. The rest were opening wine and unboxing the food with teamwork as coordinated as in the finest of kitchens.

And...she felt awfully like a stranger.

A low *whuff* caught her attention a second before Gryff

barreled out from behind the island. He slid to a stop in front of her.

"Hey, you! I missed you this morning." His enthusiastic greeting made her feel at home, and she bent down. As he snuffled her cheek, she gave him a good back scratch.

There was a moment of silence around her, and she noticed several people were giving Bull...and her...speculative looks.

Perhaps he hadn't mentioned he was banging his new server. She almost laughed when Bull winked at her.

"Frankie, we have wine, soda, iced tea, milk, and water." Caz stood by the fridge. "What would you like?"

Most of the adults appeared to have wine—totally her preference. "Wine would be lovely." She set her box on the counter.

"What happened that made you set dinner back an hour?" Gabe asked Bull.

"Nothing of note," Bull said.

Frankie liked him all the better for not talking about Harvey and Amka. No matter how much she loved gossip—she blamed Nonna for that trait—some kinds shouldn't be shared.

"Not that we're complaining about the delay. It actually worked out better." JJ gave Gabe an amused glance. "The chief is just snoopy."

Audrey snickered and elbowed JJ, before telling Frankie, "JJ and Gabe are both snoopy. It must be a cop trait."

Frankie froze. "Excuse me...cop? I know Gabe is the Chief, but...?"

"Guess you didn't get much time for introductions," Bull said. "JJ is Gabe's one and only patrol officer until he hires an additional temporary LEO for the tourist season. JJ's been away for the last couple of weeks at a law enforcement class in Sitka."

JJ was a police officer. The only other police officer. The warning in Kit's letter played in Frankie's head: *One of the Rescue police is a member of the Patriot Zealots.*

Bull set his hand on her shoulder in concern. Both the chief and his officer were watching her, their cop instincts obviously on alert.

I'm an idiot. "Sorry, I was trying to seem innocent in hopes you guys hadn't noticed my lousy driving."

Gabe blinked and glanced at JJ. "No, can't say we have. Did we miss an accident?"

Whew, he bought it. Frankie shook her head. "No, I've escaped that fate. So far."

"New York drivers are almost as aggressive as Bostonians but lack any experience to go with it." Audrey grinned at Frankie. "Do you even own a car?"

"No way. The subway and taxis, even the buses, are far less stressful."

Such appalled stares. She started laughing, partly in relief that she hadn't gotten more questions.

JJ seemed awfully nice and not like some wide-eyed fanatic. Could Kit be wrong? Frankie would have to be careful about what she said.

"Here, *chiquita*." Caz handed her a glass of wine.

She took a sip. It was a traditional chianti, rich and fruity with an edge of tannin. "Perfect."

"I'm glad you like it." His voice softened. "The family is a bit overwhelming, *sí?*"

Oh, dear, she'd let her distress show. Bull was also watching her with concern.

Down, emotions, down. This was supposed to be a fun dinner. She managed a smile. "You are all actually making me a bit home-sick for my Nonna's house in Italy. Only she was a very traditional Italian, and her gatherings were even bigger. I have cousins out to the nth degree and aunts and uncles...and there were a lot of raised voices."

"The guys don't shout much." Audrey motioned with her glass toward the door. "They just go outside and pound on each other."

"Seriously?" She glanced at Bull.

His dimple appeared. "Flattening someone is more effective than yelling."

Madonna.

Urged by a hungry Regan, they were soon seated around the big table. Even though Frankie knew she was an excellent cook, she still worried. Even the best chefs could mess up—and somehow, today, it mattered more than normal.

This was Bull's family.

Moving the food around on her plate, she pretended to eat as she watched.

Bull sampled each dish slowly, making a sound that was almost a purr, before digging in with open enjoyment.

Caz ate with a smile, urging his daughter and JJ to try this and that.

Regan went back for seconds on the lasagna before finishing anything else on her plate.

Gabe stole an extra bite of lasagna off Audrey's plate with a wicked smile, then fed her a bite from his herbed trout, whereupon she dished herself a helping of the fish.

Hawk showed no expression and made no appreciative—or disgusted—sounds. Having been the least attractive daughter, Frankie wondered what it'd been like to grow up with three "brothers" who were each man candy in different ways.

Gabe was roughly handsome with a commanding presence. If he gave an order, probably every person in town would obey. Caz was as gorgeous as any Latino movie star she'd ever seen—with an equally deadly charm.

Bull was...more. Totally hot in an over-the-top tough guy sense. Huge and powerful. Deep voiced. Maybe he didn't have Caz's charm, but he was a magnetic extrovert with an easy-going personality. He enjoyed people—and they liked him back.

Hawk was scarred, tattooed, taciturn. How could the guy compete with his brothers? After watching her male cousins, Frankie had learned brothers could be incredibly competitive.

Then again, she'd learned appearances were deceiving. His brothers loved and respected him—that was very clear.

He must have felt her gaze. Catching her eye, Hawk glanced down at his plate—which was now empty—and gave her a nod. Approval.

When she smiled back, his expression changed to one of masculine interest.

Oops. How awkward was this? She averted her gaze.

"Frankie, everything is amazing," JJ said. "And now I have to ask, if you can cook like this, what are you doing in this little place—Rescue?"

"*Tesoro,* no." Caz shook his head at his woman.

"Why are you frowning at her?" Frankie realized the others held the same disapproving expressions.

"In Alaska, it's frowned on to ask about a person's past. In some ways, our state is like the old west that Hawk loves." Bull shot a smile at his brother. "Quite a few people are here to escape something in the Lower 48."

"Interesting. In New York, people come for the size of it, or they want Broadway, or the jobs." Because they were searching *for* something.

It was a relief she wouldn't be asked more questions about what brought her to Rescue. However, she could reassure the law enforcement types. "I'm not fleeing from anything." She grinned at JJ, then the chief of police. "I have no crime or Mafia connections or whatever in my past, either."

Amusement lit in Gabe's blue eyes. "I know."

"What? You ran a background check on *me*?"

He grinned. "I'm taking the Fifth."

That *stronzo.*

She eyed Bull.

Framed by the black goatee, his mouth tipped up at the corners. He knew what his brother had done. Not that there was anything to find, but *still.*

She gave him a frown, too.

"Wasn't it hard to leave New York? And come here? Rescue's so little." Regan's nose wrinkled.

Such an intelligent girl. Bull said the child lost her mother last year, and Caz had brought her to Alaska. For someone coming late to the parenthood game, the doc seemed like an amazing father.

Frankie smiled at the girl. "Aside from Italy, I haven't spent much time outside the city." Seeing the worry in Caz's eyes, she asked for him, "Don't you like living in Rescue?"

"Oh, yeah, I do. It's a lot cooler than LA. But I'm a kid."

Caz gave Frankie a grateful nod.

"I was ready to explore somewhere different," Frankie said, "so I took a couple of months off from my job and came to Alaska."

"For the summer, like we do in school." Regan nodded. "What's your job?"

Oh, *merda*. An executive wouldn't be likely to pick up a minimum wage job. Well, a vague answer never hurt anyone. "I work in a modeling agency, but not as a model. I'm kind of a helper, not a booker or manager, but I smooth the path between the models and their managers and photographers and stylists."

Bull was studying her. "That sounds like a rather high-powered occupation."

He wasn't buying her helper spiel.

"Is it fun?" Regan asked.

Frankie dug for a truth she could use. "In a way. I like making sure everything flows well, but I don't like the advertising indus-try. Everything they do—using stunningly beautiful models and photography tricks—is to make regular people feel inadequate so they'll buy more clothing, accessories, makeup, or hair products."

"Oh. Huh." Regan sat back, obviously needing to think about what Frankie had said.

Frankie might need to do the same. Her words had come from

a truth that had been stewing for a while. One that felt dismayingly valid.

A well-paying job wasn't necessarily a rewarding one. But it was also what her family expected of her. A Bocelli worked for the company.

"Whatever brought you here, we're glad, and we love the meal you made us today." Audrey raised her glass. "To Frankie."

The chorus of appreciative comments set up a glow inside Frankie. "Thank you. And...it sounds as if this is the right time for dessert."

The delighted "*yay*" from Regan made her laugh.

In the kitchen a while later, Bull was pleasantly full, having topped off the excellent meal with a helping of tiramisu.

The Italian theme night was going to be a success at the roadhouse.

"She's an interesting woman," Caz said.

Bull put another plate into the large dishwasher. It was good they'd overruled Mako and installed it when the building was constructed. "Frankie, you mean?"

"Sí." After handing Bull more plates, Caz glanced toward the giant U-shaped sectional where the women were. "I was tempted to let JJ dig for the story of what brought her to Alaska."

So was Bull. He closed the dishwasher door and started the cycle. "She's allowed her secrets, bro."

Caz grinned. "I'm surprised you don't know everything already."

"I'm not the old man." As their leader, Gabe had been labeled the "old man" before they even reached their teens—and the cop went after secrets like a hound on a blood trail. "I don't need to know everything."

"Maybe you do. You want her for your roadhouse, which might mean helping with whatever's bothering her from her past. You're a fixer, 'mano." Caz poured himself a glass of iced tea.

Bull frowned. He did want Frankie for the roadhouse...and for himself. "You might have a point."

Hearing Frankie's open laughter, Bull smiled. She had a hell of a laugh. "By the way, bro. Do you happen to know what *orso-key-AH-toe* means?"

Caz chuckled. "Bear is *oso* in Spanish, and I think it's *orso* in Italian. I'm guessing she called you a teddy bear."

"Did she now?" His heart lightened. Teddy bears were cuddled and cried on if someone needed comforting. "I can work with that."

With Caz beside him, Bull leaned on the island to watch the group.

Everyone was on the comfortable, massive sectional. Mako'd set up the downstairs figuring on bringing them all together. An oversized flat-screen TV for movies and sports. A spacious kitchen with an equally big pantry. A gym with a fancy weight room. The sarge had known them well.

There were times Bull wondered what the paranoid survivalist would have thought of Audrey and JJ...and Frankie. Of the sweet sound of women's voices in his house.

You missed a lot, Sarge.

On one end of the sectional, as far away from the women as possible, Hawk had his violin and was teaching Regan. With her violin tucked beneath her chin, the girl was growing frustrated.

The song—"The Impossible Dream"—was older. It'd been one of Mako's favorite songs, one he'd played when he was feeling melancholy—a soldier's song, he'd called it.

Had Regan even heard it before? Hawk sure wouldn't sing the tune for her, not with his ruined voice. Bull shrugged. It wasn't as if they lacked people to demonstrate the tune. He raised his voice. "Take it from the top, Hawk."

Hawk shot him a glare for interrupting, then one of his rare smiles as he caught on. He raised his violin. "You heard him, girl. Lead off with me."

The two violins started the intro. Bull felt like a proud father. Regan was getting damned good. "Go, Caz. I'll jump in."

Caz grinned, and when the violins reached the part for vocals, he sang, "*To dream the impossible dream...*"

Bull came in, hitting the low notes.

After a minute, Gabe handed a guitar to Audrey, picked his up, and they strummed an accompaniment. Over the winter, Audrey had discovered she loved playing the guitar.

Her clear soprano, then JJ's alto blended with the melody.

When Bull gave Frankie a *jump in* gesture, she hesitated a bare second and joined with a rich, beautiful alto. Unlike Audrey, she wasn't shy—and he loved that.

After a few measures, Gabe grinned at Bull in approval. The little Italian had a lovely voice.

They sang that song and a couple more before Hawk declared Regan's lesson to be over and strolled into the kitchen for a glass of water. None of Mako's sons drank much; alcohol greased the way for flashbacks.

"The yorkie's a pretty woman." Hawk leaned on the island beside Bull, watching Frankie in a way that Bull recognized. A man-woman way.

Oh, hell. While here, Bull had restrained himself from a lot of touching—partly because of the crap with Harvey earlier. But his restraint might have led Hawk to think Frankie was merely an employee to Bull.

"She's beautiful, yeah." And he should have made his interest obvious. "I plan to lure her back into my bed after this is over."

A muscle tensed in Hawk's cheek. "*Back* into bed?"

Frankie laughed at something JJ said, the rippling sound running over Bull's skin like sunlight.

Bull shook his head at Hawk. "Sorry, bro. I'm calling dibs."

"I might have known." Hawk lifted his hands, palms out,

acknowledging Bull's claim, the gesture bringing back their younger days when they'd worked out their bro-code protocols. In their family, up until sex occurred, competition was fine. Once a guy got physically involved, the woman was off-limits to his brothers.

When it came to Frankie, it needed to be clear he was damn well invested.

How in the world did I end up in Bull's bed? Not only in his bed, but on top, with him throbbing and hot and huge, inside her.

As another rush of excitement lashed her body, Frankie pushed her damp hair from her face and glared down at his hard, carved face. "Either I move, or you move."

He was half-sitting, propped against the headboard, and his muscular hands were curved around her hips, holding her immobile. "No."

She didn't...quite...scream.

A dimple appeared in his cheek, and his hands rotated inward. Something touched her pussy—on each side of her exposed clit—vibrating fast. Buzzing. She looked down.

Ring vibes over his thumbs were just barely brushing her sensitive nub.

"Oh, ohhhhh." The sensations intensified, and the need to come grew and grew. She tried to wiggle, to move.

Even with his thumbs against her there, his hands could extend over the tops of her thighs and hold her in place.

"Buuuuullll." Her heartrate quickened, her muscles went taut. She hovered on the precipice, every nerve screaming.

He pressed the vibes against her harder, even as his merciless grip tightened on her thighs. "I want to watch you come. Feel you quivering around my dick."

His black eyes held hers as the orgasm crashed over her,

consumed her, and she shuddered with mind-shattering pleasure around the thick unmoving shaft deep inside her.

Discarding the ring vibes, he set his hands on her breasts, roughly pinching and rolling her nipples, overloading her nerves with the devastating sensations.

Before the climaxing waves slowed, he grasped her ass and lifted her up, then yanked her down onto his cock.

A moan burst from her at the stunning pleasure. Madonna, he was so *big*.

Her orgasm went on and on as she drove down on him over and over, feeling each impact through her whole body. His gaze was on her bouncing breasts, and his smile was purely carnal.

"My turn, woman." Gripping her hips, he lifted his ass up to grind into her, sending searing pleasure across her engorged clit. Then he took control, lifting her like a doll, pulling her down, hammering into her, deep and hard, taking his own pleasure with a fierce need that satisfied something inside her.

The cords in his neck stood out, and she reveled in hearing his low growl of satisfaction as he came inside her.

After a bit, he drew her down on top of him. With a sigh, she laid her head on his wide chest. Her heart was still racing, and her muscles felt limper than over-cooked pasta.

"Mmm." His purr of satisfaction was something she'd never tire of hearing.

Before she drifted off completely, he gently pulled out, eased from under her to dispose of the condom, then cleaned them both up.

She should get up, too. She needed to get back to her own place. Somehow, she'd stayed longer at the dinner than she'd planned. Caz kept refilling her wine glass, and Audrey brought out a board game she thought Regan would like. It felt so much like being at Nonna's that Frankie hadn't been able to leave.

"You're thinking too hard, sweetheart." Pulling back the

covers, Bull slid her under and tucked her against his side, his body dwarfing hers.

"I should be going," she whispered.

"I want you to stay." Bull pressed a kiss to the top of her head. "*We* want you to stay."

She lifted her head to stare at him. "We? Your family tells you what women to take to bed? That's simply wrong."

He was laughing too hard to speak for a moment. Then he snapped his fingers, and Gryff planted two paws on the mattress. "Gryff, tell Frankie you want her to stay. Howl, buddy."

Nose in the air, Gryff let out a long wolf-like howl, then waited for praise.

"Good job, Gryff. Perfect." Bull scratched behind one fluffy ear and grinned at Frankie. "He's been practicing."

Laughing, Frankie patted the fluffy fur. "That was amazing, Gryff. You're a great dog."

"*We* want you to stay," Bull said in a smug voice. "You wouldn't want to hurt Gryff's feelings, would you?"

Hearing his name, Gryff wagged his tail and licked her hand. He had the pleading-brown-eyes down to an art.

She scowled. "Using a dog is an underhanded technique, *Skull*."

With a whine, Gryff decided the bed shouldn't be only for humans and jumped up, curling in a circle at the foot.

Frankie eyed him. What a smug expression on the furry face.

"Ah...does having Gryff on the bed bother you?" Bull asked— and she had to suppress a smile. The man was so damned self-confident that a bit of worry looked good on him.

Now how would Mama say this? Frankie assumed the ice queen's expression and voice. "You do know that animals don't belong on the furniture."

"Right." Bull sighed. "Gryff, buddy, you—"

She burst out laughing.

"Fuck, woman, you played me?" Bull's eyes crinkled.

Still laughing, Frankie sat up long enough to tousle Gryff's fur and kiss his fuzzy head before nestling back against Bull's side. "I love that he sleeps on your bed."

"I'll be damned."

She sighed. "I used to beg for a dog or cat; there were so many that needed homes. As far as Mama was concerned, the only fur in a house should be the kind worn as a cape."

"I can just see you dragging home some stray and asking to keep it." Bull cupped her cheek in his palm, grazing his thumb over her skin, and the sympathy in his voice was almost her undoing.

She swallowed. "Anyway, I'm glad you have Gryff and that he gets to be on the bed."

"There's a relief." Bull relaxed, pulling her up and closer.

"However, I really shouldn't spend the night." She rubbed her face against his shoulder. "You know how I feel. Morning sex is like friends with benefits. Spending nights, sleeping together leads to relationships and—"

"Sweetheart." The amusement in his voice stopped her cold.

She eyed him.

"You're too late. We already have a relationship, no matter how you label it. Making love is just that—whether the sun is up or not." He stroked her back.

Her breathing stopped as she heard the certainty in his words. He was right. They didn't fuck; they made love.

"I know you plan to leave at the end of summer," he said gently. "Let's be together while we can."

"Yes." The word slipped out of her, because there was nowhere else she'd rather be than with him. In his bed with his arms around her, with Gryff's head resting on her foot.

It felt like a perfect moment of pure contentment and happiness. Like there should be starry skies and haunting violins and...

She blinked. "I thought I was half-dreaming, but that's a violin. For real."

Bull chuckled. "For real. Hawk sits on his deck and plays when he's having trouble sleeping or a bad day. We all..."

With a frown, Frankie braced an arm across his chest so she could lift up and watch Bull in the shadowy light. It must be extremely late if the sun had finally set. "You all...*what?*"

He sighed. "We all served. Saw action overseas. Ugly shit, Frankie. And we all have the odd nightmare or bad day because of what we saw. And did."

As her heart went all melty with tenderness, she caressed his face in a futile attempt to soothe. "It's not fair that being brave and risking your life can mean suffering for it afterward. It should be a one-time mess, then over and done."

He snorted. "I agree."

If only she could wave a magic wand and make it all better. This must be how mothers felt when their babies got hurt. Yet it turned her all warm 'n' fuzzy that her tough guy had admitted to not being a superman. She lightened her tone to half-teasing and half-serious. "Do you all play the violin?"

"Jesus, that *would* be a nightmare. No. But we've all spent hours under the stars, on the deck or in the gazebo. Waiting for the memories to fade, soaking in the peace." He ran a finger along the curve of her ear. "If I get up at night, that's why."

"Okay. But, be warned, my *orsacchiotto*. Since this is now a *relationship*, if you stay out too long, I'll come and find you."

"Will you now?" His voice had the rumbling purr he used when he was pleased. And he pulled her down for a tender kiss.

CHAPTER FIFTEEN

K eeping up the appearance of having all your marbles is hard work, but important. - Sara Gruen

On a sunny afternoon two days later, Hawk sat with his feet up on his deck railing. Gryff lay beside his chair. If Bull wasn't home, the dog would latch onto whoever was outside—even Hawk.

Hawk studied the mutt. "Haven't I mentioned I don't like dogs?"

Big brown eyes met his, calling him on the lie, and Hawk dropped a hand over the side of his chair to ruffle the soft fur.

Gryff thumped his tail on the planking then laid his head down with a contented sigh.

Hawk shook his head. He had company while playing. *Huh.* He tucked his violin back under his chin. He'd been playing for the past hour. Serenading the lady of the lake.

Years ago, a pagan co-pilot had said everything on earth had its own spirit—trees and lakes and mountains—and Hawk had scoffed.

Then came years of wading through blood, surrounded by

death...and the man's quiet belief in...life...had grown on Hawk. Who knew? It was a comfort to think the lake's spirit enjoyed his music. He'd even composed a few tunes for her.

The quiet was disturbed by the sound of a vehicle on their private road and the opening and closing of a garage door.

Gryff gave a low woof and raced across the grass onto Bull's deck. Nose against the glass, the dog quivered with anticipation.

Guess Bull was back. Probably to get ready for work.

Was he alone or with the yorkie? She'd spent the night after the Italian meal and last night, as well.

Hawk's mouth twisted. His brothers had found themselves girlfriends. Not surprising. They were damned good-looking. Got on with people. Women pursued all three of them with the tenacity of a coyote pack after rabbits.

Must be nice to be the focus of that kind of attention.

Not that *Bull* appreciated it. Not in the fucking least. Hawk eyed Gryff, still waiting at the door. Bull was completely comfortable with a dog pawing him, demanding attention, leaning against him. He didn't appreciate it from a female.

No, that was wrong. Bull had been openly affectionate with that ex-wife of his. Hawk shook his head. He'd only met Paisley once, but she'd seemed to be all surface beauty with nothing underneath. From Bull's silence about his marriage, the woman had probably screwed him over.

Sympathy made Hawk feel, maybe, less annoyed Bull had secured the woman Hawk had ever-so-briefly considered making a move on.

Stupid idea, really. He couldn't compete with his brothers. Like what'd happened when—

Bull came out on the deck, and Gryff started turning in spirals of happiness. Bending, Bull gave the mutt a rough scratching along his ribs and butt, then picked up his egg basket. They rotated egg-collection days, giving each of them a chance to restock their own larders.

As Bull crossed the lawn, he spotted Hawk. "Yo, bro. Having a quiet day?"

"Yeah." Hawk frowned, seeing his brother's strained expression—the same one he often saw in his own mirror. But...Bull? "You okay?"

"Sure, sure." Bull started to walk on, stopped, and shook his head. "No, that's a bullshit cover-up. That macho crap is partly why Mako was such a mess. Gabe, too. Hell, all of us are fucked-up in different ways."

Hawk stared at him in shock. "What?"

Putting a foot on Hawk's steps, Bull set his elbows on the railing and gazed out at the lake where a float plane was coming in for a landing. "Mako had PTSD. We all knew it, but he avoided like hell discussing it with us. He taught us that bullshit—not to talk about our problems. When Gabe came back with his head on wrong, he spent the winter alone in Sarge's old cabin instead of coming to one of us for help."

Hawk's mouth tightened. Hiding out was pretty much what he'd done a time or two.

But...Bull hadn't really answered his question. "What about you?"

"I'm mostly all right, but...not always. Had a few missions where everything went south—and yeah, they come back and haunt me." Bull turned to face him. "A couple of months ago, Dante took me to a counselor buddy in Anchorage. The guy's a vet—and uses some weird machine that helps to integrate the memories."

"It works?" That'd be the day.

Bull nodded. "For me, at least. It's not easy. Couple of times, I almost puked. But the flashbacks and nightmares and feeling of falling into a black hole? It's getting better."

"Huh." Hawk stared at the sunlight rippling on the water.

Bull cleared his throat. "As it happens, Doc Grayson was asking about you. Said you made him a promise last year that you'd see a therapist. Said if you didn't, he'd come up and you two would...chat."

"Fuck." The psychologist never made threats he didn't keep.

Even worse, Hawk had promised. Guess he'd better man up.

Pulling himself together, Hawk realized his brother had moved silently away, heading for the chicken coop.

A few minutes later, on the way back, Bull slowed. "Let me know when you have an appointment. I'll take you there the first time or two." He didn't wait for an answer.

The bull knew him well.

Her laptop in front of her, Frankie listened with half an ear to the activity in the coffee shop. And sniffed appreciatively at the chocolatey aroma of a mocha coffee.

Scowling at her emails, she thought she could use some chocolate. Two of her friends in New York had married military guys; a couple of the Bocelli models had lovers in the security business. Another friend worked in defense. After the book club meeting, she'd asked them all about finding a reputable mercenary team. Their replies were discouraging, filled with warnings about the various mercenary outfits for various reasons—bad reps, incompetent, rip-offs, criminals. Some guy named deVries had quit the business. She still had a couple of her friends who hadn't weighed in...and really, she was only checking into mercenaries as a worst-case scenario.

Maybe the next chore on her to-do list would go better. That was doubtful, though. She picked up her cell phone, selected a contact, and tried to bolster her courage. Speaking with her family seemed to get more difficult the longer she was in Alaska. Maybe because—aside from her trips to see Nonna—this was the longest she'd ever spent away from them. She missed them, but watching Bull with his family made her see that hers wasn't very loving. Or supportive of anything unrelated to their own interests.

Sure, she knew that...in a way. Most of her friends had wonderful parents. But she'd never stepped back and really considered hers.

She tapped the CALL square.

"Francesca, it's about time you returned my call."

"Mama, hi. I saw you'd called a couple of times. I'm sorry, but the cell reception at the cabin is crummy. I waited to call you from town."

The atmosphere in the little coffee shop seemed to darken with the spew of irritated language coming from the phone.

"Mama—"

"Just tell me when you're returning. Nyla can't handle your job. We've had two models quit and a photographer has refused to work with Jaxson. Birgit wants a new makeup artist, and..."

As her mother continued, Frankie thought of how she'd read about criminals killed by having stones piled on them. Until the weight slowly suffocated them. As her mother complained that Frankie's absence had affected the entire family and the company, she felt her lungs struggle for air.

She needed to be here for Kit—and in New York for her family.

She couldn't be both places.

Her stomach tightened until nausea swamped her. She didn't even know if Kit was still in the compound. What if Obadiah had taken her back to Texas?

"I'm sorry, Mama, but I'm not going to fly right back. I haven't had a vacation since I left college. Not one. For the last two years, I've asked to hire an assistant—someone I could train to fill my shoes when I can't be there."

"That's unreasonable, Francesca. We can't afford to have an assistant for you. Your job isn't that essential and if—"

If my position isn't essential, then why are you so angry that I'm gone?
"Mama, listen—"

"No, you will return. You've had your vacation and..."

As the words poured over her, Frankie could feel her muscles getting tenser. Turning sideways, she bumped her wounded arm on the back of the booth. *Ow.* Caz had just taken the stitches out an hour ago.

All too easily, she could feel how the bullet had sliced through her arm. If the shot had been more accurate, she wouldn't be here at all. And she was done. Just done with all the complaints.

"You know, Mama, if I was dead, you'd manage without me. So, since my job isn't that essential, just suck it up and manage."

There was a shocked silence on the phone. Frankie was the good child, not a prima donna model, but the one everyone could count on. She didn't have moods, didn't have temper tantrums.

Didn't have needs.

To hell with that.

"Sorry, Mama, but I need to go. I'll be back when my vacation is over. If you don't think Nyla can handle the job, then hire someone else." Before Mama could respond, Frankie said firmly, "I love you, bye."

With a long sigh, she banged her head against the back of the booth. "*Porca miseria.*"

"I know a bit of Italian. '*Damn me*', right?" The owner of the coffee shop set Frankie's cappuccino, as well as a cinnamon roll, down.

"That's right." Frankie eyed the plate. "I only ordered coffee."

"On the house. It sounded like you could use something sweet."

"Could I ever." With a half-bitter laugh, Frankie nibbled on the roll. "Mmm, this is decadent. I'm Frankie, by the way."

"One of the roadhouse's new servers, I know. I'm Sarah. My husband Uriah and I own this place." With stylish short brown hair, the petite woman was around forty. Frankie'd seen her with her young daughter and a baby. Two children, a business, and living in Alaska would explain why she was so lean, despite making scrumptious desserts.

"It's good to meet you. I mean with names and all."

Sarah laughed. "After, what, three weeks, you're almost a regular. How do you like our small town?"

"Rescue is great." Frankie grinned. "Being so far from home, I love the sound of a fellow New Yorker's accent."

"You're from New York? I heard that rumor and didn't believe it." Grinning, Sarah sat down across from Frankie in the booth. "How'd you escape without an accent?"

"It took some work. It returns if I get upset, although usually the Italian one overpowers it."

"Italian, hmm?" Sarah lifted her eyebrows. "I had a guy in here last week Googling Italian swear words on his phone. Something like 'tessydee cah-so'?"

Frankie felt her face flush. "*Testa di cazzo.* It's...um...equivalent to calling someone an asshole."

"I had a feeling he heard it from you. Was he a bad date?" Sarah grinned. "Sorry, but I love gossip."

"Since I do, too, it'd be hypocritical to complain." Frankie shook her head. "He wasn't a date—at least, not mine. I caught the man banging a woman in the roadhouse bathroom, and he called me the c-word for interrupting before he finished."

"Interrupting a banging? How rude of you." Sarah burst out laughing.

"Guys don't change no matter the size of the city." Neither did women, actually. Frankie considered the coffee shop owner...who liked gossip. "I must say, I've never met any men who are quite like those Patriot Zealots. What's with them?"

"*Them.*" The word held a super-helping of disgust. "They believe every word of their so-called prophet, Parrish, and they treat women like shit. Don't use them as an example of normal Alaskan guys."

"Ah, another example of a messed-up navigation system."

Sarah gave her a puzzled look. "Navigation system. What?"

"It's like...ideas originate in a man's *little* head"—Frankie motioned toward her crotch—"and go through the pelvic round-about before reaching the *big* head"—she tapped her forehead —"so they can think before acting. Unfortunately, some men's thoughts never make it out of the round-about."

"That's a scary analysis and too true." Sarah had a beautiful laugh. "The PZs lose a lot of brainpower in that sex roundabout."

"Huh." *Hmm.* If sexual stuff made them brainless, would that be a way to get more information? She needed to know Kit was still there. She'd said they might send Obadiah, her, and Aric back to Texas.

It would be awful to break into the compound and find out Kit wasn't even in the state.

"I could have called the police, rather than shouting at the restroom lothario," Frankie said. "But I don't know JJ well or how she'd react."

Sarah smiled. "Officer JJ would have hauled his bare ass out through the bar, pitched him into the parking lot, and given him a reaming out...without raising her voice."

"Huh. I raised my voice. I guess Alaskans are less rude—or does she like the lothario types like the PZs?"

"JJ?" Sarah burst out laughing. "She's a female in what the idiots consider a man's profession and has suffered for it from day one of her career. She's only been in Alaska since last fall—she's from Nevada—but I know she'd love to kick some PZ butts."

That sounded good. Still...she'd best be sure. Frankie shook her head. "It's odd, but I swear I heard one of the police officers was a Patriot Zealot."

"Oh, you're thinking of the patrol officer whose place she took. Officer Baumer was a PZ...right up until the bars closed behind him."

Neither JJ nor Gabe were Patriot Zealots. Relief swept

through Frankie; she liked them both. And the last officer was in jail. "I'm sure Officer Baumer is getting lonely. We should send some of his fanatic friends to keep him company."

Sarah snickered. "For JJ, the woman has a talent at diffusing situations. She's incredibly controlled. She doesn't even swear much...unlike certain Italians I've heard of." Sarah winked, and Frankie knew she'd found another possible friend.

Frankie wrinkled her nose. "At least I swear in another language to keep from offending all the English-speaking people."

"You're going to have to give me a translation guide," Sarah said. "Just for...educational...purposes."

Frankie laughed.

Expression sobering, Sarah traced a finger in a wet spot on the table. "I spoke with Harvey, the other day. About you and Bull doing that role-play intervention."

Uh-oh. Frankie waited, hoping the conversation wasn't about to turn ugly.

"Harvey has been our friend since my husband and I arrived in Rescue." Sarah half-smiled. "He said his behavior had been totally out of line, and most places would either have condoned his assholery or fired him. You and Bull educated him and gave him a chance to make things right. He really does appreciate it."

Frankie relaxed. "He's working hard to make amends. Even better, he's turned into the sexual harassment police. No one steps over the line in the kitchen, and the young women told me they're a lot happier at work."

Sarah grinned. "He was horrified to think they saw him as a dirty old man. He said he's going for a *knight protector* title instead."

"We're all grateful he feels that way." Poor Bull was still unhappy he hadn't caught the problem before.

A customer entered the shop, and Sarah rose. "It was nice to finally get a chance to talk with you. We're glad you're here."

What a sweet thing to say. "Thank you."

Nibbling on the pastry, Frankie watched Sarah serve the steady stream of customers. Some came in for coffee, some for bakery goods. A person could have a pastry and coffee, or take a pie or loaf of bread home for the family. Unlike New York where every tiny shop had a specialty, the Rescue stores often merged a couple of businesses into one. There was an art gallery with crafting and hobby supplies. The sports store that catered to fishermen also rented ski equipment and bikes. The hardware store sold lumber.

Everyone was friendly. She couldn't recall a time in New York, ever, when a store owner came out for an introduction and gossip session.

If it weren't for worrying about Kit, she'd be more content in Rescue than she'd ever been in her life. The town itself was great. Like with that woman who'd twisted her ankle. After seeing her in the health clinic, Caz had told his brothers she needed help. Bull, naturally, volunteered to do a food run. All his family had taken turns visiting the woman, then the town found out, and the woman had more help than she knew what to do with.

Frankie smiled. She'd gone with Bull on the food run...because just being with him was wonderful.

She'd sure failed at keeping their relationship casual. Guilt swept over her. The minute she had Kit and Aric in her car, she was out of here, probably without saying any goodbyes, and then she'd be back in New York. But...he knew their time would end.

She was past the point of no return; any attempt to shield her heart from being broken was useless.

So, she would simply savor every moment she could spend with him.

Because he was worth the pain.

In the roadhouse, Bull waited for Frankie to arrive. Yesterday, the contractors had finished remodeling the echoingly large room that had held only his desk and filing cabinets. Now there was a conference area with a round table that could seat a dozen people. The back was divided into two offices with sound absorbing partition walls. One was his. The other was equipped with a desk, computer, phone, and the usual office accoutrements. Ready for a manager, whoever they might be.

He knew who he wanted.

Frankie would make an excellent manager, and he hoped the position gave her an incentive to stay. Maybe the position would show her how she could fit in at the roadhouse. With the town. With him.

He wanted to let her know how much he trusted her...and needed her—yeah, that, too.

Work had taken over his life, and he hadn't realized it until he couldn't find enough minutes in his days to spend with her. He was overloaded, no doubt about it. Sarge's Investment Group—all the businesses and buildings Mako had willed them—required restoration, leasing, selling, managing.

And he had his own businesses. Thankfully, his Bull's Moose brewery in Anchorage and his restaurants in Anchorage and Homer had managers. But he needed help with the roadhouse here. Ordering napkins and silverware, scheduling staff, the day-to-day organizing? Nothing he enjoyed.

Bartending, though, was enjoyable—and owning a business meant he should get to do the fun stuff.

Working all hours needed to stop. He needed time to hang out with his brothers, to teach Regan to cook, and to be with Frankie for more than sparring and sex.

Although...the sparring and sex were unrivaled. He grinned. Good times.

The crunching sound of tires on gravel came through the open window, and Frankie parked her car beside his pickup.

Opening the office's rear door, he motioned for Frankie to come in. As she walked in, he started to bend down to kiss her. *No*. They'd agreed to keep business and relationships separate.

Guess that meant no sex on the office desk, dammit, which was a shame because she smelled like she'd just gotten out of the shower. Her soap that made him think of dark forests and full moons—and making love outside.

Concentrate.

"Thanks for coming in today." He gestured her toward the conference area. "I wanted this discussion in a more formal location."

Her brows drew together. "Is there a problem? Is this the Alaska version of a pink slip?"

"No, not even close." At her worried expression, he barely kept from hugging her.

After she sat at the table, he took a seat. "The only problem I have with you is that you're far too qualified to be a server. Since the week you started, you've taken on more and more responsibility—coming up with innovative ideas, working on the décor, teaching the new waitstaff. You're performing as a manager, and I'd like you to have the title and salary."

She stared at him. "You what?"

"This can't come as a surprise. Not with what I've been having you do."

She'd gone pale. "I thought you were just short-handed. Wanted me to help out."

"I *am* short-handed. I lack a manager. I want you to do it."

She shook her head. "I...I can't. I have a job back in New York. I can't stay here."

Dammit. "Can't—or won't? Why are you here, anyway?"

"It's a vacation." Her jaw was tight. "The modeling agency hired me the day after I left college, and the only vacation I've taken since was to attend a friend's wedding in Texas." She stared down at her hands, clasped on the table.

"Most people don't pick up a job during their vacation." He kept his voice level. Non-confrontational.

She pushed her hair back, her gaze still averted. "I wanted to meet people. I like people. Working is the easiest way."

"I see." If he'd learned nothing else in his life, it was that telling someone they were full of shit shut down a conversation real fast. But...*for fuck's sake.*

This was no vacation to Frankie. Aside from that hike when she'd been shot outside the PZ compound, she'd never even gone sightseeing. "Do you have any idea how long you'll be in Rescue?"

"Um..." She bit her lip. "I'm not ready to go back to New York. Not yet. But I'll have to, eventually."

Not yet was good. Never would be better. He barely managed to resist reaching for her hand. "You said '*have to*', not *want to*. Maybe you should pursue what makes you happy rather than what you think you're obligated to do?"

Her head tilted. "Is this a case of "do as I say and not as I do"?

"You lost me." Bull straightened. "I love my work."

"Yes, you're happy at work. But you want more than just work. I've seen your expression when Regan jumps into Caz's lap, when your brothers are cuddling with their girlfriends. You want a family of your own. Why aren't you going after that rather than working all the time?"

She was right. He did want what Caz and Gabe had. And...if he answered that honestly, he might scare her right back to the East Coast.

Instead, he smiled. "I'll do just that when the time is right. We were discussing your happiness and... Let's just say you don't seem eager to return to New York."

Her mouth tightened, and unhappiness flitted over her face again.

Leaning back, he looked deeper, studying her body language. She wasn't fearful about what awaited her in New York. She hadn't fled the city like Audrey had from Chicago.

But Frankie wasn't here to have fun, either. If anything, she appeared...determined. Like when he and his SEAL team had reconnoitered a city, taking jobs, assuming personas, waiting until the mission was a go. Not knowing when that would be.

She was here for a reason, but pushing her for answers would force her to lie to him. It was time to take a leap of faith.

"Frankie." He waited until she finally met his gaze. "I'd still like to offer you the job of manager, even knowing you'll leave when the time comes. You're doing most of the work already. I'd like to dump the rest on you."

She exhaled slowly. "You're crazy, Bull. You don't know me."

"But I'm trying to." He laid his hand over hers. "Someday, I hope you'll trust me enough to tell me what really brought you here."

She blinked hard, dropping her gaze. "It's not... I do trust you."

There was that, at least.

As though unhappy with what she'd said, she rose hastily. "I'll take the position. Show me what I need to know and what my duties are."

Cheering would probably scare his little prey right out of the room.

She frowned. "I still want to put in time as a server in the bar. I won't give that up."

Interesting. Why so adamant? "You'll be doing the scheduling. That will be in your control."

"Oh. All right then."

As he led the way to her office space, he felt his own determination rising inside him. Damned if he wasn't going to figure out what was going on with her.

CHAPTER SIXTEEN

T here are two ways to do something...the right way, and again - US Navy SEALS

In the city park woods, Frankie tripped over a root and used her staff to catch herself. Whew. Face-planting would really hurt, since she was wearing something that resembled a mini-telescope over her left eye. The head mount, which consisted of a bunch of straps around her head, held the night vision monocular device— the NVM—over her left eye. It felt like she was peering at a glowing green world through a toilet paper roll. No wonder she was still tripping now and then. *Grrr.*

It was totally amazing. She could actually see even in this thick forest where the light of the moon barely penetrated.

After a few days of practice, she'd gotten a lot better. Her lips firmed. She needed to be perfect if she was going to lead Kit and Aric out of the compound in a week. Even with the awkward bolt cutters and gear going to the compound and Aric in a child carrier on her back on the way out, she'd have to be fast and silent.

But things were coming together...and, to her surprise, she'd come to love the quiet of the deep forest, the tiny rustles of animals, the smell of evergreens, the patterns of light and shadow. There was a kind of peace here she'd never found anywhere else.

It would have been even better if her hikes had nothing to do with the fanatic cult members.

Yesterday, when she'd parked near Chevy's cabin, she'd had a chance to ask Tina if she should worry about running into PZs if she was there at night.

To Frankie's relief, the Zealots patrolled their perimeters during the day, never after dark. Which meant less chance of getting caught when Kit and Aric came through the fence.

Having learned a painful lesson about getting too close to the compound, Frankie had been extremely careful to stay out of sight.

Tomorrow, she'd do another daytime hike to the compound and this time would mark the trail with the transparent reflective paint. She'd tested a couple of spots here in the park—it made a glowing white blotch when she was using the NVM—and was invisible during daylight. If the PZs weren't out there at night, they'd never see the paint.

In the center of the woods, she grinned and did a quick happy dance.

Then froze. What was that?

Yelling, hoots...and gunfire. Still, it didn't seem too close, and the shouts sounded like a bunch of drunks having a good time. Well, it *was* Saturday night.

She made one more circuit inside the woods, this time striving for both grace—*ha!*—and silence.

Good job, Frankie.

A glance at her phone—using the unaided eye—showed she needed to leave. The roadhouse would be closed, and Bull would be coming to pick her up soon. After stowing everything in her small backpack, she jogged down the wide gravel trail toward home.

Almost there, she slowed at the sound of shouting.

Outside of the end cabin, several men were throwing their luggage into two vehicles while someone yelled at them.

After a second, she recognized Dante's voice. "Don't need no drugged-up assholes shootin' up the area. The cost of repairing the windows and doors and picnic tables will be on your credit cards, and you'll damn well pay the bill, or I'll send the police to collect."

"You'll regret throwing us out, you bastard," one yelled back.

"Fucking old fart," one man said to another. "Send the fucking police, see if we care." Steel from the man's numerous piercings glinted in the lights from the cabin.

Frankie shook her head and decided to stay inside the shelter of the trees until they were gone. Even from here, the men appeared violent. Dante apparently felt the same since his shotgun stayed on target the entire time.

She frowned and hoped it hadn't been her windows that'd been shot out.

CHAPTER SEVENTEEN

*I*t is necessary for us to learn from others' mistakes. You will not live
long enough to make them all yourself. - ADM Hyman G. Rick-
over, US Navy

Frankie hadn't been manager for quite a week yet, but she already
loved it.

On Tuesday night, she strolled through the restaurant section
of the roadhouse, checking that the hostess was equitably seating
people so no server got overloaded, the busser was speedy and
thorough in cleaning off tables, glasses were kept filled, food was
served promptly when up. And the customers were smiling. Definitely that.

She still couldn't believe Bull had given her the position,
despite knowing she would return to New York.

And would leave him. She didn't want to. Just...didn't. Not see
him every day? Not be able to curl up against him in the night? Or
hear his lower-than-low voice when he teased her during their
sparring sessions? She wasn't sure she could bear it.

On top of that...the thought of returning to Bocelli's made her stomach churn like she'd been drinking battery acid.

The atmosphere here was everything that the Bocelli Agency wasn't. Sure, she had to deal with obnoxious customers and drunks in the roadhouse, but they were nothing compared to advertising and photo shoot clients, all cologne and bleached-white smiles and hidden animosity.

Roadhouse staff made the few customer annoyances seem irrelevant. The waitstaff and chefs weren't family—she wouldn't go that far—but were more than mere co-workers. They bickered, certainly, but there was no cutthroat competition, no backstabbing. If she got swamped, Felix would notice and pick up some of her tables. If a drunk tried to harass her, either Bull or Raymond would notice.

Like when a pushy fisherman grabbed her hand. Before she could clout him over the head with her tray, Bull had bellowed, "Asshole, let'er go, or I'll rip your dick off and shove it down your throat." The fisherman saw Bull's glare. With a squeak, he'd released her and fallen all over himself apologizing.

Bull had studied her for a long minute, then smiled and nodded, leaving it up to her whether to pitch the guy out.

She loved that too—that he trusted her to deal with things. As he'd warned, he dumped all the administrative problems on her. In the last week, she'd nailed down the Italian night menu, the design, and the décor. Hired more seasonal staff. Instructed and evaluated new bar and restaurant servers and busboys. Made purchase and replacement lists.

Rather than feeling stressed, she was having fun in a way she hadn't since starting at Mama's company. How had she let herself get trapped in a job that she didn't enjoy?

Because of family expectations and pressure.

Her mouth tightened. Mama's lecture last week was akin to one she'd delivered when Frankie was little and had skipped dance class to get ice cream with a friend. How she'd hated dance classes. Mama said dance taught the posture and grace needed for modeling, something else Frankie hadn't wanted. Even as a child, she'd considered it to be a boring job.

Her mother hadn't listened until two bullies messed up Frankie's face. What with Mama's horror of scars and her father's intervention, she'd been allowed to take martial arts instead of dance.

What would it take to convince her mother to listen to her?

Pushing the unhappy thoughts away, Frankie smiled at the next table of tourists. "How was your meal today?"

This might be her favorite part of the job. Or maybe it was figuring out the scheduling software and talking to the staff, so everyone was 90% satisfied with their time on and off. One hundred percent wasn't achievable—life happened—but from the happy smiles when people saw the schedules, she'd done better than Bull. It helped that everyone was willing to talk to her and make requests. No matter how friendly and reasonable, Bull really was intimidating, even without adding in that he was the owner.

Since she had control of the schedule, she'd assigned herself the hours she wanted to work in the bar—her best chance to talk to the Patriot Zealots. It'd almost been two weeks since their lockdown started. Surely their training exercises were done.

In between her quality assurance visits with the customers, she arbitrated a dispute over cooking responsibilities on the line, arranged to get Wylie a cabled cooking probe, and indulged herself by ordering candle holders that would be amazing for the romantic theme nights. Whether Bull realized it or not, Italian night was going to be the time townspeople brought their special someones here for romantic dinners.

By the time the restaurant started to close, her feet hurt—and she was still happy. Pulling off her name badge—the one that said MANAGER—she stopped beside Wylie who was shutting equipment down. "I'm off to work in the bar for a while."

He frowned. "Bouncing back and forth between jobs isn't healthy. Bull shouldn't ask you to do that."

"He didn't." Frankie smiled at the wave of sound coming from the bar section. "I like working in the bar."

"Jesus, girl, you're as crazy as he is. First, the owner wants to be a bartender, now, the manager wants to serve drinks?"

"My dear chef, I've decided all you Alaskans are crazy—and since I live here now, I'm embracing that mindset."

The rest of the kitchen staff burst out laughing.

In the bar section, Felix greeted her arrival with a wide, relieved smile. "You're my hero, girl. It's insane tonight. Could we add another server on for the midweek shifts?"

"I'll get that fixed." Pulling out her phone, she added it to her to-do list.

So, who was here tonight? There was the usual scattering of locals and fishermen in boots, jeans, and T-shirts. A third or so were tourists in flamboyant attire. A few of the McNally's resort employees were present—out for a good time and dressed to appeal.

Frankie noticed a blonde's high-heeled footwear and sighed in envy. "Check out those boots."

Felix followed her gaze. "Oooh, nice. It sucks that the prettiest shoes never come in my size. At least, not here in Alaska. San Francisco, though..."

"You shop online instead?"

"Oh sure, but it lacks the whole vibe of shopping for sexy stuff, you know?" He waggled his eyebrows. "Computers don't flirt like store clerks."

He was the biggest flirt she knew, much like fashion photographers who'd elevated sexy banter to an art form.

As she patted his arm in sympathy, she saw the men she'd been hoping to see—the PZs—and her pulse sped up. Their training scenarios must be over now. Was Kit still there in the compound?

"Felix." Frankie nodded toward the front wall with the

mounted caribou antlers and photos. "I'll handle the Rudolph section."

"The fanatics are there." His brows drew down. "Girl, you pick their section every time you have a choice. You shouldn't get involved with those people."

"You think I'd take their bullshit seriously?" She blew a raspberry. "When I see them, all I can think is that somewhere a circus is missing its clowns."

Felix snorted. "Okay then. I won't worry even if I don't get it."

She smiled. "Like all clowns, they're entertaining."

"Not the word I'd use, but the section is yours."

Frankie checked in with the bartender, then started to work. It was good Bull wasn't here. She really didn't want him to see her near the PZs.

As soon as she could, Frankie went to the PZ table. After taking their drink requests, she backed up...and deliberately tripped over the older man's long legs.

He caught her by the waist, his hands lingering before he let her go.

"I-I'm so sorry." She made her voice sound all choked-up. "I'm just having such a bad month."

"No problem, girlie," the black-bearded guy said. "Don't get your pretty self all upset."

"It's b-because..." The way she used her oh-pitiful-me eyes on him would've gotten her high points from her sister. "My parents were killed in a car crash last month and...and sometimes it just comes back to me."

Now, what could they do except say they were sorry for her loss?

Once she'd gotten them engaged, she blinked hard—*c'mon, tears*—and sniffled. "I probably shouldn't even be working, it's not like I need to, anymore."

That got a spark of interest. "Then why are you here?" Black-beard asked.

"It's...it keeps me from sitting at home and just crying. I feel so lost sometimes, you know? Like, what's the point?"

If she were a fisherperson, she'd have said the guy swallowed her bait—hook, line, and sinker. Come to think of it, what was a sinker?

"Ah, girlie, that's a shame, now." He took her hand and pulled her closer. "Sounds to me like you need to find a new purpose, don't you? Someone to help you find the way."

Don't jump too fast, Frankie. "I...I"—she looked down, trying for humble modesty—"I guess. Maybe."

"I remember you from a while back. You asked what the Patriot Zealots were." The man who spoke was clean-shaven with a buzz cut.

Here was her chance to bring up Kit. "I was curious. Still am... maybe. Kinda. A couple of your women were at the grocery, and I asked them if they liked being with you." Frankie tried for a shy expression. "They said yes. They were older, you know, not much like me, but they had a younger woman with them. And...wait, is she still there?"

Buzzcut narrowed his eyes. "Why do you ask?"

Frankie put on an unsure expression. "It's...I mean the older women were really kind, but I just hoped that there were younger people there, my age, you know. Because...I guess I've never gotten very close to older people.

The man she was talking with frowned. "Did she have a name?"

"No, she never even spoke, but..." *Please, don't let me get Kit into trouble.* Frankie tapped her lips as if thinking. "Maybe a little shorter than me, really slender, fair skin, brown eyes, streaky long brown hair."

"Sounds like Kirsten," a man with a long red beard said.

"There was that day we took her with us to buy bareroot trees and seedlings for the gardens." Buzzcut nodded at Frankie. "She's still at the compound."

Suppressing a shout of glee, Frankie bounced on her toes like a little girl. "Awesome."

When Blackbeard seemed surprised at her enthusiasm, she confided, "I'm really, like, more comfortable around girls my age. More than older women."

His gaze ran over her body. "What about older men?"

"Um. I..." She put her finger in her mouth and cast him a hesitant, not quite flirty glance. *Men like you make me want to throw up.* "They're... That's different."

He half smiled, took her hand, and ran his thumb over her palm.

She barely kept from jerking away.

He squeezed her hand. "I think we should talk. I might be able to point you in a good direction. The right direction."

She shook her head. "I can't talk now; I have to work."

"When do you get off work?" He fondled her hip, way too familiarly, the *bastardo*, and slid his hand down to squeeze her butt.

Don't punch him; don't punch him.

Should she encourage him? It might be a way to get into the compound. *No, don't be stupid.* She wouldn't be able to conceal her loathing, especially since just letting him touch her ass felt far too much like cheating on Bull.

There was only one pair of hands she wanted on her.

Shaking her head, she pushed at Blackbeard's arm. Weakly. "Oh, please, don't. I'm a good girl."

When the ginger across the table snorted, Blackbeard shot him a chiding frown before moving his hand back up to her waist. "Yes, I can see you are. I'm glad to know that. I think you'll fit in well with us. How about you—"

"Oh!" She checked over her shoulder, as if just remembering that she had a job. "I need to get back to work.

After another shy look, she hurried away. And tried to suppress her anger. The we-have-all-the-answers and the controlling behavior would have worked like a charm on Kit, especially right after her husband died. That was how Obadiah had snowed Kit.

"Frankie, nachos up in the kitchen," Felix called across the room.

She saluted to show she'd heard him and turned to head that way. She could make a quick dash to the kitchen to get the platter before it got cold, and then—

A man stood in the doorway of the roadhouse. Was that Obadiah?

She hastily turned away. No, it probably wasn't him. He didn't drink—and Kit'd said she stopped drinking, too. Even wine. Because whatever he wanted, Kit would do.

Frankie growled. Her fingers tightened on the tray she wanted to break over his head.

A glance over her shoulder showed that the man hadn't entered the bar. She let out a breath. Even if it was him, he wouldn't recognize her. Not from the few seconds in a wedding reception line. And dark-haired, brown-eyed women were a dime a dozen in Alaska.

She sped up her pace toward the kitchen.

Someone blocked her path.

"Bull." Her heart did a happy little spin rather like Gryff's dancing paws. "What are you doing here?"

"Coming to rescue you, but it seems you didn't need any help. At all."

Oh, *merda*, he'd seen her with the Patriot Zealots. "Actually, the *stronzi* were fairly nice for a change."

His eyes were the black of a moonless night—and far too perceptive. "I noticed."

"Waitress!" The call pierced the noise in the room.

Frankie turned to see a table of impatient tourists.

"I need to get moving." She'd spent too much time with the PZs.

Brows pulled together, Bull nodded. "If you're all right, I'll get to work."

"I'm fine, thanks." She gave him what felt like the most insincere smile in the history of mankind.

The guilt pinching her muscles was far weaker than the longing to bury her face against his neck and beg him for help.

Instead, she waved at the tourists, told them she'd be right there, and went to retrieve the nachos.

Nabera walked out of the roadhouse in a good mood. Before leaving, he'd had Luka ask about the sweet little barmaid, the one who was ripe for the plucking. Naïve, with inherited money and no relatives.

Luka had learned her name was Frankie, and she lived in one of the old Okie's cabins on the lake. Nabera sneered at the thought of Dante, the owner of the market and the cabins. The nonbeliever was on the town council and licked the uppity libtard mayor's ass more like a trained dog than a *man*.

Nabera glanced around for their driver. After some of their intoxicated Zealots had run-ins with the hard-ass police chief, the Prophet decreed that members coming to the roadhouse must be dropped off and picked up. Earlier, Obadiah had stuck his head in the door to let them know he'd arrived.

At the car, Obadiah opened the door for him, then cleared his throat. "Captain, I wasn't sure if I should mention this, but..." He scowled at the roadhouse.

"Spit it out," Nabera ordered.

"It's about Kirsten. In a way. See, last year, Kirsten's friend came from New York for our wedding. That was before we moved to the compound in Texas."

Nabera sighed. Was this going to take much longer? He had a nice buzz on and was impatient to select a woman to fuck tonight. "Get to the point, Lieutenant. Was there a problem when the friend visited?"

"Nah, I only saw her for a second. She's all about women's rights and that bullshit. Not a suitable person to be in my wife's life." Obadiah shrugged. "After she went back to New York, I exerted my authority, and Kirsten dropped her."

"As it should be." Nabera nodded approval. Unbelievers were an unacceptable diversion from the Prophet's way. "I don't see what the problem is."

"I just saw her in the roadhouse." Obadiah pointed to the roadhouse.

His lieutenants moved closer, and Conrad sneered, "Like you'd recognize someone you met for a second?"

"Kit had a ton of pictures of her. Hanging on the walls in her apartment. In photo albums," Obadiah said doggedly. "I'd recognize Frankie, even in that roadhouse barmaid outfit."

Nabera stiffened. "Frankie?"

"Yeah. She even uses a man's name. Could she be here to try to get Kirsten away from me? From us?"

Luka and Conrad moved closer as Nabera spat out, "Describe her."

"She's part spic," Obadiah said slowly. "Dark brown hair, brown eyes, full rack, mouthy."

The description matched, and Frankie wasn't a common name for a woman. "She lives in New York?"

"Yes, sir. She works—worked—at some fancy-ass job for her rich family."

Now she was in Alaska working a minimum wage job? Not fucking likely. His teeth ground together. "She knows Kirsten is in Rescue. She was trying to get information about her. And about our compound."

He'd thought she was tempting—innocent and stupid.

The filthy, lying bitch.

Luka's mouth dropped open. "Captain, could she be the one

who operated the drone?"

It got worse and worse. "The operator's footprints were from a woman's shoe. She's snooping around, all right." Nabera's mouth thinned. "If we're not careful, the feds will show up with search warrants. They'll take our weapons. Remove our women."

Conrad glared at Obadiah. "Your woman needs—"

"She's not involved." Obadiah snarled, his teeth barely visible behind his yellow-brown beard. "She knows if she's stupid, her whiny-ass boy will *accidentally* fall off a cliff."

Nabera wasn't so sure. The barmaid—Frankie—had said, "*A couple of your women were at the grocery,*" and spoke about the younger woman with them. She'd seen Kirsten. "The snoopy 'friend' already knows too much about us. If she's not stopped, she'll learn more."

Luka stiffened. "The chief of police is just waiting for us to put a foot wrong."

Nabera growled under his breath. One day that cop would drive down the wrong back road, and his head would get blown off. "Let me think."

The others waited respectfully as he considered.

They couldn't leave the busybody alive. That was obvious. But if she disappeared, there would be a search. Awkward questions of why she was here.

A car accident might work, but...there still might be questions.

What if it appeared as if the target was someone else and she was—what was that big city term?—collateral damage.

She was staying in one of the Okie's rental cabins. "Luka, didn't you tell me about Dante fighting with someone?"

"Yes, bunch of wannabe gangsters from Anchorage. They got high and were shooting things up. He kicked them out of the cabin they'd rented." Luka smiled. "They almost shot him as they drove away."

Conrad spat on the ground. "City assholes can't shoot for

shit."

"Just as well." No one would question that the city thugs would want revenge—and would love to burn all four of those nice wooden cabins.

With some money as incentive, a few Anchorage scumbags could be found to pay a visit to the cabins. Nabera smiled. It would be worth the money to fuck up the old Okie who'd given the Prophet so much trouble.

Nabera told his lieutenants, "Change in plans. A quick trip to Anchorage right now. No point in putting this off." Who knew what the cunt might get up to next?

"Anchorage, sir?" Luka asked.

"There are times it's better to hire things out. Keep your own hands clean." Law enforcement must not trace anything back to the Zealots.

Nabera glanced at Obadiah. "When we get back, we need to speak to Kirsten. The New Yorker couldn't have discovered that Kirsten is here unless she was told."

Killing the New Yorker would have been enjoyable but hearing Obadiah's disobedient wife scream would make up for it.

The roadhouse was closed.

The night had been profitable, Bull thought as he finished with the bar receipts. Near the center of the empty room, Frankie waited for him at a table, doing her own paperwork.

The routine let them leave together so she could spend the night at his house. Even though he liked her little cabin, it wasn't good to leave Gryff alone too long. The traumatized rescue needed more than his snug doghouse on the deck—he needed people.

After putting his paperwork away, Bull leaned on the bar top to watch Frankie work. Such a beautiful woman. Although when he called her that, she'd laugh and say she was pretty enough, but her sisters were the beauties. Not to gain herself compliments, just stating what she believed.

He didn't agree. Maybe society considered her sisters to be more attractive than she was, but as a man, he had his own opinion.

Francesca Bocelli was beautiful.

However...

His jaw tightened. He might not know her as well as he'd thought. He'd figured her to be honest and straightforward. But tonight, her behavior with the PZs had him questioning his ability to read people.

Usually when men tried to touch Frankie, she sidestepped and called them on it. Effortlessly. Yet, earlier tonight, Nabera had held her hand, put his arm around her waist, even squeezed her ass. She'd not only let him but leaned in closer.

Her flirting had roused ugly feelings in Bull. Ones that hadn't died down in the hours since.

Done with closing, Bull walked over to her table.

She rose and smiled. "Ready to go?"

"In a minute."

Her smile faltered. "What?"

"Want to tell me what was going on with you and Captain Nabera?"

"That was Nabera?"

He blinked. She didn't know who the guy was? Maybe he'd misread the situation. "It was Nabera who held your hand. Who squeezed your ass."

Dark color rose in her cheeks, and his indecision faded away. That was guilt in her face.

Dammit. He'd been through this before, back when Paisley had taught him not to ignore his gut. *"Oh, Bull, I was just flirting a smidgeon with the buyer. Everybody does it."* Only her flirting had been a prelude to fucking her clients.

Then again, his past might have skewed his judgment. "Maybe I'm too sensitive because of my ex." His brows drew together. "Both ex's, actually, since my first wife messed around when I was deployed."

"While you were risking your life, she..." Frankie shook her head, her dark eyes softening with concern. "That must have been horrible."

"Yeah. It was. But now..." He ran a hand over his head, feeling the first signs of roughness. Much like this relationship, eh? "I know we've never talked about how this relationship should work." He'd been pleased she even recognized it as one. "But no matter how short-lived our time together might be, I have certain expectations of...loyalty."

"What?"

"Loyalty for both of us," Bull added. "For instance, that we only have sex with each other."

Her eyes widened, then narrowed. She jumped to her feet, hands lifting in the air. "I didn't fuck the man. He just held my *hand*."

"He fondled your ass, woman, and you let him. You've never let anyone else touch you like that." So why now? What was he missing here?

Her mouth opened—and he expected some good Italian cursing. But she sighed and her shoulders sagged.

Surprised, Bull stepped closer to her. "What's going on, sweetheart? Tell me so I can understand."

She retreated a step, blinking hard, then shook her head, and looked him in the face.

And lied. "Nothing. Nothing is going on. And I'm going home. It's been a long night."

Feeling as if he'd been punched in the gut, he stared at her. Feeling as if he was back watching a marriage dissolve. Just like Paisley, she wasn't going to talk. Explain. Work on making it right.

When she walked out of the roadhouse, he stayed silent.

CHAPTER EIGHTEEN

E very time someone says, "Expect the unexpected", the best course of action is to test that quote by punching them in the face. - Unknown

Frankie was still awake. She punched up the pillow again and curled into a tighter ball.

Her eyes burned. From crying. And crying. And crying.

How could she have messed up so badly? Handled Bull's questions so clumsily? When reading romance novels, she'd snicker at the messes the heroines fell into and call them idiots. All those complications because the man and woman didn't talk about the problem.

Isn't this great. I've fallen right into the you-are-really-dumb category.

She couldn't blame Bull for being unhappy that she'd let Nabera grope her. She slept with Bull, made love with him, spent hours with him every day. Certainly, he'd feel as if they were exclusive.

It was how she felt, too. It was why when she'd flirted with the PZ and let him touch her, she'd felt sick—and guilty.

What if Bull let some woman hold his hand or fondle him? What if he flirted with a woman?

I'd kill him dead.

Bull had only asked her why. Normally, she wouldn't have gotten upset...but she'd felt cornered. Of *course*, she wanted to share everything with him, but it wasn't her life on the line. How could she live with herself if she asked Bull for help and he went to the police? To his brother, the chief.

Once told, Gabe would have to do what the law required, even if a little boy might be hurt. Oh, the hard-faced law officer was a kind man. Hadn't she seen how he was with Regan?

But he'd have to call in help. Matters would be taken out of his hands—and completely out of hers.

Nabera was a fanatic. Batshit crazy. She'd seen it in his eyes. It would be a slaughter.

"I can't risk it," Frankie whispered, "not even for you, Bull." Even for what they had. Might have had. Wanted to have. Tears pooled in her eyes again.

The way she felt now was no surprise. She'd always known her heart would get broken.

She pressed her hand to her aching chest. It was past broken. Crushed into painful splinters.

Because...she loved him. Oh, Madonna, she really did.

She rolled onto her back. What would he be doing now? Trying to sleep—and staring at the ceiling like her? Or sitting with Gryff on his deck, watching the lake.

Her wine was gone, but still, she could go outside to the dark water. Whisper goodbye and see if the sound carried across to the Hermitage.

Right, and how pitiful would that make her?

And maybe—

What is that?

A rustling noise came from outside. *Bull?* Her hopes rose so high they bounced off the ceiling.

No, silly. He wouldn't be walking around the back of her cabin.

Sitting up in bed, she listened to more rustling. The crunch of gravel. Other nights, hearing the same noises, she'd peeked out the window and seen a bear. The next time, it'd been a moose.

So amazing. So Alaska.

Her New York pride roused a bit. There were bears in her state—up in the Adirondacks. Not that she'd ever seen any.

She moved a little and realized that having an oversized glass of wine before bed wasn't clever—not if one possessed only a teacup-sized bladder. Boy, did she have to pee.

She made a beeline into the bathroom across from her tiny bedroom corner. Her fingers searched for the light switch.

In the living area at the front—and behind her—glass crashed, and things thudded on the wood flooring.

What? She spun, half in, half out of the bathroom.

PHOOM! PHOOM! PHOOM! The explosions were in the living space *and* her bedroom area. The black interior of the cabin lit up like the sun had risen.

Her whole left side stung and burned. What was *happening?*

She stepped farther out of the bathroom to see—and her breathing stopped.

Her cabin was on *fire*. Flames streaked up the walls, raging across her sofa and rug. And her bed—her bed was burning.

Cazzo! I have to get out of here.

What the fuck time was it anyway? In the gazebo by the lake, Bull scowled at how the sky was lightening to predawn gray. Meant it was after 3:00 or so. He should be sleeping. So should Gabe.

At least Gryff was smarter. The dog was sprawled out, head on Bull's feet.

Unable to settle after getting home from the roadhouse, Bull had carried a cooler with the brewery's new seasonal beers to the screened gazebo and lit the firepit.

Wasn't *this* a perfect time to do taste testing...his temper was so foul nothing would taste good. Yeah, he was a dumbass.

Earlier, before Bull had even finished one bottle, Gabe had appeared, prowling around the courtyard as he was wont to do when plagued with nightmares. Combat vets—fucked to hell and gone, all of them. Taking a chair across from Bull, the old man had accepted a beer with a grunt and hadn't asked what was wrong. That wasn't their way.

Silently, they'd shared the darkest hour of the night.

Bull spent the time thinking about Frankie. She was one of the most up-front people he'd ever met—except for a few things. Such as why she was in Rescue. Why she'd hidden her car and gone hiking around the PZ compound. Why she'd flirted with Nabera.

What was the connection between her and the fanatics? It was more than curiosity.

His mouth tightened. He'd have to ask again, as many times as was necessary to get an answer. What was the worst that could happen? She'd walk away? She intended to do just that, so he might as well flatten this roadblock. How else would they get a chance to see what they had together?

She'd over-reacted when he questioned her, but...his lips quirked up. That was Frankie. Her feelings were out there, and when she was upset, her emotions boiled right over. He loved that about her...and yeah, he loved her.

Fuck, he was in deep, and he knew it. So if she thought she'd just walk away, it wasn't happening.

He frowned. Walking away wasn't like her. He would've expected her to blow her top rather than fold up and leave. Maybe because of whatever she was hiding.

So. A visit tomorrow and a long talk. A chat. The word

reminded him of Mako's psych buddy who'd show up and take Bull or one of his brothers for a hike. It'd been years before they'd realized those chats had helped straighten out their heads. Mako had saved them. Doc Grayson had screwed their heads on straight.

Bull took a sip of his beer. Maybe he'd take Frankie out for a long ramble through the forest. It'd worked for Grayson, right?

Mission planned, he glanced over at his brother.

Beer in hand, Gabe was watching the mist floating over the still lake. Over the last hour or so, the lines of tension had disappeared from his face.

"Won't Audrey notice you're not in bed?" Bull asked.

"She woke up as I was leaving, which means I have about another hour before she'll hunt me down." His smile indicated he liked that his woman would come after him, even in the dead of night.

Bull suppressed a sigh. Frankie had said she'd do that.

No, he wasn't giving up on what they had.

"Are those new trial beers?" Caz stepped into the gazebo.

"Yeah. Why don't you try Old Baldy for me?" Apparently, it was a rough night for more than just Bull. He picked out a bottle from the cooler and handed it over.

"You didn't offer me that one," Gabe commented.

"You wouldn't like it," Bull said. "There's extra hops and wheat. More fruity and spicy to give a summery feeling."

"Summery beer?" Gabe snorted. "Yeah, no. I'll take my fruit salad on a plate, not in my beer."

After moving his chair closer to the firepit, Caz took a sip and savored it. "Very nice, 'mano. It does taste like summer. This one is a winner."

The gazebo screen door opened, and Hawk scowled at them. "Noisy bastards." Obviously not intending to stay long, he wore only a pair of jeans and an unbuttoned flannel shirt.

"Evening." Bull studied him quickly. For the past weeks, they'd been doing spring chores—cleaning the chicken coop, turning compost, washing windows, repairing snow damage. It appeared Hawk had also done personal spring cleaning. His blond hair, still shoulder-length, was evened out, and his beard trimmed to hug his jaw.

The sarge would be pleased.

"Try this." He handed Hawk an Old Baldy.

Hawk sampled. "Not bad. More hops would be better"— he sneered at Gabe—"but it'd work for a sunny afternoon grill."

"That was the idea." Bull nodded. "I'll feature it when I get the roadhouse patio opened up."

"When you do, then—" Gabe leaned forward. "What the hell is that?"

Bull turned to follow his brother's gaze. Across the lake, a red light flickered and grew. Another light on the shore grew bright, then another.

"That's fire," Hawk said. "More than one."

"*Fuck.*" Bull jumped to his feet. "Those are Dante's cabins." *Frankie.*

Gabe started snapping orders. "Caz, call the fire department— and tell JJ she's on duty. Bull, make sure your New Yorker's safe. Hawk and I'll take the rest of the cabins." He sprinted toward his house.

"Hawk, I'll drive." Fear tightening his guts, Bull ran across the lawn to the house with Gryff at his heels. "Buddy, guard the place."

He got an acknowledging *woof.*

With Hawk in the passenger seat, Bull drove his pickup down the road. Ahead of him, Gabe's Jeep turned onto Swan Avenue. They went past the lake and onto Lake Road. The vehicle skidded to a stop at Frankie's as Gabe kept going to the last of the four blazing buildings.

In the few minutes it'd taken to get there, flames had engulfed Frankie's cabin.

"You see her?" Hawk jumped out.

Throat-clogging smoke filled the air, and Bull coughed as he scanned for her small figure.

No one. Fear rose even higher inside him.

Her door and windows were aflame, bright orange against the dark cabin walls. The heavy logs shouldn't have caught fire so quickly. The pattern was too deliberate.

This was arson.

Outside the light cast by the flames, the shadows were thick enough to hide...anyone. Bull's pulse quickened as his lizard brain awoke, screaming about danger. He silenced the little voice and stayed focused on the goal: find his woman. "Go on. I got this."

As Hawk ran for the next cabin, Bull jogged around Frankie's. A waft of wind sent embers through the air. "Frankie!"

"Here!"

At the sound of her voice, relief punched into his chest like a bullet. "Where?"

"In here." A hand appeared through a busted-out window. "I can't g—" Coughing interrupted her. Flames from behind silhouetted Frankie—but she was alive and on her feet.

For the moment. *Fuck.* The rectangular bathroom window was far too small for a person. Probably why it hadn't been lit on fire. His gut tightened. The door and other windows were burning. This was the only way out—or she'd die. "Hold on, sweetheart."

He grabbed the sill and yanked. Not quite enough. He roared, "Hawk, need you!"

"Coming!" As Hawk appeared from around the corner, Bull moved his grip to one side of the window frame. "Need an assist."

Hawk grabbed the other side of the sill.

"*Now.*"

They yanked together—and ripped out the sill as well as the wood below it. *Thank fuck.*

"You good?" Hawk caught Bull's nod, then sprinted toward the other cabins.

Coughing as smoke eddied around him, Bull punched out the last of the jagged glass. "Turn sideways, sweetheart. I'll brace you."

Still coughing, she nodded. It was going to be a tight fit.

From the direction of Rescue, sirens were approaching, barely audible over the roaring crackle of the fire.

Frankie tried to squirm out the narrow window but turned sideways; she couldn't use her feet to push.

"Here we go." Bull gripped her waist, supporting her as he pulled. Her curvy ass caught for a second, and then he had an armload of woman. She was dressed only in one of his old flannel shirts—the one she'd laughingly stolen to use as a robe.

"*Orsacchiotto,* thank you." Arms around him, she pressed her face against his neck. "I didn't think I'd be able to get out."

If he and Hawk hadn't been here to rip away the window frame, she wouldn't have. The knowledge was a shard of ice in his guts.

Scooping her up, Bull carried her away from the overwhelming heat pouring from the cabin. The heaviest logs forming the walls hadn't ignited, but everything inside the building was going to be incinerated.

She could've been...

Bull hauled in a breath. He had her in his arms. Could hear her voice.

Even her coughing felt reassuring.

He searched for something to say...other than *you almost died.* "Dante's going to be pissed off." Despite his efforts, his voice came out guttural and ragged.

She buried her face against his shoulder. "Uh-huh."

Setting her on the passenger seat in his truck, Bull checked her over. No blood gushing. Nothing busted. He brushed her hair back off her face. "Fuck, I was scared. For you."

Tears filled her eyes, and she pressed her cheek against his hand. "Me, too."

He turned to check the other three buildings. Who needed help?

Caz and JJ had arrived and were assisting an older man who was staggering. Hawk was between two men in their thirties, both coughing violently.

Fire extinguisher in his hand, Gabe appeared with his arm around another guy. From the scorch marks on the renter's clothing, Gabe had needed to spray down some flames to get the guy out.

All four cabins were in flames. "Any more?" Bull yelled.

"This is it," Gabe called back.

"Three-o'clock!" Hawk shouted.

Ambush.

Bull grabbed Frankie and dove for the ground. Why the fuck hadn't he come armed? He checked the woods down the road.

The bushes were moving. There was a flash of clothing. Moving away.

Not an ambush. The bastards were fleeing. Two men—no, three.

Gabe snapped, "Doc, Hawk. Take guard." Even before he'd taken off running, Bull had charged after the men.

Hawk and the doc would watch over the civilians—and Frankie. Bull would eliminate the threat. He roared.

His targets panicked, fighting to get through the thick undergrowth at the forest edge. Breaking from concealment, they fled down the road toward the park. Probably where their car was parked.

Catching up to the first man, Bull grabbed his shoulder, then heaved and spun, tossing him back to Gabe before continuing after the rest.

A glance showed him that Hawk was stationed in front of Frankie. She'd be safe.

. . .

Sitting in the pickup, Frankie stared as Bull, JJ, and Gabe chased whoever'd been in the underbrush. She'd never seen anyone react as fast as Bull had.

He'd thrown that man to Gabe as casually as she'd have tossed her sister a scarf.

Be careful, Bull. She sucked in a breath and broke into more coughing.

By Gabe's Jeep, her cabin neighbors were sitting on the ground. Standing guard over them with a knife in hand, Caz scanned the surroundings.

Beside Bull's pickup, Hawk was doing the same...only he held a pistol.

"Where'd the gun come from?" she asked.

His sharp eyes paused on her for a second. "Just part of getting dressed in the morning."

Now...there was a scary habit.

"You saw them first. Why didn't you chase them or shoot them or something?" Not that she ever, ever wanted anyone to shoot someone.

"I'm the slowest runner." He glanced at her. "And I don't shoot unless I know they need to die."

"Oh." Fear for Bull had shut her brain off. What if they were simply scared drunks or something? She shivered because...what if they weren't?

Bull was almost to the second man with JJ right behind him.

"I don't shoot," Hawk said. Like he'd done it before. Bull said they'd all seen action. Ugly shit. And Hawk played his violin at night.

"Don't shoot anyone, Hawk. I don't want you to shoot anyone."

"Good to know." The amusement in his eyes died when he realized she was serious.

240

Arms around herself, she shivered and helplessly watched the chase. The light from the flames lit up the entire area—and showed Bull catch up to the next man as easily as if the guy hadn't been full-out running.

Bull swung his arm, and it seemed as if he'd merely swatted the man's shoulders, but the guy left the ground like a pigeon taking flight.

JJ took him on, and Bull continued.

The last man spun. Knife in hand, he lunged at Bull. "Die, asshole!"

"No!" Panicking, Frankie grabbed Hawk's arm. "Help him!"

"Eh, Bull'd get upset if I butt in." Hawk just stood there.

Frankie pushed him to one side and ran forward. If nothing else, she could distract the—

"*Civilians.*" Hawk grabbed the back of her shirt, jerking her to a stop. "Stay put, yorkie."

"*Vai all'inferno!* Yes, go to *hell.*" She tried to wrench away and couldn't. Tears burned her eyes as she stared at the men fighting. *Please, don't let him be hurt. Please.*

The man lunged, and Bull sidestepped the knife, gripped his opponent's wrist, and brought his knee up. The man screamed, and Bull plucked the knife from his hand. The guy crumpled to the ground, cursing up a storm, and holding his quite obviously broken arm.

Relief hit Frankie like a tsunami, leaving her shaking.

"C'mon, woman." Hawk pulled her back to Bull's pickup so she could lean against the door.

As she watched, Bull yanked the guy up, gripped his uninjured arm, and walked him back. As they approached the pickup, she could hear Bull's deep voice with that impossible-to-shake calm. "A shame about your arm, but you hurried me. Why'd you burn the cabin anyway?"

After a pat down and search, JJ forced her handcuffed man to kneel next to Bull's prisoner. She glanced at Bull, snorted, and shook her head. "You broke this one, Bull. Caz's going to be annoyed."

"Yeah, my bad." Glancing over at his brother, Bull called, "Sorry, Doc."

Checking over one of her neighbors, Caz turned, saw the obviously broken arm. "*No mames.*" He scowled at Bull. "*Vales verga.*"

"Hey, at least I caught the bastard," Bull grumbled.

Che cavolo, the man was crazy. He acted like he'd just gone out for ice cream, not been in a knife fight. Hysterical giggles welled up, and Frankie put her hands over her mouth to hold them back.

As a fire engine pulled up, and firefighters jumped out, Gabe dragged his handcuffed man over. "Down, mister."

"You figure this is a PZ thing?" JJ asked Gabe.

"I wouldn't put it past the assholes, but arson isn't usually their MO," he said.

Arson? Frankie turned toward her cabin. Firefighters were spraying water on the buildings and the fires were starting to go out.

Arson. She stood up. Took a couple of steps forward.

Hawk frowned. "Yorkie, stay—"

"They threw something into my cabin to start the fire."

"Yeah?" He turned to where Gabe was talking to a firefighter. "Yo, old man. You got info here."

Old man? Gabe was...at most...a few years older than his brothers. Probably not even that. "Old man?"

"Means he's a bossy bastard," Hawk growled.

"What information?" Gabe walked over.

So did Bull.

"I was in the bathroom, and I heard the windows break, and something—several things—landed inside, and then everything was burning."

"Sounds like they tossed in Molotov cocktails." A firefighter joined them. "From the scorch marks and stink, I'm guessing they splashed gas on the outside around the windows and doors."

Those three men had wanted her to...to burn? Her knees buckled, and Hawk grabbed her. Held her up.

Bull pulled a blanket out of the back of his cab and wrapped it around her. "I'll take her, bro. Thanks for watching her for me."

"Yeah. Sure." Releasing her, Hawk moved away.

Feeling chilled as cold air wafted over her burned skin, Frankie pulled the blanket tighter.

Bull pulled her back against his chest. His right arm crossed over her breasts and the other around her waist. So strong, so warm.

She leaned back against him, and he didn't even rock as he took her weight. He bent to whisper in her ear, "You all right?"

Her hands curled over his scarred forearms, holding him to her. Here was safety. "Thanks to you, yes."

"You think the weird militia group did this?" the firefighter asked.

"I don't think they're with the Pissers." JJ joined them.

"The...what? Pissers?" The firefighter laughed.

Gabe snorted. "Lot of people refer to Patriot Zealots as PZs, and somehow—I'm blaming my niece—that's been transformed to *Pissers*. Don't tell anyone, but I rather like it."

As the fireman snickered, JJ sighed. "Regan started it. And after laughing my ass off when she said it the first time, I lacked the moral high ground to tell her to stop."

Gabe gave Bull a half-smile before asking her, "Any idea why the cabins would be burned?"

"I don't know." She studied the three guys on the ground who appeared more like gang members than the PZs. "Dante had a fight with some renters a few days ago. He kicked them out."

"Fishermen did this?" The firefighter lifted his eyebrows.

"The renters were a bunch of Anchorage's gangsters. They got high and started shooting up everything, including the other cabins. Someone called Dante"—JJ's frown showed what she thought about the police not getting called first—"and he showed up with a shotgun and booted them out. Insults and threats were exchanged."

"Gangsters versus redneck veteran." The firefighter grinned. "Go, Dante."

JJ told Gabe, "The state troopers are on the way to take them. Caz will have time to splint that arm."

Gabe studied Frankie for a moment, then told Bull, "She can leave. I'll get a formal statement later."

"I'm good with that. Just let us know what you find, Chief." The firefighter scowled at the burning cabins. "Good thing it rained yesterday, or we'd be battling a forest fire, too."

"*Chiquita.*" Caz stepped in front of her. "Where are you burned or hurt?"

"I…" Was she hurt? She wasn't sure. "I-I think I'm all right."

"Let's be sure, *sí?*" With someone holding a flashlight for him and Bull blocking anyone's view, the doc was gentle, but thorough, finding burns on her left arm and leg. At least the right side wasn't too bad; she'd been half inside the bathroom when the Molotov cocktails exploded. Being pulled through the window had scraped up her shoulders, back, arms, and even her butt.

He listened to her lungs, mentioning the other renters would be spending the night in the Soldotna hospital. She'd gotten lucky there, having closed the bathroom door quickly enough to avoid inhaling much smoke.

"All right, Frankie." The sympathy in Caz's dark eyes and voice was incredibly soothing. "Shower, then apply antibiotic ointment to the scrapes. You can use an aloe vera gel on the burns—or nothing. Cover any blisters that might get irritated."

"I will. Thank you, Doc." The need to leave, to get away from all the smoke and burning and violence filled her until she started to shake.

Only where could she go to shower? What would she wear? She stared at her cabin that was still aflame.

My clothes are...gone. So was her laptop and her purse and her credit cards and...everything. How could she even get a hotel room with no ID or money?

It was...was too much. *I can't do this.* Tears burned her eyes. *No, don't cry; don't cry.* "D-do you think the bed and breakfast will take me on credit until I c-can get—"

"You're coming home with me, sweetheart," Bull interrupted.

"But... We aren't..." He didn't like her any longer. He thought she was—

He pulled her close and kissed the top of her head. "We'll work it out." Not giving her time to object, he gently helped her into his pickup and buckled her in, using the blanket for extra padding under the strap.

She shouldn't go with him. This was foolish and cruel to him. Only... Her breathing hitched as she stared at her cabin. What would she do otherwise?

Bull turned to Hawk. "You ready to go?"

His brother's expression was unreadable. "I'll catch a ride with Caz."

"Fuck," Bull said under his breath. "Sure, bro. See you tomorrow."

As the pickup bounced around the lake and to the Hermitage, she struggled to stay calm. To not cry.

The thought of everything she'd have to do now was overwhelming. How could she put her life together and still get Kit out?

Those men had burned the cabins and tried to make sure she and the other renters would burn to death. Just because they'd fought with Dante? That was just...incomprehensible. Shivers shook her.

I want to go home, to my own bright apartment, my plants in the windows. Where things sound right and smell right. The need rose inside her so hard she felt like she was five again, lost on the streets of New York, the noise and people and sights too much to handle. All turned around with no way to get home.

She'd cried that day.

Tears pooled in her eyes as the world outside turned into a blur.

For the few minutes of the drive, she managed to keep it together.

When Bull let Gryff into the house, the dog was all wagging tail and little whines because she was upset. Burying her face in his soft fur, she hugged him.

"Come, Frankie. You'll feel better once you're cleaned up." Bull helped her to her feet and took her upstairs to his giant bathroom. He turned on the shower, checking the temperature with a hand.

Unable to even think, she simply stood. But when he turned and studied her, she squared her shoulders. "I'm good. Really."

"Yes, you are. You're tough." He dropped a light kiss on her mouth and left, leaving the door slightly ajar behind him.

The sound of water reminded her that she'd really needed to pee for, like, forever. A minute later, she felt so much better.

In the shower, the hot water ran over her, sluicing away dirt. Despite the stinging of her burns and scrapes, she washed and shampooed until the clean, crisp scent of Bull's soap replaced the stink of smoke. And she felt...better, like she was getting things under control.

Wrapping a huge towel around herself, Frankie stepped out of the big shower stall and found Bull leaning against the counter. Clean and in fresh clothes, he must have taken a shower downstairs. She pulled the towel tighter. "I'm not dressed."

His firm lips edged upward. "I hate to tell you this, Ms. Bocelli, but I'm pretty sure I've not only seen everything you've got—but nibbled on it, too."

He had, of course he had, but that was then. Things were

different now. So horribly, sadly different. She shook her head at him.

His black eyes softened to liquid night. "I'm sorry. I didn't mean to make you uncomfortable." He ran his hand over his shaved skull. "However, we need to get those burns and scrapes taken care of, and there are some I don't think you can reach."

"No, it's me who's sorry." She looked down. Along with the dirt, it seemed her energy had washed away in the shower. "I appreciate everything you've done. I don't mean to act like you're some bad guy."

She blinked hard as a lump filled her throat. *Cazzo, not again.*

His callused hand cupped her chin, and he lifted her head. Saw her eyes swimming in tears.

"Hell." Very, very gently, he pulled her into his arms, holding her against his chest, all his virile power shut down for the moment. "You sure had a crappy day."

The sympathy in his dark, deep voice was too much. Her shoulders started to shake as she battled the tears—and lost.

She cried, big noisy sobs, as he held her, stroked her hair, and told her she was brave. That she'd be fine. That she was safe. With him. Low, quiet murmurs. Impossibly solid strength. And warm arms around her.

Why did he have to be so truly kind?

She dragged in a breath and another before pulling back. He released her immediately.

"I... Thank you. I needed that, I guess." She had. Her head no longer felt as if it was filled with molasses. The weight was gone from her chest.

Unfortunately, the damage to her skin hadn't disappeared. The shower had irritated all the scrapes and blisters until everything burned and stung. "Can we...?" She motioned to the assortment of first aid supplies laid out on the counter as tidily as in an ER.

"That's the plan. After that, I have a Pinot Noir from Oregon you might like. We can sit and settle." He made a motion with his finger—*turn around*—and she faced away from him.

Moving the towel off her upper back, he tended the scrapes on her shoulders, upper back, and upper arms. Going down on one knee, he spread the ointment on her raw butt, upper thighs, and hips. How did such a big man have such gentle hands?

"I asked Audrey for her baggiest sweatpants." He turned Frankie around to face him. "She thought you probably wear about the same size."

Frankie nodded. They both possessed ample hips and ass. "Sweatpants sound good." She hissed as he applied a burn gel to the scorched blisters down her left side.

"Wear this, too." He drew one of his T-shirts over her head. It was so old the fabric was worn to softness.

"Thank you." She managed to smile at him.

"I like seeing you in my clothes." From the counter drawer, he pulled out her little bag with overnight items in it—deodorant, comb, toothbrush. Touching her cheek gently, he smiled and withdrew.

She stared after him and realized she was all right again. His concern and care had eased the hollow place in her center.

Usually, she was the person everyone relied on for calm and for fixing problems. She was strong because if she broke down, none of her diva-filled family could take her place.

Wasn't it amazing to be able to lean on someone?

She gave her head a shake. *Don't get used to it, Frankie.*

But...just for tonight, she'd let herself indulge.

After gathering blankets, wine, and glasses, Bull went out onto his deck. Frankie would come when she was ready. Damn, but it was difficult to know when to push and when to back off.

Then again, except for times like now, she was up-front about what she wanted. It was just one more thing he liked about her. Some men enjoyed shy women. Quiet Audrey was perfect for Gabe who found her reserve an intriguing challenge.

Bull preferred Frankie's openness. With her words, with her body language, she...shared. What she felt was what she said. If someone screwed up at work, she let them know—however tactfully. If they did good, she told them that, too.

In his arms, in his bed, she told him what she wanted.

He settled into a chair with a weary grunt. The mournful wail of a loon drifted across the lake. The cool air held the moist scent of the lake shallows. Hidden behind a bank of fog, the sun was already topping the mountains to the east.

The sliding glass door opened, and Frankie stepped out, wearing his old T-shirt, the loose sweatpants, and the thick, fluffy socks he'd left on the counter. Her almost dry hair tumbled down her back. She'd found the hair dryer Audrey had lent him.

Sitting in the single chair across from him, she ignored the blanket and set her hands on her knees. "I'd like to..." Expression serious, she shook her head. "This is difficult."

Leaning forward, Bull took her hand. "Spit it out, sweetheart."

"Tonight, at the roadhouse with Nabera, I didn't want to flirt with him. Letting him touch me..." She swallowed. "I almost puked. I felt guilty because you're right. We have something between us, and even knowing it has an end date, we're together. Messing around with other people would be wrong—and I'd be upset with you if you did it."

It wasn't easy, but he stayed silent. Just nodded. The relief that she was willing to talk, to share, felt as if a bomb had been dismantled.

She shoved her hair out of her face. "When I was in bed earlier, I worked out this whole explanation, only now I can't remember it. What am I missing?"

"Perhaps the reason you let him touch you?"

She winced. "Right. I can't tell you. I want to, but what I was doing was... I guess I can share that I was trying to get information from the PZs. For a friend."

"A friend." As worry exploded inside him, Bull kept his voice even.

"I sound insane, don't I? I'm trying to help a friend, and it's not my secret to share, and I know it's not fair to you. But...I won't flirt or anything like that again. It feels too wrong. And horrible."

Frustration, remorse, and unhappiness were all too evident in her face.

As Bull studied her, any lingering anger fizzled and died. "I'm surprised Nabera could be taken in so easily."

"I'm not one to hide my feelings, but I do know how to play a role, at least for a short time. All Mama's children learned that." She pulled in a breath, straightened, raised her chin, and transformed into a cool, self-possessed, unapproachable woman. "This is the businesswoman face I wear during meetings."

With another breath, she dropped years to appear both innocent and vulnerable. "This is what I showed Nabera."

For fuck's sake. "Bet that façade gave Nabera a hard-on."

"You'd be right on that count." Disgust slimed every word. Dropping the mask, she was his Frankie again. "I guess I'm not all that honest."

Her lying was for a friend. That changed things. As for her emotions... "Who are you pretending to be when you're role-playing?"

She nodded. "In hostile meetings at work, I'm pretending to be Mama—who can be a real ice queen. For the PZs, I acted like one of my younger cousins who just turned sixteen."

Yes, that would get Nabera's attention.

Her nose wrinkled. "Never again."

Bull smiled slightly. She was as transparent as he'd thought. When she pretended to be someone else, her eyes changed and grew distant. Because it wasn't her.

He squeezed her fingers. "Have you ever assumed a role with me?"

"No." She frowned. "Not a role. When we met, I wanted to slap your face because I thought you were a total *bastardo*—and I hated that I noticed how sexy you were. I didn't want you to see that I was attracted to you."

Yet she hadn't been able to hide it completely. The spark had been there, beneath the simmering anger in her gaze.

He leaned forward and took her lips in a slow, soft kiss. "Thank you for the honesty and the explanation."

Her eyes gleamed with tears, and she swallowed.

"Hey, hey, hey. What's wrong?"

She shook her head. "I just...I hate that I can't tell you everything and I didn't think you'd forgive me and that you'd hate me and I couldn't stand that." A tear ran down her face.

Hell, she was going to smash his heart into little bits.

Unable to help himself, he plucked her from her chair and moved to the double Adirondack chair so he could have her in his lap and cuddle. "We're good. I'm not angry. Or upset."

Her breathing held tiny sobs as she tried to keep from crying.

Here was the downside of a woman who didn't hide her emotions. There would be tears.

Far better than lies.

So, he held her, enjoying how she fit on his lap, how she was small enough that their heads were almost even, and he could rub his cheek against her damp one.

"I'm so sorry," she whispered.

"Forgiven." He kissed her again, trying to convey how he felt. That she was cared-for, safe, wanted.

When she relaxed, he shifted her so she could sit beside him, then curled her fingers around a glass of wine. In his shirt and the fuzzy socks, she was fucking adorable.

Catching his smile, she glanced down at herself and smiled ruefully. "Nothing like being braless and scruffy.

"I was just thinking how beautiful you are, no matter what you go through."

She made a scoffing sound. "I've been around the modeling business since I was born. My siblings are gorgeous. I don't make babies cry, but there's quite a gap before men will be falling at my feet."

She looked up at him, melting brown eyes framed in black lashes, the curve of her cheek heartbreakingly lovely as she smiled.

He could only stare in bemusement that she was so clueless about the basics. Finally, he touched her chin, resting his thumb on those full, incredibly kissable lips. "On cold, hard photographs, you might not have the draw of your siblings and professional models. In person... Frankie, beauty isn't restricted to two dimensions. It encompasses more than high cheekbones and perfect hair. When your eyes, possibly the loveliest eyes I've ever seen, hold laughter, everyone around you smiles. When they hold sadness, you take everyone with you.

Those perfect eyes widened in surprise.

He smiled. "Your voice makes me think of soft blankets and the warmth of a fireplace on a drizzly cold evening."

Her eyes started to gleam with tears.

No, that wasn't what he wanted. He squeezed her waist. "Your body makes me think of..." He skimmed his thumb over her full lower lip and felt it quiver. "Of stripping you right down to bare skin and discovering every dirty thing I could do to you."

As hoped, she burst out laughing. "You...you're such a man."

He grinned, because she was the type of woman who would laugh at her lover saying things like that.

And her lover was exactly what he intended to stay.

A light wind off the lake ruffled her hair and clothes, and she caught the scent of smoke, unsettling her. "Um, Bull. Why are we outside?"

It was relatively warm with the temperature in the high

forties. "After battles, it takes a while to settle." Bull picked up the soft, plush blanket he'd brought out before. After wrapping it around her, he pulled her against his side. "I've found that sitting outside or by a fire helps."

"You've fought a lot. I mean, yes, I knew that, but I didn't *know* it. That guy tonight had a knife, and you didn't hesitate." She frowned and made a tossing gesture. "The way you just threw the other man to Gabe was crazy."

Bull shrugged. "My brothers and I were fighting as a team even before our teenage years. I learned to toss one or two to whoever was bored."

"Bored," she said under her breath. "You seem like such an easy-going guy, but you're a lot scarier than I realized."

That sounded half complimentary and half worried. "I'm very easy-going," he said firmly. "Is that clear?"

"Yes, without a doubt...*Skull.*" She snickered and wiggled closer until her ultra-soft breasts pressed against his side.

His dick hardened to discomfort. "Now, sit here—stop making me hard—and just breathe. Listen to the sound of the wind. During the quietest nights, you might even hear the stars sing."

With a sigh, she leaned her head against his shoulder.

Overhead, a few clouds drifted over the brightening sky. The smell of lake water and plants held a touch of the acrid smoke of the fire.

In the forest surrounding the Hermitage, leaves rustled softly, branches squeaking with the gustier breezes.

Farther from the grassy courtyard, a patch of horsetails sighed in the wind. When camping with Mako, they'd eat new horsetail shoots like asparagus—and use the stringy older plants to scrub the tin dishes.

Birds twittered and sang. In the dark lake water, a fish surfaced with a quiet splash.

Frankie's breathing slowed. Her body grew even softer as the tension drained from her.

Eventually, she stirred. "I better get to bed. Tomorrow will be a mess. Shopping, replace my license and cards, find a place to stay, and—"

"You'll stay here. With me."

"For tonight."

"For the rest of your time in Alaska." Which he was very much hoping would be longer than a couple of months.

"What? No, I couldn't."

"Sure, you could." He smiled down at her concerned expression. "I'm not being all that selfless, Frankie. Since I'm not sure why you're here, I can't know when you might decide to leave."

Ah, that made her tense up again. Apparently, she didn't know the date she would leave, either. She was operating on someone else's timetable—the friend.

For fuck's sake, he needed to know more. But...loyalty to a friend was something he respected.

"I'll sleep better if you're here and protected." He ran his fingers through her hair. "And I wouldn't mind spending more time with you. More than we've had so far."

There it was—the same desire in her beautiful eyes.

He took her hand and kissed her palm. "Say you'll stay here, Frankie. No strings. I'll help you find a place if it doesn't work out."

"Yes." She closed her eyes for a moment. "I want to stay, too."

"Let's call it a night." He rose, took her inside—and took her upstairs to his bed.

They'd never made love so very slowly before. Oh, Bull usually took his time; in fact, he loved making her come first, sometimes several times, before he finished.

But now, he moved at an incredibly slow, heartrendingly sensuous pace. Even as he kissed her, he'd pressed a palm against her pussy. As he moved down to her neck and his lips started to brush over every inch of her skin, his fingers teased her clit. Slowly. Rousing her even as he licked and suckled her nipples. He nibbled on the undersides of her breasts, her belly, avoiding burns and scrapes, then he moved down her legs and back up.

His fingers never stopped circling her, and as she arched and came so sweetly, he never stopped kissing her. Calves, thighs, belly, breasts, her face.

His fingers found her core again. Began to arouse her. To drive her steadily toward another peak.

Her hips strained upward. "Bull..." She wasn't sure if she was protesting or—

"I love you, you know." He kissed her gently, his fingers on the center of her. "In case you haven't figured it out."

Joy filled her...and then she shook her head. It couldn't be true. "It was a scary night. You won't feel the same tom—"

He chuckled. "Woman, I've felt this way for a while. I love you."

"You...you..." How could she *think*? She stared at him, saw his slow smile as he shifted, pressed his cock at her entrance, and ever so slowly filled her. All the nerves inside her sparkled like the stars they'd watched earlier.

Her hands slid over his rock-hard biceps, over the striated deltoids, and to his muscled back.

His black-as-sin eyes held hers. "Tell me, Frankie." His voice dropped, lower, the order inescapable. "What do you feel for me?"

"I love you." The words were out, impossible to recall. And she'd spoken a truth she couldn't deny. "I didn't want to love you. I *don't* want to." She glared at him.

"But you do." He laughed, the sound so impossibly compelling she had to grin.

"I do." She ran her hands behind his neck, up over the soft skin of his scalp. "I love you so, so much."

"Since I need to hear that some more"—he smiled, his dark eyes wicked—"keep saying it...or I'll stop."

He moved inside her, hard and fast, filling her full, sliding out, driving her up and up and up.

As long as she kept saying how she felt.

And when she came, when he came, when he was so deep inside her they were one, and he said it to her again, the tenderness in his voice made her weep.

CHAPTER NINETEEN

I *n the cookie of life, friends are the chocolate chips.* - Salman Rushdie

Since Bull had lowered the blackout curtains, they'd slept late, and then he taught her to kayak. It was such a peaceful way to exercise and so beautiful with only the sounds of the oars and water and birds. New York was never quiet.

When they returned and shared a shower, Bull started to leave to get a condom, but she stopped him. "I'm on birth control pills...and I get tested for STDs regularly." When he said he had been tested and was clean, the condoms were left in a drawer— and oh, the extra closeness was worth the awkward conversation.

During their late breakfast, Gabe dropped by to make up his official police report and left Frankie a copy. It was good he had, since she spent the rest of the morning using Bull's laptop to get replacements for her driver's license, credit cards, and everything else.

There were moments of accomplishment...and moments of pure self-pity. The copies of Kit's guardianship papers had been burned to ash. So had her phone and laptop. That had been a really bad moment. Her *phone*.

When the rental company said they'd send her an undamaged vehicle, she unloaded her poor scorched car that, once again, Hawk had driven to the Hermitage for her. Then she got all teary-eyed because her jo hadn't burned up in the cabin.

She also hauled in the brand-new backpack that contained the equipment to rescue Kit—giant bolt cutters, hunting knife, rope. The navigation equipment, first aid kit, travel-at-night stuff.

Three more days, Kit, and I'll be there the second it's dark.

A tap at the sliding glass deck door made her jump.

"Frankie?" Audrey stood outside. "It's me and JJ and Regan."

"C'mon in." At the dining room table, Frankie waved to them. "Give me one second to get this form sent off."

The SUBMIT button appeared on the laptop display. She clicked on it and leaned back in the chair with a relieved sigh. "Done. You know, in all my years in so-called crime-ridden New York City, I never had my purse stolen."

They laughed.

JJ patted her shoulder. "It's good you started on replacing your documents right away. Some of those agencies move pretty slowly."

"Speaking of replacements," Audrey said. "How about we take you to Soldotna to get clothes and personal stuff? Or if you want more variety, we can go to Anchorage."

Audrey and JJ were smiling; Regan was bouncing a little.

"Really?" Frankie pulled in a breath. "You guys are a miracle. Only...I don't even have shoes. They won't let me in—"

"You have shoes." JJ held up a pair of battered black high-top sneakers. "Bull said you're a size seven, but Audrey wears a six, and my shoes would fall right off your feet. We checked around. These are from Regina, our municipal building receptionist."

Last week, when Bull said he planned to teach her to fish, he'd asked her shoe size so he could borrow waders for her. "He got me shoes." Frankie swallowed hard. "I knew I could borrow his clothes, but I felt so...defenseless...not having any shoes."

Audrey gave her a sympathetic look. "Last year, I...let's just say I kind of know how you feel."

There'd been a few hints that Audrey'd arrived in Rescue when running from someone. One of these days, Frankie needed the whole story. She rose and rubbed her hands together. "Shopping. I'm in."

JJ tucked an arm around Regan's shoulders. "While we're in a shoe store, Regan here could use a pair. She's outgrowing everything."

Regan shook her head. "Papá just got me shoes last winter. I don't need—"

"You do need." JJ kissed the top of her head. "Don't be so worried. Every kid outgrows clothes and shoes until...oh, until around seventeen or so."

Regan didn't relax.

Aw. Bull said Regan hadn't even met Caz until last fall. How long would it be until she felt as if he truly was her father? Frankie felt the ache of empathy. Sometimes it felt as if her family weighed out love on a scale. How much worse would it be to have not grown up there?

JJ gave Regan a squeeze. "Your father expects you to need new clothes. However, he's male, which means he's blind when it comes to women's clothing, so it's my job to keep you outfitted. As it happens, I think that's a great job. You wouldn't deprive me of a fun time, would you?"

Now worried she'd hurt JJ's feelings, Regan started assuring JJ she really liked getting new clothes.

Frankie glanced at Audrey and said in a low voice, "That was one smooth snow job."

Audrey covered her mouth, but a laugh escaped. "JJ is as good at smoothing out problems as you are at managing people. By the way, we're all glad Bull is getting a break from managing the roadhouse."

"Let's get moving," JJ said. "Frankie, gather what you might need."

Frankie automatically checked for her purse and groaned. "Wait, I don't have money or credit cards or even a phone."

"Obviously, you wouldn't. We should stop at a phone store, though." Audrey patted her purse. "We'll use our credit cards, and Bull will reimburse us and take it out of your salary. All arranged."

Frankie stared. "Seriously?"

"He knew you wouldn't let him pay for everything, so he arranged it the best way he could." Audrey snorted. "However feminist Mako's sons may be, they have cavemen-worthy protective instincts. You were in danger; Bull's protective instincts were triggered. This is what happens."

"Sometimes, it's really clear you majored in biology, professor." JJ walked around, making sure everything was locked up, then glanced at Frankie. "She's right about them trying to shield us. Caz and I get into some pretty vehement discussions about me being in danger."

Regan giggled. "He yelled at you last time. A lot."

"Troublesome child." JJ tugged on her braid. "You got the same lecture when you and Delaney rolled down that steep hill in a cardboard box. You almost spent your summer break in the doghouse with Gryff."

Audrey's smothered giggles sounded like little snorts. Frankie just laughed.

As Frankie pulled on her loaned sneakers, Audrey smiled. "For someone with no clothing that fits, you're remarkably put together."

"Mostly because I'm trying to hide the lack of a bra," Frankie admitted. Bull's plain black T-shirt made a mid-thigh-length dress. Over that was his dark gray and black flannel shirt with the sleeves rolled up. She'd braided his black and silver ties into a silky belt. With Regina's high-top black sneakers, it was a rather unique outfit. "My Italian grandmother taught me that a belt adds class to anything."

JJ grinned. "I agree. Of course, my belt usually has my firearm, Taser, cuffs, and—"

Regan bumped her hip against JJ's. "You're such a cop."

And a really nice one. Frankie eyed her. Maybe during the shopping trip, she could get a better idea of what might happen if the Rescue police were called on for help. Just in case.

Sure, she'd researched and practiced night hiking, but her reading had also shown that, even with an experienced woodsman, things went wrong.

On top of that, the PZs might catch on, either as Kit and Aric were trying to reach the fence or after, during the escape.

If something happened, Kit and Aric might need the police.

After helping get Frankie squared away that morning, Bull spent the rest of the day making phone calls and doing paperwork. Damned paperwork. There was no end. Talk about frustrating. All he wanted to do was go home and be there for his woman.

Finally, he called it quits and returned to the Hermitage only to discover he'd been drafted to grill for everyone, including Lillian and Dante.

Normally, he loved cooking for the family, but fuck, he was tired. He'd hoped to spend a quiet evening with Frankie.

Instead... Eh, maybe it wouldn't be quiet, but at least, she was here.

It seemed his cooking wouldn't require much effort. While catching him up on her day—between kisses—Frankie said she'd marinated the chicken and made a dessert. All he had to do was the actual grilling.

Yeah, he loved her.

An hour later, after piling a platter high with lemon-garlic grilled chicken, Bull set it on the table. Already seated, Caz and JJ, Gabe and Audrey, Dante and Lillian had all brought side dishes and served up drinks. Hawk came out of his cabin with a stack of baked potatoes and fixings.

Gryff and Sirius were strategically placed between the humans easiest to con out of tidbits—Regan and Frankie.

As Bull sat beside Frankie, he realized cooking and then listening to the women's shopping trip tales had eased his frustration and anger.

At least until Lillian spoke to him. "My boy, was there a problem at the roadhouse? Is that why you got home so late?"

"No," he growled. "It was because I was trying to wade through everything for SIG and—"

"What's SIG?" Frankie asked.

"Stands for Sarge's Investment Group. A corporation to handle all the properties Mako bought up around Rescue."

She frowned. "I thought he was a retired military officer."

"Yeah, but one who didn't spend much when serving, then as a twenty-plus year man, he had a decent pension and lived off the land in a cabin with no utilities for years afterward. Once we were grown, we all sent him money, thinking he was using it to live on." Bull found his throat getting tight.

After a glance at Bull, Caz stepped in. "When Mako moved to Rescue, the town was dying, and he bought properties from the residents who needed to leave. To help them. But before he died, McNally's ski resort opened, and he realized the town might come back to life."

Gabe cleared his throat. "He left us instructions with his will. Gave us a mission—to restore the town."

"He... Seriously?" Frankie gave Bull an incredulous stare. "Is that why you're all here after living everywhere else?"

"That's why. It's a worthwhile goal." There was a satisfaction in seeing the town come back to life. Become a community.

Lillian frowned. "He bought a lot of properties."

No shit. "I can't keep up with all of the work: renting and selling the properties, managing the rentals, bringing older buildings up to code, taxes, and contractors and all that." Just like that, Bull's mood went sour again. No, past sour into pissed-the-fuck-off. He growled under his breath.

Regan's eyes went wide. "I didn't know you got mad like that."

Rein it in, asshole. "Sorry, little mite."

Frankie put her hand over his. Her eyebrows lifted as she asked Gabe, "Are all of you guys overloaded with the SIG stuff?"

"Hardly." Bull snorted. "They dumped everything on my plate."

"Are my ears failing me?" Lillian straightened. "When did Mako's chosen offspring become work-shy, bed-pressing loiter-sacks?"

Bull's brothers winced.

"It's not like that, Lillian." Gabe shook his head. "He's—"

"No, don't start with the '*he's this or that*'." Frankie's expression resembled the sarge's after they'd majorly screwed up. "Why are you making Bull do everything?"

Caz held up his hands defensively before frowning at Bull. "You're the one with the business degree, 'mano. I'm swamped with the health clinic funding and paperwork."

"Same with me." Gabe shook his head. "I can't keep up with the police station budgets and paperwork. Being the chief involved more of it than I expected."

Bull eyed Hawk who never did paperwork if he could avoid it. He was a hands-on guy, could fix just about anything, from broken buildings to broken machines, and did all the maintenance for the Hermitage and their vehicles.

As expected, Hawk shook his head. "You don't want me doing accounting shit. Trust me. You like that stuff—and you know it."

"I do, but I don't want to spend 24/7 doing it," Bull said.

With a disgusted sound, Frankie turned to the other women.

"Maybe I'm blind, but I'm not seeing the teamwork Bull keeps boasting about."

"What teamwork?" JJ tilted her head. "That sarge of theirs obviously made this a one-man mission."

Caz's brows drew together.

"I thought there was a *no man left behind* rule," Audrey said. "Or is that only when the soldier is dead?"

Gabe scowled.

Bull blinked at the harshness of the comments delivered in soft female voices. But...when he sized up what he'd been doing from an outside point of view, well, yeah. He'd been screwed. By his brothers.

Dante shook his head. "He taught y'all better."

"F—" Gabe cut the profanity short after a glance at Regan. "You're right, Frankie. All of you. I'm sorry, Bull. Mako left the mission to all of us and that includes the properties—and the paperwork. Let's figure out how to divide up the work."

Audrey took Gabe's hand and smiled her approval.

JJ raised her eyes at Caz...who gave a pitiful sigh before nodding in resignation. "Sí."

A glimmer of hope rose inside Bull.

Frankie turned her gaze to Hawk who scowled, then sighed.

"Sorry, Bull." Hawk rubbed the scar that pulled his lip slightly upward, then made a harsh sound. "If you keep the damned renters and buyers away from me, I'll take over the maintenance and upgrades. I can deal with contractors and repair people. And Knox and Chevy, too. They're okay."

Damn, he'd never expected the hawk to step forward. "It'll be a relief to get maintenance off my back," Bull said. "You can take charge of all the physical upkeep."

"Renters and buyers—give them to me and Caz," Gabe said. "We'll work out how to deal with appointments and showings and complaints."

Caz nodded. "Sí, we can do that. We're both on-call, anyway. If it's repair problems, we'll toss the problem to Hawk and his group."

Hawk grunted his agreement.

Audrey tapped her lips as she thought. "You can give me the rental screenings and backgrounds. I can also take on the website and advertising."

Bull frowned. "I can't ask you to do—"

"Actually, you can." Audrey's voice quavered. "Being part of the family means pitching in." She held up her hand and turned a ring around. A diamond glinted at them.

Silence fell as everyone stared at the engagement ring.

Then Regan squealed in delight and rushed around to hug Audrey. "Now, I'll have an *aunt*!"

"'Mano, about time." With a wide grin, Caz slapped Gabe on the back of the head, then pulled Audrey into a hug and told her, "He talked to us a while ago, but...he's slow, the *viejo* is. He always has to think out his plan of action first."

To Bull's surprise, Hawk hugged Audrey, too, before shoving Gabe's shoulder. "Took you long enough."

Gabe laughed. "I asked her a few days ago. On the anniversary of our first meeting. It seemed...right."

Bull grinned. "Next, you'll start reading romances."

"Don't diss romance." Frankie's sharp elbow impacted Bull's ribs before she smiled at Audrey. "Was your first meeting amazing?"

Audrey burst out laughing. "He terrified me and then accused me of shoplifting." She gave Gabe a scorching glare before kissing him. "But you're *my* cop now."

The love in her eyes sent a pang of envy through Bull's heart. But, damn, he was glad his brother had found himself such a good woman. Someone to walk beside him, be with him for the long haul, and have his back when needed.

Bull pulled Audrey into a hearty hug. "Welcome to the family, champ."

He felt her tears on his shirt—sentimental little female—and handed her back to Gabe.

As he sat down beside Frankie, she was wiping under her eyes.

Make that two sentimental females.

Slinging an arm around Frankie's shoulders, he pulled her against his chest. And realized what she'd just done for him. Somehow, she'd saved him from death by paperwork by guilting his brothers into stepping up.

Last month, after Paisley's diva-act in the roadhouse parking lot, Dante said a lover was like a teammate on steroids. He was beginning to see what the Okie meant.

"Are you all right?" Frankie asked softly.

He kissed her lightly. "Thanks for having my back. I might have retreated otherwise."

"You probably would have," she agreed. "Family expectations can mess a person up."

Her tone wasn't bitter, but...resigned. Unhappy.

Frowning, he rested his chin on her head and wondered what expectations her family was forcing her to fulfill.

Perhaps he should investigate—and see what he could do to intervene. Because damned if he wasn't going to do his fucking best to keep her right here where she belonged.

He brushed his lips against hers and murmured in a voice for her ears only, "I love you, Frankie Bocelli."

And saw her eyes light up.

CHAPTER TWENTY

*I*f *you find yourself in a fair fight, you didn't plan your mission properly.* ~ David Hackworth

While Bull helped Hawk repair a lawn mower, Frankie joined Lillian and Audrey in the garden. The soil was warm and fragrant and soothing, and the small plants simply adorable. Baby greens were the best.

After that, Regan dragged her off for a quick aikido lesson while Sirius, the girl's cat, supervised.

"Frankie," Caz called from his deck. "I have something for you."

He met her at the foot of the steps and handed her a folded strip of paper. GIVE TO FRANKIE was written on the outside.

"What's this?" she asked.

"*No sé.* I was tossing the clothes I'd worn earlier into the laundry and found it in my lab coat pocket."

He wore a white lab coat at the health clinic. "Maybe a patient put the note into your pocket?"

"That would be my guess. It would have happened today since I change lab coats daily."

A chill ran up her spine. She knew only one person who might need to sneak her a message. "Well, thank you." Ignoring the curiosity in his gaze, she headed for the center of the lawn and away from everyone.

She opened the folded-up paper.

F,

They know you're here. Get out before they find you. I won't be here. O takes us away tomorrow. He won't tell me where.

Please, please, go home and be safe. Thank you for trying. It means everything.

Love you...and I'm sorry,

K

Frankie stared at the note. Read it again. Scowled at the misshapen letters. That wasn't Kit's writing. Was this a trick?

Or...

She ran onto Caz's deck and pounded on the door until he slid it open.

"Frankie, what's wrong?"

She waved the note. "Did you have a Patriot Zealot as a patient today? A young woman?"

His expression darkened. "Sí."

"Was something wrong with her right hand? A reason she couldn't write with it?"

He hesitated.

"Please, Doc," she pleaded. "It's not her writing, so I need to know."

"Ah." His face was grim. "The Patriot Zealots don't often come to me, but her right arm was broken. They tried to set it themselves but couldn't."

Broken. *Broken.* Oh, *Kit.* Those *bastardi* had hurt her. "Was she all right? Was she—"

Caz shook his head. "If your friend hadn't used me to convey her note—and if you didn't have a valid concern over who might have written it—I couldn't have told you even that much, *chica.* There are privacy rules. Don't ask me for more."

Of course, there were rules. All the rules. Nothing to protect Kit and Aric.

She clamped her jaw over the angry words. It wasn't his fault, and he'd told her what she needed to know. "Thanks. Really, Thanks, Doc." At least, for a while today, Kit had experienced some loving care.

Caz put his hand on her shoulder. "Frankie, talk to me. We can—"

She fled off the steps, her thoughts too frantic to even think about talking more.

The PZs knew Frankie was here. How had they found out? Was it something Kit had let slip? Had they realized who operated the drone or seen Frankie sneaking around the compound? Maybe Nabera realized why she'd been asking him questions. What if Obadiah had recognized her?

The reason how didn't really matter, though.

Nausea churned her stomach. Was this why the cabins had been burned?

She paced in circles on the lawn. *Think, Frankie, think.*

If they knew Frankie was here, they'd know Kit had called her here.

Kit had a broken arm.

They beat Kit up to punish her.

"Oh, *amica mia*, I'm sorry." The sick feeling in her stomach grew stronger.

If Obadiah planned to take Kit and Aric somewhere else, was it to kill her?

Fear buzzed in Frankie's ears, drowning out the sounds of everything else.

Keep it together. She mustn't panic. "It's up to me." But all of her backup plans would take time to implement.

She had the originals of the guardianship papers—in New York—but the same problems would apply. Even if she could get the cops here to move quickly, if they showed up at the gate, the PZs would simply eliminate Kit and Aric. If they attacked, well, a SWAT team, if Anchorage had one, would be up against a bunch of armed militia guys.

Everything would take too long.

Kit was out of time.

She stopped pacing and stared at the blue-green lake. Bull would help. She hadn't wanted to involve him when she had other alternatives—because he'd have insisted on helping. Risking his life. And her plan would've risked only her. But now...

Now it was a woman's and child's lives, and Frankie had no way to get them out. She needed his help.

She headed across the lawn and saw him standing by his deck. Waiting. He would've seen she was upset...and he'd given her space.

He walked down the steps to meet her.

"Bull."

He ran his hands up and down her upper arms, steadying her with just his touch. "Tell me, sweetheart."

"I need your help. Lots of help." She tried to slow her breathing. "Everything is a mess, and I think they're going to kill my friend. Please help us."

"Always. What do you need?"

Madonna, no wonder she loved him. "I have a friend who married a guy who is in the PZs and—"

"'*Mano*," Caz called. He and Gabe walked up. "I gave Frankie a message from a PZ woman who had bruises and a fractured arm."

"You..." Frankie frowned at the doc. "What about privacy?"

His mouth curled up. "Messages sneaked into my lab coat aren't covered under patient confidentiality, and I am mandated to report suspicion of abuse to local law enforcement." He tilted his head at Gabe.

"Do you want privacy—or assistance, bro?" Gabe asked.

"Could they be of help, sweetheart?" Bull motioned to his brothers. "They're offering."

Offering to help? Just like that? Her family wouldn't have helped. "Really?" Hope bloomed inside her.

Bull glanced at his brothers. "Let's talk at Mako's place."

"Yeah." Gabe's gaze dropped to the paper in Frankie's hand. "This smells a lot like a goatfuck. Caz, leave Regan at your place, but fetch Hawk and JJ. I'll get everyone else."

As she and Bull walked across the lawn to Mako's house, she tried to think—and was so incredibly grateful for the hard arm around her waist, the strength of Bull's body against hers. He guided her to a seat on the sectional and sat beside her.

She remembered the last time she was here—when she'd served them the Italian meal. Somehow it seemed as if music still lingered in the air. She'd spent that night with Bull and all the nights since.

She reached up to touch his jaw. His muscles were tense. Was he... *Oh, cavolo.* "Are you wondering how much of what was between us is a lie?"

His eyes were black when he looked down at her. "I had a moment of concern." His gaze softened. "But even though you didn't trust me with everything, I don't think you lied about how you feel about me."

"I didn't. I w-wouldn't. I thought I could get her out of there on my own and not risk you getting hurt." She blinked hard because...she knew, oh, she knew, how much it hurt to learn that love was a lie. Her voice came out a ragged whisper. "I love you. I *do*."

"*Shhh.* I believe you." He tucked her tightly against his side. "We'll figure out what to do."

In the next few minutes, the rest gathered. Gabe with Audrey, Lillian, and Dante. Caz brought JJ and Hawk.

Lillian took one glance at Frankie and settled beside her, taking her hand. "Now, love, what's this mess we're here to fix?"

The brisk question was like a crisp wind blowing away the cloudy fears.

Time to be clear and concise. *Focus, Frankie.* She drew a slow breath and started. "I have a friend, Kit, my bestie through college and after, and I'm godmother to her son, Aric. He's four now. In Texas, she married Obadiah, one of the Patriot Zealots."

Frankie rested her head against Bull's shoulder, so very comforted just to have him beside her. "I got a letter from Kit asking for help..." She continued to explain how she'd ended up in Rescue and how the children were held hostage to ensure their mothers' cooperation. "Kit was terrified that the police or FBI would try to get into the compound and get into a battle and the children would get hurt."

Gabe rubbed his chin. "Like the siege at Waco."

"And Ruby Ridge," Dante added. "She has a point."

"Is Kit the person who is on my records as Kirsten Traeger?" When Frankie nodded, Caz motioned to the paper she still held. "What did the message say?"

Unable to say the words out loud, Frankie handed it to Bull. He read it, his jaw turning hard, then gave the paper to Caz.

"I saw Kit at the grocery when I first got here. We planned that I'd cut the fence behind the children's barracks on a Saturday night. She'd sneak out with Aric, and I'd guide them out of the forest."

"That's how you got shot." Hawk snorted and looked at Bull. "She's gonna run you ragged."

Bull sighed. "Yep."

"It's not like I wanted to get shot," Frankie said. "I needed to locate the right trail and what guards might be able to see the barracks and—"

"The compound is huge, dear. You could circle it for hours

without learning what you needed to know." Lillian made a tsking sound.

"Actually, I'd already narrowed the location down to a couple of buildings near the east fence."

"Had you," Bull murmured. He tilted her chin up. "And how *exactly* did you do that?"

His face had the same expression as Nonna's when her grandmother found Frankie playing with a scorpion. In fact, all of Bull's brothers appeared dismayed.

Che palle, over-protective men. "I flew a drone over the compound and mapped part of it. There were children playing between two buildings. One of them would be the children's dorm."

"A drone." Audrey grinned. "That's really smart."

"Have you got the photos?" JJ asked. "I'd like to see them."

"I didn't get pictures of the entire compound." Frankie pulled out her new phone to flip through the photo gallery. Thank goodness she'd had everything backed up in the cloud. "They killed my poor drone. Shot it ri..."

The silence registered.

Oops.

Anger radiated off Bull's powerful body like heat waves off a New York sidewalk in summer. More than enough to scorch a person.

Jumping up, she handed JJ her phone.

"Thanks," JJ lowered her voice to a whisper. "You're in deep shit with the bull, I hope you know."

When Frankie rolled her eyes, the cop snorted a laugh...and grinned.

Maybe Bull's attitude was a touch insulting, yet his protectiveness warmed her more than the blanket he'd wrapped around her last night.

The patrol officer studied the phone's photos and enlarged a portion of one. "I see the children outside the buildings. You called them barracks. Does that mean the women don't live with their kids?"

"Kit said the women's barracks is next door to the children's. The kids have a matron in charge of their building."

"That might complicate matters." Caz turned to Gabe. "So, *viejo*, how're we going to do this?"

Frankie clasped her hands in her lap, hope and fear mingling. Because, unlike with her plan, the rescuers would have to go into the compound. "You do know—obviously—that they have guns."

"They have *rifles*, woman. I doubt they have artillery," Bull said.

Dante shook his head. "Let's hope not. Artillery would be bad."

They were correcting her grammar? Frankie stared at the two idiots—who both smiled at her.

Beside JJ, Caz flipped through the phone's photos. "We can get to the southeast fence and those buildings using the trail from Chevy and Knox's land."

Frankie nodded. "That's the one I'd planned to use."

"It goes past the corner watchtowers, though." He handed the phone to Gabe.

Gabe's brows drew together. "This is too small to see—"

"Eff-it-all, give me that." Audrey plucked the phone from his hand. "I'll run over to our cabin, download the photos, and enlarge the best ones."

"Perfect." Gabe pulled her down for a quick kiss. "You're my favorite tech goddess."

"I'm your favorite everything, Chief." Audrey hurried out of the house.

"Rather than rescuing just one boy and woman, seems like we should get them all out," Bull said.

"All?" Frankie held her breath. That would be wonderful.

"Hmm." Gabe leaned back on the sectional and stared at the ceiling for a silent minute. "It has possibilities. Remove the children—as well as any women who want to leave—would keep the PZs from using them as hostages. Handing the victims over to the authorities would minimize the legal problems."

JJ frowned. "We'll want social workers as well as law enforcement involved. If a mother is brainwashed or pressured, we don't want a child yanked back into an abusive situation."

Picking her hand up, Caz kissed her fingers. "Sí. That will keep the children safe."

Legal problems? Gabe and JJ were cops. Caz was a licensed health professional. Frankie chewed on her lip before asking, "Can we do this without breaking a million laws and getting you all in trouble?"

"We won't break more than a handful or so," Gabe said with a half-smile. "You can testify we have a reasonable belief that a child's life is at risk. Do you still have the letter Kit mailed you, or did it burn with your cabin?"

"It's in my office in New York. Safe." She relaxed slightly.

"Getting out intact is going to be a problem though. Herding women and children through a dark forest will take time," Bull said.

Dante nodded. "As Frankie pointed out, the PZs have *guns*." Despite the teasing words, his tone was serious.

He was right. Frankie considered and said, "A diversion?" even as Bull suggested, "Let's draw the sentries away."

"Yes." Gabe turned to Dante. "Could you round up some rowdy folks to create a diversion near their gate?"

"You betcha." Dante smiled at Lillian. "We know just the people."

Hurrying inside, Audrey laid an oversized map on the coffee table. "This is the best overall view of the compound. At least, most of it." She set a smaller one next to it. "This one shows the buildings with the children. I'll print off more for you, but these will get you started."

"That's perfect," Caz said. "Just what we need."

Audrey grinned. "I've learned how the *old man* likes to make plans."

Gabe shot her a chiding look, then chuckled. "Thank you, Goldilocks." He pulled forward the map that showed Dall Road and the turnoff to the PZ compound as well as the neighboring roads and cabins. His finger traced a route from the children's barracks, through the fence, then southward along the east to two cabins at the end of a road. "That's not an easy walk to Knox's and Chevy's, especially at night. We'll need woods-savvy volunteers to escort the rescues out so we can fight a rearguard action."

Rearguard action. She should have thought of that. The PZs would undoubtedly come after them. Frankie felt her spine straighten. They damn well wouldn't get near Kit or Aric.

"Could get messy." Hawk gave her a nod before leaning over the map. "I'll move the helicopter to the meadow behind Chevy's cabin. I'll come in without lights, so light me up a landing spot."

Madonna, they were *all* going to help her. She looked around the room. "Thank y-you." Her voice cracked.

Lillian squeezed her hand. "This is what families do."

"We have the helicopter for seriously wounded," Caz said. "For the rest, I'll load extra medic kits in my car."

Medic kits. Helicopters for the wounded. *Wounded.*

Bull could die. His family could die. She could still feel the impact of the bullet hitting her arm, see the red pouring over her skin. "Bull." His name came out almost inaudible, and she took his arm in her hands, trying not to shake.

There was no choice. This was the best plan to save little Aric. Save all those women and children. But the risk was... Guilt and fear and determination roiled together.

Caz was watching her. "I wondered how long it would take to hit her," he said to his brothers.

Hawk's snort sounded like a laugh.

Half-smiling, Gabe shook his head.

Bull lifted her into his lap and rubbed his cheek against hers. "Hey, it's been far too boring around here. This'll be fun."

"*Deficiente*." She yanked on his shirt to get him to listen. "You will be careful and take no chances. You will all be careful."

Bull gripped her wrists, and his gaze turned serious. "There is always a danger of being hurt when on a mission, but we've wanted to go after the Zealots for a good while now. Thank you for the perfect reason."

When she blinked in disbelief, Hawk moved his shoulders. "What he said."

"Exactly." Gabe smiled at her. "While we're setting up, I'll talk to the DEA and FBI. By the time their agents arrive, we should be back in Rescue with the women and children—and the PZs will have the feds to worry about. Now, let's finish getting this planned out."

Caz frowned. "They have dogs and wandering sentries."

Frankie leaned forward and set her finger on a square. "Here, this is the corner watchtower guard that overlooks the area behind the women's barracks."

Hawk stretched his legs out and smiled slightly. "Watchtower's mine."

Before she could respond, Bull said, "Gryff and I might have an idea or two about the dogs. Gryff'll want to play." His dark eyes glinted with laughter.

Frankie shook her head. Mako must have had an...interesting...sense of humor because his sons seemed to have inherited it.

At Obadiah's small prefab, Kit was trying to make his bed with one hand. Her right arm was in a sling and ached like...like a broken bone. God, it had hurt so much worse than when he'd snapped two of her fingers. Even more than when he'd broken one of her ribs. The memory, the sound of her arm breaking still echoed within her other bones, leaving a shivery feeling inside.

Her husband sat at the small table and ate the pie she'd brought him from the cafeteria. He liked making her wait on him. Especially on the nights he wasn't on sentry duty and he could fuck her before he went to bed.

Oh, Frankie, you were so right about him.

Fear for her friend made her fidget. They knew about Frankie, and Obadiah had asked over and over why she'd have come to Alaska. Kit kept repeating that Frankie'd always wanted to vacation in Alaska. Obadiah had lost his temper and broken her arm, ending the questions.

Because she'd passed out.

They knew, though. They knew Frankie was here for Kit. If Nabera thought Frankie had learned too much, he'd hurt her, even kill her.

How could I have been so selfish to put Frankie's life at risk?

Pattering footsteps sounded outside, then Aric raced through the door, slamming into her legs.

He's why.

She bent to hug her son, breathing in the wild fragrance of little boy. Oh, she would risk Frankie's life, her own life, the whole world for him.

"What are you doing here, you little bastard?" Obadiah slammed his fist on the table, making Aric jump.

Stepping away, her boy clasped his hands at his waist and bowed his head.

"He's finished his work and came to say good night." Kit tried for a light tone, then turned to Aric. "Get on back to your barracks, honey." She hugged him with her uninjured arm and whispered, "Sweet dreams, my baby."

Be safe. Oh, please, be safe.

Without speaking—something he did less and less—Aric trotted out the door. He might go back to the barracks; he might not. Within a month of being here, her son had found every hiding place possible. Other children tried to hide; Aric succeeded.

"Whiny-ass brat." Obadiah turned his attention back to his food, chewing it thoroughly. Crumbs tangled in his yellow-brown beard.

Hoping not to attract his attention—his interest—she concentrated on tucking in the blankets.

With a loud belch, Obadiah pushed the empty plate away. "Clean up good before you go to bed. Captain Nabera's going to pay you a visit some time tonight. When he gets back."

Her balance wavered, like the floor had sagged beneath her. "Why?"

"He says you know more 'n you're saying." Her husband's jaw jutted forward. "You better not lie to him, or you'll learn what a real beatin' is."

"I told you the truth," she whispered, going clammy with fear.

"If so, he'll probably reward you with a cleansing."

She'd undergone those "cleansings" before with Nabera. With Parrish.

Frankie would call those sessions rape.

Me, too. As sickness welled inside her, Kit started to gag.

Obadiah slapped her to the floor, and pain exploded in her head. "Get those sinful, hate-filled thoughts out of your head. The Captain is right. You need to be purified."

Holding her hand to her burning face, Kit regained her feet. Her arm throbbed, but she kept her head bowed.

She probably wouldn't survive the next twenty-four hours.

What will happen to my baby?

Damn. Bull had known Frankie had secrets, ones that involved the PZs. The truth, though, was a hell of a lot more than he figured.

"We're going downstairs," he told her and held open the door to the stairway for her.

He might've been angrier except he understood her reasons. If she'd told him, he would have insisted on going with her, and she hadn't wanted to put him at risk. Not if she could accomplish the mission herself. He'd have felt the same.

Her loyalty to her friend? Well, fuck, he had to love that about her. Who wouldn't?

With her behind him, he led the way down to the tunnels that connected the five houses together. The cool, damp air held the harsh tang of minerals...and weaponry.

Because, naturally, the sarge had built a bomb shelter as well as an armory beneath his house. *Mako, you were one crazy bastard.*

His brothers and JJ were already in the room, pulling out what they wanted to take.

A few feet past the thick armory door, Frankie stopped to stare.

Bull smiled. "Impressive, isn't it? Mako did most of the construction himself."

Rough-cut wood panels with iron brackets lined the walls. One side held semi-automatic handguns and revolvers like the S&W Magnums and Glocks. The adjacent wall displayed semi-automatic shotguns like Kalashnikovs. There were AK-47s, AR-15s. Hunting rifles like the Ruger 10/22 as well as old-fashioned Mossbergs and Remington pump shotguns.

Naturally, the paranoid survivalist had also accumulated anything a soldier needed for an apocalypse—from grenades to night vision goggles.

Okay, so maybe Sarge wasn't the only crazy one.

Over the years, they'd all contributed to the fun.

The hip-high counters held pull-out drawers with ammunition. The far corner had reloading equipment and supplies. An oversized table in the center of the room was for cleaning and assembling.

"This is... Is this stuff even legal?" After dropping the backpack she'd retrieved from his house, Frankie turned in a circle.

JJ glanced over. "Most of it. When it comes to preppers in Alaska, it's apparently 'don't ask, don't tell'. However, unless civilization collapses, using things like explosives in inhabited areas is called terrorism and wins the user many years of free meals behind bars."

"Oh. Okay," Frankie said in a faint voice.

Gabe looked over. "Gear up, bro."

"Yeah." Bull grabbed a body-armor vest in dark camo.

Around him, his brothers and JJ were doing the same.

In the short time before arming up, Gabe and Caz made calls and pulled strings. They'd done all they could, and now it was up to Audrey to organize the incoming health professionals, social services, and law enforcement. Bull didn't worry; the woman was superb at juggling resources.

Lillian and Dante had already left, taking Regan with them. His niece would spend the night with her bestie.

The two seniors were recruiting trustworthy people and getting them to the right place at the right time. The plan called for a lot of volunteers, some for the distraction, others to guide the women and children out. Even more would help transport everyone to town.

The mission was organized with Gabe's usual attention to detail. They'd penetrate the compound during the darkest hours of the night—between 1:00 and 3:30 a.m. Before and after that, the twilight-gray sky would be too light for covert endeavors.

The narrow window of opportunity was worrisome.

"If we—" Bull's mind stuttered to a stop.

Frankie was trying on a small bulletproof vest—the one Caz had worn as a skinny teenager.

Jesus fuck. "What are you doing?" He thought that was a very reasonable question.

"You're all wearing body armor. I thought you'd want me to wear one, too."

"I would if you were going on this op. But you'll be in town with Audrey and coordinating the agencies." Bull's voice hadn't risen; he was sure it hadn't, but Caz turned away hastily with a smothered snicker.

"Shh." JJ punched the doc in the belly.

"Frankie, you'll be in town. Safe in town," Bull repeated, in case she didn't understand what he'd just said.

"No. I'm going with you to the compound." Frankie settled the vest on her shoulders.

Bull's gut clenched like he'd eaten a barrel of green apples. Like his woman had just told him she planned to walk into what would likely turn into a fucking firefight. "No. No, you're not."

When she rolled her eyes and eyed the handguns, he turned to the one person to whom she might listen. "Gabe. You're in charge."

His brother folded his arms over his chest and eyed Frankie. "Convince me."

"Easy enough." She set her hands on her hips like Mom had done when squaring off against Dad. Bull's heart gave a painful twang.

"You guys are huge, even before you add the armor. All in black. Deadly." Frankie shook her head, frowned, and started to braid her hair back. "You're forgetting these women have been abused. Why in the world would they go with you? You're going to come across as even more terrifying than the cult fanatics."

Bull opened his mouth, closed it. Cleared his throat. "We'll tell Kit that you sent us."

"Maybe she would believe you...eventually." Frankie looked at Gabe. "In that plan of yours, did you build in time to explain matters?"

The sour expression on Gabe's face said she was right.

She'd be coming with them.

"God-fucking-son-of-a-*bitch*." Bull heard the echo off the walls and winced. Hell, that was his raised voice.

Frankie didn't even flinch, just chuckled. "I love you, too. And I know I'm no soldier, and I'm scared spitless, but I need to be there so Kit trusts you. If she does, maybe the rest will, too."

She loved him. Said it out loud in front of his brothers. Fuck, but he'd never tire of hearing that no matter how many years they lived.

She was scared...and going along anyway. Her loyalty to a friend left him in awe.

Bull gripped her arms, and the feeling of her tense muscles was its own reassurance. She did know how to fight. Could hold her own. He leaned his forehead against hers. "Jesus, woman."

"Yeah, I know."

Hauling in a breath, he fixed her with a hard stare. "You'll obey orders. From Gabe, me, Caz, Hawk, and JJ. Immediately. No questions or arguments. Immediately."

She glanced at the weaponry covering the armory walls. Her lips tilted slightly. "Don't worry, *orsacchiotto*. I know when I'm at the bottom of the rank and file."

CHAPTER TWENTY-ONE

If you are going through hell, keep going. ~ Winston Churchill

Frankie's world had shrunk to the narrow trail and to Bull who was in front of her. Thank heavens she'd become proficient at hiking while wearing her night vision monocular. Using her jo as a walking stick also helped.

As she'd learned on her previous forays, the trail at night was vastly different than during the daytime. The scents of spruce and damp undergrowth were more pungent. There were noises—owls hooting or worse, the whap-whap sound of big wings overhead. Startled animals crashed away through the bushes. One big animal could sound like a whole stampede.

Overhead, the tree canopy was dense, giving only glimpses of the three-quarters-full moon.

Everyone wore night vision equipment. Bull and his brothers had their own and handed out extras to the volunteers who needed them. Not many did. The guys who hunted had their own, as did JJ as part of her cop gear.

When Bull offered Frankie a pair, she'd pulled out her own along with the head mount—and shown she was familiar with it all. She was gifted quite the measuring stare.

Near the beginning of the path, she received another long look from all four of the guys when they saw the line of glowing spots that marked the trail to the compound.

That reflective paint worked well.

Nevertheless, it was still a long hike. Her legs were tired. Her neck ached from the weight of the NVM that pulled her head sideways. She was relieved when Gabe halted the line.

They were still far enough in the forest to remain hidden from the compound but much closer than she'd dared since the first time.

Bull came to stand beside her and gave her a warm squeeze around the waist. He bent to whisper, "Rest and I'll be back soon," then disappeared down another trail with Gryff at his heels.

Waiting time.

Being patient really sucked. Especially alone. Only, she really wasn't, not with all the others around her. Now that she'd stopped, she could feel the fine tremor in her hands. Her lungs felt constricted; her heart was beating too fast.

We're coming, Kit.

She squeezed her paint-darkened staff. No firearms for her. Not after Hawk mentioned that people unused to combat tended to hose down everything around them—including their team.

She'd stick to the non-lethal jo. *I don't want to kill anyone.* But she would if it meant keeping her people alive.

Rifle in hand, Hawk moved silently away, his objective a tall tree across from the corner watchtower. Bull called him a sniper and said he was the finest shot of any of them.

Good luck, Hawk.

His first job was to shoot the watchtower guard with a tranquilizer. His second... Bull had suggested that, since Hawk would be climbing a tree, he might as well set up the remote-activated device containing a recording of Gabe's voice. Hawk's response had been rude, but he agreed.

A touch on her shoulder made her jump.

The eerie night vision goggles he wore made Caz look like an alien. He set a hand on her arm reassuringly before checking on JJ who was hunkered down under a different tree.

Frankie glanced over her shoulder. All the people behind her were also taking the opportunity to rest. Chevy and Knox nodded to her. The helicopter and cars were parked at their properties. She could barely see Uriah, who owned the coffee shop, or the group of backwoods guys like Tucker, Guzman, Harvey, and Rasmussen who she knew from the bar. The school principal and the old hippie gas station owner were at the rear of the line.

These men, as well as the diversion group, had volunteered simply because Mako's sons, Audrey, and JJ had asked for help.

Frankie shook her head, thinking of the stories shared while waiting at Chevy's place for everyone to arrive. She'd heard how Gabe and Bull found Chevy's lost son after a bear attack. How JJ saved Rasmussen's life after an earthquake, then risked her life to rescue trapped schoolchildren. Audrey taught Knox how to read. Caz tended their illnesses. Hawk flew emergency flights to the city hospitals. The Hermitage family was...there...for the community. Feeding people, helping with repairs for people down on their luck, organizing community events, improving the town.

The volunteers were delighted that Bull and his brothers had asked them for help. Frankie smiled slightly. And all of them were pleased to thwart the Patriot Zealots.

Suddenly, a long howl from the southwest, broke the silence.

Go, Gryff.

Inside the compound, the dogs went crazy, barking and howling and yipping. Guards shouted irately.

Frankie turned her gaze toward the watchtower and caught the greenish outline of the guard. He was standing where he could monitor the area where Gryff was howling. No matter what kind of vision enhancement he had, it wouldn't do him any good if he was turned away from the forest where Hawk would be climbing that tree.

During the planning, the Hermitage guys had discussed using tranquilizers. How no tranq worked immediately, but would take a few minutes, the danger to the guard, that Hawk would have to climb a tree to shoot. But they didn't have much choice. None of them were willing to kill the guard.

But the corner watchtower overlooked the area where they'd be cutting the fence. Mako's sons could sneak in, but the guard couldn't miss seeing the untrained women and children escaping.

If Hawk couldn't silence the guard, the mission would be aborted.

Frankie crossed her fingers.

A few minutes later, Gryff started howling again. Again, there was a cacophony of barking from the PZ's guard dogs.

Frankie checked the watchtower. The silhouette of the guard had disappeared. *Way to go, Hawk!* He must be as good a sniper as the guys had claimed.

In front of Frankie, Gabe headed for the fence, crossing the open area between the tree line and the PZ fence. Branches inserted in his jacket broke up his silhouette, and the two huge bolt cutters he carried were painted black and wrapped in dark mottled fabric. The Hermitage had one set of bolt cutters. She contributed the other.

Moving slowly, somehow, he disappeared right into the shadows. That camo stuff was really effective. At the fence, he met up with Hawk, the two men creating a slightly darker spot against the silvery fence wires. They would be using the bolt-cutters now, the sound covered by the barking and yelling.

When the noise died, the two crouched and went motionless.

Gryff set off the dogs two more times.

"Put the fucking beasts in their kennels. I am done with this shit." Someone yelled from inside the compound. A chill ran through Frankie at the sound of Nabera's voice.

"Yes, Captain!" one of the guards shouted.

Frankie exchanged grim nods with JJ. Goal achieved. *Gryff, you are such a good dog.* There would be no dogs running loose in the compound. Perfect.

A few minutes later, Bull and Gryff ghosted back, getting silent nods and approving grins as they squeezed past the line of men.

When Bull put his arm around her shoulders, she leaned against him, and a knot in her stomach relaxed. He was all right. After giving her a squeeze, he nudged Caz, then made a soft sound like one of the birds she'd heard by the lake.

Letting Gabe know he was back.

No one moved.

They waited.

Soon, soon.

The sound of approaching cars from the other side of the compound was the first warning of the main diversion. Brakes squealed. Metal screeched and clanged. Glass broke. People were shouting.

"Time to party," Bull whispered and moved out. He'd already put on a camo balaclava with the night vision goggles over it.

Unless they found Kit and thus had proof she was held against her will, the rescuers would keep their faces covered. Since they were, after all, breaking and entering.

Slow and silent, she reminded herself, rolling down her own balaclava and following him toward the fence. Balance on one foot, set the other down, adding weight while feeling for anything that might snap. Rinse and repeat. Squint eyes to hide the whites. At least, the balaclava hid her white teeth.

The guard in the watchtower was tranked, but there might— probably would be—people moving around inside the compound.

Probably even some guards to keep the women inside, if nothing else.

The fence loomed up with Gabe, Hawk, and Bull crouched at the base, tucking their night vision goggles and head mounts away inside various pockets. She settled beside Bull and did the same. His squeeze on her shoulder, in an obvious *well done,* eased the fear flooding her bloodstream. JJ appeared, going down on one knee beside Hawk. A few seconds later, another shadow joined them, and Frankie jumped. She hadn't seen or heard Caz's approach at all.

Then again, there was a *lot* of shouting and banging and honking coming from the front gate. The diversion volunteers had been very enthusiastic about their job, especially after Zappa, the gas station owner, had donated two beat-up cars for them to crash.

Against the fence, the transportation volunteers hunkered down to wait until summoned. Bull handed Gryff's leash to Knox and got a betrayed look from the dog.

Rising, Gabe slipped through the opened flap of fence. He'd left some top links to hold up the person-sized cut section. The fence still appeared intact to all but a close inspection.

After checking the area, Gabe motioned for the assault team. As Hawk held the fence open, Caz, JJ, Bull, and Frankie side-stepped into the compound.

Gabe led them toward the back of two shabby prefabs—the barracks for the women and children.

Lights on the corners of the buildings made bright pools on the ground, leaving the rest in shadow. At least they were out of sight of the watchtowers on the corners of the fence. Frankie tried to swallow, but her mouth was too dry.

Children's quiet voices came from the building to the left. Thumps and a woman's hoarse cries sounded from the right, which must be the women's barracks. Surely, they didn't have sex in there with others watching.

Aric and Kit would be in these buildings. Almost too afraid to hope, Frankie reached out, and Bull took her hand, squeezing it in reassurance.

A closer examination showed the back doors were secured with heavy iron grillwork. So were the windows. Anger shunted aside Frankie's fear for a moment. The *bastardi* obviously didn't want anyone leaving the buildings—even if it meant the occupants would burn if there was a fire.

Having checked the door and grillwork, Gabe shook his head and whispered, "It'd be too noisy to break in here. Bull, you and Frankie take left. Caz and JJ, right. Hawk and I'll go in the front door and open this from the inside."

As Gabe and Hawk went between the two buildings, Frankie followed Bull. Her legs felt like wooden pegs, as if they didn't belong to her at all. Her heart pounded so hard it seemed like any guards inside the compound would hear it.

Thankfully, the diversion was still noisy. From the front gate came Felix's distinctive voice. "I'm saying that you crashed my car, you scum-sucking, boot-licking turd, and I'm taking you to court."

"This isn't the fucking courthouse," another man yelled. "Get yer asses out of here. This's a private road."

"It's not private on this side of the gate. We can be here if we want to." That was a young woman. Erica, maybe? Or Amka? "What an asshole."

Frankie almost snorted. *Okay, not shy Amka.*

Peering around the rightmost building's corner, Bull held up his hand with two fingers extended. *Two guards.*

Frankie cringed, then firmed her resolve. She'd do what she had to do. Around the corner, she stayed in the darkness beside the building. The dark camo made Bull hard to see—so very reassuring since she was dressed the same way.

A short distance away, their targets stood together, listening to the altercation on the road. "Maybe we should go help?" one said.

In the shadows, Bull moved past the two men and turned, ready to attack from that side.

Noiselessly, Frankie gripped her jo and steadied her breathing. She found the calm space where her mind flowed together with her body and her energy.

This was what must be done, and she'd do it well.

In silence, Bull charged.

Just as quietly, Frankie sped the few steps to hit her target from behind. The short staff came down right on Mr. Spock's favorite spot—the brachial plexus pressure point near where his neck met his shoulder.

The man dropped like a rock.

She had only seconds before he'd recover and yell. Even as she yanked his arms back and into the tactical zip tie cuffs, Bull was doing the same with his downed opponent.

Shoving a wad of cloth into her *bastardo's* mouth, she secured it with duct tape. According to Hawk, duct tape was easy to get rid of, but Chevy would watch over the captive guards during the mission.

Please, let this all be over quickly.

Inside the building, there were thumping sounds and squeaks of frightened children. Gabe and Hawk must have entered.

At the front gate, the altercation had grown louder.

"You're gonna have to pay for this!" Was that Raymond, the bartender? "Are you drunk? You bitches shouldn't be allowed to drink. Or drive. Hell, or vote, either."

He got a rousing cheer from what sounded like more guys than in the diversion group. Some PZ men must have joined in. Frankie almost laughed, knowing Raymond was more of a feminist than she was.

Grabbing her opponent's jacket, she dragged him into the shadows, following Bull to the back of the building. The PZ really needed to lose some weight. Sweating, she reached the now open back door.

The transporters were already running up to get a child and hauling ass back to the forest. Her heart squeezed in hope—and worry. *Keep them safe, guys.*

In the doorway, Gabe handed a wide-eyed little girl to Rasmussen who immediately turned and headed for the opening in the fence. All in silence.

Caz handed over the next child to Knox.

Frankie shook her head. Anywhere else, children would be screaming bloody murder at being handled by strangers. Not here in this abusive place. Heartrending as it was, the abuse worked in the rescuer's favor. The children were more afraid of making noise than of the balaclava-masked men.

With a grunt, Bull tossed his man through the door.

Show off. Frankie tried to drag her man up the single step—and got stuck.

Bull's eyes crinkled, and he threw her guy inside, too.

Approaching with another couple of children, Gabe side-stepped the trussed-up PZs. He nodded at Bull and Frankie. "Good job. We only had the matron and a PZ guard in here."

Frankie stopped beside Caz. "Did Aric get out?" They'd all studied her godson's picture and promised to watch for him.

"No, *chica*. We haven't seen him yet." His dark eyes were worried.

More children were given over to the rescuers until, aside from the tied-up PZ, the room was empty.

Fear squeezed Frankie's heart. She stalked over to the matron. "Where is Aric?"

The woman shook her head frantically.

"I already asked." Gabe set a hand on Frankie's shoulder. "She doesn't know, but he often sneaks out to be with his mama. He's probably in the women's building."

Another man entered from the back door, camo balaclava firmly in place. Frankie recognized short-statured Chevy only because his impressive musculature made him almost as wide as he was tall. He nodded to Bull. "I'm your asshole-sitter for the evening."

"Good timing." Bull motioned to the row of tied-up PZs on the floor. "Watch for breathing or gagging problems. Give him a knife, bro."

Caz handed Chevy one of the myriad of knives he carried.

Bull continued. "A knife gives them an incentive to stay quiet. Slashing faces—or balls—works well."

One of the tied-up men paled and drew his legs together.

"Fun times." Chevy thumbed the blade carefully. "Nice. Even nicer that I won't get stuck cleaning up blood this time around."

Frankie blinked. He sure didn't sound like the cheerful handyman she'd met in the roadhouse.

His act worked. From the way the prisoners stared at him, they wouldn't make a peep.

"Listen for the signal to leave," Bull instructed, got an affirming nod, and went out the back door with Frankie.

Outside, JJ had appropriated a guard's jacket and had changed the balaclava to a stocking hose to blur her facial features. Pretending to be one of their guards, she strolled casually around the area.

Between the two buildings, Gabe waited at the front corner with Hawk and Caz. He glanced over and tapped his ear.

Tilting her head, Frankie listened and heard men's voices coming from inside the building. Her stomach sank. They'd hoped the building would contain only women, not men.

Shades blocked any view of the inside. And the front door was the only entry. There was no way to take the men by surprise, and a noisy fight would alert the rest of the compound.

Bull shrugged as if to say no choice.

When Gabe took a step, Frankie grabbed his arm and whispered, "Let me go first. It'll take a second for them to notice my clothing. If I keep their attention, you might be able to deal with them without too much noise."

All four men frowned at her. So protective.

Well, she probably appeared terrified...because she was. She lifted her chin and glared. Letting Bull—any of them—get killed, wasn't going to happen if she could prevent it.

Gabe nodded. "Safest option."

"Dammit." Bull set his hand on her arm. "Do it."

"I love you," she breathed. She yanked off her balaclava and stuffed it inside her vest. After tugging her hair out of the braid, she mussed it up. Bedroom hair.

Hawk chuckled. A faint rasp. "Clever girl."

Caz squeezed her shoulder in reassurance. "We'll be right after you."

"I'll draw their attention to the right." *Okay, okay, I can do this.* Using her short staff as if she were injured, she limped into the women's building. A quick glance took in the women sitting on the bunk beds that lined the right and left walls. She headed right.

Three men stood in the center of the room. Two looked over at her.

Frankie raised her voice. "Mary? I was told to get you and—" As if she'd just noticed the men, she waved her free hand in the air in an eye-catching gesture. "Oh, hey, sorry."

And now, she saw that the third man in the room was Obadiah. Not even noticing her entry, he scowled down at—

Covered in blood, Kit lay curled in a shuddering ball on the floor.

"Stupid bitch." Obadiah drew his booted foot back.

"*No!*" Frankie charged him. Too far. She'd never get there—

Hawk dove through the doorway and slammed into Obadiah. The two flew back, hitting a heavy bunk bed with a crash.

Bull lunged across the room. His punch knocked one man to the floor. Gabe took out the other.

Kit. Oh, Kit. Dropping her staff, Frankie knelt, afraid to even touch her friend. So much blood. "*Cazzo*, what did they do to you?"

Kit was making little grunts of pain, her breathing far too fast and shallow. Blood poured from a long gash down her face and covered her clothing. A cast on her arm was half-shattered. Her eyes opened.

Gently squeezing her hand, Frankie leaned down. "I'm here, *amica mia*. We're getting you and Aric out of this place."

Kit blinked. "Fran—I didn't tell. Didn't." The awareness faded from her eyes.

When Caz crouched beside Frankie, Bull gripped her shoulder. "Let the doc work, sweetheart. We need you to ask if anyone is coming with us."

But...Kit. Frankie watched for a few seconds as Caz's hands moved over her friend's body. The doc was caring and competent and gentle. Kit was safe with him.

Right. She tried to stand, but all the strength had left her legs. She took Bull's hand. "Help?"

"Always." He pulled her to her feet and kept a steadying hand under her arm.

"We have to find Aric," she told him.

"We will."

Gabe joined them. "The bastards welded the back door of *this* building shut. Didn't trust the women, I guess. You'll have to exit out the front." Gabe's voice lowered. "We have too many men in here—I'll send JJ in and take watch."

"Got it." Bull drew Frankie forward toward the women on the bunk beds.

Over to the left, Hawk pushed to his feet. Obadiah lay on the floor, unmoving.

The two men who Bull and Gabe had downed also lay on the floor, already zip tied. She blinked in surprise, realizing one was Captain Nabera, the black-bearded older man from the bar. He'd been watching Obadiah kick Kit? To make an example of her. Frankie's hands fisted.

Her gaze ran around the room, seeing the women on the beds.

The cowards had just sat there, letting the men hurt Kit. Frankie had half a mind to just walk out of the place and let them rot.

She started to glare at them.

But...they didn't even notice her. All of them were cringing, shaking, and staring at Hawk, Caz, and Bull. At the male rescuers.

Their faces were wet with tears, eyes reddened and puffy. They'd been crying for Kit and...were too frightened to help. Frankie's anger snuffed out. How long could courage last in the face of pain. Of threats to children? The only blame should go to where it belonged, to the abusers.

Okay, I'll get you out. If you'll come.

Could she talk them into leaving?

Maybe. After all, she'd been reassuring Bocelli's timid new hires since she was sixteen. She took a slow breath, found the calm at her center, and let it flow into her voice. "Ladies, I'm Kit's friend. She asked me to get her and Aric away from this prison, away from being beat up and hurt. We're leaving with her now, but if you want, we'll take you with us."

Silence. Then one woman whispered. "They have my daughter."

Frankie expected Bull to speak, but he inclined his head toward JJ who stood in the doorway.

JJ's features were blurred by the stocking mask—but she was visibly female as was her strong, husky voice. "All the children from the barracks are already out. They're being taken to town and to the authorities where they'll be safe. If you want out of this place, come now."

Two women stood up.

The others shook their heads, and their frightened voices filled the room.

"They won't let us go."

"They'll come after us."

"We'll never get away."

Yanking off her stocking mask, JJ set her hand on her weapons belt, her posture military straight. "I'm Officer Jayden with the Rescue Police Department. If you want to leave, we *will* keep you safe. But you come with us right now...or stay here. Your choice."

Three more rose and stepped forward.

"How do we know it's not a trick?" whispered a very battered young woman.

Frankie's heart broke. But she lifted her chin. "I'm Kit's friend, and I arranged this. It's no trick."

Could they find the courage to leave?

With a moan of pain, Kit opened her eyes. She swallowed, then glared half-blindly at the women. Her voice was barely a whisper. "Go with Frankie, you idiots."

So that was Frankie's buddy, Hawk thought. The woman couldn't even see straight, could barely talk, but her thoughts were for her fellow women.

He had to respect that kind of loyalty.

Bending, Hawk checked the pulse of the bastard at his feet. Nothing. He'd tackled the asshole, and they'd hit the bedframe so hard it'd busted the guy's neck.

It was a righteous kill—the asshole had been trying to kick the woman to death—yet it was one more body to add to the total on Hawk's soul.

With an effort, Hawk shook loose of the guilt and checked out the situation.

With her staff in hand, Frankie was chivvying the PZ women out of the building after JJ who'd taken the lead. The terrified little flock detoured widely around Bull and Caz and were holding onto each other.

A few were still on their beds, unwilling to leave—true believers who'd downed the Kool-Aid.

Bull went outside to guard them until they reached the fence where the transport team would guide them through the forest.

Hawk didn't try to help. Hell, he terrified normal women with his scars and tats. If he tried to help this batch, they'd scatter into hiding like a flock of ptarmigans.

But he could serve as a pack mule for Frankie's damaged friend.

Caz looked up. "Need to find the child, 'mano." He was applying field dressings to stop the worst of the bleeding.

Fuck, they'd worked her over good. Hawk scowled.

No one, especially not a woman, should be brutalized like that. Just seeing her bruises brought back the shocking pain of his father's big fist hitting his face. The way a kick in the belly had left him curled up, unable to even breathe. The nauseating agony of a busted bone.

With a low grunt, he shook himself free of the fucked-up memories. "I'll check the ro—"

A movement caught his eye.

A little boy wiggled out from under a bed and darted toward the woman.

Hawk grabbed the kid before he landed on her. "Uh-uh. She's hurt, buddy."

The boy went nuts, squirming and kicking and fighting to get to Kit—and yeah, this must be her son. "Aric."

At his name, the kid went limp, staring up at Hawk with the biggest blue eyes he'd ever seen. Haunted, terrified eyes. His high voice was the merest whisper. "Mommy's hurt."

Jesus. Hawk felt like someone had stabbed him right in the chest. "Yeah, she's hurt. But we'll take her to the hospital. Get her help."

On the floor, Kit opened her eyes. "Aric." Her voice wasn't any louder than her son's. She blinked, trying to focus. Saw her boy in Hawk's arms. Her gaze rose to meet Hawk's and she...looked...at him. The kind of look that penetrated past the surface. Her voice was barely a whisper. "Keep him safe."

Before he could answer, tell her that no kid would want to be around him, her gaze dropped to her son. "Aric, stay with him."

A second later, she was out cold.

"*Cabrones*," Caz was muttering as he rose.

Bull and Frankie appeared in the doorway—and Frankie stared at the child in Hawk's arms. "You found him."

Hawk nodded.

Caz turned to Bull and motioned to the unconscious woman. "'Mano, you carry her. We'll take guard."

"On it." Bull lifted Kit gently.

"I can take the boy," Caz said to Hawk.

Hawk tried to hand him over, but the kid had a death grip on his vest, and his little mouth was compressed with determination.

He didn't make a sound, though—a lesson often learned from catching a backhand to the mouth for speaking. That's how Hawk had learned.

"We're good," Hawk muttered.

Caz blinked in surprise before smiling in agreement. "Then I'll guard your six, 'mano."

"*We.* We'll guard." Frankie swept up her staff and gave Hawk a firm nod.

As he walked past her with the boy, she followed, ready to defend them with everything she had.

Hawk snorted softly. Bull had found himself a stand-up woman.

The PZ women had already disappeared into the night when Frankie followed the others out of the building with Caz bringing up the rear.

Shivering, she pulled in a long breath of the cold, clean night air, free of the stink of blood and fear. Somewhere closer to the center of the compound, men were talking quietly. Off in the forest, an owl hooted.

Her gait faltered. The noise at the front gate had stopped. Their diversion was gone.

Merda. Everything inside her wanted to run...run out the fence to the shelter of the forest. She mustn't.

Gabe led the way at a measured pace—because running would instantly draw attention. The fence seemed so far away. The tension in her muscles made it difficult to even move. *Please, don't let us be discovered now.*

Trying to saunter, she followed the others into the shadows between the two buildings. Gabe thumped on the side of the children's barracks, and at the rear, Chevy came out the back door.

At last, they reached the opening in the fence where JJ kept watch. *Almost to safety. Almost.* Chevy edged out, then held the cut chain-link section open for the rest of them.

Bull went next. Kit lay unconscious in his arms, her breathing labored. Frankie's hands fisted. Caz said her ribs were cracked and broken. If Obadiah's kick had hit her, she would've died.

Bless you, Hawk.

Bull passed Kit to Chevy. "Move fast—and carefully." The muscular woodworker headed for the forest at a quick, smooth pace.

Get her out, Chevy. Please.

Frankie slipped through the fence and held it as Hawk went through with Aric, clinging like a little monkey, in his arms. She felt a pang, wanting to reassure the child, but it wouldn't help. He was so young he probably didn't even remember her.

JJ and Gabe came through, and Gabe leaned forward to tell Hawk, "Move out and catch up with Chevy. Precious cargo."

"Yeah." Hawk took off, sliding from shadow to shadow.

Meanwhile, Caz snapped on two padlocks to pull the cut fencing edges together at knee height.

As they all headed for the open area, Frankie took up position just behind Bull.

"Intruders!" A shout shattered the quiet. "Back of the women's barracks!"

The alarm spread. Men yelled. Ran toward the fence.

"Spread out and get to the forest!" Gabe pushed JJ after Frankie.

Gripping her staff, Frankie tore across the open area, arms pumping, shoulders hunched as if she could make herself a smaller target.

Loud swearing filled the air as the PZs were forced to squirm through the fence opening that'd been constricted by the padlocks.

The crack of gunfire sounded, and terror made Frankie almost drop to the ground.

"Zigzag," Bull yelled.

She veered right, then left. Bullets hit the ground near her, and dirt sprayed up. *Zig.* A tree in the forest splintered. *Zag. Don't be predictable.* She lunged left again. A sharp sound came from her right as a bullet hit a rock.

On one side, Gabe cursed, staggered, and ran again. Ahead of them, JJ reached the forest. Off to the left, Caz disappeared into the undergrowth.

Even as Frankie picked a possible opening, it felt as if a staff had whipped across her back flank. Staggering, she plunged into the foliage, arms up to protect her eyes as branches whipped against her clothing. A second later, someone followed almost on her heels.

She spun, jo rising.

"Run," Bull snapped.

Oh, thank God.

She ran again.

From the forest across from the watchtower—where none of the rescuers were—the recording of Gabe's warning boomed out over the gunfire.

The PZs stopped shooting to listen.

"Patriot Zealots, we broke into your compound to free a woman who was held against her will. The women with us requested to leave. Be warned, you are now off your property and on public land. If you attack, we will defend ourselves—and then press charges with the law."

Frankie glanced back long enough to see some PZs break off and head for what they'd think was a person rather than a recording. *Hah!*

A couple more slowed as if unsure whether to continue. *Good!*

Unfortunately, the rest kept on at a full run.

"Veer right" came Bull's instructions.

Thank heaven he knew where he was going. She angled that direction, tripping over the roots and stubby bushes. She dodged a low branch and...*oh, no.* She'd actually seen the branch. Could make out the trees in the shadowy forest gloom. The skies were lightening, and dawn would arrive in an hour or so. The rescue had taken longer than they'd planned.

Bull turned, heading another direction. From the myriad of boot marks in the dirt, she knew they'd reached the trail used on the way in. A minute later, Gabe limped out of the forest onto the trail. Two other dark forms resolved into Caz with JJ, who had her left hand clamped over her right upper arm.

"Caz, set the trip line," Gabe said quietly. "Everyone else, keep going."

Frankie glanced back, seeing Caz at a tree, pulling the pre-attached wire tight. Anyone moving fast would hit the taut, shin-high wire and fall.

The PZs were approaching fast. She could hear branches breaking, angry yells and curses.

Frankie sped up, running right on Bull's heels.

Behind them, someone yelled in pain, then there were a bunch of yelps and curses. A gun fired. More moans.

A man shouted, "Holster your weapons when you're running, assholes!"

Frankie heard Bull snort a laugh. She kept moving.

"JJ, when we get around the next corner, throw a flashbang back at them," Gabe ordered. Knowing the trail better than any of them, he was in the lead.

"Yes, sir."

Cops and their flashbangs.

The yelling of their pursuers grew louder.

Frankie tried to find more air, to move faster, but the damp track was slippery. She fell onto her knees. "*Merda.*" What she'd give for a city sidewalk...

Bull yanked her up onto her feet. "Okay?"

"I'm good. Go." She shoved her staff into the dirt and waved him on. This was like following an unstoppable tank. Panting, she lurched into a run again. They sped around a corner.

At a hoot from behind, Gabe stopped, as did Bull.

Catching Frankie, Bull tucked her against his side. "Cover your ears; close your eyes."

In the dim light, she saw him put his thumbs in his ears, fingers over his eyes. She tucked her staff under her arm and imitated him.

Bang! Even with her eyes covered, her ears plugged, the world went white. And the sound was like being in a room with a giant firecracker.

Trying to blink away the glowing after-images, she felt Bull take her hand. Gripping her staff, she jogged forward. Behind them were shouts and curses, a couple of screams of pain.

Caz and JJ caught up quickly.

Ahead on the trail, there was movement, and Frankie gasped. No, not the PZs. *Worse.* They'd caught up to the slow-moving line of women with the guide crew.

The sounds of the PZs grew closer.

Gabe held up his hand, and the assault team stopped.

"Persistent bastards." He ran an assessing gaze over them. "You up to an ambush?"

Oh, Madonna, no. Frankie nodded with the rest.

Gabe pointed toward the rear. "Bull, take the rearmost enemy from the left. Frankie—stand there"—he pointed to a dark patch of brush on the left—"and attack when the middle reaches you."

"Got it," came Bull's rumbled acknowledgment.

She added her whispered, "Yes, sir."

"Caz, rear on the right. JJ, middle right. Take them down hard. I'll play bait and deal with the front."

As Frankie edged into the shadows, Bull moved farther down and disappeared into the brush.

Flickering lights showed through the trees, approaching fast. The PZs were using flashlights—no wonder they'd caught up.

Rounding the bend, the beams flashed across Gabe.

So many PZs. A dozen, at least. A whimper edged into Frankie's throat. Too many.

But on the trail ahead was Kit, unconscious in Chevy's arms, little Aric with Hawk, and all the Rescue people who'd risked their lives.

Mouth flattening as determination filled her, she gripped her staff harder.

Lit up by the flashlights, Gabe glanced over his shoulder at the PZ horde and broke into a limping flight.

Like a pack of wolves, the *bastardi* howled and chased, blind to everything else.

To her left, Frankie saw a glint of steel in the air. Another. Two men in the rear fell. Caz stepped out of the undergrowth, holding another throwing knife.

Fight, Frankie. Her heart had crammed into her throat so tightly she could barely breathe. She crouched. *Now.*

Her feet wouldn't move.

Now!

A man pulled his pistol out and aimed at Gabe. With a frenzied scream, Frankie charged out of the brush and slammed her staff down onto his forearm. Bones cracked. Screeching, he dropped the gun and hunched over his arm.

The guy behind him lunged at Frankie, and her body took over. Spinning, she roundhouse-kicked him upside the temple, knocking him into another man. She drove her staff into the belly of a third.

No time to think. It was all yelling and blocking and striking, reacting instinctively with hard-won muscle memory. *Lean back, pull opponent off balance and twist to throw him into another. Regain balance, spin, and leg straightens into a side kick to another man's belly. Foot touches the dirt; weight shifts forward enabling a rear kick into the PZ behind her. Lean away from a knife and swing jo into his head. Move with the rebound to swing at another. Sway with his block and snap kick into his belly.*

A firearm cracked. A PZ yelled in pain.

Shooting in this tangle of people? They could hit their own men.

Moonlight gleamed along a pistol...that was aimed at Bull.

"No!" She dove at the man. Her shoulder hit his chest, knocking him back, their fall halted by a tree. With an ear-deafening bang, the weapon fired.

Pain burned down her calf, and she yelped.

The man backhanded her to the ground. His boot caught her in the belly, knocking her sideways. On his feet, he aimed the pistol at her.

Gryff sprang from nowhere and latched onto his arm. Murderous growls filled the air as the dog shook the man's arm as if it was a rodent.

Gasping for air, almost crying, Frankie scrambled away on hands and knees.

"Cunt!" A PZ swung a baton at her head. On her knees, she swayed sideways and slapped his arm to one side. Turning her hand over, she gripped his forearm and yanked him toward her. Then drove her knuckles into his throat. He fell.

Scrambling to her feet, she caught a kick to her ribs that sent her backpedaling until she could regain her balance. Eyes wild, the *bastardo* swung his knife in a move that would've cut her face open. Sidestepping the blade, she captured his wrist, twisted, and threw him headfirst into a tree.

Another man bent to pick up the fallen pistol. She snap-kicked him in the face, and her stomach lurched at the crunch of a bone. As he fell, she punted the handgun into the underbrush.

A knife swung at her, and she raised her arm to—

Bull grabbed the man's wrist, broke it, and elbowed him in the face. The man landed on his back, out cold.

Turning, Frankie braced for the next PZ.

They were all down. Groaning. Whimpering. Crying. Some holding broken arms and legs. One was throwing up. A few lay too still, either out cold or...

Her mind fled the alternative.

Holding her arm again, JJ leaned against a tree as Gabe, Caz, and Bull walked through the downed fanatics, tossing firearms and knives into the underbrush.

Whining, Gryff ran to Bull, obviously worried he'd be in trouble for fighting.

"You did good, buddy." Bull ruffled the dog's fur. "Good dog."

"You were amazing, Gryff." Frankie joined them, bending to give the dog a hug and whisper in his furry ear, "You saved me."

When she straightened, the dog's ears were up, the tail waving proudly.

"How bad are you hurt, Frankie?" Bull swept her with a quick gaze, then pulled her against him and rested his cheek on the top of her head. "Fuck, you scared me—saved me from getting shot, thank you—but *fuck*. How badly are you hurt?"

"Not bad. Mostly my calf." Her voice cracked. She'd never felt anything as reassuring as his arms around her. She was starting to shake.

"Let's see. Yeah, you're bleeding." He pulled a bandana out of one of the pockets on his personal armor and wrapped her leg tightly enough to make her squeak.

When he straightened, she gripped his arm so she could give him a quick survey. Nothing pouring blood, nothing obviously broken. She went up on tiptoes and kissed his jaw. "Thanks."

"Always." He turned at a call from Gabe.

Frankie took a step and realized something was missing. Her jo. Wiping sweat and blood from her face, she spotted it off to one side. Dark, wet streaks smeared the wood. Breathing through her nose, she picked it up.

"Done, *mamita.*" Caz had finished tying a bandage around JJ's arm. They headed toward Gabe.

"Fucking bitch." A PZ on the ground grabbed JJ's ankle.

Yanking her leg out of his grip, JJ kicked him in the gut.

"*Güey.*" Caz shook his head reprovingly at the puking man. "Such poor life choices."

It wasn't funny, but Frankie started to laugh, half-hysterically, and had to grit her teeth to stop.

"Move out." Gabe signaled something to Bull, then took the lead at a fast walk, limping worse than before.

Caz and JJ followed Gabe.

Gryff at his side, Bull watched them move out, then motioned to her. "I've got rear guard. Go in front of me, sweetheart."

Frankie kept her mind on moving forward. Her injured leg was on fire, and...*cazzo*, more and more aches kept rising. Shivers coursed across her body until it was hard to hold her staff.

She'd never wanted to be safe and snuggled down in her New York condo so much in her whole life.

Yet...

She heard Bull's soft footsteps behind her. Guarding from the rear. The man who'd risked his life for Kit and Aric, for the PZ's victims.

For her.

And she knew there was nowhere she'd rather be than with him.

———

It had been a fucking long walk back to Chevy's place, Bull thought.

In the back of Hawk's helicopter, he helped Caz strap Frankie's friend down on the cushioned stretcher. The trip out hadn't done her any good, and she was still unconscious, dammit.

What would Frankie do if her friend died?

"Hang in there, Kit," Bull murmured.

"Sí," Caz agreed. He turned to Hawk in the pilot's chair. "Get her there quickly. She's bleeding inside."

Already doing the preflight, Hawk simply showed a thumbs-up.

After a last glance at the IV he'd started, Caz slapped Bull's shoulder. "Later, 'mano. JJ and I'll make sure Gryff gets back safe." He jumped out to deal with the minor injuries incurred during the retreat through the forest.

In the passenger seats, Frankie had Aric buckled in beside her. Neither she nor Aric would leave Kit. Although the kid had been cooperative enough until Hawk had set him down.

Bull eased down on the seat beside them and strapped in. A couple of the bullets had hit his vest in the back. Nothing penetrated, but Jesus, he hurt. Then again, the sarge used to tell them *if you're hurting, you know you're alive, and it sure as hell beats being dead.*

After donning headphones, Bull put a set on Frankie. It was the only way to hear anything in a noisy copter.

"Good to go back here," he told Hawk who already had the rotors spinning.

He got a typical Hawk answer—a grunt.

Bull put protective earmuffs on Aric. Half-asleep, the boy had snuggled as close as possible to Frankie who had her arm around him.

As the helicopter lifted off, Bull saw Dante matching up the rescued with transportation. Clipboard in hand, Lillian was designating escorts, ensuring that each woman and child would be accompanied until the proper authority took charge of them.

Cars were slowly moving down the dirt road, and yes, more of them were on Dall Road, heading for Rescue's municipal building. By now, the municipal building would be swarming with health professionals as well as the FBI and Alaska State Troopers.

Yeah, the survivors would be handled. For the moment, Bull could focus on Kit, Aric, and Frankie.

"You all right?" Bull stroked his hand over Frankie's hair. He'd have to make sure someone checked her leg—all of her—while they were in the hospital.

"Sure." She looked up at him. "You're moving funny. How about you?"

"Just bruises." He half smiled. "You did good, woman. And you were right to insist on coming with us."

"I know. But it helps to hear it from you." She rubbed her head against his shoulder with a sigh. "Thanks."

He kissed the top of her head. She was pale, scratched, shot, battered, but still upright. Still watching out for her godson and her friend.

And him.

Burned into his memory was the sight of the pistol turning toward him, and how Frankie abandoned all sense of self-preservation and slammed into the PZ. He could go an entire lifetime without seeing that again or hearing the crack of the pistol as the bastard fired. *Jesus.*

However, seeing her risk her life for her friend. For him? It was as if the universe had slapped him upside the head, saying, "You think women don't have the loyalty gene? Here, meet Frankie."

Who would've thought he'd fall for a city girl? A New Yorker, for fuck's sake.

But she was *his* city girl, and he'd do his damnedest to talk her into staying in Rescue.

If not...?

Well, maybe he'd like New York.

The anti-Christ libtards had invaded their sacred soil. Stolen their women and children. Killed some of their men.

Put their sinner hands on him.

Fury boiled inside Nabera until he felt as if his head would explode.

Around him, his men were loading up the trucks. Patriots, every one of them. Loyal to the Prophet. To him.

He'd already handed out the directions to the homes of other members, of other properties where they could hunker down and hide until this test of their faith was over.

With a roar, one vehicle started up and moved out.

To think they'd been reduced to fleeing in the middle of the night. His lieutenants had argued with him, wanting to hold the Feds off with their guns and courage.

Fools. The Feds had them outgunned, outnumbered. And the Patriot Zealots no longer had the women or children. The only reason the sieges at Waco and Ruby Ridge were noteworthy was because the bleeding-heart libs hadn't been willing to sacrifice what they called the "innocent".

As if a woman with her foul nature and carnal thoughts could be considered innocent.

Nabera had ordered the evacuation. With Parrish in Texas, the compound was his to command.

They'd always been prepared for this eventuality.

He watched as the building holding their weaponry was

emptied. Carrying rucksacks, men and the very few women remaining climbed into the trucks.

Luka walked out of the building. "Empty, sir."

"No one is left, sir," Conrad called, jogging up.

Nabera nodded. "You have done well. Go, now. I'll be in contact after I speak to the Prophet."

"Yes, sir," his subordinates chorused.

"Keep your heads down, stay safe." His mouth tightened as fresh anger burned him like hellfire. In one truck were the bodies of those who'd fallen in the forest. And Obadiah.

Nabera would say prayers over them as they were flung over the cliff to the depths below. Dust to dust, as it should be.

They'd failed him by not recovering the women and children.

Obadiah had failed him by choosing a sinful woman. A stubborn one. She'd not confessed her crimes, not even when Nabera beat her. When he told Obadiah to kill her.

His men waited, and he could see their faith in the Prophet was unshaken.

"We'll be back, and we'll make these unbelievers regret what they did. But we'll do it in our own time. At the best time." Nabera gazed at the empty compound, and his teeth ground together. "And blood will flow."

CHAPTER TWENTY-TWO

When the reptile brain takes over in battle, there's no room for guilt. After combat is when the darkness hits. You gotta remember the faces of who you fought for. Your team, your woman, and the children. All the children. - First Sergeant Michael "Mako" Tyne

Cazzo, she hurt. In the quiet room, Frankie shifted in her chair, trying to find a position that didn't hurt. Her face was all scraped up, her lower lip puffy from a punch. A scraped spot over her eyebrow burned where a branch had nailed her. Really, she was lucky it hadn't put her eye out...and didn't that sound like something Nonna would've said?

Her side ached with each breath. The emergency room doctor had said one of her ribs was cracked, but the body armor had kept her torso unperforated. A shame there wasn't body armor for legs. Her calf had a hole right through the meat. *Ow, ow, ow.* There was no place on her body that wasn't bruised.

Again, she glanced through the doorway and across the hall at the surgery department's double doors. Somewhere in there, surgeons were doing their best to keep Kit alive and to repair the damage. Kit had been so very—

"Ms. Bocelli?"

Oh, oops. Someone had been talking to her... She shook her mind back to the moment and the two FBI agents who sat in front of her. A few minutes before, they'd brought her from the surgery waiting room to the adjacent "quiet" room. So, they could talk. "Sorry. I keep losing track of..." the conversation, the location, everything. She sighed.

It was like someone had opened the faucet to her energy and drained her empty.

"You just told us why you didn't call us in when you got your friend's letter or even later on." In dark pants and a white button-up shirt, Special Agent Langford leaned forward, resting his elbows on his thighs. "You made sense."

His partner, Special Agent Acosta nodded, his brown eyes sympathetic.

They'd been exceedingly kind to her, considering that they could have intimidated the heck out of her if they'd wanted. Especially since she kept dodging some of their questions.

Like who'd helped during the rescue.

Bull had warned her that a whole bunch of the volunteer transport crew were off-the-gridders—the kind to go ballistic if feds showed up at their doors. They deserved better than to be bothered.

Leaning her head back, she watched the agents. She had a feeling they were friends of Gabe's. If they wanted more information, they'd have to get it from him.

"It would help if"—Langford frowned—"did you happen to keep that letter from your friend?

"Certainly. It's in New York." With an exasperated breath, she pulled out her phone and flipped to the photo gallery. Not being an idiot, she'd taken pictures of each document Kit had sent before locking everything up in her office safe. "Here—this is the letter—with her request that I care for Aric, my godson. The other documents are there, also. When I got the letter, I knew I had to do something."

She shrugged. "My family is Italian and Catholic. We take that sort of commitment seriously."

"Understood." He gave her a respectful nod as Langford flipped screens on her phone.

A noise at the door had her standing before she even realized she'd moved. Still in scrubs, the surgeon walked through the doorway. The woman looked almost as exhausted as Frankie felt.

"How is Kit? Is she all right?" Frankie clasped her hands in front of her chest. *Please.*

"I think she's going to make it, although, it was far too close. She has a concussion. Just about every rib on the left side of her body is cracked or broken. Bleeding was impacting her heart. Her spleen was lacerated. The broken arm—that was the least of her problems."

"What happens now?"

"We're not going to let her wake up for a while. After that, she'll be here in the hospital for at least a few days. With this much damage, it's going to take her a while to heal." The surgeon rubbed her face. "No visitors until this afternoon, so go home and get some sleep, eh?"

Tears prickled Frankie's eyes at the disappointment. But she found her manners somewhere. "Thank you, doctor."

The surgeon nodded, smiled back, and disappeared into the surgical suite.

Feeling as if she was ready to sack out on the floor, Frankie turned to the special agents. "Can I go now?"

"Yes. For now." After handing her phone back, Acosta gave her a conciliatory smile. "We might have more questions later, but you're half asleep."

Thank heaven. She forced her brain to work long enough to

ask her own question. "What are you guys going to do about the Patriot Zealots?"

"We have agents and police talking with the women you brought out. And the children." Acosta's mouth flattened. "We're still coming up with charges. Unlawful imprisonment is a given. Kidnapping has been added. Assault, battery."

"And the list goes on," Langford said. "The state troopers discovered the arsonists who burned your cabin were hired by the Patriot Zealots."

Sheer fatigue blunted the revelation. And really, she wasn't all that surprised. Those *bastardi*.

"It'll take time to figure out who to charge with what," Langford added with a sigh.

"If you can even get to them." Frankie scowled. "They'll probably either hole up in a siege or disappear like cockroaches when the lights come on."

"They already took the cockroach approach." Acosta growled, then smiled slightly. "However, the unfortunate Reverend Parrish with his wife and children were intercepted in a Texas airport an hour ago. He's under arrest."

"Really?" Frankie realized she was smiling. Maybe the PZs had scattered, but the *bastardo* who'd created the fanatical cult would be doing his praying behind bars.

Hawk was showered, dressed in sweatpants, and had pulled an aged sweatshirt over his favorite long-sleeved T-shirt. He needed the familiarity of the old clothes that were worn to softness.

Opening the fridge, he saw the six-pack of beer and grunted. *Uh-uh, that's not what I need.*

The oblivion of alcohol was a fucking trap. Besides, the last thing a vet needed was to lose track of his surroundings. Or himself. Better to deal with the ugly memories—and yeah, those he had in plenty.

He shut the fridge door and headed for the deck, picking up his violin on the way. Leaning against the railing, he started to play—no real song, just the music that came to him. A tune to join with the way gray-gold mist rose off the dark waters, how the mountains glowed in the dawn.

Slowly the music changed, the strings turning to a dirge for the man he'd killed, worthless bastard that the guy had been. The dead man was another weight to carry until Hawk answered for him in the next life, whatever the fuck that would be. Guilt for the PZ wasn't all that heavy, though. The bastard had been kicking a woman to death.

A damn brave woman.

Her kid had inherited her courage. The stubborn little guy hadn't wanted to leave Kit, not until Frankie sat on the floor with him and explained how the doctors were going to fix his mom.

Hawk's playing faltered for a moment. The woman had taken a fucking lot of damage. What would the kid do if his mother didn't make it?

Guilt swept over him because that mother had told him to take care of her son. And Hawk had agreed.

I did take care of him, dammit. He'd brought the kid home and fed him a peanut butter sandwich and everything. But when Caz came back with Gryff, Hawk had taken Aric over there. The doc knew kids, hell, he had one himself, and everyone knew JJ was great with rugrats. The two would take care of Aric far better than Hawk ever could.

But Jesus, when he'd turned to leave, the kid looked like Hawk had tossed him into the lake instead of leaving him with someone who liked children.

Fuck, he kept listening, worrying that he'd hear the boy crying. With a sigh, Hawk turned to go into the house and stopped dead.

A little body sat huddled in front of his sliding glass door. Aric's big blue eyes watched Hawk's every move.

"How the fuck did you get out of Caz's house?" Hawk growled. And winced. The sound of his fucked-up voice would scare any—

The kid wasn't scared. He didn't move or speak. Just watched Hawk.

Amusement trickled in. "Snuck out, did you?" That'd teach the doc. Caz'd always figured he was best at sneaking around. "You know, the doc's better with kids than I am."

"Mama *said*." Aric's mouth set in a stubborn line. And his expression conveyed that Aric's mama had given Hawk orders, too.

"Yeah, she did. Fine." Hawk slid open the door and let the boy in. He'd have to call Caz and let him know about his crappy kid-watching.

After Aric was asleep, it'd be time to call Zachary Grayson. Maybe the psychologist could figure out what should be done with a stray boy and a mother's insane notion to hand her son over to a fucked-up asshole like Hawk.

A light drizzle blotted out the morning sun as Bull opened his garage door and drove in. "We're here, sweetheart."

Frankie'd been dozing on the way home. She was exhausted—and he was damn proud of how she'd held it together until the FBI agents were done.

As she struggled awake, he helped her out, half holding her up as they walked inside.

When they reached the living room, he heard a whuff. Gryff was pressing his nose against the sliding glass door, tail wagging ferociously.

Frankie chuckled as Bull opened the door and Gryff barreled

in, spinning in excited circles between his two humans. It took a fair bit of petting to calm him down.

And then the dog helped Bull steer Frankie upstairs and into the shower. Leaving her there, he knelt in front of the pup. "You did a great job, buddy. You saved our girl. Brave dog, good dog."

Leaning against Bull, Gryff ate up the praise as if he could understand every word.

"Your previous owner was an idiot. You're no coward. You just didn't have a good reason to fight before." Bull hugged the furry dog. "You did good, my friend. Incredibly good."

Gryff licked Bull's chin, making him laugh.

"Okay, I'm going to go help Frankie." Help her. Hold her. Reassure himself she was all right.

When he stepped into the shower, she was sitting on the tile under the water, head in hands. Crying.

His heart cracked in half.

"Frankie." He knelt beside her, so small. So valiant. "Are you in pain?"

"I'm fine."

"Bullshit." Bull turned her face toward him. "Tell me what's wrong."

She was shaking despite the hot water pouring down on her. "It's... I hit them so hard. To make them stop. I felt bones...break. And the man's throat. I think I must have killed him, and...and... right then, I was okay with it. Wanting it. So, he—they—wouldn't hurt me or you or anyone."

Combat fever, eventually, came to an end and left a soldier sick right to his soul. "Yeah, I get it. It's part of war."

"I can still hear the screams and yelling, and it won't stop, and I want to throw up and hide. That wasn't me hurting those men. It *wasn't*."

He ached for her. Hell, she'd chosen aikido because it was the least aggressive of the martial arts, because she didn't like attacking anyone. "I know."

It's how he felt about killing. "The aftermath still hits me hard, too. Some soldiers adapt; I never did."

She leaned against him, taking his hand, silently offering sympathy in return.

After a minute, she took a deep breath. "I suppose we should wash up before the water turns cold."

"Let's do that." He lifted her to her feet. A sweetly curved bundle of competence and courage with a temper worthy of her ancestors, and a swathe of compassion wider than the ocean. "I love you, Francesca Bocelli."

"I love you, too," she whispered. Turning in his arms, she pulled him down for a kiss.

Carefully, he removed the dressing on her leg. It was stitched up and no longer bleeding. Gently, he washed her, cataloging each darkening bruise and gash, then realized as she ran her hands over his back and made sympathetic sounds that she was doing the same.

Her fingers circled some damned painful places. "These are where bullets hit your vest, aren't they?"

At the odd sound in her voice, he turned.

She'd pulled her lips in and blinked hard, obviously trying not to cry again. Because he'd been hit.

Gently, he touched the darker blotch over her ribs where a bullet had cracked her rib. "Good thing we armored up, huh?"

Her voice cracked as she whispered, "Uh-huh."

It was time to leave the past.

He leaned against the wall and smiled at her. "As I recall, there's a post-combat exercise you might enjoy. You know... because you like traditions."

He ran a finger over her slick shoulder, traced over her collarbone, and circled a lush breast.

Her nipple tightened.

Her beautiful brown eyes dropped to where his dick was lengthening.

"It's traditional, hmm?" Her voice had turned husky.

"Oh, yeah." His heart rate was increasing.

"Well. I'm an old-fashioned girl." She curled her hand around his erection and squeezed.

His cock turned hard enough to break rocks.

"But I'm new to fighting." She pumped him once and then rubbed her thumb over the head. "Perhaps you could show me the...tradition...of which you speak?"

He chuckled. "I can take this duty on, I suppose."

The rest of the shower was a blur of sensations. Her breasts, heavy in his hands. The velvety feel of her nipples. The taste of her, warm and wet on his tongue. The way her hands gripped his head, holding him to her as she cried out and came. The sweetness of her mouth closing on him—and her curse when he pulled away and lifted her...high enough to impale on his cock. Her gasp, and the tension, then reception of her body around him, welcoming him. How she wrapped arms and legs around him, enfolding him in heat—and love—as he gave her all that he was.

CHAPTER TWENTY-THREE

*I*n a forest, keep your focus wide. Take it all in—the sounds of birds and insects, every set of tracks, the smells, how the vegetation moves in the wind. Then, if something is wrong—if there's an ambush set up—you'll know. Do that same shit when you're looking at a person. - First Sergeant Michael "Mako" Tyne

That evening, Frankie slid out of Bull's pickup and was grateful he'd parked it right by the back door of the municipal building. Her leg hurt like someone was stabbing her calf with a knife. Maybe she should have brought her jo and used it as a cane.

She'd have to remember when she visited the hospital tomorrow. Earlier, she'd called, and the nurse had said the swelling in Kit's brain was going down, and she'd probably be allowed to wake up tomorrow some time. That she was doing all right.

Kit was going to live. Frankie clung to the door a minute and blinked away the blurriness in her vision.

As Bull came around the vehicle, she noticed the uniformed state trooper at the back door was frowning at them. The building was well guarded. When they drove past on Main Street, there had been a couple of troopers barring the way to the front door.

The trooper came down a step. "I'm sorry, people, but only authorized persons—"

"I know, I know." Bull took Frankie's arm, lending support as they moved closer. "As it happens, the Chief of Police asked us to bring food for everyone...including the support staff."

The trooper blinked, then hope filled his face. "Food?"

"Lots of food. Can you give Gabe a ring to get his ass out here and identify us?"

"Hell, yes. I'm starving." The young man talked into his radio for a moment, laughed, and said, "I'll let them through."

Frankie blinked. "You're not going to make Gabe come out here?"

The trooper shook his head, his gaze on Bull. "He gave me a description."

Gabe had probably said something like huge and muscular, with a shaved head and goatee. There weren't many like Bull.

"Good." Bull grinned and headed back to the pickup. "If you draft people to carry in the coolers and boxes, I'll get an area set up for food."

"I'm on it." The trooper lifted his radio again.

After lowering the tailgate, Bull handed her a sack. "You can take that one in."

Full of bread, it weighed almost nothing. She wrinkled her nose at him. So over-protective. "Thanks, Skull."

Chuckling, he grabbed a cooler, then left the hand trolley sitting beside the back for whoever would bring in the heaviest of the coolers and boxes.

Once inside the wide reception area, Bull slowed. "We should probably find Gabe or Caz."

There were people everywhere, mostly law enforcement and health professionals, including social workers, as well as the survivors of the PZs. Caz had said the women and children would be interviewed, then if they had no other family, would go to shelters in Anchorage where they'd get counseling and help. If a child appeared abused—or if the woman wanted to return to the PZ, more evaluations would be done.

What a mess. At least, the news media hadn't sniffed this out yet.

"Bull, Frankie." At the receptionist counter, Audrey beamed at them. "Gabe said you were bringing in food. We cleared a space over there."

Next to the police station doors, Chevy and Knox were already setting up a long table against the wall.

"Did you get any sleep at all?" Frankie asked, noting the dark circles under her friend's eyes.

"A couple of hours." Audrey sighed ruefully. "Gabe wouldn't take a break unless I did, so we sacked out together on a couple of the police station cots. He made JJ take a nap, too, once we got up."

"Oh, that's good." The police station had showers, so Gabe and JJ would've had a chance to clean up.

When Caz took Gryff back to the Hermitage, he caught some sleep there before coming in.

Audrey's mouth twisted. "You know, I've been attacked, kidnapped, shot—and I'm not sure if it wasn't worse waiting here, all safe and sound, and worrying about you all."

Especially Gabe, Frankie knew. *If I'd had to sit in this place, waiting for word about Bull?* She shook her head. "You're braver than I am, Audrey."

Across the reception area, a clatter came from the stairs as several people descended. A state trooper, a gray-haired woman and two skinny, terrified children, followed by a man in a black suit. The trooper herded the woman and children toward the rear, while the man headed for the health clinic.

Beside Frankie, Bull inhaled sharply, then called, "Zachary Grayson, how the hell did you get here so quickly?" Taking

Frankie's hand, he crossed the room, pulling her with him at a pace too fast for comfort.

Cavolo, his legs were just too long. Normally, he didn't forget that hers weren't.

The man in the suit turned toward them. Tall and leanly muscular with silvering black hair and gray eyes, he held out a hand. "Bull, it's good to see you." His voice was rich and deep, almost compelling.

"And you. I didn't expect you until tomorrow at the earliest."

Laugh lines crinkled at the corners of the man's eyes. "I have a friend with a jet."

"Why am I not surprised?" Bull grinned. "Thank you for coming."

"Indeed, how could I refuse when every single one of you phoned?" The man tilted his head at Frankie, then lifted an eyebrow at Bull. "I also heard a rumor that you had a partner in your endeavors last night."

"So discreetly phrased." Bull squeezed her hand. "Frankie, I'd like you to meet Dr. Zachary Grayson, a psychologist who works with traumatized children and an old friend of Mako's. He'd fly up from Florida to make sure the sarge wasn't in over his head with the four of us."

A corner of Grayson's mouth lifted. "Mako was in over his head the moment he met you all."

Frankie almost laughed, because the four guys were impossible now. As children...? That poor sergeant.

Chuckling, Bull pulled her closer. "Zachary, this is Frankie Bocelli, who's taken over managing the roadhouse—and my heart."

Frankie's own heart simply melted.

Dr. Grayson held out his hand. "It's good to meet you, Ms. Bocelli."

"It's Frankie, please." Frankie took his hand, surprised when he didn't shake and let go, but held it for a moment as he studied her with a disconcertingly perceptive gaze.

When he turned to Bull, his smile transformed his face from handsome to lethally gorgeous. "I not only approve—although you didn't ask—but I'm very pleased for you."

"Thanks, Doc." Bull's own grin was just as devastating and still made her feel all gooey inside. And...he didn't contradict Zachary's assumption that they were together. Would be together. *Wow.*

Frankie cleared the thickness from her throat. "Um, Dr. Grayson. Zachary. My friend's son—Aric—my godson isn't here. He's at the Hermitage, and he's...had a rough time. Could you speak with him, too?"

Zachary's eyes softened. "Bull and Hawk called me for exactly that purpose. Caz and Gabe asked me to check on the survivors here, too, but I'll be heading for the Hermitage in an hour or so."

Bull smiled slightly, dimples appearing. "You should check on Hawk, too. He's pretty freaked out—the kid won't let him out of his sight."

The psychologist nodded. "Indeed. We'll be having a chat."

The way he said that, as if he had no doubt that Hawk would cooperate, reminded her of Gabe. Both men were commanders, used to giving orders and being obeyed.

Bull wasn't like that, and without thinking, she moved closer to him. He didn't have any driving need to be in charge, yet had no problem taking the reins if it was needed. And he'd decimate anyone and anything that threatened the people he protected.

He was simply amazing. Was it any wonder how much she loved him?

Hawk was damned grateful the kid had slept most of the day. So had he...in between getting up and pacing now and then.

He had no fucking clue what to do with a rugrat, especially one that was... "How old are you anyway?"

Aric was sitting at the kitchen table munching on a carrot. Hopefully, the snack would tide him over, since Gabe wanted everyone together for a late supper at Mako's.

Aric held up four fingers. The kid didn't speak if gestures could be used, and if he did speak, it was in a whisper. Yeah, the kid was a mess.

Four years old. Would he be in kindergarten this year? He sure seemed awful small.

"C'mon, let's go feed the chickens and collect eggs." Hawk held his hand out, because otherwise the boy would latch onto his leg.

Walking with a kid wrapped around his leg was not happening.

Aric grabbed his hand, and Hawk felt a pang inside at how tiny the fingers were. On Caz's orders, he'd had Aric take a bath before fixing him a bed on the couch. And again following Caz's advice, had dumped in enough shampoo to make bubbles. While the kid played—with worried glances at Hawk between each splash—he had a chance to check the damages.

The pale little body was covered in bruises and gashes.

Hawk scowled. It'd brought back too many memories of his childhood.

He'd been a brave rugrat, though, taking the soap and scrubbing down. And he'd let Hawk wash his hair. Whoever'd beat the shit out of the child probably hadn't been a pedophile.

Thank fuck.

They fed the chickens and left a basket of eggs outside Gabe's door. It was Gabe and Audrey's day to tend the chickens, but they were in town with the rescued women.

On the way back to the house, Hawk glanced over his shoulder to see Gryff trailing them at a short distance. Earlier, the dog had been heartbroken when Aric backed away from him.

Hawk was betting the mutt would eventually win the kid over. Gryff had a way about him.

The sound of cars coming up their road made Hawk stiffen until Gryff gave a happy woof. Only Bull's pickup got that greeting.

Looking up, Aric was studying Hawk's face in an all-too-familiar way.

Decades ago, Hawk had watched Pa like that to catch the first hint of his mouth tightening, or eyes hardening, or muscles tensing. Anger had signs—and kids who wanted to stay alive learned to read them.

"You're a survivor, kid. I approve." With a half-smile, Hawk slowly set his hand on Aric's head and ruffled his hair.

The boy didn't dodge.

As two garage doors sounded, Hawk automatically noted the locations. Bull and Frankie. But who'd opened the sarge's garage? Surely, they wouldn't let the PZ women come here. Talk about a security disaster.

Lights came on in Mako's house. Yeah, someone was there.

"Son of a—" *Shit, the kid. Stop swearing, asshole.* That meant he'd have to kick out whoever was in Mako's house without any colorful language.

Aric's face was scrunched up anxiously, and Hawk winced. *Way to scare the boy.* "Sorry, kid."

"Hawk."

What the fuck? Hawk froze as the sound of the dark smooth voice brought back memories of long walks in the forest. Of the one person he'd ever let see him cry—and the one who'd taught him how to rein in his anger...at least most of the time.

The tension drained out of him in a rush. Of course, Gabe had offered Mako's cabin to Doc Grayson. Mako would have it no other way. Despite the difference in their ages, he'd considered Grayson a good friend.

Hawk turned. "Doc."

The psychologist hadn't changed much over the years. He still looked like he could make it through basic training without breaking a sweat. He had more gray in his hair and a few more lines on his face. Not surprising. People unloaded a lot of shit on a psychologist. Hell, cleaning latrines would be easier.

Grayson came down the steps off the deck, and then a smile flickered over his face as his gaze dropped to...Hawk's legs?

What the hell? Hawk looked down and snorted. Aric was hiding behind him with a firm grip on his jeans. "Hey, kid. That's Doc Grayson. He's okay." Hawk rested his hand on Aric's shoulder, feeling only bone. No meat on the boy at all. "I liked talking to him when I was little."

That was a stretch of the truth. Under the guise of searching for herbs, Grayson had taken Hawk out into the forest for long, long walks. On a later visit, the shrink wanted photographs of the bald eagles—because he'd learned that Hawk loved the big predators.

More long walks. Sneaky bastard.

"It's good to see you, Hawk," Grayson said. "You appear well."

Hawk shook hands and ignored the way the doc studied his face. "And you. This is Aric. Frankie's godson."

"Ah." Zachary nodded at Aric...and didn't press further. "Join me on Mako's deck? I could use something cold."

"Sure." Hawk hadn't considered when he made the early morning call that maybe Grayson's conversations would include him as well as Aric. *Fuck.*

Still, he wanted Grayson's opinion. Surely, the doc would say the kid would be better off with women. With someone nice. With anyone but a fucked-up, antisocial vet.

With Aric not venturing more than a few inches from his side, Hawk went into Mako's kitchen and brought out sodas for all three of them. He took a chair beside Grayson.

Any other kid would crawl up on a chair. Aric remained standing. Yeah, it was a lot easier to flee that way.

With a snort, Hawk lifted the boy onto his lap, opened a can, and handed it to him. "Use both hands."

Watching Grayson with wary eyes, Aric took a sip.

His shocked expression made the doc chuckle. "I doubt your religious militia allowed carbonated beverages."

"Seems not." Amusement roused as Aric took another sip, so very carefully, and blinked. "Like the bubbles, kid?"

Aric looked up with eyes the clear blue of an autumn sky. His lips tilted barely upward as he nodded.

Grayson leaned back in his chair with a tired sigh—and Hawk felt a twinge of guilt. The man must've jumped a plane right away to get here so fast. It would help that Rescue was four hours later than Tampa. Still, long fucking flight, long fucking day.

"I spoke with the doctors at Kirsten's hospital and—"

"Kirsten?" Hawk frowned.

"Kirsten Traeger—Aric's mother. I believe Frankie calls her Kit." Grayson disliked nicknames. He could be almost as stubborn as the sarge.

"Got it. What'd the docs say?"

"The brain swelling is coming down adequately, and they'll let her wake. However, even if there's no neurological damage, she'll be in the hospital for a while, then need a stay in rehab after that. Quite simply, she's taken too much damage and will require treatments she can't get at home." Grayson's gaze darkened.

Hawk grunted. He turned his gaze toward Aric and lifted his eyebrows.

"That's the question, yes," Grayson agreed.

For a minute, there was quiet.

Grayson smiled at him. "You know, back when I was Aric's age, my mother would read to me every night." The psychologist was watching the lake as he continued, "I remember *Goodnight, Moon*. And *Red Shoe, Blue Shoe* and..."

Hawk felt a tiny bounce, and Aric's wary expression disappeared.

Grayson glanced over and nodded. "Ah, your mom likes to read to you, too." And he continued with a rambling, easy discussion of things his mother had done with him. The doc never asked a question, just...talked.

With Aric on his lap, Hawk could feel the tension come and go in the little body. The kid reacted to a lot of what Grayson said. But...if Hawk was reading things right, it seemed like Kit was a damned fine mother.

Or she had been before she was sucked into the PZs. *What about then, Grayson?*

Before Hawk could think of a way to ask that, the doc glanced at him, then Aric. "Now Hawk, *his* parents could be mean. His dad hit him. So did his momma."

Aric's eyes widened, and he gave Hawk a horrified look and patted his chest.

Grayson leaned forward and set a hand on Aric's shoulder, capturing his attention. "I know the mean man hit you, Aric. Did your momma ever hurt you?"

Aric shook his head vehemently and scowled at the shrink. Then he flinched, obviously remembering that grownups would hit children who glared at them.

Releasing Aric, Grayson leaned back.

Hawk nodded. That was the question he'd worried about. It seemed as if Aric could go back to his mom when she was able to care for him. Good. It would have broken Frankie's heart if her friend had turned abusive.

But...what the fuck was Aric going to do until Kit was up to caring for her kid?

The sound of garage doors rising came from Caz's place this time. And Gabe's.

Hawk glanced at Grayson. "Sounds like everyone's home."

A couple of minutes later, Regan walked out of Caz's house. The girl had grown since coming to live with Caz last fall.

Grown in other ways, too. For the first month or so, she'd

been as timid as Aric was now. She sure wasn't timid any longer. Spotting Hawk, she came running. "Hi, Uncle Hawk!"

Climbing the steps, Regan eyed Grayson then smiled at him before turning to study Aric who still sat in Hawk's lap. "Who're you?"

After a moment, he whispered, "Aric."

"Aric, this is Regan. She lives in that house." Hawk pointed to Caz's place.

"So, where do you live?" Regan asked the boy.

There was no pause this time. Aric pointed right at Hawk's house.

Oh, fuck.

All evening, Frankie watched how the psychologist managed to put almost everyone at ease. Even Regan.

Aric, though... No matter the enticement—games or food or even the cat—the boy never moved farther than three feet from Hawk. When Hawk used the bathroom, the kid waited outside the door. If Hawk went into the kitchen for something, he had a tiny escort.

Aric's fearfulness simply broke Frankie's heart.

And, hard as it was to admit, she was maybe a little jealous of Hawk. She'd thought *she* would be Aric's support.

Yet it was a miracle that the child could trust anyone other than Kit, and Frankie was profoundly grateful that he had Hawk.

Hawk might not feel the same way.

Following Frankie's gaze, JJ studied Aric. Sleeping, he was curled up on Mako's huge sectional. Half on Hawk's lap, the boy hadn't let go of Hawk's T-shirt. "I haven't heard him speak above a whisper."

"He did once." Hawk lay his hand on Aric's shoulder in a way that melted Frankie's heart. "Then he hid under the bed."

"Bet that bunch believed children should be seen and not heard." Bull sounded as if he wanted to punch someone. "He probably got punished if he made any noise."

"All of the children appeared to have suffered from abuse. Some more than others." Caz turned to the psychologist. "What do you think, Zachary?"

"He was abused by adults, especially men. No matter how much his mother tried, she couldn't protect him...or herself, either."

Cazzo, Frankie wanted to go back and pound on every one of those fanatics.

Hawk's sand-colored brows drew together. "I'm an adult. A man. But he's latched on."

"Of course he did." Zachary's gray eyes went soft as he studied Aric. "You took down his worst abuser and saved his mother. Then she told Aric to stay with you."

Hawk shook his head as if he was trying to deny that.

"Even more, Hawk," Zachary said. "His instincts agree with his mother's orders. Because you're strong enough to protect him."

The poor ex-mercenary looked trapped, and Frankie almost laughed.

"Even before I mentioned your parents, I think Aric already realized you are kindred spirits. You, more than anyone here, understand what he's been through. What he needs." Zachary steepled his fingers in front of his chest and spoke to all of them. "The boy is fragile right now. Let him adjust at his own pace. As he gets to know you and learns he's safe here, his grip on Hawk will relax."

"Makes sense," Gabe said.

Hawk protested. "His mother will recover and—"

Zachary shook his head. "Even when she is ready to take him back, she can't give him the same sense of safety that he gets with Hawk. Not right away."

"But..." Frankie bit her lip. What had she done? How could she possibly fix this? Pulling in a breath, she faced the one man she'd never have matched with a little boy. "I'm so sorry, Hawk. It's bad enough I asked you all to risk your lives, but now, I've messed up your life completely."

"Bullshit." Blue-gray eyes, hard as New York pavement, met her gaze. "If you hadn't asked, we'd've insisted." Hawk's gaze was on Aric, and a corner of his mouth turned up. "And you're not messing up my life, yorkie. He is."

"But—"

"Kit's yours. You're Bull's. Makes the kid family." Hawk shrugged. "I can deal."

And finally, she understood why—although Hawk was so adamantly solitary and taciturn— his brothers never doubted he'd be there for them.

"Are the rest of the women and children settled?" Frankie asked. There were still a few in the municipal building when she and Bull left.

"Everyone has been taken to Anchorage and Soldotna." Caz had one arm around JJ, the other around Regan.

"What will happen to them?" Audrey asked Zachary. "I saw you talking with the social workers. Making recommendations. Will they be all right?"

"Softie," Gabe murmured and hugged her.

"Some have families to take them in. The rest will be in women's shelters, getting help as they figure out how to move on and build new lives." Zachary's expression was sad. "Many had been searching for solutions and easy answers, which left them vulnerable to the cult. It will take them time to find their balance again."

Frankie frowned. "What about the women who stayed at the compound and didn't come with us."

"Ah, you probably didn't hear," Gabe said. "When the FBI and state troopers got there—maybe a couple of hours after us—the compound was empty of people."

Frankie stared at him. That was what the Feds meant about the cockroaches scattering.

"I missed that?" Bull glanced at Hawk. "Was *everything* gone?"

He meant bodies, didn't he? Frankie remembered Hawk's expression when he realized Obadiah was dead.

Gabe understood the question. "Yes. All that we left behind and on the trail. There were a few personal possessions, but their weapons were gone. The paranoid bastards had probably planned for when they'd have to abandon the place."

"But that means they're loose and can...come after us. After Kit." Frankie felt Bull's hand cover hers and realized her fingers had clenched into fists.

"They won't be free for long." Gabe gave her a reassuring smile. "There are warrants being written up for the leaders, including Nabera and his lieutenants."

"I don't like knowing Nabera isn't locked up," JJ said. "He's not exactly stable."

Hawk frowned and placed his hand on Aric's shoulder. "Tighten security?"

"Yes. We'll keep the Hermitage locked down. Just in case." Gabe shook his head. "Fanatics are unpredictable."

"The feds told me they picked up Parrish." Frankie said to Bull. "I forgot to tell you last night."

"There's good news." Bull squeezed her hand. "Without the leader, everything else will probably collapse."

Nabera was loose. "Maybe it's good Kit will be in a hospital and safe until the rest of them are arrested."

"I'd hoped to meet your friend, but my flight leaves tomorrow morning." Zachary gave Frankie a long look. "When you're helping her mend from all this, remind her as often as needed that she wasn't entirely helpless. That her courage and ingenuity in contacting you was what saved her and Aric—and the other women as well. Her actions—and yours, Frankie—broke the Patriot Zealots."

He'd called her Frankie. Because that was who she was. She caught the psychologist's gaze, and his eyes crinkled. Because when he asked her what her full name was, she'd scowled as she told him "Francesca". He'd chuckled and said he preferred to take the time to say a person's entire name, but in her case, "Frankie" was less of a nickname and more of a statement of identity. And he liked who she was.

She really liked this psychologist.

Just then, he rose. "I need to stretch my legs, especially since I'll be on a plane for hours tomorrow. Regan, I hear you have a cat. Might I have an introduction to him? I'm in need of hearing some purrs."

Regan jumped up. "Sure. Sirius likes getting petted."

As the two of them headed out the door, Frankie saw Mako's sons exchanging grins. "What?"

Bull chuckled. "We all remember Grayson's chats. Because of him, we're probably less fucked-up than we might've been." As the others chimed in with snorts of agreement, Bull gave her a light kiss and added, "Now, it seems he's planning to steer the next generation."

CHAPTER TWENTY-FOUR

W *hen everything goes to hell, the people who stand by you without flinching—they are your family.* - Jim Butcher

Gusty winds slapped rain against the window of Kit's hospital room, almost drowning out the beeps of various medical devices in the unit, carts rolling past, and voices from the hallway.

Maybe it was a bit noisy, but to her, all the sounds spelled out safety.

Kit rubbed her face and winced when her fingers ran into the coarse stitches down one cheek. They hurt. *Oh, admit it, everything hurt.* Her broken arm they'd had to set again. Her belly where they'd had to deal with stuff a broken rib had punctured. And, more than anything, her side with the cracked and broken ribs. The surgeon said she was lucky the fractured bones hadn't pierced a lung.

She didn't feel particularly lucky. More like stupid.

Her idiocy had almost gotten Frankie—and lots of other people—killed trying to rescue her from her mistakes. If she'd been smarter, maybe—

"Hey." Bringing in the scent of rain and forest, Frankie limped into the hospital room and rolled her eyes. "Whatever you're thinking about, you should stop."

Kit tried to smile, felt the stitches pull, and sighed. "I'm a mess."

Tilting her head to one side, Frankie tugged on her chin in an imitation of their elderly, persnickety, college history professor. "Ms. Traeger, I believe you might have a point."

Kit giggled, then clutched her side. "Oh, blessings, don't make me laugh. Please."

"Sorry, sorry." Frankie held up her hands. "I solemnly swear to be tedious and boring."

Trying not to laugh almost hurt worse. *Ouch, ouch, ouch.* "You're so mean."

"That's me." Arm pressed to her side in a way Kit recognized, Frankie gingerly settled on the bedside chair.

Because she'd been hurt, too. Frankie'd made light of it, but the FBI agents told Kit that everyone who'd come into the compound had been injured in some way.

Nevertheless, Frankie hadn't let it stop her from visiting. She wouldn't, because Kit was all alone here. And scared. Dear God, she was scared sometimes. Having Frankie close was like a lifeline...and one she shouldn't cling to.

Instead, concentrate on gratitude. "The Feds said a lot of people were involved in the rescue. Since I'm stuck here, could you tell them" —a lump in her throat choked off the words for a moment—"h-how very thankful I am for their help? How sorry I am they were hurt?"

When she was out of the hospital, she'd find a way to repay those amazing rescuers who'd risked their lives for strangers.

"Sure. You don't need to feel guilty. On the transport team, the injuries were mostly scrapes and a few turned ankles." Frankie's eyes lit with laughter. "The diversion team, however, had such bad hangovers the next day that the whining never stopped."

"They were drunk when they faked the crash at the gate?"

"Not then. Later. Felix said they had so much fun messing with the guards that they partied the rest of the night at his place." Frankie giggled. "After dropping off the women and children in town, half the transport team joined the party. There were many tall tales of courage told that night."

Kit relaxed back onto her pillows with a smile. "Well. Okay then." It was an oddly satisfying picture, a celebration of bravery. And life.

"Did Hawk bring Aric in this morning?" Frankie asked, derailing her thoughts.

"He did." Her poor baby had almost burst into tears at seeing her stitches. How many times had he seen her after a beating? She shook her head. "I'm worried...he's still whispering."

"Naturally."

"What?" How could Frankie sound so nonchalant?

"It'll take time to believe he's safe and even longer to let go of the habits he learned." Frankie's gaze was level, her tone even. She was always honest with her friends, no matter how unpalatable the truth.

Kit swallowed. Aric whispered because children who made noise would be switched. "I hate that you're right."

Aric would eventually move past his fears. Would she ever move past her guilt? Look at the damage she'd done to her son's childhood. All because she thought it would be good for him— and herself—to have a strong man in their lives.

Stupid. Yes, she really was.

Thinking of the harm done to others, Kit considered Frankie.

The letter asking for help had brought Frankie running. Leaving her job, her home, her friends. Risking her life. And undoubtedly upsetting her family. "How upset is your family that you're here?"

Frankie averted her gaze. "A bit. But, hey, I was due a vacation."

"Way past due," Kit said lightly. As if this mess had been much of a vacation.

Way to mess up your bestie's life, Kit. She pulled in a careful breath —because big ones made it feel as if someone was stabbing her right in the side. It was time to put on her adulting cap so Frankie knew she could go back to her real life.

The thought of managing without Frankie here was...frightening. Even so, she owed it to Frankie to let her go. "Did you know, the two women who live next door to Hawk stopped by. They said they'd keep an eye on Aric. Then Hawk actually came into my room for a whole minute today."

That was one minute longer than he ever had before. For the previous two days, she'd only seen him when he let Aric into the room, then he'd wait outside in the hallway.

"Huh. Progress."

Kit huffed, which didn't hurt nearly as much as laughing. "He came in to tell me that Aric still won't let anyone else take care of him, but it was okay, since his current jobs mean Aric can be with him. What does he do, anyway?"

"He manages the repairs for their family businesses and takes bush piloting jobs." Frankie's eyes grew soft. "Aric loves flying and gets all puffed up when someone calls him Hawk's co-pilot."

A co-pilot. Her little boy. She blinked back the tears. "He's getting so big."

He should start kindergarten this fall—and wasn't it wonderful that he wouldn't be subjected to the Patriot Zealot propaganda during their version of homeschooling. He'd go to a real school. Her baby.

"I..." She winced at the patient expression on Frankie's face. "What were we talking about?"

"Flutter-brain." Frankie smirked. "I'd blame it on the concussion, only you were like this before."

"And you're a total brat." The insult escaped before Kit

thought, and she froze in anticipation of a blow. Dear God, how had she relaxed so much as to—

No, wait...this is Frankie who loves a good insult. Kit used to deliberately annoy her—especially when they were both under the influence—just to see the sparks fly and the hand-waving begin. Sweet heavens, when Frankie started cursing in Italian, everyone loved it.

Frankie's dark eyes held sympathy, but she simply resumed the conversation. "You were telling me that Hawk came in to say you shouldn't worry about Aric."

"Oh, right." That was where she was going. "The doctor said I'd be discharged soon but have to go to a rehab facility for the respiratory treatments and all the physical therapy and stuff. They don't trust me not to get pneumonia."

Frankie made a face. "*Girl.* Coughing with broken ribs would really hurt."

It totally did. "Anyway, things are pretty much arranged." She hauled in a breath and said the words she so didn't want to say. "Frankie, it means...everything...that you came here, that you got me and Aric out. I owe you so big and—" She caught Frankie's annoyance. "I know, I know, friends don't do the owe thing, but I have no way to tell you how much it means."

"You'd do the same for me."

I would. Kit nodded. "But, after Hawk came in, I started thinking. I've upset your life long enough. With JJ and Audrey helping Hawk with Aric, he'll be all right."

Her throat tightened. They weren't Frankie, and she couldn't trust them like she did her friend. But...her comfort was irrelevant. The police chief and the doctor lived out there wherever Hawk was. Aric would be safe. "Anyway, I'm going to be in that rehab place."

She studied the sheet, crumpled in her clenched hand. "I don't want to get you into too much trouble with your family."

Frankie's mother and sisters made Kit want to slap them. All three were rich, famous, beautiful...and entitled. They did work hard; she had to give them that. But with Frankie, they doled out affection only in return for what she did for them...rather like an employer would hand out bonuses. Love should flow like the Mississippi to the Gulf, not turn off and on like a faulty faucet.

"I know I have to go back sooner or later." Frankie walked over to the window and traced a finger down the glass, following the raindrops. "I'm not sure... But probably sooner would be better. Or not."

Kit tucked her hand over her sore ribs that had started to throb and burn. "That doesn't sound like you." Frankie was the least indecisive person she knew. "What's going on?"

"I'm just having—" Frankie frowned. "You're hurting. Are you due for your pain meds?"

"The stuff puts me to sleep. I wanted to be awake to talk to you."

"Tell you what"—Frankie gave her a wry smile—"take your meds and I promise to be back tomorrow and tell you about my sad, sad life."

"Story time." Kit started to laugh and at the knife in her side and gut, shut it right down. "I love stories. Promise?"

"You're as bad as Aric." Frankie smiled. "He demanded a story —and Hawk demanded I do the reading, so he sat in Hawk's lap while I read one story. And then he insisted on another."

"Which you read." At Frankie's shrugged agreement, Kit's eyes filled. "You're the best godmother ever."

"I am."

"But, bestie, remember, we'll manage. If you need to go home, it's all right." And if she did, Kit was going to feel incredibly lost and alone. She made herself smile confidently as Frankie nodded and headed out.

The door closed behind her muffling the sounds of nurses and visitors, of carts going past. Kit closed her eyes. In all the bustle of the hospital, how could she feel so very lost and alone?

That evening, Frankie was sitting beside Bull in the big lakeside gazebo. She leaned toward the blazing firepit, trying to warm her cold fingers. Around her, his family chatted, but she couldn't manage to follow the conversation. No, she was still trying to work things out in her head.

Kit and Aric were rescued. It was difficult to get past that since fear for their safety had been so much a part of Frankie's days. Now...now, what was she going to do?

I want to stay. Four short one-syllable words. Add two more. *I want to stay with Bull.* No question, no indecision. Just truth.

What about Mama, Papà, her sisters? Her job at Bocelli's?

As if her mother could hear her thinking—something Frankie'd been convinced of as a child—her cell rang. She blinked, then remembered that the Hermitage had internet service, and she'd connected her phone.

Yes, it was Mama.

Everyone in the gazebo was watching her. Probably wondering why she didn't answer it.

With an apologetic smile, she picked up the phone. "Hi, Mama. How's the company doing?"

As usual, her mother went into how her day had been, what new models had been acquired, the successes she'd had getting her models—especially Birgit and Anja—into choice commercials and events.

The monologue gave Frankie time to limp down to the wooden dock and maybe out of hearing. The Hermitage was awfully quiet.

"Sounds wonderful." Frankie paused. If she'd been talking to a friend, now was when she'd get questions about how her day had gone. Her month. What Alaska was like.

Frankie frowned, an uncomfortable feeling growing inside her.

No one in her family had ever asked about her trip. Or how she was doing.

In fact, did they...ever?

Her mother's voice grew louder. "Francesca, did you hear me? I asked what day you're coming back. When can I expect to see you at your desk?"

That was the only question her mother ever asked on these phone calls. Frankie sighed. "I'm glad to hear everything is going so well."

"Until it isn't. We need you back here, Francesca. Birgit has lost two bookings and Anja's favorite hair stylist said she won't work with her any longer. I want you back here tomorrow."

What a great incentive to return. Not. "Actually, I think I might stay in Alaska. I like it here."

Mama's gasp was horrified. "You can't. Absolutely not. Your job is here."

"I have a job here. One I like better."

Rather than asking what the job was, her mother gave a flat, "No." Then a screech came over the phone followed by shouting.

Frankie suppressed a laugh. Mama must still be at work, and from the noise, a model was having a meltdown. The shouting was Jaxson and an outraged female.

Frankie almost laughed. "You better go deal with that."

The phone went silent.

Frankie considered her cell. Despite the small size, the device felt heavy, weighed down by uncomfortable conversations, expectations. The dark lake water seemed to be issuing an invitation: toss it in and break that connection.

Such an appealing thought, but that connection was to her family.

She looked toward the gazebo and sighed. Did she have the courage to fight her whole family to make a life here?

A life with Bull?

He was watching her, then came down the slope to join her on the dock. Putting her jacket around her shoulders, he settled beside her. As their feet bumped together, dangling over the water, he put an arm around her.

Up in the gazebo, the conversation continued in a low murmur. Gabe and JJ were discussing where the PZs might have holed up and what the town might need to worry about.

Leaning her head on Bull's arm, Frankie watched Aric. The little boy was sound asleep in Hawk's lap. His little face still had the shadow of a bruise on one side, but the strain was gone from his expression. He felt safe.

"What's the matter, sweetheart?" Bull brushed her hair from her face. His hand was so big, so powerful. So gentle. "Was it bad news?"

"No, not really. My mother wants me back in New York."

"There's no surprise. Do you want to go back?"

"No. No, I don't."

After a pause, Bull said very quietly, "Stay. Be with me."

Happiness rose inside.

He took her hand. "I realize your modeling agency job is more exciting and fulfilling—"

Her snort cut him off. "It's not that. I like working with people, but not in the fashion or advertising industries. It's so sexist. If men's clothing changed like women's, your dress pants would be above your knees some years."

Bull's laugh rang out, and Frankie grinned reluctantly. "The whole industry is designed to manipulate women into spending more money—by making them think they're not attractive enough as they are. I guess I have an ethical problem with pushing that agenda."

"Then why haven't you changed jobs?" Bull asked.

"My family needs me." She shrugged. "I'm good at what I do. Things run better when I'm there."

Bull studied her. "You've been in Rescue quite a while. Has your family been calling and putting the pressure on?"

"Oh, have they. I just told Mama I wanted to stay here. She and the rest, they won't understand not returning to them and my job… They'll see it as a betrayal." Her voice cracked with the last word. "I don't want to lose them. I don't want to lose you."

His arm tightened around her.

"Bull, I don't know what to do."

No, that was a lie, wasn't it? She knew what she wanted to do. With a sigh, she leaned her head against his wide chest. In the lake shallows, a mother duck was teaching her fuzzy babies to swim.

My mother was never that attentive.

Yet… they were her family. What would they do if she left? Would she get cut away completely?

CHAPTER TWENTY-FIVE

D iplomacy - the art of saying "nice doggie" till you can find a stick. -
Wynn Catlin

A few days later, Bull dropped onto the couch. *What a fucked-up world, dammit.*

"Dios, 'mano." Caz strode in, followed by...Jesus, everybody except Hawk who'd taken Aric to the hospital to see his mama. "We saw you put your fist through the railing."

The doc sat down, tsked, and started pulling splinters out of Bull's knuckles. "What set you off?"

"Frankie." The heat of anger couldn't compete with the chilling cold of loss. "She called to say her family is here, staying at the Swan B&B. They want to take her home with them tomorrow."

"But she wants to stay here." Gabe smiled at Bull's raised eyebrows. "I'm not blind, bro. She loves you."

"Typical move," JJ said. "If phone calls aren't enough, it's time for in-person pressure. They brought everyone so they'll out-number her."

Audrey frowned at the officer. "Was your mother manipulative? I thought you said she was wonderful."

"She was." JJ shook her head. "On the Weiler police force, I got stuck with family dispute problems. I learned to recognize the tactics used to strong-arm a rebel into line."

"Strong-arm?" Bull's jaw tightened. *Over my dead body.*

"Bro." Gabe sat down on the woodstove hearth. "How serious are you about her?"

"Very serious." Bull scrubbed his hands over his face. Dammit, he'd thought they'd have a little more time to work things out. "This is your warning. If she goes back to New York, I'll follow her."

Gabe and Caz nodded in complete understanding.

"I think JJ and I are seeing a different side of this." Audrey leaned forward. "Will Frankie really be content in New York? Or is she being guilted into returning—and she'd be happier here."

He knew the answer to that—or was it merely his own wishes? Because his thoughts had been going in a circle for days now. And what he'd decided was... "If she loses her family by staying, I doubt she'll be happy."

"Sí, your Frankie is the kind to sacrifice herself for her family." Caz tilted his head. "But 'mano, does that family realize what they're asking her to give up? A job she loves, a man she loves, a life she loves?"

Setting his fears to one side, Bull considered. When Frankie spoke of her family, they didn't sound particularly loving. More like they were oblivious to anything unrelated to modeling. Since Frankie didn't fit into their worldview, they discounted her opinions as unimportant. Did the same with her, too, he thought.

So...if they actually loved her, perhaps if they saw what Frankie would be losing, they might halt the pressure.

If they didn't love her, then showing them they'd have a fight on their hands might also work.

Gabe had been watching Bull, and now he smiled slowly. "Let's do some planning. Caz and JJ, you're in charge of the psychological warfare. Audrey, identify the personnel and resources available. Hawk will probably remain here with Aric and Regan, so don't include them in the mission. Bull, pick the field of battle."

"Frankie said they'd eat at the roadhouse," Bull said, feeling the rightness of his decision. "Let's set up on home ground."

Gabe nodded approval.

"Felix will want to help," Audrey offered.

"Perfect." Bull gave her a smile. "He can do a sneak and peak."

"Good." Gabe had a pad of paper in his hand. "That's advance recon nailed down. What do we know about Frankie's family?"

"I'm going to get my laptop," Audrey called, already on her way out the door.

The blood started to move faster in Bull's veins. Frankie's family didn't understand her. Didn't value her.

He did. And so did his family.

At the roadhouse, Frankie smiled at her father. "While you wait for the hostess to set up the table, I'm going to run out and get my jacket. It's chillier in here than I thought."

Before he could respond, she slipped out the door into the quiet night. *Cavolo*, but her ears needed a rest. Did Birgit ever stop talking?

Still, it was wonderful to see them all. She really did love them.

Crossing the parking lot, she grabbed her coat out of her little car.

After her time in Alaska, Frankie could see her family more clearly...her very work-obsessed family.

Papà loved her but couldn't think of anything except his photography for longer than a few minutes.

Her sisters' lives revolved around their modeling careers.

That was a given. Still, they could be loving siblings at times. Birgit was always delighted to fix Frankie's makeup before an event. Anja loved being asked for help when deciding on what to wear.

Pulling on her coat, Frankie leaned against the giant chain saw-carved moose at the corner of the building. Her heart ached as she considered the fourth member of her family.

Mama had a reserved, chilly personality. Bemoaning that was futile. Her mother's priority was—and would always be—the business she'd built from scratch.

With all of them, relationships came second.

Frankie needed to accept that what she wanted from them was something that wouldn't happen. Something she needed to stop trying to get.

Being here with Bull's family had let her see that the lack wasn't her. She was who she was, and she really was quite lovable. There were just some people who measured love out in smaller portions.

Unlike Bull, who poured out love like a wide river.

She smiled as just the thought of him renewed her resolve.

The night wasn't going well. Mama's dedication was to her company, and that meant she was pushing Frankie to return with all her might...because that was what was best for her business.

Just before they left for the roadhouse, Mama mentioned how they'd supported Frankie in college...and with the expectation she'd pay them back by working at the company.

Another wave of guilt swept over Frankie. So far, she'd managed to stand her ground, but...it really was difficult. Was she being as ungrateful as Mama said?

She told them she had a job here, a life...and a man she loved. They ignored or discounted everything she said.

After all, Birgit had said in a disparaging voice, Frankie didn't have good taste in men. Look at what'd happened with Jaxson.

"Francesca, we're being seated," Anja called from the door.

"Coming." Frankie patted the moose's huge head and strode into the roadhouse.

Shortly, Amka, the night's hostess, took them to their table. "Enjoy your meal, Frankie and family."

As Amka moved away, Frankie frowned at the large round table they'd been given. Yes, it was in a quiet corner, but...the table seated twelve and was reserved for people who wanted to conduct a meeting and eat at the same time. Her family wouldn't even fill half of the table.

But no point in asking Amka what she'd been thinking. Papà'd already sat down with Mama on his right.

"Hi there, everyone. Welcome to Alaska." Felix gave the group his most charming smile. "I'm Felix, and I'll be your server tonight."

"Felix?" Frankie raised her eyebrows. "Since when have you waited tables in the restaurant?"

"Girl, I lost my waitstaff-virginity over here in the restaurant section." He tucked an arm around her and kissed her cheek, then firmly seated her where she had an empty chair on each side of her.

He kept talking as he handed out menus. "Bull—the owner of the restaurant—heard our Frankie's family was here. He plans to come over and say hi. When you see a huge guy with a shaved head, don't panic. He's ours."

"That's very kind of him." Papà's expression was pleased. "I'm sure he's a busy man."

"Oh, very. He has another restaurant in Homer and one in Anchorage. We're gratified he prefers to live in Rescue." Felix beamed at them all. "Who wants a pre-dinner drink?"

Her mother and sisters ordered wine, but Papà loved beer. "I'll have a Beartooth from Bull's Moose Brewery. Is there any connection to this roadhouse?"

"Excellent choice," Felix said. "And yes, Bull owns the brewery."

As her sisters and parents opened their menus, Frankie looked around the roadhouse. So familiar, so dear. No, she didn't want to leave it.

How was she going to get that through to everyone?

Would they hate her forever if she stuck to her resolve?

But...just the thought of saying goodbye to Bull left her feeling as if her heart and lungs had been scooped out.

Her jaw tightened. *I'm going to stay here.*

Operation planned. Contingencies accounted for. Advance recon done.

An hour later, having debriefed Felix about his impressions of Frankie's family, Bull studied the group from across the room.

Probably in her fifties, the mother was still a spectacularly beautiful blonde. Her two daughters, also blondes, had inherited her high cheekbones, pointed chin, big blue eyes.

Frankie's heritage obviously came from her dark-haired, brown-eyed father.

They were all chattering away while Frankie sat quietly. Seeing her so subdued pissed him right the fuck off.

Ignoring the momentary wish for his old assault rifle, Bull strolled across the room. Stuffed full of good food, the opposing force sat, pinned at a table, square in his sights.

"Sweetheart." Leaning over, Bull kissed the top of Frankie's head—warning shot delivered across the bow—and ignored her parents' startled expressions. "Welcome to Alaska, Bocelli family. I'm Bull Peleki, the owner of this establishment. How's the food?"

After listening to their compliments—sincere, to his surprise —he smiled and initiated the attack. "You must be Frankie's mother."

When he glanced at Frankie and raised a brow, her color deepened. "Oh, excuse me. Bull, I'd like you to meet my mother and father, Sigrid and Giorgio Bocelli."

Before she could introduce her sisters, Bull interrupted. "It's good to finally meet you. Frankie has talked about you all quite a bit. I'm sure she's told you she is staying with my family out at our property—what we call the Hermitage."

Giorgio appeared surprised.

Sigrid didn't. So, the mom knew about Frankie being with him, and dad didn't? How much had Frankie told them about Mako's sons and the Hermitage?

"When we heard you were here," Bull continued, "my family hoped to meet you."

Her mother was frowning at Frankie, but her father, who, from all reports, had a personality like Frankie's said, "We'd be delighted."

They were probably thinking a meeting would happen sometime in the future, but nope. Bull raised his hand and motioned.

Time for the psychological warfare.

From the bar where they'd been waiting, his family sauntered over. They were missing only Hawk and the children; Aric was still uncomfortable away from the Hermitage, and Hawk already had too many internal scars from family conflict.

Gabe and Audrey took seats directly opposite the parents; Caz and JJ sat down across from the sisters.

Bull slid into the empty chair next to Frankie. Felix was an excellent conspirator.

Reaching under the table, Bull appropriated Frankie's cold little hand.

After studying his family, she narrowed her eyes at him.

Yes, sweetheart. The sarge's sons are conducting a rescue, using words instead of bullets.

Rising, Bull launched into introductions. "On the New York side, we have Sigrid Bocelli—owner of the Bocelli Modeling Agency. Giorgio Bocelli, renowned for fashion photography. Anja"—he nodded at the oldest sister—"and Birgit, world famous models."

He managed to suppress his smirk when Frankie's siblings realized he knew who they were without any introduction. Audrey was truly excellent at research.

He continued. "On the Alaska family side, we have Audrey Hamilton who runs our library. Gabe MacNair, Chief of Police. Police Officer Jayden Jenner. And Caz Ramirez who runs the town's health clinic. We all live out at the Hermitage."

"You live together in one house?" Birgit asked in confusion.

"No, we own a fair amount of acreage on Lynx Lake and built our houses there with a shared courtyard," Gabe explained. "Frankie came to live with us after her rental cabin was torched."

"*Torched.*" Her father almost stood. "*Merda*, my daughter's house was *burned?*"

Nope, she hadn't told them about the arson. And here was where Frankie's temper and emotions came from. He leaned into Frankie. "I like your father."

Her eyes shot sparks at him. "*Deficiente*, what have you done?" Her voice dropped. "They didn't need to know that."

His grin widened. Yep, one Italian temper.

Across the table, JJ asked Caz, "Did she just call him an idiot?"

"Francesca, you will explain this torching. Now." Her father pointed to Frankie.

She kicked Bull's shin hard enough to make him wince. "Papà, Kit's husband was abusive and involved with a horrible cult, and he dragged her into it. I came here to help get her free, and the cult burned my cabin to make me leave."

The father turned angry eyes toward Gabe. "Shouldn't the police have been dealing with such a cult?"

Gabe gave him a sympathetic look. "Although the cult has been a problem, they're outside of my town limits and quite good at not being caught breaking the law. The ones who burned her cabin were hired through a third party. However, last week, that all changed."

"What happened last week?" Anja's sharp blue eyes were bright with curiosity.

"The women in the cult got free, and the fanatics fled the area." Gabe went on to explain more, including that Kit was in the hospital in Anchorage.

The sisters were wide-eyed, the mother obviously unhappy. "Francesca, this was most irresponsible of you. What were you thinking?"

Frankie stiffened. "That Kit needed help."

"And helping is what friends do," JJ said. "Your Frankie is a daughter to be proud of."

Sigrid's mouth pursed like she'd been sucking on a lemon. "Her name is Francesca. Why do you all persist in calling her Frankie?"

Perfect, the mom was getting irritated. That was what Caz had told them to strive for.

Time to toss the first grenade. "Our father was a traditionalist who taught us to address people by the name they prefer to use. It's a form of respect." Bull said politely. "And your daughter is very worthy of respect."

The muscles in Sigrid's face and neck tightened, exposing the fine white lines of a facelift.

Giorgio eyed Bull. "It is difficult for a family who called a child by one name to change to another."

"True enough," Caz said with his white smile. "It does take thought. However, since Frankie has a generous heart, I'm certain she would overlook a few mistakes."

Slight color rose in...damn, everyone's faces. No one called her by the name she preferred? Anger roused inside Bull.

Did they think her wishes weren't worth considering because she was the baby of the family? Or was it because she wasn't blonde and classically beautiful?

But this skirmish had been won. Bull sat back. A battle, like a river, would surge strongly, then slow into eddies while combatants recovered. This was often when unwary opponents let their guard down.

So, with a sweet smile, JJ asked the two siblings about how they'd developed such unique catwalk styles. Birgit and Anja jumped into the discussion. Despite sounding good-natured, their bickering held the edge of performers in competition with each other.

No wonder Frankie had superb negotiation and peacemaking skills.

Living in a world of prima donnas must chafe at her soul. Bull ran his hand over Frankie's shoulder in a caress that was as much for her as it was for him.

She was so much better a fit with his family...and she knew it.

The trick would be making her parents and siblings see it, too.

When she felt Bull's hand on her shoulder, Frankie started to lean into him, as she did so naturally now. He enjoyed being her support and protector, almost as much as she liked giving him the open affection he needed...even if he didn't admit it to her.

Just like he hadn't mentioned that he'd be here tonight. Despite the unsettled feeling in her stomach, she had to admire his facility with verbal warfare. And from the light in his gaze, that was what he was conducting.

With an effort, she focused on the conversation at the table, then realized Papà was studying her.

"Despite the strain of freeing Kit, you're particularly lovely today." Her father rubbed a finger over his chin. "I should do a series of photographs, perhaps with a theme of—"

"No." She shook her head. "I haven't changed my mind about how I feel about photographs of me hanging on a wall. Sorry, Papà."

"Her beauty isn't skin deep; it goes right to her heart and

soul," Bull rumbled. "Even your photographs, Giorgio, can't capture that essence."

Cazzo, she loved him, and she knew she was probably blushing.

Then he added, "Undoubtedly, her happiness at being here in Alaska—and with me—adds a glow."

She had to suppress a laugh. Such conceit.

Birgit sniffed. "Or maybe she's glowing because she finally got laid."

Ouch. Frankie winced, and Bull stiffened.

"You know, I once thought I wanted a sister." JJ gave Birgit her pissed-off cop stare. "I guess I got lucky being a single child."

Birgit flushed a bright red. "I didn't—" Her gaze dropped. "I did say that, and it was really petty."

She looked at Frankie. "I'm sorry, Francesca. I can't find a man I want to see for longer than a date or two, and you have"—she gestured toward Bull—"and he's so into you."

Birgit's mouth often ran ahead of her brain. It was why she caused so many problems at work. Understanding melted Frankie's anger because... *Anyone would envy me having Bull.* "It's okay. I—"

"Shit, I called you Francesca, and you've asked us over and over to call you Frankie." Birgit scowled. "When my BFF thought it was cute to call me Bibi, I slapped her to make her stop. Why do we do it to you?"

"Because Mama said we had to since it's her given name." Anja frowned at Mama. "When I was oh, maybe twelve, and my friends called their mothers, *mom*, and I wanted to call you that, you said *absolutely not*. You even sent me to my room when I kept trying."

That'd been quite the week. Papà had called it the battle of the frost giants.

Mama's blue eyes held anger. She opened her mouth. Closed it. Sat back and stared at nothing. Then she turned to Frankie.

"They're correct. I'm sorry. *Frankie*. One's name is a personal choice."

Cribbio, Bull had accomplished in one night what she'd not managed in years. "Thanks, Mama."

"So, if Kit's out of the cult, you've achieved your goal. I'm glad you're coming back to work." Anja had obviously blown off everything Frankie had said at the B&B about being in love and planning to stay in Alaska.

"Oh, me, too." Birgit tossed her hair back with a flirtatious look at Bull before telling Frankie, "The makeup people keep messing up my eyeliner before a shoot. And my agent is being a total asshole. You need to talk to him and—"

"Is that what you do all day?" Bull gave Frankie's hair a light tug. "Deal with quarrels?"

She sighed, because it sounded awful, didn't it? "That's the job description, yes. I'm essentially a diplomat in a war zone filled with models and advertising people."

"*Chiquita*." Caz's voice was smooth and concerned. "You love being with people, I know that. I've seen how much you enjoy managing the roadhouse and making the customers and staff happy. You have a sweet, good-natured personality. Enduring hours of angry, frustrated people must feel like you were tossed into a blackberry bush. Do you truly like doing that?"

Papà frowned...and Mama acted as if *she* was the one tossed into a blackberry bush.

Feeling as if she'd let them down and hurt their feelings, Frankie stared at the table. What Caz said was the truth, but it wasn't what they needed or wanted to hear.

Bull lifted their clasped hands, resting them on the table. "Sweetheart?"

Why could she deal with everyone else in the world, but not her family? She hadn't changed her mind, still wanted to stay, but her family had decided different. And was making their claim on her clear.

Did she want to start this fight here, in the restaurant? "Bull, it's not..."

His black eyes captured hers. "So, when we have children, you're going to tell them they must work at Bocelli's, whether they want to or not. Even if it makes them unhappy."

"Of *course* not." Her answer came a second before her brain told her that she'd just opened the can of worms she wanted to handle in private.

"I fear you don't understand," Mama said, her voice frozen.

"Ah, the ice queen," Frankie heard Caz say under his breath.

"We supported our daughter in college with the understanding she'd return to work for the company."

Actually, that'd never been stated. Just understood.

"Ah, many of my friends in the medical professions have done the same as Frankie—accepted help, then worked in a less...pleasant...work environment for a couple of years." Caz smiled at Frankie. "Is your two years not up yet, chica?"

If she wasn't totally in love with Bull—and if JJ wasn't usually carrying a gun—Frankie would kiss the doc right on the mouth.

"I'm not sure when I should start counting." She tapped her fingers on her lips. "Should it be at twelve when I started helping after school. Or when I worked there every weekend in college? Or just the four years I've worked there after I got my MBA?"

There was silence around the table.

And, okay, she was done with this. "However, if you think I still owe you, then send me a bill, and I'll pay you back. We'll pretend it was a loan."

"Wait—does that mean I'd have to pay you back for the money you've given me?" Birgit asked, appalled.

"No. No, you do not. None of you do." Her father rubbed his face. "This is a night for uncomfortable insights, is it not?"

"Uncomfortable?" Anja said. "You mean hearing that we've all been shitting on F—on Frankie. Because we can."

"Anja! Language," Mama snapped.

"The word bothers you, but making your daughter eat it doesn't?" Anja gave Mama a hard look. "Mama, I know you love her as much as you do me and Birgit, but you treat her differently. Probably because she doesn't want to be a model. She's put up with being treated like a...a servant because, like Papà's side of the family, she's a lot nicer than your side."

The air left Frankie's lungs. That was way too much honesty for Mama. She opened her mouth to say...something.

"Shhh," Bull cautioned under his breath.

Mama's eyes filled with tears. "Francesca. Frankie. I...no. I don't mean to..."

Cavolo, Mama was going to cry, and she never cried. Aghast, Frankie started to rise. "Mama—"

"My dear, I'm so glad you're here," Regina, the municipal building receptionist called as she and her husband walked into the restaurant. "Thank you so much for the other night. You made our anniversary incredibly special. One we'll never forget."

After giving Frankie a warm hug, Regina joined her beaming husband, and they headed into the bar.

"Frankie's here?" From a nearby table, Tina, Chevy's wife, half rose. "Girl, don't forget we're reading *The Handmaid's Tale* this week."

Small towns. Frankie stole a glance at her mother who was regaining her composure. *Okay, then.*

Rising, Frankie called back. "I'm halfway done, Tina. It's a great book." When she sat back down, she felt more centered. As Bull took her hand again, she smiled at her mother. "Mama. It's all right."

"No. No, it's not." Eyes now dry, Mama set her jaw. "I need to think about this, but you are not less. Different, yes. Not less. And never a servant. Not my daughter." Her fingers were tapping on the table.

Her gaze came to Bull and where he held Frankie's hand. A very blatant possessive hold, Frankie realized.

Before she could move, Lillian swooped down. "Love, I'd hoped to run into you tonight. Don't forget poker night is next week. Also, for the Harry Potter reading, could you bring yourself to wear black robes?"

"Hey, wait, is this reading for the library? *My* library?" Audrey asked, frowning.

"But, certainly, my child. Frankie and I intend to add some stage props," Lillian said. Dante stepped up behind her.

Frankie eyed the petite woman. It was very unlike the British actress to bust into a dinner party like this.

Lillian cast a gracious smile over the table. "Please excuse the interruption. Frankie and I have been reading to the elementary children and showing them how literature gets turned into theater."

Dante laughed. "Lillian went and left the Broadway stage, but acting is in her blood."

"Lillian Gainsborough?" Papà's eyes widened. "I saw you in *Macbeth*. No one has played the Lady better, before or since."

Beaming, Lillian gave a slight bow. "Thank you, my good sir."

Frankie suppressed a smile at her sisters' wide eyes.

"Now, Frankie." Lillian patted her shoulder. "I have robes for you. Come over early, and we'll get dressed. We'll have ever so much fun."

"I'll be there." But...they'd discussed robes and times yesterday. There was no way Lillian had forgotten.

Cazzo, Bull had drafted more than just his family for this meeting with her family. Felix, Regina, Tina, Lillian...? Ohhh, this was such a set up.

Lillian smiled at Frankie's family. "It's lovely that you came to visit her. I know she's missed you all."

As Lillian and Dante moved away, Anja snorted. "Missed us? When would you have had time?"

Birgit sniffed. "She doesn't put in hours at the gym like we do. This place probably doesn't even have a gym."

"We have a home gym," Gabe said mildly. "I've noticed Bull and Frankie seem to prefer jogging and sparring in our park."

Bull shrugged. "There's nothing like running beside the lake at sunrise."

"Oh." Anja sighed. "That does sound nice."

"By the way, Frankie, can you give me some lessons with that staff of yours? Some of your blocks and strikes would work great with the police baton," JJ said.

"Sure. I'd love to."

Papà didn't seem upset, but Birgit and Mama were frowning. Because none of Frankie's plans included returning to New York.

"Only, you'll have to tell Gryff not to bite me—that we're friends, right?" JJ added with a smile.

"Bite you?" Birgit stared. "What?"

"Our dog," Bull said. "He's ninety pounds of fur that tries to crawl into Frankie's lap every chance he gets—and will guard her with his life."

Mama looked appalled, then her eyes softened. "You've always wanted a dog."

"One like Nonna's," Papà said. "Back when you'd help her in her gardens."

"We have a huge garden." Audrey smiled at Papà. "Frankie was singing as she harvested baby salad greens."

Frankie smiled at the memory. She'd been singing "Yesterday", the old Beatles' tune when everyone had joined in to create a lovely four-part harmony.

"You're part of his family—and this town, aren't you?" Anja said, and Frankie could hear a note of envy. "It suits you, too. No wonder you're so happy here."

"Now," Frankie heard Caz whisper to JJ, "now, they finally see her clearly."

Birgit pursed her lips. "You actually found a guy who has no intention of being part of Bocelli's."

Mama made an appalled sound, then sighed. A sigh of acceptance.

Bull only laughed. "I like to think that I found her, and I'm doing my best to convince her to stay here." His voice dropped, and he cupped her cheek, bringing her gaze to his dark eyes. "Ms. Bocelli, I'll follow you to New York if I have to, but I'm pretty convinced you'd be happier here in Alaska."

He'd move to New York to be with her? She stared at him, seeing the firm line of his mouth, the set of his jaw. The honesty.

He'd go with her, even though he belonged here in Alaska.

She belonged here, too. This was her place.

Eyes filling with tears, she saw Gabe starting to smile, Audrey beaming. Caz nodded at her, and JJ grinned because they knew her decision without her speaking.

Because they knew her. They saw *her*.

They were her family.

And Bull was her man. She looked up at him, into eyes the color of the darkest sky. "I love you. And I belong here."

"Yeah, you do." He leaned down, forehead against hers, and whispered. "Here, with me."

EPILOGUE

Where thou art, that is home. ~ Emily Dickinson

In the kitchen at the roadhouse, Frankie sucked down a glass of soda. Caffeinated soda, because she totally needed it. *What a day.*

This morning, Kit had moved into the rehab hospital. *Progress.* Frankie had taken in clothing and books and anything she could think of that her friend might need. Kit had been exhausted and in pain, but the stubborn woman refused to take pain meds unless she was in agony.

Somehow, Hawk had anticipated the problem and said he'd take Aric to visit tomorrow when Kit wouldn't be stressed.

Poor Aric. He was still whispering and hiding whenever he made any noise. Or anytime there was the least upset—like when Bull had dropped a pot, it'd taken an hour to find Aric, who'd holed up under a bed.

Hawk planned to take him out more often. In fact, the two planned to pop into the roadhouse tonight and take a dessert back to the Hermitage. She'd watch for them so Aric would have someone he knew.

Her soda finished, Frankie set the glass down, then checked her hair. Her old-fashioned braid-coronet was more suited to a date night than work, but her Hermitage girl-gang had wanted to learn the style Nonna had taught her. Regan was going to a birthday party and sleep-over at her bestie's house. JJ and Audrey had dates planned with their men. So, they'd had a girls' hour before Frankie came to work.

Frankie smiled. Regan was such an appealing mixture of intelligent and innocent and sturdily practical. Audrey was brilliant and sweet. JJ was the voice of reason and the one who balanced them all out.

They were becoming good friends.

On her way to work, Frankie had dashed off to Bull's house —*her* house, too—while answering a call from Birgit.

It was the first time she'd heard from her sister since her family returned to New York. Honestly, that night at the restaurant, they'd been almost as shell-shocked as the PZs were after Mako's sons dealt with them. Yet, at the airport, they seemed pleased she'd found Bull and was happy.

She cried when she sent them off.

Today, though, Birgit whined that Frankie's replacement wasn't good enough and never would be. So, Frankie said since the replacement wasn't up to the job, someone in the family should take over. Since Birgit was the youngest...

It was the fastest end to a phone call on record.

"What're you laughing about, Ms. Boss?" Felix called from where he was waiting for a platter of nachos.

"I was—"

Shouting came from outside the kitchen, then a crash.

Crashes were bad, very bad.

Frankie hurried out and into the barroom. "No, no, *no*."

A fight, in *her* bar. A broken chair lay on a crushed barstool with a short, stocky man sprawled beside the mess.

Gabe punched a bearded blond man who stank like dead fish, then shoved a lanky rat-nosed one at JJ.

So many people—did they bring an entire fish camp here to brawl?

Yelling, a barrel-chested, bald man raised a chair, planning to hit JJ from behind, then staggered back with a knife in his shoulder.

Caz, seriously?

When a thickset man with a receding chin lunged for Gabe, a heavy mug bounced off the guy's forehead. Mr. No Chin landed on his ass.

The glass mug shattered on the floor.

Che palle! Frankie scowled as she looked around.

Bull stood off to one side, two men at his feet. He'd probably thumped their heads together. At least, he'd been tidy about it. He smiled sweetly at her.

She stomped through the battlegrounds, seeing how the regulars had simply moved their tables and chairs away, treating the fight like the best entertainment ever.

Alaskans.

The bald fisherman with a knife in his shoulder tried to stand.

She grabbed his ear and twisted. "Sit. Back. Down."

When Caz pulled out another knife, she pointed her finger at him. "*Basta.*" Enough was *enough*. "You got blood all over my clean floor."

Caz sighed, and the knife disappeared.

"Jesus." The idiot whose ear she had grabbed shuddered and held his hands up. "You sound like my mama."

"I am far meaner than your mama." Releasing him, she said without bothering to look. "Felix, the first aid kit, please."

"Yes'm, boss lady, ma'am," he answered from beside her.

"*Tonto.*" She slapped the back of his head affectionately, and he laughed.

Felix wasn't the only idiot—they abounded in this place. She eyed the shattered glass on the floor.

Someone had thrown it. Someone with particularly good aim.

Turning in the direction from which the mug had flown, she spotted Hawk at the hostess station with Aric in his arms. Whatever he was whispering in the boy's ear made the child smile.

"You're a good boy, Aric," Frankie called, then gave Hawk her meanest frown. "If it's glass, it does *not* get thrown."

The *bastardo* grinned at her.

She put her hands on her hips and surveyed the miscreants. "Who broke the chair and stool?"

"He busted the stool." The groggy chinless fishermen pointed to his stocky friend who sat beside the broken furniture.

Gabe raised his hand like a grade schooler. "The chair."

The Chief of Police broke her chair? "*Che schifo*, that is absolutely disgusting. You are the law in this town, not some...some hoodlum. And those chairs and stools come out of my budget."

She heard a laugh, Bull's very deep, resonant laugh. He'd been very tidy—and took two out. She would claim a kiss from her hero...later.

"Right," Gabe said. "I'll pay for the chair. Bull can add the stool to the asshole's bar bill."

The stocky asshole scowled at Gabe, then Frankie. "No fucking way. I'm not gonna pay for—"

"*Vai a farti fottere*," Frankie gritted out and glared at the man.

His eyes widened, and he scooted back several inches. "Uh... Right. On my card. Sure thing."

She huffed in satisfaction. Men were so fragile. Tell them to fuck themselves, and they caved immediately...even if they couldn't speak the language.

Although Nonna would be horrified that her granddaughter sounded like a fish wife.

Well, the fight was over, at least. She sighed, her anger cooling. "Do I even want to know what the problem was?"

"We just stepped in to break the fight up, actually," JJ said as she righted chairs and tables. "That one"—she pointed to the bulldog-jawed one Hawk had nailed with a mug—"he started it because the others said he hadn't caught the biggest salmon."

"Seriously?" They messed up her bar for a fish? Frankie threw her hands in the air, then glared at the instigator. "*Ficcati una barca in culo con i remi aperti.*"

"Dios," Caz's eyes widened.

Gabe and Bull both edged closer to him. Bull asked in a whisper, "What'd she say?"

"She told him to insert a boat...anally...with the oars out. Medically speaking, that is very...unhealthy." Caz shook his head. "I think I'll just do a bit of first aid now." He knelt by the man with the knife in him.

"Fuck," Gabe muttered.

And Bull, her Bull, started laughing—that infectious booming sound that had everyone in the place smiling.

He walked over and put his arms around her. "I love you, New York. You fit in here like you were made for us." He looked around at the room. "Yeah?"

Cazzo, the entire bar was listening to them now, and the room roared back, "Yeah!"

"But...see what they broke," she protested.

"Sweetheart, we can live without chairs and barstools. Beer, now that's a necessity."

There was another chorus of, "Yeah!"

Bull leaned down. "Have I mentioned how much I love you?"

The last traces of her anger disappeared under the warmest of waves. "I love you, too, *orsacchiotto.*" Wrapping her arms around his neck, she went up on tiptoes and kissed him until hoots and whistles filled the room.

"Go, Frankie!"

"Atta-girl, New York!"

Home is the place where you're loved for simply being yourself.

She was home.

ALSO BY CHERISE SINCLAIR

Masters of the Shadowlands Series

Club Shadowlands

Dark Citadel

Breaking Free

Lean on Me

Make Me, Sir

To Command and Collar

This Is Who I Am

If Only

Show Me, Baby

Servicing the Target

Protecting His Own

Mischief and the Masters

Beneath the Scars

Defiance

Mountain Masters & Dark Haven Series

Master of the Mountain

Simon Says: Mine

Master of the Abyss

Master of the Dark Side
My Liege of Dark Haven
Edge of the Enforcer
Master of Freedom
Master of Solitude
I Will Not Beg

The Wild Hunt Legacy

Hour of the Lion
Winter of the Wolf
Eventide of the Bear
Leap of the Lion
Healing of the Wolf

Sons of the Survivalist Series

Not a Hero
Lethal Balance
What You See

Standalone Books

The Dom's Dungeon
The Starlight Rite

ABOUT THE AUTHOR

Cherise Sinclair is a *New York Times* and *USA Today* bestselling author of emotional, suspenseful romance. She loves to match up devastatingly powerful males with heroines who can hold their own against the subtle—and not-so-subtle—alpha male pressure.

Fledglings having flown the nest, Cherise, her beloved husband, an eighty-pound lap-puppy, and one fussy feline live in the Pacific Northwest where nothing is cozier than a rainy day spent writing.

Made in the USA
Middletown, DE
04 December 2022

16548946R00215